WILLIAM CHRISTOPHER SPREADBURY

THE NAME
of the
BOOK

A Collection of Short Stories, Interesting Concepts, and Self-Serving Rants

PART OF THE *CF FICTION SERIES*

From Foster & VonCharles Publishing

CONTENTS

Non-Introduction. ix

Look What Terry Made. 1

"About Love" 31

Do You Feel The If? 87

True Fables From Interstate 90 91

"Things I've Heard" 153

Happy Birthday Roger 163

The Uncredible Shrinking Man. .197

The Absent Pretender 235

Lucky. 283

What Is Water?. 321

About The Author. 338

Dedicated to my children,
Riley Lyn & Trevor Joseph

"Do you realize that all great Literature is all about what a Bummer it is to be a Human Being? Isn't it such a relief to have somebody say that?"
Kurt Vonnegut

"That's one thing Earthlings might learn to do, If they tried hard enough: Ignore all the awful Times and concentrate on the good ones."
Kurt Vonnegut

NON-INTRODUCTION

WELCOME TO *The Name Of The Book*. I'm glad you are here. This may sound odd, but at this time, would you please allow me to not introduce myself. Not yet at least. I am William's partner. William is our author. The two of us collaborated on this project. I promise to properly introduce myself later, but doing so now I fear would lessen the experience you are optimistically about to enjoy. The stories both William and I sincerely hope you are about to read are *my stories*. Unfortunately, I do not possess the talent necessary to transform them into the written word. William appears to have the necessary skills to make him adequate at this endeavor. Let's hope so. If not, I most genuinely apologize for wasting all of our time. Especially mine.

Not to be rude, but let's be honest, I have invested far more time in this project than you will. That is something I hope to do throughout *The Name Of The Book*. Be honest, that is. Which reminds me, this is the part of the book where William, and the fine folks at Foster and VonCharles Publishing require me to inform you that this is a work of fiction. That none of it is true and if anything or anybody in our stories resembles something that is factual it is purely coincidental. Even what you are reading right now is fully and completely a product of William's imagination. Don't you get it? All of this is Bullshit. There, I said it.

Now that being said, I would also like to say that I feel the previous statements that I was forced to say are rather deceptive to you, the reader. It is not my wish to bamboozle you with tomfoolery or poppycock. My wish is to develop a strong relationship with you and the foundation of any solid relationship is truth. I can assure you despite what William and his conservative cohorts at Foster and VonCharles lead you to believe, everything you are about to read is 100% true. Or at least 98%. Granted I took some creative license and William sprinkled in a touch of writers embellishment here and there, but for the most part, all of it really happened and I have first-hand knowledge of it. Even the stuff that didn't happen yet. This I promise you.

Please take a moment to breathe deep and expel your conscious of all that makes you anxious or upsets your constitution. Open your mind and allow me to place something fresh into it. Pour a glass of your favorite beverage and get comfortable. It's time to Read On...

LOOK WHAT TERRY MADE

OAKIE ROBERTSON SUCKED in as much air as his abused and tired lungs would allow. He held it as long as he could, until the thoughts that now crowded his mind took control, and then expelled his breath. Slowly he exhaled as his nephew, Todd Robertson, awaited his answer on the other end of the telephone. "Okay… sure I'll come Todd. I'll be there tomorrow."

Oakie only knew his nephew as much as his fragmented memory would allow. The memories were distant, foggy, and inaccurate. Through no fault of his own, Oakie had not seen his brother's oldest child in many years. *The fault of our nonexistent relationship is definitely owned by Terry. Not me.* Oakie thought.

After hanging up the phone, Oakie sat and stared at the silence that surrounded him. He wanted desperately to share this news with someone for no other reason than to hear himself say the words aloud. But he spoke not a word. He lit a cigarette. He poured three fingers of Beefeater Gin. He told no one. He added one finger of olive juice. There was no one to tell. He dropped one olive into his drink and shoved another into his mouth. He chewed. He thought. He tried to rationalize his feelings. Terry was Oakie's younger brother by two and a half years. Terry had always been a thorn in Oakie's side. Terry was Lucky. Terry was blessed. Everything Terry touched turned to gold. Terry was the exact opposite of Oakie and he always made sure the world knew it. Terry was an asshole. Terry was dying. Terry was at home and his time on Earth was almost complete. Oakie took a generous swig of his drink and smiled. *Well little brother, I guess we finally found something that I am better than you at...*

It was an early March morning. Oakie pulled out of his driveway and began his long journey. The air was too cool to roll the windows down and too warm to run the heat, so he sat in the still quiet. He decided not to play the radio, but instead consider the life and times that he and his brother had shared. Oakie felt guilty for not feeling sad and wondered if that guilt was warranted. The brothers had not talked or seen each other very often in the last three decades and now Terry was requesting an audience with his older brother as he lay dying. *I didn't even know he was sick,* Oakie's mind asserted. When Todd called Oakie it took him a moment to even realize who he was. *My long forgotten nothing.* Todd was the oldest of Terry's four children. Oakie always refered to him as Little Shit One. *Wow, Little Shit One must be in his forties.* As Oakie's car entered the expressway, his thoughts traveled as far back as the corrosive signals of a worn-out mind would allow. He remembered the excitement that went along with becoming a big brother. At least he thought he remembered. Most of his early recollections were manufactured by photographs and stories and old home movies, not actual memories. While searching the ancient files of his mind, one event seemed far more vibrant than the rest. It was Oakie's earliest true memory of life.

Oakie was four years old. He was happy. He was in kindergarten. Oakie loved school. He did very well in his early years and loved how proud that made Mommy. Oakie adored Mommy. He felt his job in life was to impress her and she made that job very simple. Oakie was also crazy about his baby brother. But he thought of him as kind of an ornament. Something for he and his mommy to enjoy together. An accessory. A toy.

Anyway, on the day of Oakie's earliest memory, he had just finished a very important school project. *A Secret Box.* It was a shoebox that he had transformed with great effort and attention into a beautiful place to keep his most cherished and personal treasures. *His secrets.* Decorated with markers and glitter and construction paper.

His Aunt Rose, Mommy's younger sister who lived with them, picked him up from school that day. Aunt Rose was six years younger than Oakie's mother and ten years younger than her actual age. She was a little too slow for a world that was way too fast. Her parents had died young and her sister now owned their burden. Aunt Rose loved the *Secret Box* and told Oakie in no uncertain terms. He gushed with pride and excitement. On the way home, his skin could barely contain the frenzy that flowed through his body. *Mommy will love it!* he thought. He felt it was the finest thing he had ever made. Perhaps the finest thing anyone had ever made.

Oakie's mother did not disappoint. She praised him as a great artist and joyfully fussed over the Secret Box. Their celebration of kindergarten art was suddenly and rudely interrupted. Terry burst into the kitchen calling out for his mother. "Mommy! Mommy, come look what I made. Mommy! Mommy!" Oakie was in the middle of describing to his mother and aunt the glitter and glue technique he used to create his masterpiece. He continued talking, undaunted by the little toy that had just intruded upon his story. He simply increased the volume of his voice while placing one of his hands across his baby brother's mouth.

"Oakie! Don't do that," Mommy scolded.

Huh? Oakie thought.

"What did you make, Terry?" Mommy continued.

"Huh?" Oakie thought out loud this time.

"I made a poopoo in the potty," little Terry now gushed with pride and excitement.

"All by yourself?" the mommy exclaimed.

Little Terry smiled a big smile, taking his mommy by the hand. "Come see, Mommy. Come see."

"Such a big boy," Aunt Rose encouraged.

"Come, Aunt Row" and as the parade of three made its way to the toilet, Mommy said, "Come on Oakie, come see what a big boy Terry is."

What?! You gotta be kidding me! Go look at Terry's poo, Oakie thought as he stood alone in the kitchen looking at his quickly forgotten *Secret Box.* Slowly he walked toward the bathroom where his mother and aunt and brother stood around the toilet staring down at Terry's impressive bowel movement. "Come see, Oakie," Terry requested.

"Terry, you're supposed to flush when you're done," Oakie commanded.

"No, I want Daddy to see."

As Oakie moved in to flush the obscene interruption out of his life forever, Mommy grabbed his hand." No Oakie. He wants to show Daddy."

"But Mommy, I have to pee," Oakie lied.

"Use the upstairs bathroom," Aunt Rose suggested.

"But Mommy, Terry's poo is gross and smelly."

He did have a point.

"Deal with it, Oakie," commanded Mommy, as his aunt sprayed lavender air freshener.

"I hate the smell of lavender," Oakie complained. "Oh no, Mommy, there's no toilet paper in there!" Oakie tattled.

Two hours later, still an hour before Daddy came home, Oakie sat at the kitchen table overflowing with jealousy and anger. His mother took the *Secret Box* off the table and put it on top of the refrigerator. "Why are you putting my *Secret Box* up there?" Oakie asked with a displeased tone.

"I'm going to set the table for dinner."

"Dinner's not for a long time." Oakie felt betrayed.

A shit! Oakie thought. *All this hoopla over a goddamn shit!* At least he thought whatever the four-year-old equivalent of that is. Oakie left the kitchen. Oakie went to the bathroom. Oakie flushed the toilet.

"Mommy!" Terry cried.

"Oakie! You know your brother was saving that!" Aunt Rose yelled.

"Go to your room right now young man," Mommy shouted.

That night at dinner, there was plenty of talk about what Terry had made. And about the defiant flushing Oakie had performed. Delightful dinner conversation. Oakie's father let him know he was upset about his actions and at the same time reveled at how very proud he was of Terry's defecation and how he would've loved to have seen it. Terry beamed. Not a word was spoken about Oakie's *Secret Box*, even though it sat only a few feet above them on the refrigerator.

Later that night, while lying in bed, Oakie created another *Secret Box*. He kept this one deep in his craw and decorated it with anger and resentment and hatred. Even though Oakie built this second *Secret Box* all by himself, he held his baby brother responsible for it. It was, after all, entirely his fault. *Look what Terry made.* Oakie knew this would not be the type of *Secret Box* of which his mother could be proud. He hoped it would be gone by morning.

Unfortunately the next morning, Oakie was still in possession of two *Secret Boxes*, one still sat atop the refrigerator, the other hidden deep inside

Oakie's fractured heart. At breakfast he could not stand the sound of his baby brother's voice. He hardly tolerated the sound of his mother's interest in the stupid things Terry had to say. There was a new dynamic at the Robertson home and Oakie did not approve. Terry was no longer an accessory. A toy. Terry was now competition. A rival. And so that's the way it went. The game was on. Anytime Terry took center stage, Oakie was quick to try and cast him out of the spotlight. And his mother or father or Aunt Rose were always quick to correct him. "Wait your turn, Oakie." "Don't interrupt, Oakie." "Quiet down, Oakie."

And then two years after the incredible bowel movement incident, the most terrible thing happened. Terry came home from school beaming with pride, carrying his own *Secret Box*. Terry's *Secret Box* was bigger than Oakie's. And more colorful. And it had twice as much glitter. "Look Oakie. Look what I made. A *Secret Box*, just like yours. Except it wasn't just like Oakie's. It was better in every way. Oakie let some jealousy slip out of his second internal *Secret Box* and threw it at his baby brother in the form of angry words. "It's stupid, Terry! *Secret Boxes* are for babies!"

Oakie could not believe that he was considering these distant memories as he journeyed to visit his dying brother. He stopped at a gas station to fuel up, get a pack of smokes, and some coffee. He wondered why Terry wanted to see him after all these years. He wondered why he was willing to grant him an audience. *What else am I going to do? He is my brother. I guess I can let him off the hook. I could forgive him and show him that I am the better man. I mean it's not like I was busy or anything.*

That much was definitely true. Oakie was not busy. He had not worked in years. He had taken early retirement ten years ago and was on disability for five years before that. He lived on a fixed income. It wasn't very much, but it was enough. Oakie lived alone. He had no one else to support, or to worry about, or to tell he was taking a road trip to forgive his dying brother.

Oakie did not care to visit his early childhood any longer. So he hit the fast-forward button of his mind and jumped ahead to his teenage years. Not a good choice, for that was a terrible time in Oakie's life. That's when Oakie stopped being Terry's big brother.

Oakie loved sports. In eighth grade he did not have a lot of friends of his own, actually he had none, so he found himself playing baseball, basketball, and football with Terry and his friends. Terry had many friends. It seemed that once a week, Terry would make a new friend while still hanging onto the old ones. Terry was glad to have his big brother play with him and his friends. To a bunch of sixth graders it was cool to have an eighth grader hang out with them. And Oakie enjoyed it because he was by far the superior athlete of the group. Terry and his friends even accepted it when Oakie was a ball hog, as well as when he would tease them for their inferior athletic ability. That is with the exception of Jason Buckley. Terry would not tolerate his brother teasing Jason. Jason was overweight and underloved. He tried hard and failed easy. Terry liked Jason and filled the role of his protector, threatening to put an end to the games that Oakie enjoyed so much if he made *jokes* at Jason Buckley's expense. "Fine," Oakie would say "but I don't want that fatty on my team."

When Oakie started high school he tried out for all three of his favorite sports. Terry thought for sure his brother would be the school's MVP. He failed to make a single team. Too small, too slow, too weak, too Oakie. He took it hard. It made him angry. He stopped hanging out with Terry and his endless supply of friends. He started hanging out with other angry kids that also took things hard. And then, when Oakie turned sixteen, another terrible thing happened. His little brother became his bigger brother. Terry was suddenly taller than Oakie. And wider. And stronger. And... Holy shit, does he need a shave? This was not fair.

Oakie combated this the only way he could think of; He became a total dick to his brother. Terry did not take it hard. Terry never took anything hard. Terry simply rolled with it. The next four years all Oakie ever seemed to hear was, *hey everyone look what Terry made*. Terry made the basketball team. Terry made the baseball team. Terry made the varsity football team as a sophomore! Terry made the Dean's list. Terry made the National Honor Society. Terry made the game-winning shot. Terry made his high school rewrite the record books for yards and touchdowns and hits and home runs. Terry made college scouts take notice. And then soon, Terry had to make a decision as to which college scholarship he would accept.

Oakie was unimpressed. To Oakie everything Terry made was just another shit. His jealousy prevented him from being proud. Oakie would have gladly flushed all this new shit that Terry had made. And during Terry's four year high school run of unbelievable good fortune, it seemed that Oakie made nothing but mistakes. He hung out with the wrong kind of people. He barely graduated high school. He had a few brushes with the law. He had no direction. His father tried to save him by getting him a job at Standels Office Supply Company. Oakie worked in shipping and receiving for little more than minimum wage. His father had worked at Standels for twenty-five years. He also started working on the dock and then moved up to salesman, then top salesman, then regional manager, then vice president of operations. He hoped Oakie might do the same. He did not. Oakie began making life more and more difficult on his parents by continuously making poor decisions. And then, soon after Terry graduated from high school, as he counted down the days to college, and everyone gushed over his exemplary high school career, Oakie made something of his own. *Hey everyone, look what Oakie made.* Oakie made the breathalyzer register twice the legal limit. Oakie made the police officer put him in handcuffs. Then later, Oakie made bail. Oakie made his mother cry and his father yell. And although there is no way to tell for sure, later that week, Oakie always felt that his actions made his father have the massive heart attack that killed him. It was after a very intense argument. Oakie stormed out of the house feeling the way he did most of the time, angry, cheated, and misunderstood. The yelling had stopped. The house was quiet. Three hours later, Oakie's father's heart would also stop.

Oakie's hands gripped the steering wheel tightly as his lips sucked on the cancer stick that would eventually overtake his lungs. But that would be many years after his little brother was returned to the earth. He ripped the cigarette from his mouth and flicked it out his slightly opened window. A mouthful of smoke followed and quickly vanished behind the speeding car. Oakie was traveling at 73 mph on a highway that requested you not exceed 55 mph. It was the fastest his eighteen-year-old vehicle could travel. He was not in a hurry to arrive at his brother's home, as much as he was trying to outrun his thoughts. Oakie tried not to think about his father. The guilt of his death wreaked havoc on his fractured constitution. No one other than himself ever blamed Oakie for his father's early death. Most felt the man's poor diet was responsible for his premature death. It was a steady diet of red meat, brown whiskey, and forty Camels a day. Oakie shoved all that guilt into his *Secret Box*, right beside all the jealousy and resentment of his younger brother.

The death of the family's breadwinner did have one positive effect, it caused Oakie to mature quickly. At least temporarily. He worked hard on the dock at Standels. He took care of the house. He took care of his Mommy and Aunt Rose. Terry went away to play football at Michigan State, but not before asking his older brother what he should do. "Should I still go?" Terry felt as if he were abandoning his family.

"Hell yes, you should still go. This is your future. This is what Dad wanted" is what Oakie said. What Oakie meant was, *hell yes you should go. Far away. Get out of my life. I'm sick and tired of looking at you.*

Oakie considered his job a penance and he performed admirably. He was quiet. He mostly kept to himself. He began to stage deliveries by their zip code, as opposed to the order in which they were received. To Oakie it was common sense. To the loaders and drivers it was organized and efficient. To the bosses it was impressive and they let Oakie know it. Oakie was proud of himself. And with the distraction of Terry gone, his confidence began to grow. So much so that at the end of Terry's freshman year, Oakie made a request on his brother's behalf. Oakie got Terry a summer job, on the dock Oakie now supervised. It made him feel good. In a small way he thought order had been restored. On the dock at Standels, his younger brother, who excelled at everything, would be put in his place. Beneath Oakie. His subordinate. His inferior.

Things did not go the way Oakie had hoped. As was usually the case, Oakie had to look at what Terry had made. Terry made friends. Lots of them. The guys on the dock loved him. He was charismatic. Interesting. Funny. And it did not end there. Everyone loved Terry. The salesmen, the drivers, even management. Oakie could not wait for summer to end. He swore he would not make the same mistake next summer.

When the next summer arrived, Oakie did not invite his brother to join him on the loading dock. Instead, the operations manager gave Terry a call at the end of his sophomore year. "How would you like to drive for us this summer?" he asked. "It pays two dollars more an hour than on the dock."

Terry loved the idea of not being cooped up in the warehouse during the summer. More money sure sounded good, too. Management thought a good worker like Terry, with his handsome looks and engaging personality, should be out where the customers could witness him. Not on the dock with the unmotivated ex-cons, who wore their pants only halfway up their ass, and the alcoholics, who came in late and tried to sneak out early, and the Mexicans that barely spoke English, oh…and Oakie.

At first, Terry did not accept the job, because he worried about Oakie's feelings. "I told them no. I said I would rather work on the dock… with you."

"Are you nuts? It's a great offer! Take the job, you idiot." Oakie said it just like that. But what he meant was go somewhere that I don't have to see you. I'm sick and tired of looking at you.

"Did you ever consider getting off the docks and driving?" Terry asked. Oakie answered with only a look of regret and anger. It was then Terry remembered the three letters of the alphabet that would never allow Oakie to drive a truck for Standels, DWI.

Attention all drivers: *Look what Terry made.* Terry made more deliveries in a shorter amount of time than every one of you. And he has only been driving for two months. Terry made his bosses love him. Terry made customers feel compelled to call Standels and compliment the new delivery man. Terry made the other drivers hate him.

Oakie now had allies in his silent war against Terry. He found himself going out for beers after work with guys he rarely spoke to previously. Now the conversation flowed, and it always centered on a shared resentment toward an undeserving soul. They all looked forward to the end of summer when the All-American football star would leave them and order would be restored to all of their fractured constitutions. Even Terry counted down the days. He felt the acrimony of his brothers *Secret Box*. He decided next summer he would work elsewhere in an attempt to keep Oakie's *Secret Box* from totally revealing all its contents. He hoped to save the relationship he imagined, but never actually had with his older brother.

* * * * * * * * * * * * * * * * * * * * * * * * * * * * * * *

The following summer, Oakie would not have to deal with the distraction of Terry's good fortune as Terry would not work at Standels. He would instead work at a completely different type of job. He worked very hard. In fact, it would be the most difficult job he ever had. He would work in a bright clean environment surrounded by caring beautiful women. The women worked hard also. All of them toward the same goal. That goal was for Terry to be able to walk again. Terry suffered a terrible neck injury during the season's final football game. At the time of the devastating injury, the doctors believed the chances of Terry ever walking again were extremely slim. His strong will, hard work, great supporting cast, and unlimited hope and determination lowered those odds. Within a year's time, their goal would be accomplished. Terry would eventually make a full recovery. He would regain all his motor functions. But he would lose football, as well as all other contact sports, forever. The risk was far too great. He would also lose his scholarship.

Order restored, Oakie secretly thought. I have my own apartment now. I just got a twenty-five cent an hour raise. Baby brother is back at home, unemployed, unlucky, unspectacular.

"What's going on with your brother?" the owner of Standels asked Oakie.

"He's coming along, Mr. Standel. You know, one day at a time. He is all done with physical therapy and thinking about finishing school," Oakie answered.

"No no, I know all of that. I mean why would he not accept my offer?"

"Your offer?" Oakie questioned.

"Your family means a lot to us. Your dad was with me from the very beginning. And your brother, I don't have to tell you what a great guy he is… and, of course, you do a fine job for me here on the dock. Never any problems. So I just don't get it."

"What offer?"

"He didn't tell you?"

Oakie shook his curious head.

"I told him to come back to work. I would put him in sales. No heavy lifting. I even told him we would enroll him in some night classes, you know, to finish school and get his degree. I can't imagine he has a better option than that."

Oakies Secret Box was bursting at the seams.

Oakie = *a fine job, never any problems,* stay on the docks, where you belong.

Terry = *a great guy*, a promotion, an education, solutions.

They want my brother, they can have him. I'm done. Fuck this place. And fuck Terry, too. Does he think he's doing me a favor? What is he, some kind of martyr? He could have this place. I sure the hell wasn't going to work here forever.

Three days later, Oakie had a home-cooked meal at his mother's. "How was work today?" Aunt Rose asked.

"I didn't go to work today. Or yesterday."

His mother stopped in the middle of shaking some Kraft 100% grated parmesan cheese onto her spaghetti and looked at her oldest offspring with great concern. "Are you not feeling good?" she asked. "What's wrong?"

"Never better. I quit Standels."

Terry stopped in the middle of twirling far too much spaghetti onto his fork for a single bite and looked at his sibling, wondering if he had really heard what his brain had just told him he heard. There was a gasp. There was a *"What?"* There was a *"Huh?"* And there was Aunt Rose using the commotion as the perfect camouflage to quickly refill her wine glass.

"Got a new job. A better job. A lot more money. I'm in the asphalt business now, starting Monday. "

"Seriously?" Terry asked.

"That sounds dangerous." mother worried.

Gulp. Aunt Rose swallowed.

"Good Intentions Paving Company," Oakie announced.

"Seriously?" Terry re-asked. "Good Intentions?"

Now Oakie gulped down some wine as he explained, "Yeah, you know... Like the road to hell."

"The road to hell?" Again mother worried.

"It's paved with Good Intentions," Oakie says with a little laugh. "Get it?"

"That's terrible," Mother says.

Aunt Rose says, "How clever."

"That sounds like a tough job." Now Terry worried.

After dinner, after three bottles of wine, before Oakie left, he told his brother, "I know what Standel offered you. You are a fucking idiot if you don't take it."

So that's what Terry did.

And this is what Terry made.

Terry made his sales quota.

Terry made salesman of the month.

Terry made his customers very happy.

Terry made Mr. Standel very happy.

Terry made head salesman in less than two years.

Terry made Oakie sick any time his mother mentioned him.

And while Terry made things, things that Oakie felt were no different than the shit he made all those years ago. Things he wished he never had to hear about. Things he wished he could unhear. Things that Oakie wished he could simply flush away. As Terry made more and more things, Oakie got things:

Oakie got sick from the smell of asphalt.

Oakie got a bad back from the weight of asphalt.

Oakie got drunk after work.

Oakie got high before work.

Oakie got fired.

Oakie got another job, just as painful as the last one.

Oakie thought about stopping for a drink before seeing his dying brother. He thought he might need one. Or two, maybe three. The Secret Box that had been shut for a long while now hung open, pumping jealousy, resentment, and anger through his blood, in and out of his dark lonely heart. He thought about the big beautiful house his brother called home. He had not been near it in many years. He thought about the shitty little apartment he called home. *He has a beautiful house because of me. I'm the one who got him a job at Standels in the first place. And talked him into taking Standel's offer. Standel Office Supply, the company I used to work for.* The company that has grown tenfold. The company Terry has been president of for the past twenty years.

What Oakie's mind refused to consider was Terry's original refusal to take Standel's offer out of respect for his older brother. Or the possibility that Terry would have been just as successful at many other companies. Or the number of times Terry had invited Oakie back to Standels. Or that he, himself would've been just as unsuccessful had he stayed at Standels.

Oakie picked up the pint of Beefeaters. Once back in his car he took a healthy pull. His nerves steadied. He imagined looking down at his brother and his brother looking up at him. At first he could not fathom the feelings he would have seeing his brother in this position. So he instead tried to imagine what his brother would feel looking up at him. *Jealousy. Jealous of my life. As pathetic as it might have seemed to his big shooter little brother in the past, now it must look pretty damn good. No end in sight,* Oakie thought. And then Oakie realized what he would feel looking down on his brother. *Satisfaction. It's his fault.* Oakie revised their history. *He's the one that ruined my life. And after I got him his lucrative job, his degree, his everything.*

When Oakie was in his late twenties he tried to become a ghost to his family. He hardly ever saw Mommy, Terry, or Aunt Rose. Phone conversations had also become very rare and were never initiated by Oakie. He was completely burnt out on hearing about how well Terry was doing. Terry was already in management at Standels. Terry had a cute girlfriend named Claire and Terry thought he might be in love. Oakie was working for Triple B Moving and storage. The Bs stood for *Back Breaking Business*, and that, it certainly was. When Terry learned of his brother's new occupation he tried to phone him. Seven times in six days, before Oakie finally answered. "You got to meet Claire," Terry made friendly small talk. "She's great."

"That's what I hear. I'm just super busy, with work and all." Oakie politely declined his brother's request.

"So about that… Why don't you come back to Standels?"

"Huh?"

"I don't mean on the dock. I could get you in sales…or something."

"I have a job. And I'm making pretty good coin."

"I know, but you know, maybe you'd like something a little less physical."

"I'm fine, and I ain't no suit-wearing salesman."

"Well, something else then. I'm telling you Oakie, in a few years, you and I could be running this place. The potential is unlimited."

"Dude, I'm fine. I don't need anything from you."

"I know, but you've helped me out so many times, I just thought I could return the favor."

Oakie's voice raised three octaves. "That's right, Terry. Because you're my little brother. Get it. I'm your big brother. I look out for you, not the other way around."

"But Oakie -"

Click.

The nerve of that ungrateful bastard! Oakie was pissed at his brother's generous offer and he remained pissed for six days. On the seventh day he met Roxanne. He met her at work. Her work, not his. She worked on a pole that Oakie liked to admire from time to time. The pole was located at a drinking establishment that he liked to frequent because of their one dollar draft beers, tasty chicken wings, their willingness to look the other way if you wanted to snort a little coke in the bathroom, and of course, the pole. Every night the pole would be decorated with a moderately to fairly attractive, very naked woman. Roxanne was new. Roxanne was more than fairly attractive. Roxanne was *almost* beautiful. Of all the pole decorations, Roxanne had the least amount of cellulite, the least amount of scars, and the least black and blue marks.

Oakie was captivated by her *almost* beauty. It was after Roxanne's first night of work that she ran into Oakie in the parking lot. She asked him for a cigarette. She asked him for a ride home. Once in the car, after Oakie asked *where's home?* Roxanne began crying. Roxanne was in between homes. She had no place to go. Oakie gave her comfort. Oakie brought her to his home. Oakie says, *Roxanne is different. She never even stripped before that night. She was desperate. She needed money. She didn't know what else to do.* Oakie felt great sympathy for this slightly bruised *almost* beautiful woman. Oakie says *she never even did coke until that night in my apartment. She never even had sex with a guy she just met until that night in my apartment.* Oakie felt he could finally be the hero he always wanted to be. He convinced Roxanne to stay with him, indefinitely. Two weeks later, he talked her into quitting her job on the pole. Roxanne says *she had never even been in love before she met Oakie.* Oakie thought he was in love, too. The way a mouse thinks it's going to get the cheese from a spring-loaded Victor Mouse Trap.

Oakie adored the way Roxanne seemed to adore him. The way she would open his beer for him. The way she once did his laundry for him, while he was at work. Or the few times he came home to a hot cooked meal of Tuna Helper or Kraft Macaroni and Cheese. Three months and several eight balls into their relationship, Oakie decided he wanted to share his good fortune with his family.

One night, on the way home from work, Oakie stopped by his mother's house to share the good news of Roxanne. Aunt Rose and Mommy were very excited for Oakie. They could not wait to meet Roxanne. And while Oakie was there, expounding on the excellence of Roxanne, who should show up but Terry and Claire. It was Oakie's first encounter with Claire and it was not at all what he expected. Oakie was delighted. She was so plain. So ordinary. She was even a little overweight. *Not at all the type of woman you would expect a former All-American football player to be dating. Someone in management, someone climbing the corporate ladder, someone like my brother Terry, could do so much better,* Oakie thought. Their meeting was short.

Their meeting was pleasant. And during their brief encounter, all Oakie could think was *Roxanne is so much better looking. Sexier. Hotter. I have finally defeated my brother at something. I landed the far better catch. Terry has to be made aware.* So plans were made: dinner, drinks, a night of fun, a new beginning. Order had finally been restored.

The double date that Oakie had wished for soon became a reality. And Roxanne looked exactly how Oakie had hoped. Her heels were high, her skirt was short, her legs supported not only her torso, but the hopes and lust of all men that saw her. The *almost* beautiful woman wore enough make up and showed enough cleavage and had enough hair highlights to almost make the *almost* disappear. Oakie and Terry looked like men who were exactly where they wanted to be and their dates looked like models: Roxanne, a model from Maxim magazine, Claire, a model from a public service announcement.

Terry could not help but be captivated several times during the night by Roxanne's libidinous display. He tried to be inconspicuous when he looked her way a few seconds too long to be considered appropriate. He failed. He was caught six times. Twice by Roxanne, thrice by Oakie, and once by Claire. Although nothing was said, it only bothered Claire. Roxanne enjoyed capturing the attention of men and Oakie mistook Terry's lustful leers toward Roxanne as jealousy toward himself.

Oakie and Roxanne were far more accomplished drinkers than Terry and Claire. That's what made them want to end the evening far earlier than Oakie and Roxanne were accustomed. The brothers made one last deposit into the establishment's urinals before their departure. It was there that a slightly buzzed Oakie asked a very drunk Terry, "So what do you think about Roxanne?"

Terry belched. Terry steadied his feet and concentrated on comprehending Oakie's simple question. "Oh yeah. She's great."

"Sexy, huh?" Oakie hoped for validation.

Terry's balance began to forsake him. "Yeah, yeah, she is real sexy." Terry attempted to put his penis away as he asked Oakie, "What do you think of... of..." The alcohol caused Terry to temporarily forget the name of his true love. "Oh shit!" he suddenly shouted, not because of his absent-mindedness, but because his penis retrieval was premature. He was not done urinating, which his now urine-soaked right hand would confirm.

"Claire! Claire! What do you think of Claire?" Terry remembered.

"Claire?" Oakie pondered. "You mean do I think she's sexy?" Oakie considered the least insulting way to answer his brother's query.

Now Terry sort of laughed. "No, I mean do you like her?"

"Oh sure, she's fine."

As Terry clumsily washed his hands, he looked to his brother in a moment of unexplainable complete sobriety. He proclaimed, "Oakie, I think I'm in love."

"Well, then that makes two of us," Oakie answered, not about to forget his self-perceived brotherly competition.

"You're in love with Claire too?" Terry misunderstood.

"No, you dumbass, I'm talking about Roxanne. How drunk are you? Throw some water on your face."

As Terry obeyed his brother, Oakie continued, "I'm thinking about asking Roxanne to marry me."

Terry turned his dripping drunk face to his brother. He placed his wet hands on Oakies's shoulders for better support, and looking down into his eyes he said, "I was thinking about asking Claire. I mean she's great, but-" Terry broke eye contact for a second as his head became heavy, then he pulled his eyes back to Oakie's, "do you think I should?"

Oakie did not consider his brothers future for a single second. He thought about a competition that only existed in his myopic mind. He loved the idea of Terry being married to a less attractive, less sexy, less tantalizing woman than the one he was suddenly making wedding plans with. *A plain Jane. A stick-in-the-mud. Perfect. Everyone will envy me and pity Terry. I win.* He grabbed his brothers broad shoulders, gave him a vigorous shake, and looking up at Terry's drunk stained eyes, he proclaimed, "Hell yes, you should marry Claire. If you love her, fucking marry her!"

Oakie really enjoyed the evening. He got everyone home safely and soon after that night he became angry. In the months that followed, as usual, Terry continued making things. Oakie's mother made sure he heard the news.

Terry made the biggest sale in Standel's history – he landed a huge government contract. Terry made reservations at a fancy restaurant to celebrate. "Won't you and Roxanne join us? Terry really wants to see you."

"No, too busy."

Terry made a down payment on a darling little house out in the suburbs. "See you at the housewarming."

"Sorry, can't make it."

Terry made the most beautiful wedding proposal to Claire. "You guys just have to come to the engagement party. Please."

"Oh, how I wish we could. Sorry"

"Enough!" Roxanne insisted. "I had a lot of fun with Terry and Claire. He's your brother. Let's go see his house."

Oakie complied only because he feared losing Roxanne. She had become distant in the last few weeks. They had been fighting a lot. About silly stuff, Oakie thought. But serious enough to her that on a few occasions she would disappear for a couple of days. It had been over a month since she had made him a Kraft Macaroni and Cheese dinner. Oakie did not want to be alone. Again. So visit Terry they did.

"So what do you think?" Terry looked for his brother's approval.

"Kind of small, ain't it?" That's how Oakie answered, but that's not what he thought. *This place is so much better than my shitty little apartment.*

Terry's home was a cute two bedroom ranch with a generous family room and a lovely wooded backyard. It was in the middle, middle class suburb of Cavern Springs, forty miles from Chicago. Claire would be moving in after the school year. Currently she still lived with her parents on the south side of Chicago, where she taught seventh grade in a public school and was working on her masters. The young couple had a June wedding planned, followed by a two week European honeymoon, followed by Claire hopefully getting a job at Dunbar Elementary school in their new hometown.

On the other hand, Oakie's struggles to pay the rent on his shitty one bedroom apartment in an undesirable section of Chicago had become far more difficult over the past seven months, now that he had an extra person to support. He met his new financial obligations by working more hours and doing far less recreational drugs. He now drank Blatz Beer instead of PBR and it had been months since he had bought any blow. That upset Roxanne terribly. She tried to talk him into buying a different, cheaper drug, called crystal meth. She said she had never done it, but heard it was awesome. Oakie did not trust it. Roxanne called him a pussy. That was the first fight that made her disappear for two days.

"Well, it is just a starter home," Terry tried to justify something that required no justification.

"Why do you want a starter home? Now is the time to buy, brother. It's a buyers' market. You should buy one of those mini-mansions in Sequoia Hills." Oakie pretended to know what he was talking about. "Dad always said your home is your biggest investment." That much was true. Their father did truly believe that.

Claire cooked. They all ate. Terry was more careful with his libation consumption than the last time he imbibed with his older brother. He was also very cautious with his lustful leers at Roxanne. He did well. This time, only Roxanne noticed, and she appreciated it.

Terry was not the only one staring. Oakie caught Roxanne staring several times. She stared at the expensive bottles of wine that stood beside the cheap crap that Oakie brought as a housewarming gift. She stared at Claire's beautiful one point five karat diamond engagement ring. She stared at each and every room in the house. She stared at Terry's car, his television, his stereo system. *Was she staring at Terry?* Oakie asked himself. *Absolutely not,* he answered himself. But she sniffed. She definitely sniffed. Hard. Every time she came out of the bathroom, she would perform three or four deep nasal inhales. *She's doing coke. Is she? Where did she get coke? Where did she get money? Am I just imagining this?* Oakie decided to increase his drinking in an effort to decrease his imagination. "You got any whiskey?"

It was after eight when the four started playing Monopoly. It was before midnight when Claire excused herself and passed out in the master bedroom. It was just before two when Oakie's suspicions about the reasons for Roxanne's nose sniffling began to increase. He started to consider where it was that she would go when they fought. And the staring! Why was she so fixated on Terry and all his stupid shit! It was well after two when Oakie started getting obnoxious and soon after, he laid his head back on the couch that he and Roxanne shared. And then his head fell onto her uninviting shoulder, and drool began to flow past his lips. Roxanne looked across the cocktail table and made eye contact with Terry. They shared an embarrassed look followed by a little laugh. She squirmed out from under Oakie's drunken skull and freed herself from the couch. "Wow, now that's the first time I ever outlasted Oakie drinking," Terry confessed as he looked Roxanne down, then up.

She stood before him, barefoot in a short black skirt. Her blouse revealing ten percent more cleavage that it was two minutes earlier. "I bet you can outlast your brother at a lot of things."

Terry stared back, dumbfounded and slack-jawed. She let him off the hook for a second by giving him another little laugh. Terry uncomfortably returned the laugh. Then she approached him. She stood before him. Her bare knees pressed against the denim that covered his knees, her calves pushed into the cocktail table that held the Monopoly board. She gently caressed the top of her left breast with the palm of her right hand. "I see the way you look at me, Terry." Terry swallowed hard. "Do you see the way I look at you?" She asked in a soft whisper.

"Come on, stop screwin' around," Terry slurred as he began to get up. Roxanne pushed his shoulders back. She straddled his lap. Terry felt the heat of her body. It was exciting. It was inviting. It was forbidden. "Knock it off Roxanne."

Terry tried to grab her shoulders in an effort to gently discard her unwanted advances. Roxanne was not gentle. She quickly redirected Terry's hands to land on her nearly exposed breast. Terry's firm grasp of reality fought back the urges that rushed through his blood as the palms of his hands tried not to grasp the flesh they strongly desired.

"Don't fight it," Roxanne insisted as she removed her hands from Terry's and gathered his face in her palms. Her lips moved forward. Her tongue invaded Terry's mouth. Terry pushed his hands forward to expel the terrible situation he found himself in. He immediately felt he must've pushed her too hard as her body flew onto the table that held Boardwalk and Marvin Gardens. Terry was wrong. It was not his slight push alone that propelled Roxanne's body from his lap. It was his push in conjunction with Oakie pulling her by her platinum, highlighted blonde hair. "You fucking slut!" Oakie yelled.

"Oakie!" Terry yelled back.

It was seconds later Terry felt the crash of the Square Jack Daniels bottle across his face. Then Oakie was gone.

Terry would spend months trying to speak with Oakie. He even showed up at his apartment a few times. All to no avail. It would be over a year before the brothers would talk again.

* * * * * * * *　* * * * * * * * * *　* * * * * * * * *　* * * * * * * *

Oakie was now an old man. And being an old man gave him the ability to admit that some of the things he had told himself for decades were actually lies. Convenient lies. Lies that fit his agenda. As Oakie sat in a booth at Wendy's eating a cup of chili, and occasionally taking a small pull off of his Beefeaters, he thought about the lie that was Roxanne. In his mind, the lie did not absolve Terry from his terrible actions. It just made both Terry and Roxanne guilty. Oakie had seen Roxanne only once more after the incident. It was twelve years later. Oakie had spent twelve years doing pretty much the same: same apartment, same unskilled, labor-intensive jobs. Same loneliness. Roxanne had spent that same time doing crystal meth. The years had not been kind to her appearance . When she showed up at Oakie's front door, it took him a minute to realize who she was. She needed help. She was homeless. She was wanted by the police. At one time she was the best part of Oakie's life. He turned her away. She tried to use the only bargaining chip she ever had. Her sexuality. It no longer worked.

"Why don't you go ask Terry for help," Oakie suggested as he shut the door on her broken face. Oakie was proud of his response to Roxanne's plea for help. It was redemption. It made him laugh. Even now, all these years later. He laughed aloud, all alone in a booth at Wendy's. Oakie was stalling. He was very close to Terry's house. He worried how Claire would receive him. And the boys. *I wonder what terrible things Terry has said about me over the years.* As he walked through the lot to his old beater car he saw a Standels delivery truck parked in the lot. There was a guy inside eating his lunch. "Hey there, young fella," Oakie shouted out to him. That's how old Oakie had become. Where strangers used to be, *hey there, buddy,* now they were *hey there, young fella.*

"Yeah?" was the drivers reply.

"Do you know who Terry Robertson is?"

"Well, sure I do. I work for Standels."

"Whacha think of him?"

"I ain't never met him. I know he started the college work program there. And it's a pretty good deal for me. I hear he's real sick. Why?"

"Never mind."

Look what Terry made.

Terry kept right on making things after the Roxanne incident. About a year later Terry made a down payment on a huge house in Sequoia Hills.

A few years later Oakie's mom really began to push him to bury the hatchet and come see the latest thing Terry made. "Oakie you're an uncle. Don't you want to meet your nephew? Please."

Everyone come see! The proud parents begged. Look what we made. Oakie thought, *Terry finally did it. He made the ultimate shit. A mini version of himself. Not interested.*

Time passed.

Oakie's back became weak and tired. Alcohol eased the pain. One particularly painful night Oakie was pulled over in a Chicago suburb for drunk driving. He was in trouble. Hours later, Oakie's head pounded as he sat in his cell. He was scared. He was broke. He had no idea what he was going to do, but he feared he would be spending some time in jail. The Police Commander paid him a visit. "Good morning, Oakie."

Oakie sat in silence.

"You were sure pretty ripped last night."

Not a word.

"Do you remember me, Oakie?"

Oakie looked at his face. He thought. *Jason Buckley?* Terry's childhood friend that was too fat and too uncoordinated for Oakie's taste. The boy who was overweight and under-loved and always protected by Terry.

"I called your brother. I'm going to give you a huge break Oakie. Not that you ever gave me one. He is on his way here. You're going to go home with him. And all this… It goes away."

Later that day, Oakie and Terry had their much overdue reunion. Oakie finally met 'Little Shit Number One'. As well as Number Two, and Three. The children were very excited to finally meet their uncle. Oakie visited his brother's huge home and had dinner with his family. Terry pleaded with Oakie to take a job at Standels. To stay with him for a while. To go to AA. Oakie said he would think about it.

Another year passed.

Terry and Claire made another baby. Another boy.

Oakie seldom spoke to his family, but now he would visit them three times a year, Thanksgiving, Christmas and Independence Day. Fun days. Days Terry truly loved to celebrate. Days Oakie truly did not wish to spend alone. For some strange reason, Terry's boys truly enjoyed their Uncle Oakie.

As the years marched on, Terry made vice president.

Oakie got laid off.

Terry made president.

Oakie got another job.

Oakie and Terry's mother died.

Terry made the arrangements.

Oakie made an appearance.

Terry made Oakie take the money from the sale of their childhood home.

Oakie made a down payment on a small two bedroom house three hundred miles away from his little brother.

Terry made Aunt Rose move into his home.

Oakie made Beefeater gin his new best friend.

After their mother passed, Oakie slowly put an end to making his holiday visits, until they were nothing but a memory, and then a faded memory. They made him feel too inferior, too angry, too jealous.

Time passed.

Oakie parked his car. About to make his final appearance.

The driveway was full. The street was full. Oakie parked halfway down the block and began walking toward his brother's mini mansion. A couple of middle-age guys were walking the opposite way. *Someone must be having a party*, Oakie thought. *Who are these jokers? Why are they staring at me?*

"Uncle Oakie," the taller one said warmly.

"We are so glad you made it," the shorter one spoke sincerely.

These are Terry's kids? Oakie could not remember their names. The next thing Oakie knew he was being hugged and having his back slapped. The men were good-looking. Healthy.

Their eyes were swollen and glossy.

"Dad will be so happy to see you."

"You are all he's been talking about."

Oakie looked at them not knowing what to say.

"Carl," said the taller one.

Oakie looked confused.

"I'm Richard," said the shorter one. "But you used to call me little shit number three," he laughed.

"And little shit number four," Carl was now also laughing. "You were always so funny."

"You remember," Richard interrupted. "when we were little we had a band. We called ourselves The Little Shits."

"Not a real band. We played air guitar and banged on pots and pans," Carl explained.

"Mom would get so mad. We'd be like that's what Uncle Oakie calls us."

The men laughed and reminisced about the past that Oakie was part of yet had no recollection of, as they escorted him up the driveway.

The house was crowded. There were people and food everywhere. "Oakie," an elderly voice called out. Aunt Rose sat in a wheelchair covered with years. "Give me a hug, young man," she demanded.

After his hug with Aunt Rose, Terry's other two sons were there to greet their uncle with their wives and children. Todd, Terry's oldest, began to introduce Oakie to family and friends and neighbors and Claire's relatives and employees from Standels office supply. Oakie's mind spun round and round. This was not at all what he had expected.

"Dad's upstairs taking a nap."

"Mom's with him."

"The house has been packed for the last two days." A collection of unfamiliar voices bounced against Oakie's skull as he tried to take it all in.

"Are you hungry, Oakie?"

"This is how Terry wants it."

"We've all just been visiting and telling stories about Terry's life."

"And eating."

"Everybody just keeps bringing food."

"You must have a million stories." People swarmed Oakie. Patting his back, shaking his hand, and talking. And talking. And talking.

"Have something to eat, Oakie."

"I could tell you a story about Oakie and Terry," Aunt Rose tried to sneak her words in between all the others.

"Daddy, is that the uncle that used to call you the little shits?"

"Sweetheart, I told you not to say that word," a mother cautioned.

"It sure is. This is your great uncle Oakie," a father boasted.

"You know at Standels they still use your staging process. Even as big as we've become, it's still the best way."

"When these two boys were little. Real little..." Aunt Rose continued. Her mostly ignored voice began to raise above the others.

"I'll go tell Mom you're here."

"He's always sure to tell everyone that the staging system was your idea."

"I played football at Michigan State with your brother."

"It's been a long time." Retired Police Commander Buckley shook Oakie's right hand with both his hands as everyone continued talking. And talking. And talking. Including Aunt Rose. "Terry was just learning how to use the bathroom."

"We call it the Oakie System."

"Terry says it's like being able to attend his own wake."

"Dad always likes to be around a lot of people."

"Lots of them."

"Have a piece of lasagna, Oakie."

"He wanted to save it, to show his daddy..."

"Oh yes. You must be starving."

"How about a sandwich, Uncle Oakie?"

"Your brother was a hell of a ballplayer."

"Oakie thought the whole idea was just disgusting..."

"He is right over there, Mom."

Oakie's chest felt tight. His palms were sweaty. His breathing was becoming difficult. He felt dizzy. He looked for a place to sit. What he found was Claire. She stood before him with the same swollen glossy eyes as her sons. A tear rolled down her cheek. Oakie's eyes also became filled with tears. He did not know what to say. So he simply said, "Claire."

The two embraced. And then Oakie began to do something he had never done before. He fell apart. He cried. His shoulders bounced as he sobbed. As was the case from time to time over the past two days, the reality of the gathering would be realized by all in attendance. The stories would stop. The laughter, the eating, the commotion. It would all stop. Everyone would bow their heads and try to hide their tears. Silence. Except for the sound of weeping and, of course, Aunt Rose. When a woman in her nineties starts telling a story, she will not stop until she is finished, social cues be damned. As everyone rubbed their eyes and Oakie continued to fall apart in Claire's arms you heard the voice of Aunt Rose proclaim, "He flushed it. He flushed it right down the toilet."

"I'm so sorry, Claire." Oakie's knees began to buckle.

"Get him a chair," someone shouted.

As Carl and Sam helped Oakie sit down, Claire commanded, "Get him some water."

Oakie looked at all the people that filled his brother's house.

"Is he all right?" Someone handed him a glass of water. Oakie rubbed his forehead and then smeared his tears into his cheeks. Oh my God, he thought. *This is what Terry made. All of this. Everyone look. Look at what my brother made. Look what Terry made.* He looked at his hands, damp with tears. Tears of regret. *Terry made all of this and I could have been part of it, but I could not get over myself. All these years I have been ruled by jealousy. Why could I not accept that my younger brother is a better man than me. Smarter. Stronger. Kinder. Funnier. Better. How could I hold that against him? I could have been part of all of this. He invited me time and time again. And I flushed it. My entire life, I just flushed it.*

Oakie gathered himself and looked at Claire, Terry's soon to be widow and said, "If it's okay, I would like to see my brother now."

* * * * * * * * * * * * * * * * * * * * * * * * * * * * * * *

Terry sat in a recliner in his bedroom. Asleep. No tubes or machines or monitors. He wore black sweatpants and a Michigan State T-shirt. He looked weak. He looked tired. He was waiting for death to come find him, calmly and patiently. His eyes opened and beheld his brother, sitting across from him. He smiled. "You made it."

"Yeah."

"I'm glad."

Oakie fumbled for words. "There's a lot of people here."

"Well, I guess I didn't want to die alone."

"No chance of that."

Thirty-eight seconds of shared silence. "Look," the brothers chorused.

"You first," Oakie surrendered.

Terry breathed in a shallow breath. "I just wanted to say that I am sorry, Oakie."

"You're sorry. I'm the one who is sorry. What do you have to be sorry for?"

"All these years, I could've tried harder. To be a better brother," Terry's breathing was becoming labored. "And the whole Roxanne thing. I'm sorry."

"Stop. Stop it." Oakie insisted and as his brother fell silent, Oakie let out a nervous laugh.

"What?" Terry asked.

Oakie smiled, holding in his laugh.

"What? It's not polite to keep a dying man in suspense."

Oakie revealed what amused him. "It's not really funny, Terry. I say this with great regret, but do you realize the last real thing we did together was throwing that crack whore off your lap."

Terry shook his head in disbelief holding in a stupid smile. Then they both laughed a fake laugh that was really a cry.

"It's my fault Terry. I'm sorry. I'm sorry for not being a part of your life. I'm sorry for telling you your *Secret Box* was stupid. I'm sorry for everything I ever did and everything I didn't do. I'm sorry for flushing your shit." Oakie laughed to hide his sadness.

"Flushing my shit?" Terry laughed for the same reason.

"Do you remember that?"

"Heck no. I mean Aunt Rose talks about it but-"

Terry started coughing. It frightened Oakie. "Should I get someone?" Terry shook his head trying to regain some composure. Terry struggled to speak with a strained whisper, "I do remember the *Secret Box* though. It did hurt my feelings."

Oakie smiled. "You were in kindergarten. We were just kids. Get over it."

"I did." Terry smiled back.

It was true, Terry did get over it. You see that night, all those years ago, Terry created a second *Secret Box* just as his older brother did two years earlier. But he did not fill it with jealousy and anger the way Oakie did. He decided he did not want to be mad at his brother because of the hurtful things he said. So he decided to just let it go. The *Secret Box* that was deep in Terry's craw was filled with acceptance and forgiveness. All these years later Terry's *Secret Box* was still filled with an unconditional love for his older, broken brother.

Oakie took a moment to quietly reflect on all of the things in his life that he could not just let go. "Seriously, Terry, it took me my whole life to realize it, but I really do realize it now. I mean, I see it now. I wasted my entire life on jealousy and anger." Oakie began to choke up. "I wish I would have been a bigger part of the life you have made." Oakie's voice shook with weakness and regret. "I am sorry, Terry. I'm so sorry. I know it's too late now... But I want you to know...I just wish-" Oakie hung his head in shame and wept.

Terry wiped a tear that hid in the corner of his eye. "What are you talking about, the life I have made? I can't imagine what my life would have been without you." The weight of Oakie's shame kept his head facing the floor as Terry continued. "When I was a little kid I looked up to you so much. You were my big brother. You really never had any time to be bothered by your snot-nosed little brother… That was until I was in sixth grade. Do you remember, Oakie? You were in eighth grade and you started playing football with me. And baseball. And basketball. Almost every day for a whole year. It was one of the happiest years of my life. That's all we did, sports, sports, spo—" Cough. Cough. Cough. "You were so good. You're the reason I started taking sports so seriously. I wanted to be as good as you."

Oakie glanced up toward his brother. "Well you achieved that goal a thousand times over."

"Thanks to you. I was a hell of an athlete. A lot of good that did me." Terry paused for a moment of self-pity and then continued to lift his brother up. "Every major decision I've ever made was based on your advice."

Oakie rolled his eyes in disbelief, not appreciating his brother's attempt to patronize him.

"Seriously, Oakie. After Dad died I wasn't going to go away to school. Remember. You're the one who made me change my mind. And then, after I broke my goddamn neck-" Again Terry went on a coughing jag. Oakie waited patiently, interested in his brother's thoughts. "You talked me into going back to Standels. And look how much I owe to that decision."

Oakie gave an *aw shucks* smile considering the possibilities. Terry continued, "You're the one who told me to buy a big house in Sequoia Hills. Shit, Oakie you told me to marry Claire, remember."

Hey right, Oakie thought. *I did do all that.*

Oakie spent the night at his brother's side. Terry died the following afternoon. Oakie spent the next four nights at his brother's home. And as the stories of Terry's life flowed like water around the kitchen table and at the wake, and at the funeral luncheon, and the days following Terry's burial, Oakie made sure to tell everyone his new stories: how he made Terry the All-American athlete he once was, how he forced him to go to Michigan State and after his injury he did not allow his baby brother to give up, how he got him the job at Standels, how he told him he would be a fool to let a woman like Claire get away. And the house, don't forget the house. Everyone loved to listen to Oakie's stories. Terry's friends, Terry's coworkers, Terry's children, even Claire did not object. The energy, the passion, the happy endings.

Hey everyone, listen to what Oakie made.

As great a life that Terry had lived, it always bothered him deeply the misery with which his older brother surrounded himself. He always knew his blessed life was responsible for the resentment and anger Oakie carried with him. After Terry's death that resentment and anger seemed to melt away. Oakie felt relevant. Important. He was happy to portray himself as the big brother he always wanted to be. Oakie finally opened his *Secret Box* and just let go of all the jealousy and hatred he had stored there for all those many years. Oakie was suddenly a content Human Being.

Hey everybody, look what Terry made.

"ABOUT LOVE"

Excerpt from Session 3

"WE MET, WE fell in love, we got married, you hear that from couples a lot. I'll tell you something, that middle part is never true."

"You don't believe people fall in love, Ethan?"

"What actually happens is two people meet, they date, they give birth, and then they get married."

"You feel a baby is the only reason to get married?"

"No, no, not a baby. No, this happens long before a baby."

"I'm puzzled, Ethan."

"What happens is, every couple gives birth to an uncontrollable, yet all controlling entity. This new distinct creature will feed off the happy couple, and they will gladly nourish it, at first. But most of the time this… this beast will become stronger than the couple, but it won't stop feeding. It will just suck every bit of life out of them. It will get to the point that everything the couple does, it does for this god-forsaken monster. I'm talking any couple, black, white, Asian, gay, straight, doesn't matter."

"Oh my, you certainly paint a pretty picture. Does this monster have a name?"

"Sure, it does. The monster is *the relationship.*"

"Okay…?"

"You see at first when people become involved with each other, after a while they decide they want to expand that involvement, they enter a *relationship.* Which at first is fine and good. Nice and innocent. And as most couples go, they do things for one another, right? And that sometimes includes one making a sacrifice for the other one. Wouldn't you agree?"

"Certainly."

"You give up a night out with the boys or a night out with the girls, a football game, a TV show, Christmas Eve at Moms, whatever, am I right?"

"Of course, Ethan, any sustainable relationship is give and take -"

"I know, I know, I'm not disputing that, but what happens when the *relationship* becomes bigger and stronger than the individuals that make up the couple? When decisions start being made that are not in your best interest, or your partners, but they are what is best for the *relationship*. Friendships are lost, jobs are taken or not taken, homes are bought or sold, plans are made, children are created, dreams are abandoned, as the *relationship* grows and grows. We feed it with our very souls. With our once sacred individuality."

"Ethan, everybody is different and people have to decide for themselves —"

"No! That's not true! I'm sorry...I'm sorry to interrupt. I know what you're saying, but sometimes the people are too weak...And the *monster* is too strong."

Ethan felt embarrassed and somewhat, slightly ashamed for having exhibited so much dark honesty, and vulnerability. What made it more uncomfortable for him was his father. Having been raised in a very close-minded misogynistic household by a very no-nonsense, fanatically religious, physically abusive son of a bitch made it very difficult for Ethan to open up to anyone, let alone a therapist, a thirty-one-year-old female therapist at that. This was a big step for Ethan toward becoming a better Human Being. He had been a terrible one.

Ethan ended his rant to reflect on a more personal matter. "I should have left Madelyne years ago. When the boys were young. But I couldn't. How could I?"

"What is it that you regret the most Ethan?"

"What I regret the most is what I regret the least. My boys, Toby and Thad. I was blessed with two incredible sons. It wasn't until after Thad was born that I realized what Madelyne truly was. I mean...I know she has issues and it is not entirely her fault, but she is an abuser. My boys grew up in a toxic house because of her. But if I divorced her when they were young you know she would have got custody. The best I could have hoped for was joint custody and I would have had to leave my sons with a cruel abuser without me being there to protect them, or at the very least comfort them. I couldn't risk having them be alone with her. Without me. Their father. Their advocate. It's a real shame, but courts are not in the practice of taking children away from their abusive mommies, unless it's the type of abuse that leaves physical scars. Believe me, you might not be able to see them, or touch them, or take a picture of them for the judge to see, but my boys have scars. I can see them. And it eats me up inside that I could not prevent them."

* * * * * * * * * * * * * * * * * * * * * * * * * * * * * * * *

This is the story of Ethan White and his attempted journey to self-actualization. I will share with you some private conversations that I was able to obtain along with information about Ethan's past. From time to time I may also take a few moments to editorialize. Not necessarily about Ethan or his journey, but about anything, perhaps my own journey, although I'm not exactly sure what my destination is so I may not even be on a journey. Maybe you are? I may express some opinions on that. I try to never miss an opportunity to express my opinion. But I implore you, please, do not confuse my philosophies or attitudes with those of Ethan's. At times he seems to be all over the map. And if you're curious about who I am, I promise I will introduce myself at what I feel is an appropriate time. I can promise you however, I am not William.

Excerpt from Session 4

"Do you know what today is, Fabiola?"

"Yes, Ethan, Happy Valentine's Day."

"Indeed, but today would have also been my twenty-second wedding anniversary."

"I didn't realize you and Madelyne were married on Valentine's day. That must have been very romantic."

Ethan laughed a sarcastic laugh in the form of breath being spat out his nostrils as he rolled his eyes and smiled a clever smirk. He then crossed his legs in a feminine way that appeared quite masculine when he did it. He rubbed the left side of his five o'clock shadow with his right palm and fixed his ocean blue stare directly into Fabiola's rich brown eyes. He looked as though he was about to say something sincerely profound. Fabiola blinked twice and then consulted her note pad for a half a second. She was not in need of consultation from the blank page she held in her hand, but was in need of breaking Ethan's gaze. Whenever he looked at her like this, it made her feel uncomfortable because it made her feel so comfortable.

"It was very romantic. You have to remember, at that time I was rather young. I thought I was in love. In fact, it was soon after our wedding that I found myself in *true love*, although it didn't last very long."

"The way you say that, am I to assume that looking back on it now you don't think you were ever really in true love with Madelyne?"

"No and yes and no."

"Meaning…"

"Well, we all have different definitions of what love is and throughout your life the definition can change. As a mature and evolved man of fifty, I feel far different than I did at twenty-eight."

As a woman of thirty years, Fabiola could probably relate better with twenty-eight-year-old Ethan as opposed to fifty-year-old Ethan, but being a person of above average intelligence and perceived sophistication, Fabiola had subconsciously convinced herself long ago, that through the aid of her memories and her power of prognostication she could relate with anybody of any age.

"What does fifty-year-old Ethan think about *true love*?"

"It's bullshit. Maybe not for everybody, but for most of us. It's like I told you last week, the monster I call *the relationship* is quite the beast. Most people that fall prey to *the relationship monster* do so because they think they are in love. First, we believe lust is love. Funny thing about lust is it can never be truly satisfied. Maybe temporarily, but not permanently. You can really only attend to your lust. And when your lust gets attention it makes you happy. If it gets enough attention you can become downright euphoric. And I'm not just talking sex. No, no, not at all. You can lust for someone in a whole myriad of ways. Their mind, their body, their touch, their conversation, whatever. And if you're lucky enough to have the object of your lust, attend to your lust…well then you are generally unlucky enough to think you are in love. But like I said, lust can only be satisfied for a very short time. So, what happens is the time you are away from the person that attends to your lust becomes very difficult. You find yourself longing for them. Longing is the second feeling you confuse for love."

"Are there any others?"

"Yes…First we think lust is love, then we think longing is love, and finally we think obsession is love."

"Do you feel Madelyne was an obsession?"

"That's why I married her. She was my obsession. But it wasn't even her. At least not really."

"How do you mean?"

"Nothing made me feel more alive than the anticipation of seeing her." Ethan shot another stare deep into the eyes of Fabiola. She nervously fidgeted with her pen and consulted her note pad which now listed Ethan's three phases of love along with the words *true love* circled. "It was really unfair of me Fabiola…Fabiola Fabiono, such a beautiful name. Did I ever tell you how much I like your name?"

"Thank you, yes you have mentioned it."

"Fabiola Fabiono…"

"Please, continue…"

"Yeah, yeah, right, I'm sorry. It was never like I was actually obsessed with Madelyne. I was obsessed with the idea of Madelyne. Somehow my mind built her into someone nobody could possibly live up to, let alone Madelyne. Confused, depressed, suicidal, mean, nasty, abusive Madelyne. Soon after we were married I began to see the reality of Madelyne and the idea of Madelyne slowly faded away. The sad truth is I didn't marry a person. I married an idea. By the time I realized it, little Toby was on the way."

Ethan did not place his captivating gaze on the windows of Fabiola's soul. This time its audience was the tile floor.

"Are you okay, Ethan?"

"Swell as hell, Fabiola, swell as hell." He looked up with his devilish smile.

Fabiola consulted her note pad and re-circled the circled words *true love*.

"Ethan, you said soon after you and Madelyne married you found yourself in true love. What did you mean by that?"

"True love is sleep my dear. It comes after the first three phases are long gone."

"Interesting."

"Once I discovered who Madelyne really was, or actually really was not, I went to sleep. There was no more lust, longing, or obsession. I put them all to bed. I put all my dreams and desires to bed. I accepted my fate. I accepted her and she accepted me, in as much as we existed day after day after day. Under the same roof. We fought a lot. We disagreed on almost everything. But neither one of us were going anywhere. We were asleep in the back seat of the car. *The relationship monster* was doing the driving."

"I see...but you say that did not last long."

"She was very abusive to me. Emotionally. That started right after Thad, our oldest, was born. I made a strong attempt to live in denial of her behavior, but then when Thaddeus was five, I witnessed her abuse against him. My son. Our son...I woke up. We stayed married, because she wasn't gonna get my boys. But that's when I kicked the *Monster* out of the car and I started driving."

"In what way did she abuse him?"

"She manipulated him into feeling bad about himself. And doubtful about me. She was always a master manipulator."

"So, does that mean you do not believe in *true love* for anyone?"

"Not at all. *True love* exists for anyone who wants to stay asleep."

* *

Today is a momentous day in the life of Tobias White. Today is the celebration of the young Mr. White having completed eleven years of sentient existence on our planet. Our birthday boy was tucked under the blankets of his bed imagining the events of the day. His thoughts were not of birthday presents and a cake with candles, but rather of his helpless inability to keep the peace in a house of corrupt malevolence.

Tobias lived in what appeared to be an all-American, middle class, statistically average family. He lived with his older, somewhat supportive and generally confused brother Thaddeus and his two loving parents. One loved him with a self-perceived sense of helplessness and the other loved him with a self-perceived sense of entitlement which led to constant, relentless abuse. The White house was a toxic house.

Most parents claim to love their children, but in reality, many do not. When considering the love of one's offspring, it is important to realize that love must be unconditional. Love for a child with conditions is not love. Many people, many fine upstanding members of our society do not love their children. Many simply tolerate them. Some just support them with food, clothing, shelter, education etc.... Some of us just kind of like our kids a little, once in a while, when they're not being assholes or what not.

There are some that actually dread their children. They cannot stand what their children have become or are on their way to becoming, but when they are with them they still treat them respectfully and make a valid attempt to be supportive.

There is absolutely nothing wrong with any of these people. Think of it this way, according to the United States Bureau of Assholes, Jerks, and Nasty Rude Fucks, close to 25% of the US population are assholes, jerks, and nasty rude fucks. This is based on the 2004 US census. 23.6% to be precise. Every single member of that 23.6% is somebody's kid. It is very difficult to love an asshole or a jerk or a nasty rude fuck. You don't have to. And you don't have to spend the rest of your life beating yourself up over it if you don't. It's okay. What you should still do, and this is important, is treat them respectfully, attempt to maintain a relationship with them, try to see things from their perspective and absolutely, under no circumstances at any point in their lives should you abuse them. In any way.

Really, that last part can actually be said for anyone. But don't feel too bad about the not loving them thing. Maybe your kid is just part of the 23.6%. Hell, maybe you are. At birth, we all deserve to be loved unconditionally. But shit happens. Things change. As life goes on, not all of us deserve to be loved unconditionally by mom and dad. Only 76.4% of us do. Because, quite frankly, a lot of us present mom and dad with some pretty fucked up conditions. I'm just saying, don't feel too terrible about it if you don't love your kid, or your parents for that matter, you can still have a pretty good life that they are part of...unless-

Before I get to the unless, let me say one more thing on the subject... If your kid turns out to be an asshole, a jerk, or a nasty rude fuck, chances are pretty high that either mom or dad or both, had a little or a lot to do with it. That you should feel terrible about. Dr. Frankenstein should feel very bad that he created a monster, but he should not feel bad if he did not unconditionally love it. Really, what's to love?

From the safety of his bed, Tobias could hear his parents moving about the house. He interpreted the sounds as signs of a bad day on the rise. Mother always had her worst days on what were supposed to be joyous days. He heard heavy footsteps, cabinet doors closing loudly and more than likely, unnecessarily. He heard frustration. He did not hear the voices of his mother or his father. He could feel the tension of the house making its way under his bedroom door. He sat up and prepared to face his birthday celebration. The toxic fumes of an abusive parent filled the air. The beautiful hardwood floors of Toby's room were not visible. They were completely covered. Today, like most days, Tobias would be walking on eggshells.

Entitled parents are incapable of loving their children. Every single aspect of their relationship with their child is based on their perceived entitlement. This is unfortunate and sad for the child, but in many instances it can and does work. The parent is incapable of unconditional love, regardless if the child is part of the 76.4% or not. The child is cheated, but the two can learn to deal with one another and at times enjoy a satisfactory relationship unless...unless...the parent's frustrations turn to abuse. It may be emotional abuse, it may be physical abuse, it may be both. Abuse of any type destroys relationships. That is unfortunately what happened in the White house. Abuse always escalates.

Excerpt from Session 5

"There isn't much else to say about our first date. At that time my lust for her was purely physical. I enjoyed her appearance and was excited about the idea of being intimate with her. Our first few dates were fine. Personality wise she seemed fun. Beautifully average. She smiled or laughed any time

I said or did anything that she thought I thought was funny. Our conversation was basic. She didn't really share any of her opinions and didn't challenge any of mine. This was before the *relationship monster*, before I started confusing lust for love, before any of that. That all started on our historic fifth date."

"Historic in what way?"

"Well for our fifth date I thought it would be a good idea to take her to what became known as Disco Demolition."

"What exactly is a Disco Demolition?"

Ethan's wild staring eyes fixed on Fabiola's embarrassed awkward eyes. She felt she had said something wrong based on Ethan's expression. She had not. Ethan's immediate reaction to Fabiola's question was one of dismay in the same way that someone becomes perturbed that a fellow Human Being does not carry the same knowledge and appreciation that they do about a particular movie, song, band, artist, TV show, riot, etc. as they do, as in – *you never heard of Andrew Bird?*

Ethan's gaze became warm and attractive when he remembered to whom he was talking. Ethan felt his therapy sessions were beneficial and he enjoyed the company of Fabiola, but through no fault of her own she was young. And through some fault of her own she was not well traveled. She grew up in Nowhere, Iowa, went to school at the University of Iowa, and now was a psychologist in Anywhere, Iowa. Fabiola consulted her note pad, not because it had the possibility of answering the question, *what exactly is a Disco Demolition?* but because it did not have the captivating effect of Ethan's attention.

"There was only one Disco Demolition. It happened in Chicago at Comiskey Park, where the White Sox used to play…it was a big deal. Not just in Chicago, I'm sure it was on the news here in Anywhere, Iowa. But that was back in 1979. You probably weren't even born yet."

"I was born in 1973."

"Well it was an interesting choice for date number five. Steve Dahl was down on the field killing disco while I was up in the stands starting to confuse lust for love."

"What do you mean *killing disco?*"

"He was blowing up disco records."

"And people went there to watch him? Why?"

"Because disco sucks," Ethan smiled at Fabiola, his eyes laughing at the person he was and the world he lived in twenty-five years ago. He continued. "I was a card-carrying member of the Insane Coho Lips."

"Which is what exactly?"

"We'd love to take disco over, the way midgets love to bowl."

"I have no idea what that means but it certainly sounds offensive."

"Oh relax, back then there was a war against rock n roll and people were not so P.C. There was a vile stench of disco music starting to permeate the air waves. This is when people listened to the radio. Rock 'n' Rollers, real Rock 'n' Rollers were not going to take this lying down. We were going to rid the world of disco. Our army was called the Insane Coho Lips and our leader was Steve Dahl."

"This sounds like a very poor use of time and energy."

"No, it wasn't." Ethan seemed a little perturbed. "It actually worked. At the time the White Sox were suffering from poor attendance. What's new, right? So, they had this double header scheduled against the Detroit Tigers and thought they could boost attendance a bit if they allowed Dahl to blow up some disco records in between games. So, if a fan brought a disco record to blow up they got in for a buck or something. So, it was a cheap date. Madelyne was into it. She brought a Village People album."

"Was it your shared hatred for disco that made you start confusing your lust for love?"

"No, I think it was the riot."

"The riot?"

"Well the way she reacted to the riot."

"What riot?"

"The Disco Demolition Riot. It was way more than a sellout. Once the park was filled to capacity, there had to be another 25,000 people outside the gates. They stopped collecting the records. I guess they had too many. So, Dahl comes out after the first game and starts blowing up records and then it's just pandemonium. People storm the field, fans are whipping disco records around like Frisbees, the people outside are storming the gates. It was crazy. You are probably too young, but if you are ever wondering what happened to disco, that's what happened to disco."

"And what about Madelyne?"

"What about her?"

"You said your feelings changed for her that night, perhaps because of the way she reacted to the riot. How did she react?"

"Oh, she loved it."

* * * * * * * *   * * * * * * * * *   * * * * * * * * *   * * * * * * * *

Today is the eleventh birthday of Tobias White. He sat at the dining room table across from his older brother Thaddeus. Tobias had a nervous stomach. Thaddeus stared at his younger brother. His eyes looked angry. His face disgusted. Thaddeus looked as fed up as a fifteen-year-old boy could look. His stare penetrated through his brother's skull and fixated on the wall behind him. Toby's vantage point offered him a more disturbing display. A few feet beyond his brother there was a large cut-out in the wall that offered a view of the kitchen.

Tobias spied his mother, Madelyne, in the kitchen. Dinner was over and she was putting the finishing touches on his birthday cake. A birthday cake Toby had no desire to have presented to him. He just wanted the night to end so that he could return to the safety offered under his bed's blanket. Mom did not seem happy. Not at all. The tension in the house was thick and made it hard to breathe. The sounds and the vibe coming from the kitchen would make it clear to anyone that this was not the happy celebration it should be. Something was terribly wrong.

The entitled parent is incapable of unconditional love. They believe they are inherently deserving of special treatment. They believe they have an inalienable right to knowledge and involvement and acceptance in every aspect of their spouse and child's life. It generally is not limited to the lives of their spouse and children, but every Human Being they have close or common interaction with. No such right exists. Because of this, the entitled parent spends a lot of time with *hurt feelings*. Sometimes they use their *hurt feelings* as a weapon against the person they hold responsible for hurting their feelings by projecting guilt upon them so that they, too, can feel badly. This shared hardship does not offer the entitled parent happiness, but rather a strange satisfaction. Misery loves company.

Tobias watched his mother while attempting to not let her know he was watching her. Thaddeus grew more angry with every sound that came from the kitchen. Dad was in the bathroom. The boys anxiously awaited their father's return.

When the entitled parent also suffers from mental illness the situation could be far worse. No one should have to live in an abusive home. Abuse always escalates.

Excerpt from Session 2

"I should have left her so many times. I just always felt if we just stuck it out, together, at least then I would always be there for my boys."

"You felt trapped."

"I felt my boys were trapped. No judge would take children away from their mother for emotional abuse. But our house was toxic all the time. The mind games. The yelling and screaming, or the pouting and martyrism. The manipulating."

"But you were there for your boys. You explained things to them. You let them know Madelyne's behavior was not appropriate. You did what you felt was right."

"Toby's birthday. I told you about Toby's eleventh birthday. I should have got them the hell out of the house that night."

"Regretting something from ten years ago is not going to help you move forward. You have to forgive yourself."

"That was really the first time I realized it. Before that I guess I really didn't know that emotional abuse is just as bad as physical abuse, maybe even worse." Ethan shot air through his nostrils and smirked to denote bemusement. "That's kind of funny when you consider my childhood and my father. How did I not see my boys were suffering just as much as I did as a child?"

One of the first things Fabiola had noticed about Ethan when she met him, besides his very distinguished attractive looks was that he walked with a very noticeable crooked limp. It was toward the end of that first session he revealed the reason for that. Fabiola learned that Ethan grew up in an abusive home. Outside the home his father was a much-loved member of the church and an upstanding citizen, inside the home his father was a tyrant.

He abused Ethan and his mother mentally, emotionally, and at times physically. Growing up, Ethan only considered the beatings to be abuse. During his senior year of high school Ethan resolved to fight back. One night he came to the aid of his mother. He was scared, but he went on the attack and felt he got some good licks in. In the end the tyrant prevailed. He beat Ethan bloody and stabbed him in the thigh with a butcher knife. The cuts were so bad they nearly had to amputate his leg. That was the last time he saw his father. He was arrested that night and soon after killed himself in prison.

Fabiola allowed Ethan some time to collect himself.

"He was such a son of a bitch."

"I know," she replied.

"But I loved him too. When I was real little I looked up to him. That's so fucked up. I looked up to a monster."

"It's okay, Ethan. He was your father. Your house was the only house you knew."

Ethan sat in quiet reflection.

"I'm sorry Ethan, but we are going to have to end it for today. We will pick it up again next week."

"No problem, Fabiola."

"Are you okay?"

"Swell as hell."

"Okay then...see you next week...Oh Ethan, did you get me that phone number from your last therapist? I really think it would be beneficial to you if we spoke."

"Oh yeah, Mary Gibbons. Sorry, I forgot. I'll have it next week for you."

* *

Today is the eleventh birthday of Tobias White. Toby watched his mother. She was visibly upset. Toby watched his brother. He was visibly angry. Toby heard the toilet flush. Dad would be back soon.

Abuse generally follows a pattern. The abuser creates tension. They can do this in a number of ways. They could be critical or nitpicky or withdrawn or distant, while the victim attempts to keep things calm by walking on eggshells, trying so hard not to light the fuse. But the fuse always gets lit and then we have an explosion. This will eventually be followed by an apology of some type and a promise to not let such a thing happen again. This gives the victim artificial hope for a little while. But deep down they know the tension is right around the corner.

Ethan returned to the table where his boys sat quietly. He turned his attention to Madelyne in the kitchen. "How's the cake coming?" he asked.

Toby knew what was happening next. *Why would he ask such a stupid question?* he thought.

Excerpt from Session 3

"My boy Thad is a very hard worker. He always got decent grades, but he had to work his ass off for them. He graduated from ISU two years ago. Got himself a good job with U.S. Robotics."

"You must be very proud of Thaddeus and Tobias."

Ethan smirked and shot air through his nostrils to signify his amused agreement. "Sure, I'm proud, but I'm also watching Thad make the same mistakes as me."

"How so?"

"He is asleep in the backseat and the *relationship monster* is driving full speed ahead."

"I thought you approved of Elizabeth?"

"I do, she is a very smart young lady. She is the one that got him in at USR, but my approval has nothing to do with my disappointment."

"Why are you disappointed?"

Ethan stared deep into Fabiola's eyes. His gaze was warm and sympathetic. His words were bitter, but they did not sound that way. They came off his lips calm and confident. It was as if he was trying to explain a card game to a young child. "Because, Fabiola, they are making one huge mistake after another. They have been together for eight years now. And the *relationship monster* has been driving for at least seven of them. From the moment they gave up the wheel they were destined to fail. It's only a matter of time."

Fabiola did not look away. She remained locked in Ethan's stare. Her words were appropriate for the conditions and the subject at hand, the thoughts that danced in her head were not. "Do you mean because they make sacrifices for one another?"

"You are listening to me Fabiola, but you are not hearing me. Thaddeus and Elizabeth are making sacrifices for the sake of the *relationship*. Not for each other. Do you know they graduated together from ISU? High school sweethearts, then college sweethearts, now U.S. Robotic sweethearts."

"There is nothing wrong with that."

"Sure, things look great now. A good job at a good company. But good for who? Let me tell you something about Elizabeth. ISU wasn't the only school to accept her. She was accepted at MIT. And that came with a financial aid offer, that actually came out less expensive than ISU."

Fabiola was too busy thinking about what Ethan had just said to respond verbally.

"She went to ISU to stay with Thad. That *sacrifice* certainly didn't do anything positive for her and in the long run it certainly won't help Thad either. Sure, he got his knob rubbed a few extra hundred times, but as they were attending to the lust they thought was love the seeds of resentment were sown."

Fabiola remained tongue-tied.

"Not to mention that after graduation Elizabeth landed an interview with Apple out in California, but never went. Thad wants to remain in Chicago. Elizabeth is tending to a garden deep inside of her that she doesn't even know exists, all while the *relationship* appears stronger than ever."

Fabiola suddenly found herself considering her own love relationship. She sat quietly and expressionless.

"You okay, Fabiola?"

Fabiola felt unprofessional. She re-entered the conversation and attempted to sound qualified and diplomatic. "You don't know if Elizabeth even considers these sacrifices. These can very well be her wishes as well as your son's."

Ethan's smirk and nostril laugh returned. "MIT vs ISU? Apple? Sunny California vs Chicago winters?"

Fabiola's silence returned. Ethan's captivating stare returned. "Fabiola Fabiono, I really like your name."

* * * * * * * * * * * * * * * * * * * * * * * * * * * * * * * *

Today is the eleventh birthday of Tobias White and the way his mother is behaving is beginning to become quite upsetting. Ethan stood at the head of the table and observed his two sons seated on either side of him. Thaddeus appeared to be very angry. Tobias looked distressed. Ethan wondered, *Why? Why does she have to do this? Does she not care about her children? Can't she see what she is doing to them? It's Toby's birthday for Christ sake.*

He looked down at his dinner plate. He paid no attention to the few scraps of food that remained on the plate, he only noticed the shape of the plate. It brought him back to a different time and place. A time when he and Madelyne were both better people. Not broken like they were today. He thought of the album *Cruisin* by the *Village People*. He could picture Madelyne taking it out of the sleeve at Comiskey Park and flinging it like a frisbee all the way down to the mayhem down on the field. She laughed. She was so happy. Carefree. Life was so non-toxic back then. Ethan attempted to lighten the mood and cut through the tension. He spoke loudly. "Do you remember Disco Demolition?"

His question was not met with the warmth he was hoping for.

* * * * * * * *   * * * * * * * *   * * * * * * * *   * * * * * * * *

Fabiola Fabiono lived and worked in Anywhere, Iowa. That was never her plan. She always saw herself moving to Chicago and working and living in the city. She dreamed of it. But then she fell in love. *Or did she?* She decided to stay in Iowa. She and her husband decided to buy a house in Iowa and remain close to their extended families. *Or did the relationship monster decide that?* Fabiola did not like having these doubts. She was sure she was in true love. *Or was she asleep in the back seat?*

Ethan is just a man who has been hurt, she thought. He is just bitter. I bet I could make him view relationships differently. *I could teach him to love again.* Oh my God, why am I thinking like this? *It's those eyes. Those goddamned eyes.*

That night was not a restful one for Fabiola. She tossed and turned and imagined herself being with Ethan. Being held in his arms, returning his passionate stare, repairing his broken heart. Tomorrow he would be back in her office for the sixth time. She had known this man for only five hours but could not get him out of her thoughts. She remembered something

Ethan had said about his wife and a similar thought ran through her mind. She felt silly and embarrassed by the thought. It was inappropriate. It was unprofessional. She was ashamed of the way she felt. *Nothing made her feel more alive than the anticipation of seeing him again.*

Ethan's Final Session
The Old Man and Average Girl

"I learned everything I know about love and relationships when I was seventeen years old from the neighborhood drunk."

"Do you think the neighborhood drunk is a good place to get relationship advice from?"

"He never gave me advice. He just told me stories. At the time he didn't realize he was laying the foundation for my philosophy about love. Either did I. Not until many years later. Believe it or not, at the time we were both hopeless romantics.

"His name was George, and when the teenagers of the neighborhood would ask him to buy them alcohol, they would actually call him George. The rest of the time everyone would just call him the Old Man.

"The Old Man was probably only seventy, but a high mileage life made him look much older. He was always more than happy to oblige and get us our beer and Schnapps and occasional pint of Jack Daniels, provided he got a cut of the booty. It was also understood that during the warm months, when the teens were not drinking, they would sit on the Old Man's front porch with him and listen to him wax poetic. Nobody minded. He was entertaining. The Old Man was always somewhere in the spectrum of mildly buzzed or completely shit-faced. Most of his audience preferred the latter. I found his stories more appealing when he was closer to sober.

"The Old Man lived two doors down from me, so I started visiting him long before I had any interest in the *contributing to the delinquency of minors* service he offered. Not that that didn't come later, believe me it did. The Old Man got me my first pint of Mad Dog 20/20 when I was fifteen years old. Nasty shit that Mad Dog. But anyway, one day when I was seventeen, the Old Man really opened up to me. He told me about how he found *true love* and then lost it. He told me how sad this made him and it was the reason he had spent the last twenty years of his life in the state of or process of becoming inebriated. I mean this guy was really torn up…

"You know, now that I think about it, if I do the math, poor old George must have been around the age I am now when he thought he found *true love*. We both had different ideas about *true love* back then. Back then *true love* was…beautiful.

"The Old Man was pretty conservative back in the day. He was raised by devout Christian parents and lived his first few decades with little or no rebellion. He told me that when he was growing up his father had all the answers, so he never even considered that there were any questions. The Old Man had a baby brother that was a little more on the wild side. Baby Brother had some questions. But the Old Man's father didn't call them questions. He called them doubts and he would whoop those doubts right on out of Baby Brother. The Old Man's old man sounds like quite a pill, don't you think?"

"That's one way of putting it. I would prefer to call him an abusive parent."

"Yeah, well anyway, a frequent story the Old Man told quite often was about his old man. You see the Old Man served his country, just like his old man did. And after that he worked on the family farm, just like his old man did. So, when the Old Man was in his late twenties he had a beautiful wife, a baby girl named Alice, and a job and a life style that he absolutely hated. So, he decides life is too short and talks to his beautiful wife about moving to Chicago and taking their chances at life in the big city. The wife is overjoyed. Turns out she is a closet atheist and cannot stand her devout Christian in-laws. But now the Old Man has got to tell his old man. He is very nervous. The Old Man's old man is in the barn working on the tractor. He was always working on that tractor. The Old Man had a hundred tractor stories. Some of them pretty funny.

"So, the Old Man says, '*Dad, I got something to tell you.*' The Old Man's old man never looks away from the tractor. He just keeps tinkering away and says, '*So start tellin'.*' Now that was nothing new. That's the way the Old Man's old man always was. He never respected his children enough to stop what he was doing and just listen. He never cared to. You see, he was one of those holier than thou, smarter than you, supreme ruler of the house parents. The type of guy that thought he deserved complete respect and absolute obedience from his wife and children. He felt he was just naturally entitled to it. A real prick.

"The Old Man knew his father was going to take it hard, especially when you consider that Baby Brother split the day he turned eighteen and there were no other siblings. But the Old Man was brave. He was also compassionate. So, he *started tellin'*. He told his old man what his plans were and why he wanted to do them. He told him that he loved his Mom and Dad and appreciated all of the sacrifices they had made for him and his brother. He said he was sorry but that he and his beautiful wife just couldn't be happy living on the farm any longer. All the while he was *tellin'*, his old man just kept right on wrenching on that old tractor. At times the Old Man wasn't even sure if his old man was even listening. Occasionally, during the *tellin'* the Old Man's old man would actually ask the Old Man to hand him a tool off the work bench. Once the Old Man was all done talking, his father asked for one final tool, '*Son can you grab the axe off the wall?*'

"Now it didn't register to the Old Man at the time that an axe is an odd tool request while trying to repair a tractor, but being the ever obedient son, the Old Man grabbed the axe that was hanging on the wall above the workbench and when he turned to bring it to his father, he noticed for the first time since he entered the barn his father was looking at him and not the tractor. And this is what the Old Man's old man says to him. '*Now son, I want you to take that there axe you're holding and take a mighty swing and put that bit right through my heart.*'

"The Old Man just stood there, staring at his father. '*Go on, what are you waiting for?*' his father shouts at him. The Old Man cannot remember what he said; some type of apology or further explanation or promises to visit often, who knows? But he remembers what his father said next…

'*After all of the sacrifices I've made for you and your brother. You're gonna do the same as him and abandon me and your mother and the farm. Everything we've worked so hard for. All of our dreams. So, you go ahead and put that axe right on through my chest. 'Cause either way, son, you are killing me.*' After about twenty seconds of looking at each other, the Old Man's old man turned his back on his defiant son and went back to working on his tractor. That's the last thing he ever said to the Old Man."

Ethan's eyes were now fixed on something in Fabiola's office that was not her. She watched him and realized his stare was not fixed on any object but rather a different time and place. She allowed a few seconds to pass and then interrupted Ethan's silent reflection. "George's father seems to have a lot of similarities to your father."

Ethan came back to his present time and place and politely asked Fabiola to repeat her observation. He then laughed his usual laugh through his nostrils and responded with a question and then an answer. "You think? Maybe that's why I related to him so well."

Ethan continued…

"The Old Man said life was great for him and his beautiful wife and daughter Alice in the Second City. He got himself a job at United Airlines in the air freight division. Made good enough money and had a great pension plan to look forward to. The three of them were very happy. There were times the Old Man became extremely sad that he no longer had a relationship with his father, but deep down in his heart, he knew he had made the right call. He made his decision based on what was best for him, not what was best for the *relationship monster*. Funny thing is, if you think about it, the Old Man's decision would have actually been better for his father, too, if his father wasn't such an entitled selfish prick, because let's face it, if you are truly a righteous soul, how can you be happy if you are making your children miserable? You should be your children's greatest advocate, not their greatest obstacle…

"Sorry…so, the Old Man goes on to say he realized pretty early on that his little girl Alice was a bit different. She reminded him of Baby Brother. She was wild at heart. Despite having mostly conservative views the Old Man was not going to do to his daughter what his father had done to him. He loved Alice unconditionally. He says he always tried to keep an open mind and listen to what his daughter had to say. I think I believed him. At the time he first told me about his superior parenting I did not believe him. I based that on the fact that I never witnessed a visit from his precious daughter Alice, but that was before I knew the entire tragic story.

"The Old Man's conservative life style, unconditional love for his daughter and valid attempt toward open mindedness was all put to the test when Alice was seventeen years old."

Fabiola interrupted Ethan. "The same age you were when George told you this story?"

"Yeah, yeah, I guess so," Ethan responded in a way that portrayed displeasure in being interrupted for such a trivial piece of information. "Anyway, at seventeen, Alice came out of the closet so to speak."

Fabiola sought clarification. "She told her father she was gay?"

"She sure did. The mom had known for a couple of months, and now so did the Old Man."

Fabiola Fabiono was beginning to suspect the characters in Ethan's story were not who he said they were. *Was George's father actually Ethan's father? Was George Ethan? Was Alice one of Ethan's sons? Were Thaddeus or Tobias gay? Is Ethan using gay to represent something else? Is Ethan Alice?* "How did George react to his daughter's news?" Fabiola asked.

"Well, he wasn't delighted. You have to consider the way he was brought up, what was ingrained in his mind. I mean, according to the way he was raised by his asshole father, he just found out his daughter was going to burn in hell."

"Is that what he believed?"

"No, but it took some time for him to learn how to stop that thought from entering his head. It took a little while, but the Old Man was able to accept the whole gay thing and go on loving his daughter unconditionally. The problem he had was accepting who Alice was being gay with."

"So, he had a problem with the gay community?"

"No, not at all. He had a problem with this particular group of friends Alice now kept company with. There was a lot of drug and alcohol use, some petty theft, a couple of arrests. Alice even dropped out of high school. After about two years of delinquent behavior the Old Man and his beautiful wife had a come to Jesus type meeting with Alice and gave her an ultimatum."

"How did that go?"

"It worked. Alice straightened out. Well not that kind of straight, I mean she was still a full-blown lesbian, but she cleaned up her act, got her GED, started taking some classes at Sequoia Hills Community College and met a real nice young lady. The Old Man and his beautiful wife were delighted. But then something happened that the Old Man could not understand.

"Alice's new girlfriend was very nice. She had a real friendly outgoing personality. The Old Man said she was downright bubbly. She wasn't ugly, but she wasn't super attractive either. The Old Man had an old picture of her and I guess I could see if the light hit her in just the right way she might appear to be cute. I also imagined that if she spent some time dolling herself up for a special night or event or something, she could probably pass for pretty. There was nothing fantastic about her body; she was neither fat nor thin. As far as I know she had all of her lady parts, which is a plus, but I imagine her body type was closer to a twelve-year-old boy than to Pamela Anderson. Let's just say she was an average girl."

"Nothing wrong with average."

"Right, but not to the Old Man. He shows me her picture and says she is the prettiest girl of all time. She's like in her early twenties in the picture and I'm like seventeen when he shows it to me and I'm like…Her? I mean, she was all right, but why was she the prettiest girl of all time…to him?

"Anyway, the Old Man says when he first met her he didn't think much of her. Thought she seemed nice. Friendly. And like I said he and his beautiful wife were thrilled that Alice was turning her life around. But as time went on the Old Man began to feel this strange attraction to Average Girl. Unlike anything he had ever felt before. And the more he saw her the more this attraction grew. Not that they saw a lot of each other. Alice and Average Girl were always on their way to something or coming back from something. Their time in the Old Man's home was very limited. But the Old Man would always try to be around for these brief encounters. He said he began to cherish them. When Average Girl wasn't around the Old Man would ache with wonder as to when he would see her again. And when he did see her his heart would hope it would just last a little longer. He started to constantly invite the girls to do something, anything, with his beautiful wife and him. *You girls should stay for dinner. You girls should come over for a game night sometime. Your mother and I would love to take you two out for dinner.*'—'*Not tonight Dad. We are running late Dad, we got to go. Sorry Dad we have plans,*' would be Alice's response. Then one time Average Girl says, *That sounds nice, we should do that sometime.*

"The Old Man told me he clung to those words as if they were a tangible being. He brought them to bed at night and embraced them more passionately than he had ever embraced his beautiful wife.

"Eventually game night happened. And then a dinner here and there. The four of them. And the Old Man tells me that quite often he and Average Girl would be sitting or standing very near each other. Let's say their shoulders would be separated by just a couple of feet of open space. He swears to me in the space between them he could actually feel an electrical type force. A magnetism if you will. His insides would tingle. Yeah, that's what the Old Man tells me. And he says he loves it, the feeling. It absolutely overjoys him, even though every time it only leaves him wanting and hoping for more, he says it's the most satisfying thing in his life. So, I'm thinking, like wow, this poor guy has got it really bad. The most satisfying thing in his life is the feeling of not being satisfied.

"The only thing that really bothered the Old Man was he could not for the life of him figure out why he felt these insanely strong feelings for Average Girl. He knew that he had fallen fully and completely in love with her, but he did not know why. His words, by the way, not mine. At the time he told me this story I also believed that he had fallen in love. He said the whole thing made him feel silly, and embarrassed, and a little creepy. At the time I thought he sounded a little creepy, too, but the heart wants what the heart wants, right?"

Ethan laughed through his nostrils again and then glanced at Fabiola, looking for confirmation. She offered none, nor did she look away. Ethan continued...

"His daughter's significant other, nearly thirty years his junior, definitely a recipe for disaster. And the Old Man knew it. He promised himself he would never graduate his feelings into actions. He would just continue living his life being satisfied with his un-satisfaction.

"I really wish I knew then what I know now so I could have told him. But then I would have never got married to Madelyne which means my boys would have never been born. And my boys mean everything to me. Quite the conundrum."

Fabiola inquired, "What exactly is it that you wish you knew back when George was telling seventeen-year-old Ethan his love story?"

"That he wasn't in love. He couldn't be. How could he be? He didn't even know her. They never talked, I mean as in really talked. He did not know her thoughts or likes or dislikes or plans or dreams. They had barely scratched the surface on knowing anything about each other. The Old Man did not fall in love with Average Girl. He fell in love with the idea of Average Girl. His mind built her into something that he truly desired and his imagination just ran with it."

"Ethan, I'm not saying necessarily that George's story is an example of this, but isn't it possible for one person in a relationship to fulfill the other person's *ideas* of them?"

Again, the nostril laugh. This time accompanied by a shake of the head and roll of the eyes. Ethan continued without verbally answering Fabiola's question. "Poor old George was head over heels in lust. There was definitely something about Average Girl the Old Man found attractive. Maybe it was her smile, or her eyes, or her hips, or the way she walked, or the way she said his name. Maybe it was her awkwardness, or her confidence, or her youth and innocence. Maybe she reminded him of someone from his past, or she was completely unlike anyone he had ever met. Something got the ball rolling. Let's call whatever *it* is the first puzzle piece. And because she was such forbidden fruit, being so much younger and his daughter's girlfriend, he was not able to obtain the rest of the puzzle pieces in a natural and honest way, so his mind made them up. And he made every single puzzle piece to his liking. He created the perfect woman out of Average Girl and he lusted for her like a man on fire.

"Do you remember a few sessions ago I told you how I believe that the first thing most people confuse for love is lust? That was definitely the case for the Old Man. Well, I also said if that lust is tended to it will eventually evolve into the second thing that people confuse for love."

"Yes, you said people confuse longing for love," Fabiola remembered.

"Indeed. And that's exactly what happened to the Old Man. Having never sexually touched Average Girl the Old Man's lust was tended to merely by her being in his presence. Her smile, her laugh, a conversation, a simple hello, a hug goodbye, this was enough to cause the Old Man to long for his next encounter with Average Girl. He told me sometimes he would find himself staring at her for long periods of time and looking away once he realized what he was doing. He worried terribly if Alice or his beautiful wife had noticed his inappropriate leer. There were even a couple of times when he thought he had caught Average Girl staring at him. This sent shivers of excitement through his entire body, but then after some reasonable consideration the Old Man would come to the conclusion that even if it was true and she was sneaking a peek at him, it could never be for the reasons that he hoped. Imagine, a young lesbian in a committed relationship, suddenly being into a middle-aged man with nothing to offer other than the promise that his body would soon start to deteriorate.

I really felt for the guy when he was telling me. He would think about her every waking moment of every day. When he woke up in the morning she would be his first thought and he would start dreaming about her before he fell asleep. And it wasn't like he was some horny dirty old man. He said having sex with her was never forefront in his mind. Not that it wouldn't have been nice, he also said. But mostly he just thought about being with her, watching her, listening to her, touching her, being touched by her, holding each other. He couldn't get these thoughts out of his head, no matter how much he tried. And he hated himself for having them. He loved his beautiful wife so much. At least he thought he did. But he never had feelings like this about her. And he loved his daughter, Alice, and being madly *in love* with his daughter's significant other filled him with guilt and shame."

"Sounds like he was in quite a bit of pain," Fabiola sympathized.

"Well here's the weird thing. He tells me every minute of every day that Average Girl was not around, which was most of them, that the longing he felt caused him tremendous pain. He says he loved her so much that he constantly ached in agonizing torment. But then he goes on to tell me that that torment, that pain, made him feel more alive than he ever had before. As we sat there on his front porch he told me he had felt dead inside for the last twenty years. And that for the first fifty years of his life he was just going through the motions. But for that short period in his life, when Average Girl was part of it, he felt truly and completely alive. And he said he would do anything to get that pain back again."

"That's interesting."

"I really wish I could go back in time and talk to the Old Man and tell him that it was all in his head. The reason he never felt this way about his beautiful wife was because she was real. Average Girl was not. He invented her. He built her into something she could never be. No one could. He fell in love with the perfect woman in his mind and put her into Average Girl's body…

"So, then the Old Man's story takes a little bit of a twist. He kind of starts breaking bad on Alice. He tells me that Alice started treating Average Girl poorly. Sometimes she's rude and dismissive, sometimes she is downright mean. And the Old Man doesn't like that. At the time seventeen-year-old me starts wondering if the Old Man is full of shit. I mean, at this point in the story I'm kind of rooting for Alice. She is like the hero. She was on a bad path and she fixed up her life. And the Old Man, even though I feel sorry for him, he is a little creepy, right?"

Fabiola Fabiono offers no confirmation.

"Anyway, the Old Man decides to confront his daughter about her behavior toward Average Girl. At first Alice is pretty cold to her father putting his nose where it doesn't belong, but after some mild arguing, she confides in him. It seems Alice does not *love* Average Girl. She wants to move on, meet other people, do her own thing. To which I say, bravo, Alice. She is a smart girl. She is not willing to jump in the back seat and let the *relationship monster* drive the car. She is making decisions that are best for her. And in the long run, best for Average Girl. But the Old Man finds this news devastating. The non-existent, unattainable girl that he believes he is madly and deeply in love with who comes around a few times a week, to put a bandaid on his aching heart and temporarily tend to his unsatisfiable lust is about to be jettisoned from his daughter's life, which means his life as well.

"This is when the guy starts to drink. Then one night, he was drunk, he was down, he was wanderin' round his bed, he called out her name. He called out her name, with his wife laying right there. She heard him. The only thing she said was *get back in bed. You're drunk.* The Old Man knew right away what he had done. In the morning he remembered his blunder. He waited all day for his beautiful wife to confront him about his gaffe. She never did. The Old Man said it was because in her eyes the two of them were in *true love.* I agree, using my current definition of *true love,* the Old Man defined it as two people having the ability, willingness, and strength to put up with each other's bullshit. What he felt for the Average Girl was far beyond *true love.*

"A few weeks after the Old Man confronts his daughter, she dumps Average Girl. Turns out, the break up is pretty hard on Alice too. I mean she feels she made the right decision, but she also still has feelings for Average Girl and feels really guilty for breaking her heart. After a couple of weeks of watching her daughter mope around, feeling like a criminal for making a decision in her own best interest, the Old Man's beautiful wife decides to take Alice on a spa weekend. So, the ladies of the house are gone. Now the Old Man is the only moper in the house. And he is tossing back a few drinks to try and dull his pain. He is trying to convince himself that everything that happened is for the best. For everyone. But his longing for Average Girl is almost unbearable. He is trying so hard to just hold himself together. But he doesn't think he can. He feels like he is going to lose it. I mean this guy is teetering. And then the doorbell rings... Guess who?"

"Average Girl?"

"Disco."

"Disco?"

"Disco, like bingo, like yes, you are right. He opens the door and there she is. Average Girl, standing there looking like she had been crying for the last two weeks. But to him, she still looks like the prettiest girl of all time. She asks the Old Man, *'Is Alice here?'* Her voice trembling. The Old Man just stares at her, captivated by her beauty, tantalized by her vulnerability and just says, *'I'm sorry.'* She lowers her head, which cheats the Old Man of continuing to behold her perfect face and she mumbles, *'I shouldn't have even come here. I'm sorry, please don't tell Alice.'* As she turns to leave the Old Man thinks, this is it, I'll never see her again and in a panic he cries out, *'Don't go!'*

"She continues to make her way down the steps ignoring his plea. *'Please, come in for a minute. Warm up. It's so cold.'* She is halfway down the stairs and showing no signs of stopping. The Old Man continues his desperation to extend the moment. *'How did you get here? Did you walk? I can drive you home.'*

"As she hit the last step she responded without turning around. *'No thank you, it's okay, I drove.'*

'You can't drive!' the Old Man shouts. And then using his inside voice he adds, *'You're in no condition to drive.'*

"She stops. She turns to him. As her voice cracks in a poor attempt to hold back her emotional breakdown she asks, '*Why did this happen?*' She stands there weeping. The Old Man rushes to her side. He escorts her back up the stairs and into the house saying, '*I can't let you drive like this.*'

"Once inside she stands before him and continues to weep and questions, '*Did I do something wrong? What did I do?*' She looks up at him, her voice trembling, her body quivering. He puts a hand on each of her shoulders and tries to offer her comfort. He feels the electricity between their bodies stronger than he ever had before. Still having his senses about him he realizes this was a one-sided feeling and attempts to reassure her. '*You didn't do anything wrong. You're fine. You're better than fine. You're perfect. It's just sometimes...sometimes....*' He fumbles for the right words.

"She burst into tears and buries her face into his chest. George feels her arms wrap tightly around his waist. He returns her hug and keeps repeating, '*There, there, it's going to be okay.*' The electricity that was between them moments ago is now racing through his body. The charge is intoxicating. He felt like the most powerful man in the world. More than anything he had ever wanted in his entire life, he wanted to have her right there. He could barely contain himself. But contain himself he did.

Still having his senses about him he realizes the reality of the situation and it nearly destroys him. This was his daughter's brokenhearted ex-lover. He thought about Alice. He thought about his beautiful wife. He thought about the girl that he considered to be perfect, that he now held in his embrace and after holding her a little tighter than he should have and allowing it to last, perhaps, slightly longer than he should have, he decided to give Average Girl what she needed. With his chin resting on her head he said to her, '*I know how badly this hurts right now, but you will get through it. You will love again. You are smart, you are pretty, you are funny, you are such a great person. Some day you are going to make somebody a very lucky person.*'

"George should have stopped right there. But he didn't. He continued. '*My only regret,*' he says, '*my only regret is that somebody can't be me.*'

"Can you believe that? I mean can you believe he said that? The Old Man really put himself right out there."

Fabiola found herself on the edge of her seat desperate to find out what happens next. She excitedly asks, "Did she hear him?"

"Oh, she heard him all right. He said he felt her warm hands on his back and the moment those words slipped out of his mouth those hands were gone. The Old Man felt embarrassed and ashamed and stupid. He was trying to figure out what to say next. Someway to save face. When all of a sudden, her hands returned to him, but this time they were red hot and they shot under his shirt. He felt her palms gently caressing the bare skin of his back. She looked up at him and said, '*You can be that somebody.*'

"Bam! Just like that every one of the Old Man's dreams and fantasies came true. Turns out, Average Girl is a switch hitter. Ends up all those times the Old Man thought she was sneaking a peek at him, she was. Ends up she is totally fucking into him."

Ethan leans back in his chair and interlocks his fingers behind his head. His face projects a shit-eating grin which Fabiola has never witnessed on him. He had such a self-satisfied appearance you would have thought he had just told the greatest story ever told. Fabiola needed more. "So, what happened?"

"As the Old Man put it, the greatest and worst six months of his life. As I would put it, the poor Old Man went from thinking longing was love to thinking obsession was love, because after that night he was absolutely obsessed with Average Girl. They snuck around at first, but then they got busted. It destroyed his marriage, ruined his relationship with his daughter, but the obsession continued. For a while the Old Man was having the time of his life. After a few months though, the Old Man began to come to terms with certain circumstances that deep down he had always been aware of, not to mention his perfect girl was slowly becoming a real person. So, he did the exact same thing his daughter did. He was not willing to go in the back seat and let the *relationship monster* drive. No ma'am he was not. Instead of allowing things to happen that were best for the *relationship* he made a decision based on what was best for Average Girl. He dumped her. It was the right thing to do. She was young. She wanted to start a family. She wanted to do the things young people do. The Old Man did not. As he put it, he was only in love with her, not with what she wanted. So, he spent the rest of his life drinking and reaping the harvest he had sewn. He still longed for her. Their time together was so short that twenty years later, in his mind, she remained the perfect woman.

"After he told me his story, he says to me the night she showed up at his front door he thought he knew what his only regret in life was, but he was wrong. Kind of at least. It was really just the way he said it. It kind of means the same thing. It's just more definitive. Doesn't allow for any wiggle room. You see, George's only regret was that he wasn't born twenty-five years later."

"That's quite a story Ethan," Fabiola commented and then she had this question. "So, the way you see it the two of them never shared a love?"

Ethan had this answer. "Of course not. The poor girl was young and mixed up. Coming off the rebound. I guarantee she had Daddy issues that she thought the Old Man answered. Even when the Old Man told me his story, twenty years after he last saw her, he still insisted he was madly in love with her and because of her he could never love again. That's why he drank like a fish. His mind had rebuilt her back into the absolute perfect soul mate. He could call it love if he wants, and you can too, but I just say he is completely and hopelessly obsessed with a person that does not even exist."

They both sat quietly for a few seconds and then Ethan added something Fabiola found very interesting.

"I can tell you, there is no end to that pain."

"You can tell me?" Fabiola repeated.

"Huh?" Ethan did not understand the echo.

"*You can tell me there is not end to that pain* as in you are also experiencing that type of pain?"

"No, that's not what I meant by that. You are over-analyzing. I meant, I can imagine there is no end to that pain."

"What about realization? Wouldn't realizing a fantasy is just a fantasy go a long way toward at least dulling that pain?"

"Sometimes, Fabiola Fabiono, it's too late to realize."

"No, it's not, Ethan. It is never too late to realize. That's how we grow as Human Beings."

* * * * * * *   * * * * * * * *   * * * * * * * *   * * * * * * *

Today is Toby's eleventh birthday. His father, Ethan, just asked his mother Madelyne a question. "Do you remember Disco Demolition?" She remembered it, but she did not answer her husband's question. The tension in the birthday house continued to grow.

When people are abused they are frightened. Whether they are scared of being hurt physically or emotionally they spend much of their time worrying about the next time they will be attacked. Whether that attack is a violent beating, an unwanted touch, a hurtful comment, a passive aggressive statement, or a complete act of dehumanization, it is unacceptable and should not be tolerated. But more often than not it is tolerated.

Abusers have this knack for being in control of their victims. Victims generally stay silent and just wait in quiet fear of the next assault. Some do it out of complete paralyzing fear of the abuser, some mistakenly think they love the abuser, others rely on the abuser financially, and there are still others who just try to keep the peace, and even some unfortunate souls that believe it is their fault. Whatever the reason, whatever the abuse, abusers will abuse until their power is taken away, but until that happens, abuse always escalates.

Ethan continued to stare at his dinner plate thinking back to better days when his wife was not the toxic person he felt she had become. He wanted to end this. He wanted a happy family. But how?

The Final Moments of Ethan's Final Session

Fabiola Fabiono sat silently, feeling oddly titillated and regrettably unprofessional. She had allowed herself to be captivated by Ethan's story instead of better analyzing it and determining the purpose that he shared it. She actually found herself sympathizing with the Old Man. Rooting for him. Or at the very least, hoping for a happy ending for him. Now as she struggled to escape the spell Ethan had put her under, she refused to look at his lovely eyes. She opted to instead to look at the notes scribbled on her legal pad as she tried to give reason to Ethan's words.

Such a convenient story as it clearly supported all of Ethan's philosophies regarding his myth of love, she thought. *I wonder how much is even true? What is Ethan really thinking? It seems as though there is so much more to him. Could he be the Old Man and I be the Average Girl? Is that a possibility? Or am I projecting my deep desires? It cannot be that. Can it?*

"Same time next week, Fabiola," Ethan stated as he got up to leave.

Don't go, Fabiola thought. "Yes, indeed," Fabiola said. "Have a good week, Ethan."

"You, too."

"Any plans for the weekend?"

"Yeah, I told you, Toby's twenty-first birthday, remember? I'm headed to Chicago to spend some time with my boys."

"That's right, that's right, I'm sorry. Well enjoy."

Ethan walked with his crooked crutch toward the door.

"Ethan, wait," Fabiola called to him. He turned to her. "The number you gave me for your old therapist was disconnected."

"Oh, the ever-elusive Marie Gibson. Well, she was just that, an old therapist, very old. And at least five years passed between the last time I saw her and the first time I saw you so, who knows, maybe she retired?"

Fabiola considered Ethan's words as he walked out of her office for the last time. "Maybe," she agreed. "Well enjoy your children."

Fabiola was not considering Marie Gibson's retirement. She was considering that this was the first time he had called her Marie Gibson. She was sure of it. She consulted her notes to confirm. Every other time Ethan mentioned her she was Mary Gibbons. This would explain why Fabiola could not find any information about Mary Gibbons in previous attempts. Fabiola investigated the new name and before she went home that night she discovered who Marie Gibson was.

Marie Gibson was a psychology Professor at Moraine Valley Community College just outside of Chicago and was only fifty-seven years old. *Well that can't be her*, Fabiola thought, *perhaps Ethan just misspoke*. But there were a couple of other interesting things about Marie Gibson. She had only been teaching for five years and before that she was a licensed clinical social worker for fifteen years. The following day, a Thursday, Fabiola put a call in at Moraine Valley Community College and left a message for Marie Gibson.

Thursday came and went with no return call.

Friday morning Fabiola left a second message.

Late Friday afternoon she left a third.

It was 5 o'clock on Saturday when Fabiola's phone rang.

"Hello."

"Hi, this is Marie Gibson, returning the call of a Fabiola Fa…" she stumbled through the name.

"Yes, Yes, Fabiola Fabiono, thank you for—"

"Yeah, right, easy for you to say," Marie interrupted. "Anyway, if you're calling about the job you are about two weeks too late." Marie was brash, Marie was curt, Marie was no-nonsense.

"Job? What job. No, no, I'm not calling about a job."

"Really? Well if this has anything to do with Richard I've got nothing to say and you could call my law—"

"No, I don't even know what you're talking about. I'm a therapist from Anywhere, Iowa—"

"Seriously, that's a place?"

"Yes, it is."

"Well, what do you want, Anywhere, Iowa?"

"I have this client and I think at one time he may have been a client of yours, when you were a LCSW. His name is—"

"Client? That's what we're calling them now?"

"I'm sorry…a former *patient* then—"

"Oh boy, now that's rich. What did you say this person's name is?"

"I haven't yet, his name is—"

"Cause I'm probably not going to remember him. I had a lot of *patients*. 15 years' worth."

"Yes, well his name—"

"You sound young. You're probably young. It's a tough job and once you burn out you try to put it behin—"

"—Ethan White."

The abrasive Marie Gibson went silent.

"Miss Gibson? Are you there?"

"Well, you picked one that I remember. A story like that, how could you forget?"

"A story like what?"

"The whole story. The entire story. He did tell you about his childhood, right?"

"Yes. Yes he did. But—"

"Yeah, well that was some messed up shit. The kind of stuff you don't forget too easy."

"Well, I feel like Ethan definitely holds a lot back during our sessions. Sometimes I have the feeling that he is not being completely honest with me, but he did tell me that his father was quite abusive."

"To say the least. I really pitied Ethan as a young man. Could you imagine, seventeen years old."

"Are you talking about his leg?"

"His leg? No, hell no, I'm talking about Alice."

"Alice? His neighbor's daughter?"

"Alice was his sister. He told you Alice was his neighbor's kid? Now that's rich."

"His sister? Like I said, Miss Gibson I'm afraid Ethan has not been totally honest with me then. Can you please share with me what happened with his sister?"

"Oh Christ. Stories like Ethan Whites are why I got out of the business. You at least know what a terrible prick his old man was, right? Please tell me he told you that."

"Yes. Yes, that I know."

"The son of a bitch was super religious. A real church goer, but at home the prick would beat on the mother from time to time. In front of Ethan and Alice since they were little babies. Ethan never did anything about it. He was scared shitless of the old man. That really ate Ethan up inside, that he never did anything to try and stop it.

"Anyway, Ethan's sister Alice, she's about three years older than him, turns out she's a queer. She gets herself this real pretty girlfriend, Ethan says she was the prettiest girl of all time, for the life of me I can't remember her name. So, the two of them are sneaking around. She never even considers coming out of the closet or anything with this bible-thumping lunatic as a father, but somehow, he finds out. Maybe he catches them or something, I don't know, Ethan didn't know, but the old man decides he is going to beat the gay out of his daughter and he knocks the shit out of the poor girl. Puts her in the hospital."

"Oh my, how terrible."

"So, the mother, who's been quiet for years, she's not quiet anymore.

The old man's on the run and the mother is in full cooperation with the police. But there is another part of the story."

"Please, do tell."

"Alice isn't the only one sneaking around with the prettiest girl of all time—"

"Oh my God, the Old Man?"

"No, not the old man. Ethan. Seventeen-year-old Ethan was banging his sister's girlfriend. It was his first love. And the way he talked about her, I never heard anyone so madly, deeply in love before. He cherished her, but for her I think…well, I think she was just sort of a player.

"Once Alice got home from the hospital, the girlfriend moved into the house. When she wasn't nursing Alice back to health she was banging Ethan. After a couple of weeks, she must have started feeling guilty, because she decides to break things off with Ethan."

"And now she's living in the house." Fabiola imagines all the painful nuances of the situation and wonders why Ethan was not honest with her.

"Yeah, that's not the half of it. I probably shouldn't even be telling you all this, but, whatever. So then Ethan leaves. He's got nowhere to go so he fills a backpack and just starts walking. Alice and his mother have no idea what's going on. And the night Ethan leaves, the father, that goddamned prick, comes back."

"Oh no, the police never got him."

"They do, but not at this point. Turns out the priest at the old man's church was hiding the son of a bitch."

"Unbelievable. The Priest?"

"Really? You think that's unbelievable? You must not read the news very often."

"So, what happened?"

"It was terrible. The father set the house on fire. He started the fire in the front and then waited in the back with an hammer. He killed all three of the woman."

"Oh my God. Like the Taliesin murders."

"Exactly. The girlfriend put up a real good fight. When the police got there, she was still alive. The father was on top of her, choking her, when a cop blew his goddamned head off."

"This is definitely not the version Ethan told me. How incredibly tragic."

"I could tell you it's the true version. I checked it all out. Then after three nights on the streets Ethan comes home to find his family dead and his home burned to the ground. At that point the girlfriend was still holding on. Ethan sat with her for her final hours. She was unconscious, but she did speak to him just before she died."

"What did she say?"

"Poor kid, just when you think it couldn't get any worse for him, she speaks one word just before she dies. His prettiest girl of all time looks right at him and cries out...'Alice'."

"Poor Ethan."

"Back then, yes. Soon after that he joined the Marines. So, are you out at Anamosa?"

"Anamosa? The penitentiary?"

"I figured, since you were calling from Iowa. I have an acquaintance that worked there a few years back. Ramona Chworktap, do you know her?"

"No, I can't say that I do. I don't work for Anamosa."

"Which prison are you at?"

"Prison? I don't work at a prison."

"You don't?"

"No. I'm in private practice."

"Oh, I just figured...Well, I guess it's been about seven years—"

"Miss Gibson, how exactly did you counsel Ethan?"

"He went through my anger management program. Twice."

* * * * * * * *   * * * * * * * * *   * * * * * * * * *   * * * * * * * *

Today is Toby Whites eleventh birthday and his mother is really starting to piss his father off. Still staring down at his dinner plate Ethan growled at his distraught wife as she nervously tried to prepare her son's birthday cake. "I asked you a question. Do you remember Disco Demolition?"

Madelyne wanted to answer her husband. She truly did. Not because she was interested in the subject he had brought up. Not because she thought he deserved an answer, only because she wanted Ethan to stay calm. She knew all too well how he became if something made him angry.

Currently all of the emotions Madelyne possessed only wanted to make her cry. Crying made Ethan angry. The reason Madelyne was such a wreck was because of something that had occurred in the dining room a few minutes earlier, before Ethan went to the bathroom, before Madelyne went into the kitchen. As usual Ethan's dismissive tone and cruel statements toward Madelyne had been very upsetting and embarrassing to her. As usual the boys were very angered by their father's behavior. After the incident when Ethan witnessed how upset he had made his beautiful wife and children, he offered this...

"Okay, why don't you calm the fuck down and stop your goddamned martyr bullshit. I'm sorry I upset you, but now you're trying to embarrass me in front of the kids. Make me look like the fucking bad guy. Well, just stop it. Go on and get Toby's cake ready and calm yourself down before you ruin his birthday like you ruin every other fucking day."

Since then Madelyne had not said a word, but there were definitely sounds coming from the kitchen, the sounds of nervous clumsiness, the sounds of fear, the sounds of regret, the sounds of a victim desperately trying to hold back the sounds of her despair. She took in a shaky breath and tried to answer Ethan's question as she exhaled. "Yes," she said in a voice filled with painful dismay.

"Here we fuckin' go," shouted Ethan. "I said I was sorry. But you can't let it go. Can you?" He then grabbed up his plate and threw it just like a Village People album through the opening in the wall that gave access to the kitchen. The plate barely missed Madelyne's head and smashed against the cabinets behind her. Glass fell to the floor as Ethan made his way to the kitchen.

"You see what you made me do! You see what you made me fucking do!" Ethan shouted.

"Please, Dad, don't," yelled Tobias.

"I'm sorry. I'm sorry," Madelyne pleaded.

Ethan raised his fist to make her flinch but did not strike her. He instead grabbed a handful of her hair and began screaming through clenched teeth into her ear. "Why do you always have to be like this? You want to turn my children against me."

He pulled her head back and forth, up and down, as if he were the puppeteer of a demonic puppet show. He continued his horrific degrading performance by completely humiliating his beautiful wife, the mother of his children. He forced her head down toward the countertop with great strength until her face completely destroyed Toby's birthday cake. The candles snapped and broke against her forehead and cheekbones. He held her head down deep below the frosting into the cake. She could not breathe. She sucked crumbs of the cake into her trachea and began to cough violently while still being held down.

Fifteen-year-old Thaddeus wrapped his arms around his father's waist and attempted to pull him away from his mother. His efforts failed. His father easily escaped his grasp and pushed him hard. He fell hard against the wall on the opposite end of the kitchen. This made Ethan even angrier at his beautiful wife. He released his clench. Her face covered in cake and frosting mixed with blood from a cut lip and bleeding nose she started to make her way past Ethan to go to the aid of her son.

Ethan stopped her by again grabbing a fist full of hair and pulling her back. He walked her around the kitchen still yelling through clenched teeth, as drool began to seep from both sides of his mouth. Pieces of glass from the broken plate ripped through Madelyne's socks and began to cut her feet as Ethan continued to be the puppet master.

Fifteen-year-old Thaddeus again attempted to attack his father, but his father was too powerful. He shoved Madelyne down to the ground at one end of the kitchen and pushed Thaddeus hard back to the wall from which he came. Blood began to ooze through Madelyne's socks as she sat there crying with her beautiful face vandalized. Thaddeus sat on the floor opposite from her. His head had hit the wall and his perception was cloudy.

"Stop it, Dad! Please stop!" Tobias yelled.

Ethan stood in the middle of the kitchen, entirely deranged by anger. Looking down at Thaddeus he began to take off his belt.

"Dad! I called the police! They will be here any second," Tobias shouted from the dining room. His father stopped. He refastened his belt. This was the first time during Ethan's reign of terror that somebody called the police. He turned to Tobias and ran his frosting-filled fingers through his disheveled hair and in all seriousness said, "It's not me son. It's her."

* * * * * * * *   * * * * * * * * *   * * * * * * * * *   * * * * * * * *

Madelyne was raised by a set of entitled parents. She was never abused by them in the classical definition. They, as well as all of their family and friends believed them to be terrific parents. They were not. They were strict. They were stifling. They chose what parts of the world Madelyne would see and what parts she would not, even as her years advanced. They kept most of the world hidden from her. They were rewarded for their corrupt agenda with an extremely well-behaved child that never gave them any trouble. They truly believed that because she was their biological daughter that she was also their eternal property and should live her life on their terms. Their love was not unconditional, it was compromised and they were lazy in the ways they showed their affection and absent when it came to respect.

Madelyne met Ethan White when she was quite young and he was anxious to illustrate his love and affection. He was also six years her senior and offered her freedom that was previously unavailable. Living almost twenty years under the oppressive regime of her parents, she was poised for a rebellion, and Ethan White offered to lead that rebellion.

He was handsome. He had a good job and his own place. He listened to her most of the time, in the beginning, and was really grand at pretending to advocate for all of her plans and dreams. In reality, she was just entering a more oppressive regime. None of her plans or dreams actually ever came to fruition. Because of the busy day to day duties of raising children she soon found herself in the backseat, but the *relationship monster* wasn't driving, Ethan was.

By the time she reached her late twenties she had two children, no relationship with her family, no friends that were not Ethan's friends first, she had never had a job and Ethan was against her getting one. She had learned no skills and earned no degrees, she never even learned how to drive an automobile. Tobias was a baby the first time he laid hands on her. She complained that she was over-worked with the two children and insisted Ethan contribute more in raising them and she also expressed dissatisfaction in their social life and Ethan's lack of appreciation for her. She insisted he remedy both situations.

Her requests were far from inappropriate; perhaps her manner of delivering them was a little aggressive. She was stressed out from a long day with a baby and toddler and as the day went on she had a feeling of resentment toward Ethan that began to fester deep within her soul. Ethan was undeniably on the receiving end of some yelling. He slapped her hard across the face with an open palm – so hard that she fell to the floor and had a red imprint on her face for two days. He then bent over, grabbed her by the shirt and pulled her injured face close to his and through gritted teeth he insisted, "Don't you ever fucking talk to me like that again."

She did not. The next day Ethan was all apologies. *It will never happen again. I'm under a lot of stress at work, I promise to help out more at home, I love you.*

Madelyne had become a prisoner of her life with no foreseeable means of escape. Ethan had complete control and ultimate power over all their lives. When she would think back and imagine the man she used to love, she would try to figure out what happened to him. She eventually came to terms with the fact that nothing happened to him. Nothing since they met, at least. She realized she had never been in love with Ethan, she simply loved the idea of Ethan. Ethan was a way to escape her parents. Ethan was a new adventure. Ethan was a controlling abusive person since the first day she met him. Thinking back, she should have stopped seeing him after their fifth date. But her mind was already set on running away with him and she had no place to run back to. Her parents had failed her on a parent's most important job, *offering your children a soft place to land.*

There were many chinks in the armor of Madelyne's new shiny knight, but the one she kept going back to was on their fifth date at Disco Demolition. The couple thought that was the day they fell in love. They were swept away in a historical event of both rock 'n' roll and Chicago White Sox history. The *disco sucks* promotion evolved into what the police and media declared a riot. Madelyne and Ethan were having the time of their lives at that so-called riot. What better place to be a rebel than at a riot. And it was hardly a riot. A bunch of Rock 'n' Rollers stormed the field fueled by alcohol and pot. But there was really no violence to speak of. The field was wrecked, a bunch of disco records were destroyed, but the news only reported nine minor injuries in a crowd of 70,000. But there was a tenth injury that went unreported. That injury belonged to Ethan. It was after Madelyne and Ethan had stormed the field and joined in on the foolishness and nonsense. It was after they made out right on home plate, just before somebody dug it out of the ground and stole it. It was after Chicago's finest cleared the field and the White Sox announced they had to forfeit the second game. The couple lingered, sharing kisses and laughs and silliness. Just before they left Ethan used the washroom. When he finished he found Madelyne continuing to enjoy the day. She was chanting disco sucks with a group of Rock 'n' Rollers. As Ethan approached, the chant stopped and Madelyne was high-fiving a couple of guys she had never met when Ethan violently pushed the young man that had just slapped hands with his property. "What the fuck!?" The young man was not alone. He had five friends with him.

"Don't you fucking touch her!" Ethan snapped.

"Ethan, it's okay," Madelyne insisted.

The young man and his five friends all had something to say. Ethan was about to get his ass kicked. Luckily for him a group of Chicago's finest showed up at just that moment. "Let's move it along."

Ethan took Madelyne by the hand and did not say a word to her until they reached his car despite her constant inquiries. Once at the car Madelyne more aggressively insisted, "Ethan, what was all of that about?"

Madelyne was up against the car. Ethan stood in front of her with their bodies touching, he looked her in the eye and asked, "Why were you flirting with those guys?"

Madelyne nudged him away and snapped, "I was not flirting with anyone." She felt insulted.

Ethan clenched his fist and cocked his arm. Bam! He punched the car door of his Buick Skylark. It hurt. He put his fist between his thighs and winced in pain.

"Why did you do that?"

Grunting and breathing unnaturally he ran his other hand through his hair and looked at her with his magical eyes. "I just couldn't take it if you ever cheated on me."

She hugged him. She felt wanted. "Oh baby, I would never cheat on you."

Ethan had suffered two dislocated fingers from the incident.

* * * * * * * *   * * * * * * * * *   * * * * * * * * *   * * * * * * * *

Ethan was taken away in handcuffs the night of Toby's eleventh birthday. Before he went before the judge Madelyne had convinced herself and her innocent young boys that it would be better if they gave Ethan another chance. That she would insist he get help and that he would and that they needed him to survive. They would not press charges or say a word to the police. The prosecutor still sought charges against Ethan using a technique called an Evidence-Based Prosecution *or victimless prosecution*. Without the help of the family and being a former Marine, which the not so impartial judge was also, Ethan got off light. One-year probation and six months of court mandated anger management.

Marie Gibson brought Fabiola Fabiono up to speed about what happened at Toby's eleventh birthday and how it ended him up in her anger management class.

"I was an Illinois Certified Domestic Violence Professional for fifteen years and I saw a lot of terrible monsters, some worse than Ethan, some not, but make no mistake about it, I know he is charismatic and has a charming way about himself and is definitely easy on the eyes, but that man is an abuser. A violent, cruel abuser."

"This is all just very unexpected."

"Because of his eyes, right?"

"I hadn't noticed."

"Well then either he is wearing sunglasses during your visits or you're lying to me. Like I told you, Fablono, I pity Ethan as a child and as a teenager, but I despise him as an adult. He is a monster."

"And he went through your class twice?"

"Yeah, both times because of the birthday incident. We met twice a month for six months. His first group was with about five others. All twelve classes he just sits there. Never says a single word. Zero participation. I keep telling him that ain't going to fly. That I'm going to tell the judge and he'll be held in contempt of court. But he stays quiet. So, when the class is over I report him as a non-participant and I figure this idiot is going to be spending some time in the big house. But nope. For some reason the judge gives him a second go around. And this time, talk about night and day – he won't shut up. He participates more than anyone I had ever had. That's how I find out about his dad, his sister, and mom. He really opens up. Every class. He tells me how hard he is working on his coping skills and he has all these rules and philosophies about becoming a better person. And respect and love and family. I was really hopeful for him."

"So, his family took him back after the second go around?"

"He was living with them the whole time. Now who is to say what goes on behind closed doors, especially if the people behind those doors are afraid. But the police were not called back to his house until a couple years after I last saw him."

"So, there was another incident?"

"At least one that we know of. But I'm sure there were more. It was bad. Good friend of mine was the arresting officer. It took three cops to get him under control."

"How badly did he hurt his family?"

"He broke his younger sons jaw. The wife was pretty beat up. I know she had some broken ribs. The older son, he was probably like seventeen at the time, he gets home right before the cops get there. Ethan is on top of the mom, beating on her, and the son jams a butcher knife in the back of Ethan's thigh. So, he is still fighting three cops with a butcher knife sticking out of his thigh."

"This is all so shocking."

"After that, the mom and sons cooperate fully. Ethan went to prison. Well I guess he's out now, but at least he's in Iowa, far away from them."

* *

Today is the birthday of Tobias White. Despite it being his twenty-first birthday, he was planning a very low-key celebration with his mother, brother, and brother's girlfriend. They were going to all eat pizza and watch a Wes Anderson movie, Toby's favorite director. He was feeling good as he took his three block walk home from the bus stop. The temperature was just above freezing but there was no snow to be seen which was very unusual for an early March night in Chicago. Tobias was not thinking about his father. He had not seen Ethan in seven years. On his birthday last year his father was front of mind. It was forty days before Tobias' birthday last year that his father was released from prison. Now, after more than a year with absolutely no attempts at making contact in any way, Tobias had removed his father from his mind.

Tobias walked up the driveway and into his yard. The White family always used the back door. He was surprised to see Thaddeus standing on the back porch without his girlfriend. He appeared to be having trouble opening the door.

"What's up Thaddeus? You forget your key?"

Oddly, Thaddeus offered no response. Tobias continued his line of questioning, "Where's—"

Tobias was only a few feet away from the man on his back porch when he offered this, "Happy birthday, Tobias."

Tobias suddenly felt sick. All of his insides rushed to his brain and he nearly collapsed from the weight of his head. The birthday wish had not come from his brother, but from his father.

Weak and frightened, Tobias spoke. "Dad? What are you doing here?" Instantly, for the first time in seven years Tobias felt like a victim again.

"I'm just here to talk. I have some things I have to say to you...and your brother."

Tobias felt himself getting dizzy. The task of standing was becoming difficult.

"...and your mother," Ethan continued.

Hearing his father mention his mother stirred something deep within Tobias. His fear was starting to be replaced by anger. He regained his equilibrium. His blood boiled. He spoke clearly. "You're not supposed to be here."

Ethan held his ground. "Tobias...son—"

"Don't you call me son!" Tobias now spoke with great distain in the voice of an intrepid protector. "Get out of here now. Right now!"

Ethan lowered his head and mumbled, "I didn't want it to be this way." He then pulled a .44 Magnum handgun out from his waistband and held it at the bridge of his son's nose. "I will be heard. Now goddamn it, Tobias, don't make me do this."

When a violent man is out of control and holds a gun at your forehead you would be surprised how quickly the barrel of that gun can suck all of the bravery out of your body.

"Now unlock that door and let's go in and wait for your brother and mother."

With a trembling hand Tobias unlocked the door and the father and son walked into the house. From behind Ethan raised the gun high above his son's head and brought the handle down hard. For Tobias, everything went black.

* *

Today is the twenty-first birthday of Tobias White. His brother Thaddeus and his girlfriend, Elizabeth, were walking up the driveway of the family home. Thaddeus and Elizabeth lived in an apartment a few miles away. Although it was only a little after six, the winter sky was as black as midnight. Elizabeth playfully complained as they walked toward the back door.

"Are we really going to watch a movie?"

"Whatever Tobias wants. It's his birthday."

"Why don't we play a game, like Farkle?"

"You can ask him."

"Or Ship, Captain, Crew."

"Maybe we can do a movie and a game."

"If we do a movie, I'm going to fall asleep."

Thaddeus was surprised to find the back door unlocked.

Soon after that surprise came another. Tobias was duct taped to a dining room chair, unable to speak as his mouth was also bound with tape.

Then another surprise. Thaddeus' father was sitting in his old spot at the head of the table with a roll of duct tape in front of him and a gun in his hand.

"Aren't you going to wish your brother a happy birthday?"

"You son of a bitch—"

Elizabeth made her intentions to make a run for the door clear, while Thaddeus continued his verbal assault.

"Both of you shut up and don't move or I swear this will be the last birthday Tobias ever has."

It had been seven years since the brothers had seen their father and they had hoped they would never see him again. Other than the nearly six years he had spent in prison the brothers had no idea what their father had been up to. Ethan, on the other hand, had kept tabs on their lives. He had an old drinking buddy that lived across the street, another former Marine. Despite everything Ethan had done, the two still talked. This was Ethan's sole source of information on his former family. Ethan had longed for his family for the past seven years. That longing was now an obsession.

Ethan limped his way over to the young couple. "I don't want to have to hurt anybody, but if I have to…well, you know I will. I just have some things that need to be said and I will have your undivided attention. So here is what's going to happen: you are going to sit over there, across from your brother and she is going to tape you up all nice and tight."

"I got a better idea—" Thaddeus began.

"No, Thad, you don't!" Ethan shot back as he grabbed Elizabeth by the back of her hair and held the gun tight to her temple. "Now I would really be broken up about it if I had to shoot you or your brother, but I got no problem blowing the head off your little lady."

"I should have stabbed you in the back when I had the chance."

"You've been stabbing me in the back for the last seven years."

Elizabeth shook with fear as she taped Thaddeus' wrists to the arms of the chair. Thaddeus left a small gap between the chair and his left wrist as his father stood to his right, in the hopes that space would help him to escape later. Ethan's gun remained steady aimed at Elizabeth's head. She then taped his ankles to the legs of the chair and then put a piece across his mouth. She was then instructed to sit in the chair that was normally Madelyne's. Ethan placed the gun in the center of the table between his two sons and said, "Don't try anything stupid. You will not succeed."

Elizabeth took his advice. Ethan secured her to her chair, taped her mouth, and then retrieved the gun and took his old seat back at the opposite head of the table. The floor was his…

"So how did we get to this point? … I know you guys think you know, but you don't. I know you think it's all my fault, but it's not. I know I have my problems, but I have been working on them. I've been sorting things out. For the most part I have been making great strides in controlling my anger. I'm not angry right now. I'm very calm. I had to go to these lengths because it's the only way to get you guys to listen."

It was not lost on Thaddeus and Tobias that they were seated in the exact same spots as they were ten years ago today, being abused by the same man. Ethan had an intense need to be in total control of everything, and at this very moment that need was being fulfilled. Thaddeus looked at Elizabeth's eyes, which were crying. He then turned to his brother's eyes, which were trying to tell him something. Thaddeus could not decipher the message. Ethan continued...

"I know I have not given you guys the best childhood, and for that I am sorry, but you have no idea what a nightmare my childhood was. My father was the worst. I never spoke of him to you guys, or even your mother. The last thing I wanted was to become like him, but somehow, I did. And now I worry you guys are going to do the same." Ethan put the gun on the table in front of him and placed his face in his palms.

With Ethan not looking, Tobias now incorporated dramatic head movements in trying to signal Thaddeus. It was obvious he wanted Thad to look up. He did and only viewed the ceiling. His eyes relayed his confusion. Thaddeus didn't care very much about Toby's message as he was working on freeing his left hand. He looked at the gun and ran through possible scenarios in his head. His father raised his head.

"I also had some redeeming qualities. I provided for this family. But your mother...your mother always knew what buttons to press. Always knew how to make it look like it was all my fault. She turned you guys against me."

Ethan returned his face to his hands. Thaddeus pulled his wrist back as hard as he could.

"Where is she at anyway? I mean it's just like her to be late for her son's birthday. There's a box of cake mix on the kitchen counter, I'm guessing she got all ready to make you a cake and then realized she was missing something. Eggs or candles. She would never plan ahead. She has no concept of time. Anything I ever did with her, we would be late. And she knew how much—"

Just then what sounded like a box of marbles being dumped on a tile floor rang out from upstairs.

"Holy shit she's in the house. She's been up there listening all along."

Ethan grabbed the gun off the table, Tobias' eyes bulged huge. Thaddeus now understood his message. Ethan made his way upstairs. Tobias bounced around in his chair furiously trying to make as much noise as possible to warn his mother. Tears and makeup streamed down Elizabeth's face. Thaddeus pulled his left arm back and forth violently causing himself great pain trying to free his hand. The three of them soon heard the cries of Madelyne, and the enraged shouting of Ethan. There was loud pounding that somehow did not make sense in all the chaos.

"No! Please!" Madelyne cried out. Ethan said something that was muffled as the pounding returned even louder. The brothers realized the pounding was coming from outside the front door. Thaddeus and Tobias tried fruitlessly to yell out from behind their duct tape muzzles.

As Tobias continued to wildly thrash his body and chair as much as his restraints would allow, he and his chair tipped over. The tape that held the left wrist of Thaddeus had become bunched and scraped his skin as his arm moved faster and faster. Blood began to seep through his battered pores.

And then the sound of a single gunshot rang through the house. Time froze. Everything in the dining room stopped. Not a single movement could be detected nor a sound of any kind was heard. Not even a heartbeat. This deadly silence lasted somewhere between less than a second and an eternity. The concept of time had momentarily lost its value. Chicago's finest suddenly burst through the front and back doors with their weapons drawn. Upon their sight Thaddeus felt a terrible lack of relief.

They were too late.

* * * * * * *   * * * * * * * *   * * * * * * * *   * * * * * * * *

Today is the twenty-first birthday of Tobias White. His mother Madelyne, who worked two minimum wage jobs, one as a cashier at the Stop N Shop grocery store, had left work an hour earlier than her usual Saturday schedule, so that she could make her son a birthday cake.

As she rode the bus home her mind flashed to a memory that she was not fond of in any way. It was the memory of the fate of a birthday cake from the past. She dismissed the memory as best she could. That was a long time ago and life was very different. She was very different. She was no longer a victim. She was not as weak as she thought she was ten years ago. She now worked and somehow made just enough money to experience the threat of losing her home, but not have it actualized. She had friends. She was in the very early stages of developing a relationship with the new manager at the Stop N Shop, hence today's early dismissal. They had been on two dates. He was kind and gentle, a widower. They were her first dates since…Although fractured and not completely warm and fuzzy, she once again had a relationship with her parents. She drove. Well, at least she had a license. Thaddeus taught her in his car and brought her to get her license. Madelyne could not afford a car. Her sons were doing well and her youngest, the birthday boy, still lived with her. Life was good.

Once home Madelyne wanted to get the cake in the oven before Tobias got home. Because of an unusual volume of Saturday traffic and the tardiness of her bus caused by that traffic it would be close. *Perhaps Tobias will be delayed by the traffic as well,* she thought, *although he comes from the other direction.*

No sooner did Madelyne get the cake mix out of the cabinet that the phone began to ring. She went to see who was calling. She did not recognize the name on the caller ID. She decided to ignore it. More than likely a telemarketer or a bill collector she surmised. She went back to the kitchen. *What happened to my mixing bowl? I swear if Toby was using it as a chip bowl again.* The phone rang again. She investigated the receiver and found it to be the same name and number that displayed moments ago. This time she answered, but decided to remain quiet and let the other end of the line reveal themselves first.

After a brief silence on both ends…

"Is somebody there?"

Madelyne remained silent.

"Hello?"

Madelyne did not recognize the voice.

"Is this the White residence?"

Telemarketer, she thought. Click.

Before she got back to the kitchen, they called a third time. *Now this is rude, they are going to regret their persistence.*

"Whatever you're selling I don't want. Take me off your list! And if it's about a bill, do not call here again! I have a right to tell you that and you have to honor that—"

"Is this Madelyne White?"

"I think I made myself clear, good—"

"Were you married to Ethan White?"

His name made her insides shiver. It felt as if the temperature in the room had dropped by ten degrees. The memory of fear washed over her, but she swallowed hard and overcame that memory with anger. "Who is this? What do you want?" she snapped.

"Madelyne, I think you and your sons may be in danger."

* * * * * * * *   * * * * * * * *   * * * * * * * *   * * * * * * * *

After not being able to reach Ethan, Fabiola Fabiono found the phone number of and called Madelyne White to warn her of what she feared. She told her how Ethan had been in therapy with her for the past two months. She told Madelyne that he did not seem violent nor did he ever threaten any violence. She told her he had also not been very honest with her.

"Since my last visit with him on Wednesday I have discovered many truths about him. Most of them very unpleasant to say the least. The reason I decided to try and reach out to you is because on Wednesday he told me that he was going to see his boys this weekend. Now mind you, he has always placed me under the false impression that he maintains a wonderful relationship with his sons, so this could just be talk to support this delusional world he has created. I just felt in light of your past I should call you."

Throughout their short conversation, Madelyne did not say very much. She mostly just listened. At this point she was not saying anything. Complete silence.

"Miss White?"

"Madelyne?"

This increased the paranoia of Fabiola. *Did Miss White hang up on me? Or is there something more sinister at play?*

Fabiola's next conversation was with the desk Sargent at the Chicago Police Departments 8th district. He did not seem very concerned.

"So, what you are asking for is a well-being check?"

"Yes…I guess, yes, yes a well-being check."

"Okay, when I have an officer available, I'll send one over to check things out."

"When will that be?"

"Look Miss, it will be as soon as possible, Saturday nights in Chicago are a little busier than they are in Anywhere, Iowa."

* * * * * * * *   * * * * * * * * *   * * * * * * * * *   * * * * * * * *

Today is Toby White's twenty-first birthday and his father just cut his mother's phone line.

Madelyne peeked out the back window between the blinds and the wood trim and spied her ex-husband for the first time in seven years walking across the deck toward the back door. He had just cut the phone line. Her heart began to pound hard against her chest. *Does he know I'm here?* Her mind began to panic. *The blinds are all drawn. Only the kitchen light is on. I haven't touched any other lights, have I? Did he see me come in? Has he been waiting?*

Madelyne heard him trying to gain entry through the back door. Madelyne had a gun. It was upstairs in her closet. During the last seven years driving a car was not the only thing Madelyne learned. She learned how to protect herself. She could run and get the gun and be waiting for Ethan when he made his way in. Or she could run out the front door when he came in the back and call the cops from a neighbor's house. Fight or flight? That is the question. As Ethan fiddled with the door knob Madelyne chose flight, but then she heard the voice of her son Tobias from the driveway.

"What's up, Thaddeus? You forget your keys?"

Fight was now the only option. She ran upstairs with her insides shaking. She reached up onto her closet shelf and felt the cold steel of her .32-caliber double action, short barreled Colt revolver. Her outsides were now also shaking. Her stomach turned. She felt the urge to vomit. She ran back downstairs and stood before the back door. Her tremble was uncontrollable. Would she be steady enough to fire? Then something most unfortunate dawned on her.

A little over two years ago, when Thad was still at home, Elizabeth had moved into the White house for a short time. During that time her five-year-old nephew, Liam, would be over quite often. Everyone loved having an adorable child around and Elizabeth was her sister's babysitter of choice. Despite Madelyne's gun being on a high shelf in her bedroom closet, she did not want to take any chances. The bullets were taken out of the revolver. All of the gun's ammo was now kept in the master bedroom's bathroom linen closet behind the towels. Madelyne's .32 caliber double action, short-barreled Colt revolver was empty and Tobias was unlocking the back door.

Without thinking she ran to the front room, laid across the top of the couch, gun in hand, and dropped herself between the couch and wall. A rather tight squeeze, but a great hiding place. How to get out from behind there was a problem she did not consider.

Madelyne remained silent, although her insides continued to quiver. She heard Ethan calling out for her. "Madelyne. Come on out, Madelyne. I know you're here."

She heard him search the house going from room to room. She did not hear Tobias. She worried. Then she heard Ethan say something that brought her some much-needed relief. "Well, son, I guess she's not here. That's okay, we'll wait for her."

Then she heard Ethan grunting and struggling followed by the sounds of the duct tape being unrolled. She began to squirm her way forward so that her eyes were beyond the obstruction of the couch. From under the end table she could see one half of Tobias' body being taped to the dining room chair.

Her mind was hard at work trying to come up with a plan. She knew she had to get those bullets, but right now all she could do was wait. It would definitely take some time and effort to free herself from behind the couch. It was not very long before Thaddeus and Elizabeth arrived at Toby's birthday celebration.

After Thad was secured to the chair opposite Tobias, the brothers watched their father tightly roll the tape around the wrist and ankles of Elizabeth. Tobias also witnessed something beyond his father's back, but not in the view of his brother. He watched as his mother slowly and quietly squirmed her way out from behind the couch and under the end table. He worried so much that if his father turned around it would all be over.

He did not. Then Tobias realized that his mother did not make her escape alone. She had her gun with her.

Tobias felt the joy of rescue and a small taste of the sweetness of vengeance. *But wait, why is she not using the gun? Why doesn't she just shoot him right now. His back is still to her and his gun is on the table. What is she doing? Why is she hiding behind the chair now? Is she just too scared to do anything? Is she just going to wait for him to shoot one of us? We are all going to die!*

Tobias was right about his mother being scared but knew nothing else of her circumstances. Her new hiding spot was more advantageous as it offered a quick and easy escape route across the front room to the stairway that led to the master bathroom linen closet that housed the bullets required to put a final end to their abuse. But she should have gone right away, while he was finishing up his tape job on Elizabeth. Now it was too late. Now Ethan sat at the head of the table opposite Elizabeth, and the path between the chair and the stairway was right in his view.

Madelyne peeked out from the corner of the chair in the dark front room and watched her ex-husband have his moment of undivided attention. She felt she had to make a move soon, but could she run upstairs, lock herself in the bathroom, and load the gun before he kicked the door in. *But what if he just stays down here? What if he shoots the boys?* The front door was only six feet behind her, perhaps running out to get help would be a better plan? *No. I could not leave my children. I would rather die with them.*

"The last thing I wanted was to become like him," Ethan insisted, speaking about his father, "but somehow I did. And now I worry that you guys are going to do the same." Ethan placed the gun on the table and his face in his palms. This was Madelyne's chance and she knew it. But her body was shaking so badly she did not know if she could make it. She made a break for it.

Tobias watched in petrified horror as his mother staggered across the front room like a drunken sailor, barely keeping herself upright and almost collapsing before she grabbed hold of the banister and made her way up the stairs, out of his sight. Using his head and eyes he tried frantically to relay what was happening to his brother.

Veteran Chicago police officer Pryzbylewski had been on the front porch of the White home for several minutes ringing a doorbell that had not worked in several years. He was tired of being one of Chicago's finest. The job was too dangerous, the environment too political. He had multiple applications in at various affluent, quiet Chicago suburbs. He was happy to be doing a well-being check in a nicer working-class section of his precinct as opposed to a more hazardous call, or so he thought. He was now sure someone was in the house as Madelyne's escape to the upstairs produced a quick and slight change to the dim light from the kitchen that made its way through the three tiny decorative windows at the top of the door. Despite his dissatisfaction with his job, Officer Pryzbylewski was a very good police officer. Not answering the door and the detection of movement in the home warranted further investigation in the veteran's mind. Because of the step up the windows at the top of the door were too high for him to gain a peek. The rest of the home's windows appeared to have had their shades and curtains drawn.

Somehow Madelyne had made it up the stairs, even with her body forsaking her by forcing her to shake so intensely with fear that even the simplest of tasks brought great challenge. She quietly closed the bathroom door and leaned her body against it for rest and steadiness as she pressed in the privacy lock. She tried to take a deep breath which nearly caused her to cry out in desperation. She opened the linen closet with her shaking hand and grabbed the bottom towel on the top shelf, pulling it forward and allowing the entire pile to fall to the floor, giving her an unobstructed view of the box of bullets. Her entire body now shuddered to the point that she nearly dropped the gun. She tried desperately to pull her emotions together and get a hold of herself.

As Madelyne's body continued to betray her, her mind remained focused on the task at hand. She put a large bath towel in the sink and placed the gun on top of it. She put the toilet seat down, her body continuing to convulse with the anxiety of the upcoming events and their possible results. She held the bullet box with both hands and carefully took a seat on the toilet. She began to calm herself. She thought of where she was only a short time ago, pinned between the couch and the wall. She considered how far she had come from that point to make it to where she is now. The tremors became more moderate. Her breathing more stable. She sat on the toilet with a box of .32 caliber bullets on her lap with her hands cupping both sides of it. Now all she had left to do was load her revolver, go downstairs, and kill the father of her children before he killed them.

Not finding anything to stand on to give him the necessary height, Officer Pryzbylewski resorted to jumping. Each jump would afford him a split-second view of inside the house. It took several jumps for him to be able to figure out what direction he should be looking. *There are at least two people sitting at the dining room table.* He was able to see the back of Elizabeth and a good portion of Tobias. *The one with their back to me appears to be a female.* Correct. *The other one a male, thick mustache.* Yes, but not a mustache, duct tape. Pryzbylewski took a break to catch his breath. Then one final jump to confirm his suspicions. *Nobody has moved. At all. Not an inch.* Officer Pryzbylewski thought it would be wise to call for back up.

You already know this but I will tell you anyway...Despite Madelyne doing her absolute best to stay calm and focused, her physical reaction to the calamitous situation she found herself in was currently her second worst enemy, when you take Ethan into consideration. She dropped the bullets all over the bathroom floor. She should have spread the towels on the floor beneath her as she did the sink.

"Holy shit she's in the house. She's been up there listening all along."

Ethan grabbed the gun off the table, Ethan made his way upstairs. Madelyne panicked. She grabbed the gun out of the sink and fumbled to open the cylinder. She could hear Ethan coming up the stairs. She reached down between her legs and grabbed a single bullet. The shaking was increasing. She fumbled to slide it into the chamber.

Ethan shook the door knob. "Open up Madelyne!" he yelled.

She dropped the bullet to the ground. Her labored breathing returned along with the intense shaking. She began to cry.

Ethan pounded on the door. "Open the fucking door!"

She got down on her hands and knees with the gun and grabbed another bullet. Ethan gave the door a mighty kick at the same exact second she dropped a bullet into a chamber. The lock gave way, the door flung open as pieces of trim exploded into the bathroom.

As the door swung at great speed it caught the side of Madelyne's face. The impact caused two teeth to fly out of her mouth and she momentarily lost her vision and faculties. Ethan stood over her brandishing his gun. The force of the door put Madelyne in an awkward position. Her lower legs were folded back under her knees and her body lay straight back, her head against the side of the tub.

"I want you to listen to me! I've been doing a lot of thinking and I know I fucked up. I know my head's not right. But I want you to know most of the culpability lies on you. And I want the kids to know. You made me this way. The boys have to know that! It's not my fault."

Blood gushed from Madelyne's mouth where there once were teeth. Her eye began to swell. Her face was covered with tears and snot and blood. A blurry vision of Ethan began to come into focus, surrounded by the stars of a concussion. She could barely comprehend his words as her crying became louder. Somehow, miraculously, Madelyne was able to hang on to her gun.

"You don't get off scot free. You're not Miss Perfect. I shouldn't have to be the only one that has to suffer."

Madelyne noticed the gun still in her hand. The chamber was still open, as her vision became clearer she saw the bullet was still there. She had to get her wits about her.

"Listen to me, Madelyne! Listen!"

Ethan held his gun between them, aimed at her head. Madelyne knew she had to take the chance of closing her gun's cylinder and firing it until it hit the right chamber, all before he simply pulled his trigger. She would never make it.

"Madelyne, this is all your fault! You did this! This is on you!"

"No! Please!" Madelyne cried out.

Ethan then took his gun and shoved the barrel deep into the roof of his own mouth. He pulled the trigger and the sound of a single shot rang through the house.

DO YOU FEEL THE IF?

I AM SAFE.

I am warm.

I am protected.

Although I realize the barriers that offer me these pleasures are delicate and fleeting.

I feel a slight ping of uncertainty deep within my core and I recognize that it is *knowledge*. And that in a short amount of time that knowledge will make its way to my brain and the process will start all over again.

I know this because the same thing happened yesterday.

And I am fairly certain it will happen again tomorrow.

Just beyond my protective shell lies the real world and it is calling to me.

I do not wish to go, but I know I must.

The real world is demanding and cruel and chaotic and uncertain.

Here, under my blankets, I am safe and warm and protected, five more minutes, please. I hit the snooze function and the process begins.

The real world was not always like this. Was it? I don't believe that to be the case. And it does not have to continue on this way. Does it?

I stretch. It feels marvelous, but my brain is now acutely aware of what is coming next. Another day.

I am thankful to have been granted another day, but I am also filled with the illogical desire to spend it here where nothing can hurt me, or confuse me, or offend me, or claim me, or solicit me, or constrain me, or scare me, or deny me. My alarm calls to me again. My ears are no longer offering me protection from the sounds of the real world. I negotiate. Five more minutes! The process continues.

These next five minutes are not spent in slumber, they are spent in transformation. I can taste the vile vallation that was placed in my throat to protect me from saying the wrong things. I know it is time to brush it away and take my chances. I feel the dry layer of crust that restrained my eyes from witnessing the sights of this damaged world. I know it is time to wash them away and take my chances. I now smell and feel things that I did not, just a short time ago. A short wonderful time ago.

As I prepare to face another day in the real world I begin the final step of the process. I seek and find the solution. I can feel the IF. The one thing I need to accomplish to make my real world, my morning process, my life, profoundly amended and tremendously enhanced. Will today be the day? Can today be the day? Is it even possible? I'm sure you know what I'm talking about. I believe we all share this common thread. I sincerely hope that today is your day, as well as mine. The day we learn to conquer the IF. The day we destroy the conditions and achieve our intentions. The day supposing becomes realizing.

I wonder what your IF is?

If I could just get started.
If I could just lose twenty pounds.
If I could just have a chance to explain.
If I could just get one more dollar an hour.
If I could just get one more month of unemployment.
If I could just get one more chance.
If I could just maintain straight A's.
If I could just graduate.
If I could just survive this.
If I could just make her understand.
If I could just get away from him.
If I could just stop making the same mistakes.
If I could just find another job.

If I could just find a second job.
If I could just find a job.
If I could just get a C on tomorrow's test.
If I could just get through this day.
If I could just get through three more chemo's.
If I could just skip dessert.

If I just could…
If I could just keep the car running through the winter.
If I could just get her to notice me.
If I could just get them to leave me alone.
If I could just nail this presentation.
If I could just close the deal.
If I could just run away forever.
If I could just pay next month's rent.
If I could just get my security deposit back.
If I could just lose ten pounds.
If I could just tell him I'm sorry.
If I could just meet somebody.
If I could just leave him.
If I could just learn to swallow again.
If I could just get her to see he is wrong for her.
If I could just get back to a size six.
If I could just start eating healthier.
If I could just get some money for groceries.
If I could just understand you.

If you would just stop.
If you would just leave.
If you would just understand.
If you would just come back.
If you would just take better care of yourself.
If you would just listen to me.
If you would just leave him.
If you would just stay.

If you would just tell me why.
If you would just call me.
If you would just let me explain.
If you would just say something.
If you would just stop hurting me.
If you just would…

If I could just get a couple days off.
If I could just get some overtime.
If I could just win the lottery.
If I could just realize he is worth it.
If I could just have one more chance.
If I could just make her come home.
If I could just start over.
If I could just go back in time.
If I could just realize she is not worth it.
If I could just lose five pounds.
If I could just have one good day.
If I could just walk again.
If I could just realize that everything is possible.
If I could just realize that some things are out of my control.
If I could just realize some things are impossible.
If I could just get my ass out of bed and face the day, and embrace it.
And if it holds some nefarious agenda for me, if its intentions are to do harm, than if I could just outwit, transcend, and overcome its fiendish design and emerge victorious.
Or…
If I could just hit snooze one more time.
If I could just have five more minutes.
If I could just stop stalling.

Good Morning.

TRUE FABLES FROM INTERSTATE 90

FIVE DAYS EARLIER

"Do you truly not realize the sacrifices I've made for this family? What I put myself through every day for you? For the kids? I work hard every day because I have to, not because I want to. I have forced myself to work with terrible pain in my back and my legs. Pain so bad that a lesser man would not even consider dragging himself out of bed much less to work! Jesus Christ, I pulled my own tooth with a fucking pair of pliers and went to work the next day! That's how there is a roof over our heads! Food on the table! Clothes on our backs! And you sit there and say I don't love you? That I don't care that you are sick? It's killing me. Every moment of every day it is absolutely destroying me. But the bills don't stop coming because you're sick. We are barely hanging on. We are this close to losing what little we have. That's why you have to fight and I have to work."

EIGHT DAYS EARLIER

"I feel like you are taking advantage of me. You guys have already been here for two weeks. You both get drunk every night. You are constantly fighting. What kind of a relationship is that? You two are no good for each other. You are toxic together. I know, I know, you say you are trying to find a job.

Look, you are my son and I want to help you. To believe in you. But she is dragging you down. Why can't you see that? You can stay here as long as you want, but I want her gone by the end of the week."

THIRTEEN MONTHS EARLIER

"I am very sorry, but I promise you, this is more than just treatable. This is curable. It is going to be very difficult for you. At times you are going to feel like just giving up, but I promise, you can beat this. This is my plan for treatment; it is proven and has an 80% success rate. First thing Monday morning we will rip open your flesh in the shoulder area and insert a piece of plastic about the size of a quarter. This is called a port. We'll use a catheter to connect that port to a vein. Now I will tell you that it is a simple outpatient procedure and virtually painless. I will be lying when I tell you that. It will go from painful to irritating to something that just gives you the willies. For about the next year of your life you will use that port to administer chemotherapy and draw blood.

We'll start out with some low dose chemo. It will be in a bag that you get to carry around in a fanny pack. That won't be annoying at all. You could wear it Monday through Friday for about five weeks. That will make your weekends more enjoyable. That low-dose chemo will stimulate your cancer so that when we blast you with radiation five days a week for five weeks we have a better chance of destroying the cancer and not just the healthy cells around it. Now because your cancer is in your ass you're not going to want to be using it after we scorch the hell out of it on a daily basis. No big deal, we'll set you up so that you can do your business in an ileostomy bag for the next eight months to a year.

Now I will lie to you again and tell you how simple that surgery is and how quickly you will get the hang of changing your bag and that reversing this procedure when you are cancer free is easy as pie. Your body will snap right back to normal. And you lose some unwanted weight. Then after the radiation we'll do another simple surgery to remove whatever is left of the tumor and then the Big Chemo starts. Let me tell you a little about that…"

THREE MONTHS AND 14 DAYS EARLIER

"My little girl, my little princess, going to MIT! I can't believe it. I mean I can believe it because you are so smart, but…Oh my God! Congratulations sweetheart."

"Thanks, Dad."

"Imagine, the daughter of a punk rocker going to MIT. Does your brother know?"

"Not yet. You're the first person I've told."

"My sweet little princess an Ivy Leaguer."

"MIT is not an Ivy League school."

"It's not? But still, MIT. Holy shit, MIT."

"Yep."

"Like, what kind of a tuition are we talking?"

"Don't worry Dad. With our income, at a school like MIT, my financial aid will make it very manageable."

"Oh…Okay…Great. Well I guess it's a good thing my band isn't more successful, huh?"

Eyes roll upward, head slightly shakes.

"I'm going to mark this date, so we always remember it. So exciting, March 14th 2017."

"PI Day."

"Absolutely we will get some pie. Let's celebrate!"

"Not that kind of pie."

"Whatever kind you want, sweetheart."

Eyes roll again, head shakes more vigorously.

"Your Mother would have been so proud."

TWELVE MONTHS EARLIER

"I don't know…I just found her in bed…she was…when I found her she was…she wasn't breathing…I tried to…she was dead. I'm so sorry…I'm so sorry." Sobbing. Inaudible.

NOW

Myelin's boots echoed loudly as he crossed the shiny, cold tile floor. The only person in his vision was an employee. The worker was operating one of those large rotating floor waxing machines. The machine and the worker were good at their jobs as the floor shone brightly. Neither the worker nor his machine acknowledged Myelin as he passed them and entered the recently cleaned public bathroom. The condition of the bathroom made Myelin happy. It was not disgusting as so many public bathrooms are, nor was it occupied by any living soul, other than Myelin.

He was also happy to see three push button hand dryers mounted on the public bathroom wall. Myelin found the push button variety fit his needs much better than the motion activated type. He pushed all three hand dryer buttons on his way to the last of six private stalls. The hand dryers roared their hand dryer sound producing the perfect camouflage for the deed Myelin was about to perform.

The reason for this audio deception was not to spare himself or any potential innocent bystander a moment of awkward embarrassment. His reason for the sound enhancement of the public bathroom in the Interstate 90 Rest Stop was actually quite illicit. In one fluid motion Myelin latched the stall door with his left hand as his right hand went into his pocket and pulled out one of his two contact lens cases. Using only his right hand he untwisted the left lens cap and slid it in between two fingers as his left hand entered his back pocket to retrieve the tool that would aid him in completing this forbidden act.

Myelin did not wear contact lenses. Myelin had 20/20 vision. His actions were smooth and fluid. He was very practiced. It was around 11 p.m. He had been in the car for nearly eight hours. Google Maps told him he was still seven hours from his destination. Myelin felt soothed as he looked at the pure white powder in his contact lens case. He loosely gripped the shortened straw between his middle finger and his thumb and held one of his nostrils shut with his index finger. He felt the tickle and the burn rise up into his open nostril all the way to the back of his eyes.

He flushed the toilet a couple of times to create more diversion as he continued to suck air through his one open nostril to pick up any stray granules. As he put his equipment away he coughed. He licked his lips. He felt the charge. He dreaded the drive that still lay before him. He hoped that his sister would still be alive when they reached their destination. He hoped she would be resting peacefully when he got back to the car.

A BRIEF HISTORY OF MYELIN SHEATH

Melvin Smathy Jr. was one of nine children born and raised in Chicago, Illinois. They lived in a tough working-class neighborhood called Canaryville. Melvin's father worked for the railroad while his mother worked for The International Amphitheatre. Six of the nine children earned college degrees. All of them eventually moved out to the suburbs and had varying degrees of success.

Melvin, the oldest of the nine, enjoyed a lucrative career as a plastic surgeon and raised three children with his wife Peggy, two daughters, Charlotte and Camila, and a son, the youngest, Melvin Smathy III. Melvin Jr. was so proud to have a son and carry on the Melvin Smathy name. He was equally disappointed when III dropped out of high school, formed a punk rock band, and moved out of the family's palatial estate in favor of a one-bedroom apartment with his three bandmates on the north side of Chicago and legally changed his name to Myelin Sheath.

Myelin: A fatty white substance that surrounds the axon of some nerve cells.

Myelin Sheath: Medical definition: The insulating covering that surrounds an axon with multiple spiral layers of Myelin, that is discontinuous at the nodes of Ranvier, and that increases the speed at which a nerve impulse can travel along an axon.

Myelin Sheath: The person: Lead singer of the American punk rock band AMA (*American Maniac Association*) from Chicago, Illinois. The band showed a lot of promise with their debut album *Oath of Hypocrites* featuring the two critically acclaimed singles, *Dull Like a Scalpel,* and *Replace Your Face.* Their follow up album *Do More Harm* featured the bands most successful track as well as one of the bands very few songs not written by Myelin, *Not a Coward, Just Jaundice,* which was penned by AMAs cofounder and lead guitarist, Billi Rubin. The single received national air play and set the band on an eight-month nationwide tour. Although AMA remains a Chicagoland favorite, the band never lived up to its potential after the *Do More Harm* tour. Nationally they fell into obscurity. Other less successful albums include: *Femalpractice, Blown Nose Job* and *Cut Me Up and Love Me.*

So, if you feel as though you have figured out a little bit about Melvin III/Myelin's past as well as his current psyche, you would be correct. At a young age Myelin had a great appreciation for science with a great emphasis on anything medical. This made Dr. Melvin Jr. feel the proudness he felt for his son was warranted and well deserved. As time went on the young man's soul grew to be rebellious. His defiant behavior was met with much opposition in the form of discipline from the good doctor, akin to putting out a fire with gasoline. A wedge grew between them. The fast, abrasive, deliberately offensive genre of punk rock became Melvin IIIs new mentor. Music really does soothe the savage breast.

American Maniac Association had a very raw, very angry sound and were immediate favorites on Chicago's north side bar scene. The band was formed by Myelin and his best friend Dennis Craven, who later legally changed his name to Billi Rubin. The gimmick of having the band member's names, album titles and most of their song titles parody medical terminology was a good one. The fans embraced it and it went a long way in signing them to their one and only three album contract. The bass player called himself Braxton Hicks and the drummer was Type 2 Diabetes. Type 2 was not the most creative guy, but he played loud, angry, and fast.

It was at the height of AMA's popularity that a very young Myelin met the very beautiful Jody Fischer. They became a thing. They made a baby. A boy. Myelin wanted to name his son Iggy, after Iggy Pop, the godfather of punk as well as Myelin's main musical inspiration. Jody worried about her son's future with a name like Iggy. *(What if he did not embrace the punk rock life style? What if he wanted to be a businessman or a politician or doctor or who knows what? How would the name Iggy look on a college or job application?)* Jody was able to talk Myelin into naming his son James Newell Sheath *(Iggy Pop's birth name)*. Win. Win.

Five years later, as the bands popularity was rapidly fading, Myelin and

Jody became husband and wife and welcomed a second child into their punk rock family. A perfect little baby girl they called Lydia Anne Sheath (*after Jody's favorite musical talent Lydia Lunch.*) A name Jody felt would look absolutely fine on an application of any kind. She would be correct.

Although Myelin never gave up on his band or the music scene, he had to take quite a few day jobs to make ends meet. As did his wife. Security guard, dock worker, cashier, receptionist, landscaper, you name it, they did it. Myelin and Jody had a family to support. And they did it. They also had some quite nasty drug habits to support. And they did that as well.

It was far less than pretty. At times it was absolutely ugly. Every time would be the last time until the next time. As parents they provided poor little James and Lydia far more disappointment than is acceptable from a parent. Myelin's sisters, Char and Camy, filled a lot of the parental voids created by absence of proper decision making.

Things were very bad for a long while. They got better. All those years ago, when Aunt Char and Aunt Camy were saving Myelin's children, he never envisioned himself being alive and functional deep into his forties, let alone being charged with keeping his sister from dying in the back of a rented Dodge Caravan.

NOW

Two sisters sit in the way back of a brand-new 2017 Dodge Caravan rental, seats slightly reclined, middle seats stowed away, feet up on top of their suitcases.

"How is the pain?"

"It's starting again."

"I think your fever is coming back, too."

"How long since my last Tylenol?"

"Almost three hours, you should take some now."

"Supposed to wait four hours."

"Screw that, are you serious? These are extreme circumstances."

"What time you think we'll be there?"

"Don't think about that. We got a long way to go."

"Yeah and Melvy is stopping to piss every hour."

"He is making up for it with the way he's driving."

"But still…"

"Look how much coffee he's drinking. I'm surprised his heart hasn't exploded."

The sisters shared a worried silence for thirty-eight seconds.

"Do you think that's okay?"

"Do I think what's okay?"

"All that caffeine?"

"Well, yeah. It's what keeps him going."

Twelve more seconds of shared worried silence.

"I'm just saying, caffeine is a drug."

"So, he's a caffeine junkie. Better than what he was."

Five seconds.

"Give me those damn Tylenol."

TWENTY-FIVE DAYS EARLIER

When Charlotte first met Carl's newest girlfriend, Penny, three months ago, she figured it would be a short-lived relationship measured in days, not months. She was wrong. At that first meeting there was something about Penny that Char could not quite put her finger on. It was not until there third meeting that Char figured it out. *Penny is an alcoholic, slut, lying, whore, piece of shit, drug addict, scumbag.*

And now here was her son Carl, her only child, asking her if the two of them could move in with her for "a while". Carl was definitely not the smartest guy in the world. He wasn't even the smartest guy in the room. Ever. Even if he was the sole occupant of a room. Seriously. In a meta-physical sense whatever Human Being was in a room previous to Carl being there alone, would leave behind more intelligence than Carl would ever possess at one given moment. The only chance Carl would ever have at being the smartest person in the room would be if he were the first Human Being to ever enter said room. Chances of that were slim to none.

"Do you have any idea how hard it was for me to get you that job?"

"Did you think I was going to work there the rest of my life?"

"Well, I thought you would work there until you found something better."

"I will find something better."

"With your past? Really son? I mean three years on the straight and narrow, and then three months with her and you start showing up late and now no job, no rent money, no – "

"Okay forget it! I get it! You don't want to help me."

Mother's guilt. Mother's worry. Mother's unconditional love. Mother says... "No Carl. That's not it. Not at all. Of course I want to help you. I just worry about you so much and this Penny...She's just not right for you. And I got so much on my plate right now...Everything with my sister. And now your uncle wants to take this goddamned road trip."

"She gets me, Mom."

"What?"

"Penny...She gets me."

"No, I heard you. I mean what does she get you?"

"Stop it, Mom. I love her."

Spoiler Alert: Penny does not "get" Carl.

A BRIEF HISTORY OF CHAR PEACH

Char Peach was the oldest of Dr. Melvin Jr.'s three children and a very sympathetic character. The story would be much more satisfying to you, the reader if you were willing to acknowledge and accept that implication, especially when you consider some of her upcoming morally questionable decisions. I will attempt to present a quick and concise argument to support my claim.

Charlotte Smathy married Reginald Peach at a rather young age and became Char Peach. They were absolute soulmates if there ever was such a thing. They had a story book wedding followed by a storybook life. It only lasted a little over a decade. Char and Reginald loved more in that short time than most people do in a lifetime. The loving couple had more than enough love left over for their baby boy, Carl, despite his lack of proper reasoning skills and dimwittedness.

When Carl was eight years old, Reginald was involved in a terrible airplane crash. He was on a business trip in Los Angeles, California, staying on the twenty-third floor of a Marriott Hotel. He was sitting on his king-sized bed, freshly showered, in only his boxer shorts, clipping his toenails over a hotel towel strategically placed to catch the clippings, when the pilot of a Cessna single engine air plane accidently had a massive heart attack, fell forward onto the yoke, and brought the plane crashing straight through Reginald's insulated double-pane glass windows as he was clipping the baby toe of his left foot.

Amazingly, Reginald survived. He lived for close to a year after the terrible accident. His life was not ideal. Even less ideal for Char Peach. Reginald spent a good portion of that year in a state of unconsciousness. He had sustained multiple spinal cord injuries and was for the most part completely paralyzed from the neck down. He was no longer able to speak. Char would occasionally remember her husband's last words to her. "I just got out of the shower, hon. Let me dry off, clip my toenails and give you a call back." He never did finish clipping those toenails and Char often felt great resentment toward his final statement as she had always found toes to be the most creepy part of the human anatomy.

Char spent the better part of a year tending to all of Reginald's needs. Their once active and somewhat, slightly kinky sex life was now just a memory. At times Char would look through the box that remained in their closet, filled with oils and lubricants, and fur-lined hand cuffs and anal beads and scandalous photographs, and she would submerse herself in the lonely, relentless, anger, and pain she now felt. Her days were spent bathing and dressing and feeding Reginald as well as disposing of his waste. Every other day she would turn her soulmate on his side, pull up his knees, insert a suppository into his anus and wait to clean up the results. Even worse, five times per day she would have to insert a catheter into the slit of his flaccid penis and push it all the way up to his bladder and drain the urine. The same penis that once gave her so much pleasure now made her feel nauseous. Reginald communicated by blinking in Morse code, but he really never had much more to say other than "I'm sorry."

Occasionally Reginald's legs or arms would move violently with aggressive involuntary spasms. On more than a few occasions Char would take a knee or an elbow to the face. After several black eyes and a chipped tooth Char decided to unretire the fur lined handcuffs.

TWENTY-ONE DAYS EARLIER

The following statements contain a vast majority of accuracy, validity, and genuineness, to the best of the participant's knowledge. This verbal communication, however, is significantly altered by unreliable memories and/or erroneous visions of self-perceived grandeur. Nonetheless, I assure you that the following is indeed an attempt at an honest dialogue, even though the exchange also contains a smattering of sporadic exaggerations, overstatements, understatements, misgivings, and bare faced lies in an attempt to support the speakers position, retain assumed respect, and avoid embarrassment, while also devaluing the stance of the person waiting anticipatorily for their turn to speak, which is detected at varying degrees by the non-speaker as well as the speaker throughout the entire discourse. This type of event happens quite often among Human Beings. It's called a *conversation*. As a courtesy I will inject myself into said conversation in order to aid you, the reader, in cutting through the bullshit.

"You gotta be kidding me. C'mon Char, it will be a blast. The three of us on a road trip together."

True: Myelin did sincerely believe a road trip with his sisters would be a blast.

"And Lydia, don't forget Lydia."

Also, true: The point of the trip was for Myelin, Char, and Camy to drive Lydia from Chicago to Cambridge, Massachusetts for her freshman year at MIT. The plan was to make the trip there in two days, stopping overnight in East Syracuse, New York, spend almost four days in the Boston area getting Lydia settled and taking in the sights, and then drive back in two days, stopping overnight in Geneva, New York.

"Of course, Lydia. I would never forget Lydia."

False: This is a lie. In fact, there was a stretch of time in between baby and toddler where forgetting his children was almost habitual. He had accidentally abandoned both James and Lydia at more than a few gigs, the supermarket, the DMV, a carnival, and perhaps the most outrageous, he once forgot them both at Lydia's fourth birthday party at a Chuck E Cheese for over an hour and a half. Drugs or alcohol were always involved and the children would always remain forgotten until someone would inevitably say, *Hey dude, where's your kids?*

"It's just not safe, Melvy *(both Char and Camy always called Melvin III/ Myelin – Melvy. He graciously accepted that, but only from them)*, and you guys really should rethink what you're doing. I just don't think Camy is healthy enough for that long of a road trip."

True/False: Kind of a mixed bag here. Char definitely had deep concerns about Camy's health, but felt she would be fine if accompanied by a responsible adult. Myelin did not fit that bill and Char, as much as she would have loved to fulfill that role, did not feel comfortable making the journey as Carl and his alcoholic, slut, lying, whore, piece of shit, drug addict, scumbag girlfriend had just moved into her home and it was probably not the best of ideas to give them free rein.

"Camy's fine. She's cancer free. This trip is a celebration. A victory tour."

True: Camy is cancer free, that much is true, but fine is a stretch. The last year had been one of relentless torture. She was successful in defeating the rectal cancer that tried to destroy her, but there was quite a bit of collateral damage: months of poison pumped through her body, devastating rounds of radiation blasting away at one of the most sensitive of areas, shitting through an ileostomy bag for thirty-eight weeks and five surgeries, the latest an attempt to rebuild her bowels. Cancer free, yes, terrible bathroom issues, times of extreme pain, occasional uncontrollable human urgency, uncomfortable to dreadful residual side effects, also yes. As far as the trip being a celebration, true. To Myelin, everything about life was either a celebration or a journey to the next celebration.

"You know she is a long way from fine, Melvy. You just want me to go so I'll take care of her and you don't have to."

Kind of true, but…That's not the only reason.

"That's not true, Char. We need this trip. We deserve it. After everything we've all been through."

Very true: They had all been through a lot. Char had been right at her sister's side during her entire battle. From holding her hand to helping her change her ileostomy bag, from taking care of her house and children to cleaning up her sick and raising her spirits. Myelin had also suffered a terrible tragedy, one month after his sister's diagnosis he came home to find his wife Jody dead in their kitchen.

"You! Really? I don't remember seeing you at any of Camy's treatments? Or helping to take care of her after?"

True, but oops. Char did what all of us do from time to time, she let her mind run selfish.

"I was talking about my wife dying."

Here comes another oops. A lot of times when someone points out to someone that they are wrong, if that person would just step back and think in a logical and compassionate way, they would realize that they may have spoken or acted inappropriately and their best course of action would be to apologize or remain silent, but as flawed Human Beings being *right* and saving face sometimes becomes far too important and something like this happens instead...

"Oh, I'm sorry, is that what we do when our spouse dies now? Go on a celebratory road trip. Some bonding time? Support each other? Well then, I must have missed the meeting when we changed that rule, cause when my Reginald died I don't remember any support from you. No, quite the opposite. I remember having to take care of your kids because you guys were too fucked up to do it!"

I cannot dispute the accuracy of any of that.

"That's not fair, Char."

True: It was a low blow.

Quiet reflection, noticeable tension.

"I'm sorry, Melvy."

True.

"I'm sorry, too, Char."

True.

"Sometimes I can be a real bitch."

True.

"I know I have messed up a lot, but I've been drug free for eight years."

False.

"I know."

Well, she thinks she does.

"It was just such a shock when I found out Jody was still using...to come home and find her like that...to find out I was living a lie."

I'll allow it.

Char embraced her brother and offered him comfort. This is what Char did best, gave comfort to those in need of it.

"Please just think about it, Char. You and Camy have always been like Lydia's step moms and now, with Jody gone it would mean a lot to her and to me."

True.

A BRIEF HISTORY OF MYELIN AND JODY'S DRUG USE

Myelin and Jody enjoyed using drugs. It was their favorite pastime. In the early days it was plenty of Jack Daniels, pot, and LSD with the occasional bag of mushrooms. As times got better, so did the drugs. Cocaine and Molly became their drugs of choice. As times got worse they dabbled with Meth, Crack, and H. I don't believe either ever developed a physical addiction to any of their hobbies. Not saying that their usage was not destructive, it was. I think Myelin was just addicted to being fucked up. He would say he was addicted to good times, unfortunately he always equated good times to being fucked up.

Jody, on the other hand, suffered from depression and was always under the impression that a strong enough buzz would ease that suffering. It only masked it. Even if they were not drug addicts in the truest sense of the word, they were reckless drug users. Anyway, as far as most of the people in their life were concerned, they both became drug free when Lydia was eleven.

Once a child hits double digits, it is generally the time they are able to shame a semi-functional destructive parent. In this case it worked. At least for Lydia. Myelin and Jody loved their children and they cleaned up their act. Or at least gave that impression. They became extremely responsible drug users. No more dirty drugs. Pot and coke, that's all. And booze. Booze is okay, it's socially acceptable. Myelin became such a responsible cocaine user that he could buy an 8 ball on a Tuesday for an event that coming weekend and not dip into it once, not even a taste until Saturday. After dinner. That's impressive.

Jody followed Myelin's lead. Lydia was happy to cautiously welcome her parents into her life and attempt to play the role of loving caring parents. It was too late for James. Two years after his parents perceived sobriety, so to speak, he was gone at the age of eighteen. Although he maintained a relationship with his sister, his interaction with his parents became very minimal and cold. He did not even return his father's hug at his mother's wake.

When somebody tells you that *you learned something the hard way* what it really means is that *you screwed something up and are now paying the consequences.* They assume in paying those consequences you learned a lesson not to screw the same thing up again. That's not always the case. Some people have the miraculous ability to completely believe their own lies. The number one job of someone who believes in their own lies is to get others to share a belief in those lies.

Myelin had a habit. Really it was more of a philosophy. To be completely honest it was a miraculous ability, when it worked, which was often. He used it concerning all of his shortcomings: his sobriety, his parenting, and of course his band's inability to sustain continued success. *When you fail at something, instead of being ashamed that you did not succeed, attempt to trick your on lookers into being embarrassed that they failed to notice your success.*

Myelin Sheath was shocked and devastated when he came home and found Jody dead from a heroin overdose at their kitchen table, but to say he was surprised she was using drugs again is a barefaced lie.

NOW

Myelin had the Dodge Caravan rolling down I90 at 88 mph feeling like he could drive forever as he spoke loudly to his sisters sprawled out on the bench seat in the way back. He thanked them over and over again for joining him on the road trip and all of their motherly attention to detail in getting Lydia settled. He spoke candidly of Lydia's affection for both of them and waxed poetically of Lydia's imagined future as well as her imagined past. Occasionally he talked about the moon actually being a giant spaceship occupied by extraterrestrials that controlled everything, which would always cause him to get off track and end up talking about how much he missed Jody, which led him back to thanking his sisters.

Char and Camy had seen him like this before. *This is what too much coffee does to him.*

Char pretended like she was pretending to go to sleep so she would not have to engage in the mostly one-sided conversation. In reality she was very concerned. She had tried calling Carl twenty times in the last eighteen hours, all to no avail.

Camy was just as concerned if not more as she felt the pain in her side returning. *Please go away, please stop.*

"Char, do I have a temperature?"

Char grabbed the Exergen Temporal thermometer they had purchased at the Travelmart and as she scanned Camy's forehead she said, "You shouldn't, I mean you took Tylenol less than an hour ago."

Myelin continued to verbally express every thought in his head.

"Nope, you're cool as a cucumber."

Char went back to her pretending position.

The pain continued to build.

"Guys," Camy requested her brother and sister's attention.

"Guys." She had to say it five times before Myelin would shut up.

"What's up Cam?"

"If I die —"

Char snapped into action and grabbed her phone consulting her notes and google maps.

"What's the closest one?" Myelin commanded.

"Guys."

"Shit! We just passed the exit for Angel Of Penance Hospital."

"Should I get off?"

"Guys."

"No wait, Edgewater Medical might be closer."

"Should I turn around? I could turn around right here."

"Hang on, hang on."

"Guys! We are not getting off the expressway! I am being hypothetical! We are going to Chicago!"

"If we don't take you to Edgewater, the next one is Grace and that's forty-eight miles, and then-"

"Stop it, Char. Nothing has changed. We are sticking to the plan. I want to go to-"

"Why would you say-"

"I don't even have a fever anymore, remember?"

"There is a Beacon Medical Center twenty-eight miles away."

"I just wanted to say, you know, we don't know what's going to happen in Chicago."

"I'm getting you to Chicago Metro and it will be all good." Myelin insisted.

"I just wanted to say I'm really happy I took this trip with you guys."

"I'm happy I did, too," Char put her arm around Camy.

"Girls, we are doing this every year for the next three!"

"That sounds great to me."

Camy smiled in doubtful pain.

"Shit! You guys can come with me to pick her up in the spring, too."

Char sensed Camy's pain and squeezed her tighter.

"That's seven more trips."

Camy feared she was making the wrong decision.

"And I'll have you at Chicago Metro before you know it."

Char worried for her sister and son.

"But first I gotta hit the next rest stop, take a piss, and get some more java."

Camy did not reveal the conditions that haunted her thoughts of possibly dying in the near future and her brother and sister were currently too concerned with keeping her alive to ask what she was about to divulge.

TEN MONTHS EARLIER

"We've been through this already, you can't expect me to go to all your appointments "

"I don't."

"I have to work."

"I know but –"

"Bills still have to be paid. College is right around the corner."

"But you have only been to two appointments."

"What do you want me to do? I'm on track to be Vice President. Should I throw that away?"

"Of course not."

"Look, Camy, baby. It sucks and I'm really, really sorry, but you got Char, I mean thank God for Char, right?"

Eyes swell. Tears form. He turns his back and walks to the desk. Her head drops. He picks up the phone.

"Look, I'm not going to be able to make it today…No, it's Camila, she needs me…Just give it to Stefon, he'll know what to do…Stefon will be fine, don't worry."

Camy's head raises with a smile. The couple embraces.

"I'm sorry hon, I'm just trying to do too much and take care of this family. All this juggling and I dropped you. I'm sorry."

"I'm sorry, too. I was being selfish."

"No, no, not at all. I'm going to re-arrange things. I'll do some stuff at night and on the weekends…I want to be there for you."

A BRIEF HISTORY OF CAMY NEWBERG

For the most part, Camila is a swell Human Being, who lived a seemingly conventional life. She married a lovely husband, they had three adequate children, and lived well above the poverty level. One night, an average night, a night like any other, Camy went to bed, very sleepy and cancer free. She did not wake up that way.

There are many things that happen when a Human Being is at rest. You see, the human body never truly sleeps. Although our minds take a break from our perceived consciousness, I assure you there are many things going on. Your heart still beats, your lungs still take in air and expel air, your hair and fingernails and toenails continue to grow, and your cells continuously divide. Mitosis, the magnificent, remarkable dance that is constantly taking place within all of us. A majestic display that is, unfortunately at times, less than perfect. Prometaphase, metaphase, anaphase, and telophase, these are the stages of the process where a parent cell becomes two daughter cells with an identical duplication of chromosomes that takes place in our bodies billions of times each and every day. The main component of a chromosome, and the carrier of all this genetic information is deoxyribonucleic acid, better known as DNA.

The typical number of chromosomes in a human cell is forty-six, twenty-three from your mommy and twenty-three from your daddy, each one containing around 25,000 genes, and the duplication that takes place billions of times each day has to be exact. Well, at least it's supposed to be, so what happens when it is not? You become the proud owner of a mutant cell. Not to worry, more than likely that mutant cell is not going to get very far. There is a mutant war going on inside of your body. You have a well-armed, extremely trained, very protective group of assassins inside of you that hunt down and destroy mutants. This police force is known as your immune system. But once in a while, one gets away, hides out in the country and starts its own family. So, then what? Usually nothing. Over a million genes on a cell and one is mutated. No big deal. The family of mutants stay in the country, keep to themselves, eat Frogmore stew, no muss, no fuss.

But sometimes the mutants birth themselves a new mutation. A mutant's mutant. And this could happen again and again. Eventually, these mutants of mutants of mutants will get sick of life out in the country and head to the big city looking for good times, a job, and a new way of life, but nobody wants their kind. And one of the shopkeepers calls the cops, but it's too late. There are too many of them and they are too strong and the cops can no longer destroy them. But they chase them away from the city. Unfortunately, their family back in the country has enjoyed life without them and they are no longer welcome there either. So, they find their own territory and form their own nation and make their own culture and laws. This new nation is what we commonly call a tumor.

When Camy went to bed that average, ordinary night she had such a nation attached to her anus. That night the new nation had a decision to make, they could sign a treaty, and promise not to invade the surrounding tissue of Camy Newbery and be a benign nation, or refuse to sign the treaty and become a malignant nation. Unfortunately for Camila, it chose the latter. Suddenly, Camy was in need of more than a lovely husband and adequate children.

EIGHTEEN DAYS EARLIER

The following is another Smathy sibling conversation. This one is between Myelin and Camy. Once again, I feel it would be beneficial to you, the reader, if I were to provide a truth detector.

"Camy, I think it really sucks that Char isn't going. Lydia is going to be really bummed. Please tell me, you're not thinking of backing out now?"

While technically true, the Lydia comment was a passive aggressive ploy designed for Myelin to get his way.

"Of course not. Why would you even think such a thing? It's not like Char and me are attached at the hip."

Here we have both true and false. Camy was very concerned about going without Char and was strongly considering opting out. Myelin's passive aggressive ploy was really manipulating that consideration at this point. As for the second part of Camy's statement, while technically true, I find it to be both emotionally false and incredibly insensitive to conjoined twins. C'mon Camy, you're better than that. Char and Camy may not be physically connected, but Char has been her entire support system for the last year. Char cared for her after the radiation scorched the inside of her ass day after day, cleaned up after her when the chemotherapy forced all that was inside her and not essential to survival to be violently puked up through her throat with a red-hot burn that reminded her of her raw, scalded rectum. She nursed her back to health after all five of her surgeries.

No, they may not have been connected at the hip, but they definitely had a profound connection. For over five months a major aspect of that connection was only four inches away from Camy's hip. Her stoma. The stoma the sisters affectionately named Olivia. They hated Olivia. As much as all the combined Human Beings on the planet could possibly resent one entity, that's how much the Smathy sisters loathed the existence of Olivia. Olivia was a stump at the end of Camy's small intestine that would normally feed into Camy's large intestine, where liquid shit would be transformed into healthy bowel movements. But the doctors felt it would be best if Camy did not use her large intestine for a while, as they would be busy at that far end of it, cutting out tumors and blasting it with unforgiving, deadly radiation. So, this stoma, Olivia, would constantly ooze human diarrhea through an opening in Camy's stomach. But not to worry, there is a bag to put over Olivia to catch all the premature feces spewing from Olivia's mouth. A bag that has to be changed over and over again. Chances of Olivia fitting perfectly into the ileostomy bag? Zero. Chances of the tape holding the bag to her skin not causing great pain and irritation? Zero. Chances of Olivia never ever leaking? Zero. Chances of it not being a messy, disgusting, smelly job? Zero. Chances of Olivia taking a short break from puking up Camy's digestive waste while the Smathy sisters struggled to change the bag? Zero. Chances that Char will help her sister with this process over and over and over again? 100%. Chances that this type of activity between two Human Beings will form a very unusual bond? 100%.

Oh my. I have digressed considerably. All apologies. Back to the conversation.

"Great! That's great. I just don't get Char. This is the trip of a life time. Sibling bonding."

True. Although they loved and cared for each other very much, there was a lot the Smathy children did not *get* about each other. As with all siblings.

"I want to get together with Lydia soon and we can talk about bedding and decorating and all that kind of stuff."

True.

"She would love that."

True.

"Do you know any of the details of her room?"

Valid question.

"No, I don't."

Sadly, he had never asked.

Myelin continued, "Do you think Char isn't going because she is jealous?"

True, Myelin did wonder this.

"Jealous? Of Lydia?"

Camy did not understand the assertion.

"No, that you know...My kid is so smart and Carl is such an idiot."

While that is true, it had nothing to do with Char's decision.

"Well...I mean...I don't think that would keep her from going."

Also, true.

"I mean, shit, Carl probably could not even spell MIT."

I'm not entirely sure, but there is a good chance that may also be true.

CAMBRIDGE, MASSACHUSETTES

Lydia and Myelin and Camy and Char had a fantastic drive out to Cambridge. They left at 5 a.m. on a Thursday. They spent Thursday night in a Courtyard by Marriott in East Syracuse, NY. They were supposed to have a nice Italian dinner and get some sleep. Instead after their delicious dinner at the perfectly charming Grimaldi's the four of them stayed up talking and laughing and reminiscing until 3 a.m. They were back on the road by 8 a.m. and arrived in Cambridge on Friday afternoon and would spend the next four nights there.

Lydia was to spend her freshman year living in the Burton Connor House. She would be staying in a suite with six other freshman girls. It was a four-bedroom suite, two double, two singles. It was a dump. Burton Connor House opened in 1939 and was last painted soon after. It had no air conditioning and the heat ran 365 days a year. No one knew how to stop it. And we're talking about no one at MIT. The Burton Connor boiler took on a life of its own a few decades ago and everyone decided it would just be better to leave it alone and try not to agitate it.

Lydia was lucky enough to get one of the singles. It had a window. And a screen sitting on the floor next to the window. Myelin tried to install the screen but it was very ill-fitting. Char poked her head out the screenless window to get some relief from the relentless boiler on the hot August day. In doing so she noticed a couple dozen screens lying in the courtyard down below. The ill-fitting screens were an epidemic.

Camy found the phone number for maintenance but when she called, it only rang and rang. The phone associated with the number Camy was dialing sat several feet away from the boiler in the basement and had not been answered in years, although some have occasionally claimed to have had their calls answered only to hear maniacal laughter on the other end.

Despite the heat of the room, the four of them, although mostly in each other's way in the tight 10X6 bedroom, enjoyed setting up Lydia's living quarters and each other's company. The bedding and matching towels Lydia and her aunts selected were perfect, the room's decor was flawless after several return trips to Target. Myelin, with the help of a roll of wire and some duct tape, was able to secure the screen. The shithole was transformed into a comfy little nest, that would be warm and snuggly when the East Coast winter arrived.

The rest of their time in Cambridge was swell, but not fantastic. In the agenda sense it was fantastic. Lydia spent all four nights in the suite at the Residence Inn by Marriott with her father and aunts. The amenities at the Marriott were slightly better than those at BC House.

They did a lot of sight-seeing in Boston and Cambridge, although Camy stayed back at the hotel for most of that, saying that she was still too tired and too weak. They visited Bunker Hill. They walked the Freedom Trail. They dined at absolutely superb restaurants: Craigie on Main, Cuchi Cuchi, Loyal Nine, and The Asgard. Camy was present for all the dining experiences. They said tearful goodbyes to Lydia. Lydia squeezed her father and her aunts tightly and held on so long that Char and Camy felt awkward ending the embrace. They felt even more awkward persuading the end to the cradle between father and daughter, but if they did not it may very well have gone on until one of them passed out from pure hug exhaustion. After six days of being on the road and in a hotel and a 10X6 dorm room with Myelin, Lydia felt closeness to her father she had never known.

So why was their time in Cambridge simply swell and not fantastic? For reasons that they all remained very quiet about. They all had secrets. And the thing you do with secrets is hide them, no matter how much more difficult it may make your life. Somehow, sometimes, the secrets we keep become more important than the lives we live. Why is that? I said earlier in our story that there were certain things that the Smathy siblings just didn't *get* about one another. I said that was true with all siblings. Why? Don't they all kind of start out on the same wave length? Same parents, same household, same experiences? So, when things start to change with one of them - perceptions, ideas, experiences – why aren't the reasons for that change explained to the other siblings? Why isn't that information communicated? Not that the other sibling would be obliged to join in on this new way of thinking or feeling or acting, but now they would know why and would come to understand.

All that is good and enlightened and appreciated and beneficial in this world comes from understanding and secrets are a barrier to understanding. But still we keep them for fear of embarrassment, resentment, scorn, or fear of hurting other's feelings or unwanted confrontation. Many times, anger or embarrassment or hurt feelings are the first step toward understanding. And are not we all siblings in a sense? And don't we all suffer the consequences of secrets? And…Oh my, this digression has become awkward and rambling, perhaps even sappy.

I will get off my soapbox.

Do you want to know our character's secrets?

Secret # 1: Myelin Sheath had four eight balls of cocaine in two contact lens cases. Myelin loved coke, but as I have already told you he had also trained himself to be a very disciplined drug abuser. Besides slowly burning a hole in his nasal septum, this coke was also burning a hole in his pocket. He was doing it slowly and using it sparingly. This took incredible self-restraint. The benefits of this were three-fold. Of course, it made a very expensive drug last for a while, but it also made Myelin feel more like a cocaine connoisseur and less like a drug user. Much like a sommelier enjoys every aspect of wine drinking, Myelin savored every aspect of the cocaine use process. Without a doubt his favorite was the initial ingestion and its immediate effects: the vibration of the cilia in his nose, the warm surge of exuberance shooting violently up his nostril into his brain causing an involuntary smile.

Snorting coke for Myelin was very reminiscent of performing on stage, or perhaps vice versa. You see, Myelin had a rather large, but character-enhancing nose, and while singing he would often get right up on the microphone. At times it seemed he was almost consuming it rather than using it to amplify his vocal range. In doing this he would rest his significant snout right on the metal grill of the microphone. As the mic's diaphragm vibrated his cilia would dance, he felt the absurdly gratifying burn and his facial muscles would force an involuntary smile. The third benefit to Myelin's drug rationing was not getting so stoned that his travel mates would suspect his behavior was due to drug ingestion and not simply being a middle-aged punk rocker.

In the old glory days of AMA, Myelin and Jody would not have to go through the hassle of purchasing drugs. People would just give them all the drugs they desired. As the band's popularity waned so did the free drugs. The young couple quickly became purchasers of government controlled substances. There were never any dangerous, shady, back alley deals. Their providers were friends, friends of friends, fans, bandmates, sometimes even co-workers.

The blow that Myelin was currently traveling with was very difficult to obtain. Not that there was any kind of shortage. People just no longer wanted to be Myelin's provider. It was his own fault. After he and Jody did the whole fake clean thing, every time he would make a purchase he would insist to the provider that this was to be his final indulgence. Sometimes he would even make them promise to never sell to him again. Most did not honor such promises, until Jody's overdose. Then no one would sell to him, with the exception of the drummer of his band. Type 2 Diabetes would sell anything to anyone. Type 2 Diabetes didn't give a shit. The way Type 2 Diabetes figured it was if you didn't give a shit about yourself, why should he. His motto is *if you don't want to take care of yourself, Type 2 Diabetes will be right here for you.*

During their time in Cambridge Myelin would use just enough to take the edge off, make himself feel more interesting, and the world more compelling. He looked forward to the trip home. Day one they would travel to Geneva New York, dine at Kindred Fare, a seemingly hip restaurant in the middle of nowhere Camy had found on line, and spend the night at the Fairfield Inn, where Myelin planned on removing his coke sanctions and having a memorable night with his sisters doing what siblings do, complain about their parents and their childhood. That plan would not work out. Besides the eight balls Myelin was hiding behind, he had another secret that I will not tell you at this time.

Secret # 2: Lydia was afraid. She hid her fear as best she could, but she was scared shitless. She was also sad. Less than an hour after her dad and aunts left she found herself sobbing into her new hip and colorful pillow case in her comfy little lonely nest. Unlike her brother James, Lydia had a genuine need for her father no matter how poor of a father he was. She had never been away from home. Her parents or aunts had always been within reach. Soon they would be more than a thousand miles away and she would be alone. Lydia felt foolish for crying like a baby. She knew she was capable. She had been running the house long before her mother died. Her capability did not make her feel any less scared or sad.

Things would get better for her before her dad got home. She would meet a boy. A sophomore. Just a few hours after soaking her pillow, Lydia would be in a hallway of Burton Connor wearing her Chicago Bears t-shirt where she would hear, "Hey, are you from Chicago? I'm from Oak Lawn." Oak Lawn is a suburb of Chicago and happened to be where Aunt Char lived. A friendship was born and that friendship would lead to many others. The five things that establish and maintain friendships in order of importance are: common enemy, common interest, common experience/ locations, common beliefs, and common knowledge.

Secret # 3: Char Peach was also afraid. Very afraid. She was afraid of what she might find when she got home. She was afraid for Carl. She hated the way he and Penny would fight and drink and fight. She just could not understand the basis of their relationship. *Sex. It had to be sex,* she thought. *I wonder if Carl knows about masturbation? He must? Right? Everybody does…*

Secret # 4: Camy's colon could explode at any moment.

On the morning of the trip Camy woke up at 3:30 a.m. Not because she had a lot to do before Myelin and crews early arrival. She was awakened by a feeling. A strange uncomfortable feeling. Not a pain, not yet anyway, but she definitely knew something was not right. She decided to keep this new discomfort a secret. Her body had been through so much in the past year, her hourly disposition had been anywhere from excruciating, merciless pain to pleasant uncomfortableness. *What's one more odd feeling.*

The discomfort turned to occasional pain.

The next day when she woke up at The Courtyard by Marriott in East Syracuse New York, she decided to reveal her secret, not to her traveling mates, but to her doctor. "It's probably just some residual effects from the surgery. Some discomfort in the healing process. I would just stay close to home and try to take it easy and rest. Don't worry too much about it. But if it gets really bad or you develop a fever, you should go to the ER because then it can be something really serious".

Their first day in Cambridge the occasional pain turned to nagging pain and now Camy joined the ranks of the afraid, but her secret she still kept.

I'll just take it easy, she thought, *I'll stay behind and rest while they do some sight-seeing. I'll tell them I'm too tired. Too weak. They'll understand. I don't want to ruin things for Lydia.*

On the third day Camy felt a fever. The nagging pain was becoming a complete bitch, but her secret, she still kept.

The final morning in Cambridge, Camy slept in while the others went to breakfast. Sleep she did not. Instead she made phone calls.

"You should really go to the nearest ER."

"But I really want to see my doctor at my hospital."

"Well, how far are you from Chicago Metro?"

"It's a bit of a drive."

"Then I advise against it."

"What's the worst that can happen?"

"If there is some kind of post op infection in your intestines and it burst or opens or spreads in any way and gets into your blood you will become sepsis."

"Meaning?"

"Blood poisoning! Organ failure! Death!"

"___"

"Did you hear me Camy? Are you there?"

"I'm going to Metro. Please let them know."

"That's a terrible decision. When will you be there?"

"___"

"Camy?"

"Tomorrow morning. Early."

Click.

Camy then placed a call to each of her three children. She told them she loved them. She told them how proud she was of their adequacy. She did not tell them her secret. The rest of the gang entered the room as she finished her last call. It was nearly noon. On a scale of 1 to 10 Camy's pain fucking sucked.

NOW

The funny thing about *now* is it doesn't last long. You see, there, it's gone, but there is always a new *now* ready and willing to take the old *now's* place. It just occurred several times while you were reading this sentence. I decided to use *now* as one of the time frames while telling you this story in the hopes that it would summon feelings of anxiety and nervousness in you, the reader, for the three siblings as they make their way home. So, for all intents and purposes, this conversation between Camy and Char and Myelin takes place right *now*…

"Melvy is really making great time."

"Char…it's really starting to hurt, feel my head."

"You don't feel warm."

"How long since my last Tylenol?"

"A little over two hours. Try not to think about the pain. Pretty soon you'll be in the arms of your hubby at Chicago Metro and the doctors will get you all good."

"He probably won't even come."

"How you ladies doing back there?"

"Now honey, why would you say such a thing?"

"Is my music too loud?"

"Why wouldn't I?"

"I heard you on the phone with him."

"Huh?"

" '*I love you, sweetheart. You are the world to me.*' "

Those terms of endearment were to Camy's daughter, who did not even remember her Mother was on a road trip.

"Char, it hurts really bad."

"Hello ladies, no secrets. Speak up."

"Camy is really hurting right now."

"Goddammit fuck."

"Fuck, fuck."

"Honey I'm gonna give you more Tylenol now and we'll go to the closest hospital."

"No…Chicago Metro."

"Do you think Oxycodone would help?"

"Well, yes, if we had some."

"Promise me Char."

"I've got some."

"Wait, what? Why do you have oxy?"

"From my back thing."

"Char, promise."

"What back thing?"

"When I hurt my back."

"When?"

"Oh God...Char."

"Yes Melvy – give me the fuckin' oxy."

"I got to pull over. It's in the back."

"Have you been abusing oxy Melvy?"

"Wait a minute, will that be too much acetaminophen?"

"Don't answer a question with a question."

"Char."

"Pull over! Get the fucking oxy now!"

"Should we check on line? To see if it's safe?"

"Now Melvy! She is in too much pain!"

6 DAYS EARLIER

When Char Peach came home from work she was hoping to find Penny the alcoholic, slut, lying, whore, piece of shit, drug addict, scumbag gone. Her hope did not come to fruition. At that time, she also had no intention of making the road trip out to MIT. In no logical way could she even begin to imagine leaving her home in the hands of the Chaos Couple for a week's time.

But soon after she entered her home something happened. Something that completely changed her way of thinking. Her plan was to grab a bottle of Barefoot Pinot Noir and a wine glass along with a Portillos chopped salad and a large french fry she had purchased on her way home, and go upstairs to her room and lock herself in for the night. She would spend her evening eating, drinking, and Netflixing and hiding from the sight and very thought of Carl and Penny.

But there was Penny, blocking the stairway and not seeming to make any effort to get out of Char Peach's way. Penny startled Char and caused her favorite wine glass to slip out from under her arm and shatter on the hardwood floor. She also dropped her salad and french fries. She hung on to the wine though. Penny stared at Char. Penny had a goofy look on her face. Not just on her face, but the way she cocked her head. Defiantly. Silent. Making no effort to move out of Char's way. That's the thing about dead alcoholic, slut, lying, whore, piece of shit, drug addict, scumbags, - they pretty much just lay there with their heads twisted awkwardly onto their neck in a way that is defiant of the normal human biological constitution and their eyes still wide open as if their final feeling was one of shock.

Char could hear her son upstairs, his breathing labored by occasional sounds of sobbing.

"Mom, I really fucked up."

AFTER FAREWELL TO LYDIA

The Dodge Caravan rental was melancholy. The three siblings already missed their little Lydia. Where did the time go? It was around 3 p.m. when they finished their final trips to the Target and Star Market grocery store and said their goodbyes. Myelin's sullen spirits were greatly alleviated about an hour into the drive. He looked forward to a great dinner and a couple of well-deserved cocktails in Geneva New York in a little over five hours, followed by sitting around a Fairfield Inn suite with his sisters talking about what an asshole their father was while moving an eight ball from the contact lens case in his left front jean pocket to a much more internal place. His enthusiasm for the night's events were short lived though, as Camy decided to drop the bomb on her siblings.

"Guys, don't be totally mad at me, but I think maybe we should skip Geneva and drive straight back."

"Yeah right, like that's gonna happen."

"Why? What's wrong honey?"

"I'm not sure. I have a bad pain in my side."

"Wait, you're serious?"

"Yes, she's serious!"

"And I might have a little bit of a fever."

"Oh, what the fuck!"

"Shut up, Melvin. We have to call your doctors if you have a fever."

"I already did." Camy began to tear up.

"What did they say?"

"I should…get to Chicago Metro as soon as possible."

"Do they know how far away you are?"

Myelin calculated. "If I drive straight through you'll be there around 5 a.m."

"That's too long. We have to go to a nearby hospital."

"But if we still stop for dinner and a little rest in Geneva, I'll have you there by 2 p.m. tomorrow. Are you sure you don't want to try and gut it out, sis?"

"Shut the fuck up Melvin! She's not gutting it out."

"5 a.m. is good. I'll be fine. I can make it."

"No! No! We're going to a hospital right the fuck now."

"Slow down, Char. What did the doctor say could happen?"

"Well," through tearful eyes and a shaky voice, "If it gets really really bad…" swallow. "I could go sepsis, and…and I could die."

"You see! You see! Hospital! Right now!"

"But wait, just hold on a second, did he say *you could die* or did he say YOU COULD DIE!?"

"Are you a fucking idiot?"

"There's a difference! Doctors are always saying you could die."

"How can he be related to us? I'm finding the nearest hospital now."

"STOP! No, wait. My life, my decision. I want to go to Chicago Metro where my doctors are. Now he said-"

"Camy."

"NOW HE SAID, that if things started to get bad we would have warning signs. I would vomit. I would run a high fever. A fever that Tylenol would not be able to break. If things get bad, there will be plenty of time to change our plans."

Camy now had a new secret. The secret she just divulged was full of lies and half-truths. They decided, begrudgingly but united, to attempt to carry out one of Camy's all-time worst decisions. They would attempt to control the fever and pain with Tylenol, Myelin would exceed the speed limit, and Char would constantly keep track of the nearest hospitals and medical facilities. Once Myelin had overcome his initial self-centered disappointment he was all on board with the new plan. He was happy to have a pocketful of energy and willingness to help him along.

6 DAYS EARLIER

Char Peach did what she was best at, comforting those in need. She pulled a scissors out of Carl's left bicep, cleaned and bandaged the wound. She listened to Carl's tearful explanation. They had fought, like they often did, but this one had turned more physical than usual. Penny threw a cup of coffee at Carl, barely missing him. The fight escalated. Penny stabbed Carl in the arm and Carl pushed Penny. Unfortunately, the only thing there to break her fall was a staircase.

"I'm gonna go to jail, Mama. I'm gonna go to jail."

Carl's prediction was the odds-on favorite. Carl had had legal issues in the past: drunk and disorderly, possession of a controlled substance, driving under the influence, and misdemeanor theft. He once stole a live iguana from a pet shop. He just shoved it down his pants. Walked right out the door as inconspicuously as possible with a large lizard scrambling around in his crotchal area. He got away with it, too. What he did not get away with was when he returned and attempted to steal three dozen live crickets. He was unaware iguanas are mainly herbivorous. In addition to all of these indiscretions there were two arrests that would make his current involuntary manslaughter almost impossible to avoid jail time. His first assault and battery occurred when he was only eighteen. It was truly self-defense, but in the end Carl pleaded no contest and Char paid a fine and some medical bills. The twenty-five-year-old instigator definitely picked the wrong eighteen-year-old to mess with. After breaking the oppressor's jaw and making him look silly and foolish, Carl realized he had found something he was above average at. Far above average. Street fighting. From that day until this latest unfortunate incident, Carl took part in eighty-three physical altercations. Eighty times he was the ass-kicker, three times he was the ass-kickie. His stats in this area were definitely impressive and he unquestionably possessed the *Neanderthal Gene.*

These were not the type of fights or the type of people, nor did they occur in the type of places where law enforcement would be summoned. All but one. Three years ago, Carl was at a strip club with a couple of friends, where he took exception to another patron's attitude. The gentleman in question was loudly making some rather scandalous accusations as well as some absolutely pornographic suggestions to Carl's current favorite stripper. Carl's favorite stripper usually changed several times in a single visit to such an establishment. Carl took exception.

"Hey buddy, show some respect," he insisted.

"Take it easy, Carl," his chums cautioned him.

"She's a stripper, Carl," his chums reminded him.

Carl calmed momentarily.

The patron would *cat call* again.

"Watch it pal, I'm telling you," Carl warned.

This went on for about twenty minutes with the stranger trying hard to ignore Carl, avoid trouble, and continue to enjoy himself in his boorish way. Carl decided he'd had enough and placed his face inches from the stranger's face.

"You are going to apologize to her right now and then keep your goddamn mouth shut."

"Dude, calm down, I'm just havin' fun. She's a stripper."

"It's okay," insisted the naked dancer.

Carl's mates made attempts to ease his intentions.

"I don't hear you."

"Fuck man, her whole job is to be objectified."

Carl did not know what objectified meant, but he certainly did not like the sound of it.

"Oh yeah, how 'bout I punch you right in the face, champ?"

Carl did.

Repeatedly.

The very talkative, striptease enthusiast ended up in the hospital with a broken jaw. Carl really loved punching jaws. Although the fellow could not talk, he was still able to press charges, and charges he pressed. Carl spent ninety days in jail. Carl did not like jail. While in jail he got in three fist fights. Those were Carl's three ass kickings. Carl did not like ass kickings.

Char rubbed her son's back as they sat together at the top step staring down at Penny's lifeless body.

"You're not going to jail young man so get that idea out of your head right now."

"I am, I am, I know I am."

"No, you're not. Now listen to me –"

"How? I'm done. I fucked it all up."

"Listen Carl, I don't think she is going to be missed by anybody."

"I kind of miss her already."

"Besides you, look, do you remember on Breaking Bad?"

"Why can't I control my temper?"

"She fucking stabbed you."

"But I didn't have to get so mad."

"Carl concentrate. Breaking Bad."

"??"

" 'Member? Jessie, he had to get rid of those bodies, with the special plastic container and the chemicals, 'member?"

"??"

"Carl, look, I know you are upset right now. I know this is a very traumatic thing. But listen, the cold hard truth of the matter is you guys were not soulmates or anything like that. You had some fun. You fought a lot. But you had some laughs. And you fought a lot. And then this…"

"??"

"But it was an accident, Carl. An accident. Do you want to go back to jail because of one goofy old mistake?"

"? No…?"

"Of course not! That a boy. So, do you know what that means we have to do?"

"??"

"So, you don't have to go back to jail."

"…get a lawyer like Saul Goodman?"

"No! Are you kidding me? You killed her. She's dead and you have a rap sheet with some violence on it. No lawyer is keeping you out of jail."

"I can't go back to jail."

"I know honey. So that means we have to…"

"…Run!"

"No. Not fuckin' run. Get rid of the damn body."

"??"

"No dead body…no crime."

"But how -"

"That's what I was saying. Like on Breaking Bad. The special plastic barrel. The chemicals."

"…Wait? How do you know that was for real?"

"Vince Gilligan."

"??"

"Vince Gilligan, the director, I once saw an interview with him and he said they had some science guy right there on the set to make sure all the science stuff checked out."

"For real?"

"Yeah. The science had to check out. Gilligan was a real stickler for that kind of shit."

"Well, I'll be."

"Now listen to me, Carl, you have to do this right. This is very serious. You will be going to jail if you screw this up."

"So, you're gonna help me…with the…chemicals and with-"

"Hell no. I'm going to your uncle's house right now and heading to Boston with him tomorrow. I don't know anything about this. This is your mess."

"__"

Char rubbed her son's back affectionately, "Now what kind of a mother would I be if I did all the hard stuff for you." Then she jumped up and went to her bedroom and began packing. Carl followed. As she packed she continued to dole out some motherly advice and cash.

"It's all right there in season one. You can watch it on the Netflix. I'll give you my credit card. No. Cash, has to be cash. And don't buy the stuff around here. If anyone asks say you're a science teacher. No. Never mind.

Bad idea. Tell them…tell them…Don't tell them anything. It's none of their business. Just stare at em'. Intimidating like. Here. This is all my cash. That's more than enough. Just make sure no one follows you. And don't use the bathtub. That's what Jessie did and screwed it all up. I know, my emergency fund. And don't procrastinate. There are a few Lean Cuisines in the freezer. And frozen burritos. The ones you like. Here take this. Now you have way, way more than enough. I mean how much could these chemicals be? And this counts for your Christmas gift, too, young man. You just get it all cleaned up and everything will be fine. Just do it exactly how Vince Gilligan's science expert guy says. No bathtub. Seriously, no bathtub. Oh, you know what else? I got that Ghirardelli chocolate you like. Intense dark. 72%. You know, for when you're done. It's in the back of the vegetable crisper. I was hiding it from…you know who. I know, that was wrong. Sorry. I love you son. And I really, really am sorry. Watch your step. Be careful. I love you, honey. Goodbye."

2 MONTHS EARLIER

The following is one side of a telephone conversation…
"Right now, you are doing what is becoming a very bad habit for you."
(unknown)
"You're not listening. You're just waiting for your turn to talk."
(unknown)
"Just because I have had the same position on something does not mean I always say the same thing."
(unknown)
"You're the one who always says respect and listening are the cornerstones to a strong relationship."
(unknown)
"Yes, and being there. And I am always there for you. Maybe not as much as I would like to be in the physical sense, but —"
(unknown)
"Well obviously the situation became —"
(unknown)
"Do you think I wanted things to go this way!?"

(unknown)

"I know. It's okay."

(unknown)

"I get frustrated too."

(unknown)

"And I love you too. And I know how hard this last year has been on you. On me. On all of us."

(unknown)

"And of course, the kids...Oh God, the kids. They truly do complicate things, but I love them so much. They are the only part of my life that has not been a lie."

(unknown)

"Well, yes, I think they'll like you. What's not to like?"

(unknown)

"Well, that's not true. Things happen. People fall in love."

(unknown)

"I think it will be toughest on my big guy, but to be honest, I think my little princess already suspects."

(unknown)

"Just from little things she says."

(unknown)

"Well, she is a little old for imaginary tea parties, but I do miss those days."

(unknown)

"She learned a hell of a lot more about being a woman from me than from her mother."

(unknown)

"I already told you."

(unknown)

"She goes for the pet scan next week. If it's clear, I put the wheels in motion."

(unknown)

"Of course, I promise. You have to know, Stefon, I want this as bad as you."

(unknown)

"So, what's a year. Big deal, we are a year behind schedule. We have the rest of our beautiful lives ahead of us."

(unknown)

"Well it's better it happened before I made any announcement as opposed to a few weeks after…Could you imagine?"

(unknown)

"Well, either way. My God. How terrible."

(unknown)

"Could you imagine, hey kids, Daddy's leaving Mommy and he's gay, oh and Mommy has cancer. I'll be in Cancun with my lover, bye."

(unknown)

"It would have been so much better if she would have just died in a car crash or something."

(unkn—)

"Hang on, I think someone's here. Hello? Somebody there?"

(unknown)

"I better go."

(obvious)

"I love you, too."

NOW

Now Camy slept lying across the way back seat, unbelted, her pain and fever temporarily held at bay, courtesy of oxycodone. It was probably irresponsible for Char and Myelin not to secure their sister to the seat while traveling down I90 at 92 mph but they wanted her to be comfortable. It was also not very responsible of them to send so much analgesic to her liver in such a short amount of time, forcing her liver to shift into overdrive, especially when there was a very real possibility of her going sepsis at any moment, which would surely disrupt her use of her vital organs.

Now Char sat in the front passenger seat, worried about her sister, worried about her son, worried about his progress or lack thereof with his dead girlfriend's body disposal project. Char wasn't talking much as Myelin was talking too much. Her ears heard everything he had to say, her brain comprehended half of it. The Paul Thorn band played quietly through the front speakers.

Now Myelin Sheath was talking fast and driving fast. His heart was racing as were his words, which his brain gave little consideration to as they came spilling out of his pie hole. Occasionally, his eyes would sneak a peek in the rearview mirror at his sister. The middle seats were still stowed and there lay quite a mess on the Dodge Caravan rental floor between he and his resting patient.

A few minutes ago, just after Char assured herself that Camy was sleeping, some demands were made by the oldest sibling. She demanded they ignore Camy's demand and abort their mission to continue on until they arrive at Chicago Metro Hospital. She demanded that they instead go to Erie Christian Hospital in Ohio, between Cleveland and Toledo, eighteen miles from their current location and three hours and thirty-eight minutes from Chicago Metro based on their current speed and road conditions. Char also demanded that Myelin give up control of the vehicle's sound system. She had had all she could take of the Clash, Social Distortion, The Pogues, Art Brut, etc....etc.... Myelin acquiesced.

"You know she is really gonna be pissed."

"Yeah, she'll get over it. You seen how much pain she was in. And the fever."

"But still, I mean we got it under control now."

"Erie Christian Hospital, Myelin."

"I know, I know. I'm just sayin', she said we would have plenty of warning before anything bad happened."

"Yeah, and that warning started three days ago in Cambridge, so stop saying."

"All right, I'm not saying...I'm just saying."

"Myelin, I've been reading about this sepsis on my phone. She definitely has an infection somewhere in her intestines. If it gets into her blood, she is fucked. We already have the warnings. There are no more warnings. Camy lied."

Myelin checked his sister in the mirror. His eyes lingered.

"The road, Myelin. Watch the road."

They were surrounded by darkness. It was just starting to drizzle. Other than the occasional truck they would pass or see on the other side of the road, it was desolate. The road is a lonely place at 2:30 a.m. on an early Wednesday morning.

"She'll be fine, Myelin. We'll be there in like fifteen minutes."

"Why would she lie? Why would she risk it after all she's been through?"

"She wants to be with her doctors. She wants the people who fucked her up in the first place, because they have the best chance of cleaning up their mess."

"Fucked her up?"

"Goddammit, Myelin. How are you so clueless? Do you have any idea what they put our sister through? They pumped her full of poison, they fire bombed her ass, they sliced the fuck out of her, they yanked a shit-spewing piece of her intestine out of her stomach and left it there for five months. They ravaged her poor little body for a fucking year, and now this! A fucking infection because they didn't put her back together right!"

"...They got rid of the cancer."

"___"

"They saved her life."

"They better have."

As the coke raced through his bloodstream Myelin struggled not to say anything. He attempted to consider their current situation but found himself considering every situation. His heart raced.

Char's mind was keeping pace with Myelin's heart. *This could be good. They'll get Camy stable, pump her full of antibiotics, she'll have to stay there a few days, maybe a week. I'll stay with her. I sure can't go home. Not now. How can I? Why isn't Carl answering my calls? My texts? He must have got busted. I'll send Myelin on ahead, have him check on Carl. I'll just play dumb. What if he got caught? Did Carl say anything about me?*

"Let's change subjects," Char suggested.

"Okay, how in the hell do you listen to this music? I need a heart with four-wheel drive?"

"Oh, come on, Paul Thorn is great."

"I'm not feeling it."

"You know he once fought Roberto Duran?"

"The boxer?"

"No. Roberto Duran the gardener."

"Duran must have kicked his ass."

"No, well, not at first."

"What happened, did he try to make Duran listen to his music and Duran just snapped?"

"No, idiot. Thorn used to be a boxer."

"He should have kept boxing."

"You know Punk is not the only music there is?"

"But it is the only good music."

"—So how are you gonna be with Lydia so far away at school?"

"It's gonna be great, you know me, I'm a lone wolf."

"You're a narcissistic, punk rock star that craves the spotlight."

"And I'm a lone wolf, too."

"If you say so…"

"I've always lived my life on my terms."

"Can't argue that."

"Even though my terms seem to constantly change."

"And Lydia made that difficult?"

"Made what difficult?"

"Life on your terms."

"Oh, no. Not at all, but now with her a thousand miles away I'll have complete freedom."

"Please. You've had complete freedom your entire life."

"But this will be even better."

"You know you're kidding yourself. Lydia has been doing her own thing for years. And you always have. The difference now is you guys won't have that occasional dinner, or breakfast, or movie, or face to face conversation. No sir, you're not getting complete freedom, you're getting complete loneliness. Welcome to my world."

"You're lonely?"

"No. I mean yeah, not all the time, but sometimes, yeah, I'm lonely."

"Isn't everybody?"

"True, but just wait. You are about to experience the empty nest."

"But Carl just moved back in with you?"

"Yeah and that's going great."

"You don't like his girlfriend, huh?"

"Why would you say that? I never said that. I would never do anything to hurt his girlfriend."

Camy made a slight moaning sound. Char spun round to check on her. Myelin thought about his empty nest for the first time and it struck a chord. His heart raced.

"She's okay," Char assessed.

"—You're right, Char. I've got nothing. The band has become a joke. My son hasn't talked to me in years. He didn't even hug me at his mother's funeral. Now my daughter is gone. It's not an empty nest, it's an empty life."

"Oh sweetie, I know." Char reached over and caressed her brother's shoulder.

"No Char, you don't know. You don't. I know we were terrible parents, but to have nothing to do with us. Nothing! Jody just couldn't deal with it. She had always fought depression, but James just totally blocking us from his life…It was just too much."

Char took her arm back.

"The hell I don't know. That's why I called you a narcissist. Not to be cute or funny, because that's what you are and that's fucked. Nobody feels what Myelin feels. Our feelings are all inferior to his."

"Sorry, that's not what I meant. Calm down."

"It's with everything. I love Paul Thorn, you love the Pogues, can it be that we both love music? No. It has to be that my music sucks and yours is far superior."

"Whoa, slow down."

"And how can I possibly know what it's like to be disappointed by your child? Have you met Carl?"

"All right, I'm sorry."

"And there's no way I could ever relate to having a dead spouse. How could I? I'll tell you something right now, the one I lost was far better than the one you lost!"

"—"

"—"

"Sorry."

"Me, too. Sorry, I'm an idiot. I've just been under so much stress."

"—I wasn't saying you couldn't relate, it's just that…I loved Jody so much, and I know she wasn't the greatest of Human Beings, she could not hold a candle to Reginald-"

"That was wrong, I said I was -"

"But you didn't kill Reginald."

"And you didn't kill Jody. You can't blame yourself."

"I could have stopped it."

"No, you couldn't. Depression is a terrible thing -"

"Depression didn't kill Jody."

"No, but, the depression led to the drugs. You didn't know-"

"I did know."

Myelin was becoming aware of his heartbeat in an intimidating way.

"You mean you knew she was using again, well -"

"I knew she never stopped using."

"Never? But she-"

"We never stopped using."

"??"

"We cleaned up our act a lot. We used a lot less. We were careful. We made the kids, well, Lydia our number one priority instead of getting fucked up."

"You mean like once or twice?"

"Sure, like once or twice a week we would do a little blow, smoke some weed, maybe drop a hit of acid. Just to take the edge off. And if the kids were away or we were away, a little more than taking the edge off. What can I say, we really liked to party?"

"Wait a minute, you mean you would be high in front of me and I wouldn't know?"

"Not long after our new lease on life, like a couple of months into it, things were going great. The kids were with friends. I got an eight ball, laid out a couple of nice rails and in walked James. That was it. Our chances with him were over."

"He never-"

"What's that?!"

"Why are you slowing down? What's happening!?"

"Oh, fuck!"

FOUR DAYS EARLIER

It was a hot sunny day when Myelin, Char, and Lydia arrived back at the Residence Inn by Marriott at Kendall Square in Cambridge Massachusetts after some sight-seeing. Char flopped in one of the queen-sized beds with an already flopped Camy. Lydia stretched across the other bed while Myelin hit the couch. Char's rest did not last long as her cell phone interrupted. The provider of that interruption was Carl Peach. Char answered quickly and told Carl to hang on. "I'll run down to the lobby, I don't want to disturb you guys." Once in the hall...

"Is everything okay, Carl?"

"Yeah, everything is good."

"Oh, thank God, and how are you Carl? Are you okay, I mean I know you're not, but you know?"

"I'm fine, Mom. How is the trip going?"

"All good. I'm getting in the elevator, if I lose you, I'll call you-"

Once in a fairly private area of the lobby Char called Carl back.

"Hello."

"Oh sweetheart, I'm so sorry you had to do that, but I'm glad it's done."

"Well, it's not done, done."

"It's the barrel, right? I was thinking about that because they really don't say what to do with the barrel after, do they? Because Jessie screws it all up."

"I didn't get the barrel yet."

"What? Then how? You didn't use the bathtub, did you? I swear to God-"

"No, Mom, I didn't use anything yet."

"What do you mean? What's wrong?"

"I can't figure out how to get your Netflix to work."

"   "

"Mom?"

"Please tell me you're joking."

"No, I'm not. Your TV is being stupid-"

"I've been gone for two and a half days and you haven't done anything yet?"

"I've done stuff."

"What!?"

"I did the dishes, I did a load of laundry."

"I mean with Penny."

"It's all under control."

"How do you think that?"

"The house is all clean and I moved her body out to the garage."

"The garage?! Did anyone see you?"

"No, I didn't want to do the barrel acid thing in the house."

"Okay, okay, that's good. Smart thinking."

"But now this stupid Netflix."

"All right, all right, I'll walk you through it, just turn on the TV-"

"Now?"

"Yes, now."

"Oh, I'm not home right now."

"What?! Where are you?"

"I'm on my way to Pizza Plus. I'm hungry."

"Jesus, Carl! Why wouldn't you call me when you were by the TV?"

"I got hungry."

"Okay, do you remember the *stupid* TV remote has a button that says menu?"

"Yes, I hit that."

"Well then you hit the arrow down button until it highlights input."

"But nothing is highlighted."

"Well, it says input somewhere. Just listen."

"Input, right."

"Then you hit the center button."

"Which center button?"

"The one in the middle."

"The middle of what?"

"The middle of the remote!"

"I'll have a beef grinder, hot peppers, and a large fry."

"Oh my God! Are you ordering?"

"No drink."

"This is un-freaking-believable."

"But, Mom, hang on, I have a penny."

"What!?"

"Oh, not that Penny. I was talking to the cashier."

"Sweet Mother of God."

"Hang on, Mom, I have an idea."

"I can't wait."

"Maybe we should forget the whole Breaking Bad idea."

"And do what?"

"Do you remember in Pulp Fiction they called that guy and he came to their house and cleaned everything up?"

"Are you fucking out of your mind? They called Harvey Keitel, the Wolf and the key wasn't that he cleaned up, it was that he had a place to get rid of the body. Do you have a place that takes dead bodies, no questions asked?"

"No, that's not what I was thinking. Not that I do it, that I find a guy like the Wolf. Like a cleaner guy and we pay him."

"Pulp Fiction is a movie. It's make believe."

"So, Breaking Bad is a TV show."

"You're not going to find a cleaner guy, for Christ's sake you can't even figure out the Netflix."

"—Just saying, I'm sure people like that really exist."

"I'm sure, too, and if they were affordable and easy to find people would be killing each other left and right. But they're not, so we are going to do the Breaking Bad plan. So, when you get back home, call me and I will walk you through the Netflix, but I won't be able to say much else because I'll be with your aunt and uncle."

"And Lydia, right?"

"Yes, and Lydia."

"How they all doing?"

"They're fine."

"Hey, tell Uncle Myelin that I met this guy at TC's last week who is a big fan of AMA and he was saying-"

"Carl. Now is not the time. I have to go. Call me when you get home and are in front of the TV."

"But Mom."

"What?"

"Can I eat first?"

"Yes, and you could also stop being a complete idiot."

Click.

NOW

"Do you really not realize the sacrifices I've made for this family? What I put myself through for you? For the kids?" His own words from five days earlier now haunted him. He thought of how hard he had worked. The pain in his knees and back from years of dedication to his job so that he could provide for his family. How he could not afford the expense of a dentist and pulled his own tooth out with a pair of pliers. And now she accuses him of being a bad husband. Of not being there for her while she is sick. How dare her.

AFTER THE BEEF GRINDER

Carl Peach felt full, slightly bloated even, but not satisfied. He was angry. Angry at the situation he found himself in, angry at the work that was ahead of him, angry at his mother for the way she talked to him and ordered him around, angry that she called him a complete idiot. He was even angry that she would not give his Pulp Fiction idea any consideration. While Carl definitely did not personally know any 'Cleaners' he was pretty sure he probably knew the type of people that would know the type of people that would know a Cleaner or two.

Carl did not make another attempt to access the Netflix, which was probably a good idea because he was using the wrong remote. He was using a dust covered remote that sat on a shelf of the TV stand that was for an old disconnected VCR, instead of the one that sat on the end table beside his mother's favorite chair. Carl also made no attempt to contact his mother, nor did he answer any of the calls she placed to him. Carl had a new plan. It was a terrible plan.

NOW

"Oh my God, oh my God! What's happening? Get it to the shoulder, get it to the shoulder."

Myelin managed to do just that as an alarm bell on the Dodge Caravan dinged and the engine sputtered and then coughed and then sputtered again. And then nothing.

"Fuck!"

"What is it? What happened?"

"It's all right Camy…What happened, Melvy?"

"I think were out of gas."

"What's going on?" Camy's voice was groggy and half asleep.

"It's okay sweetheart…What the hell do you mean were out of-"

"I meant to fill up at the last stop."

"That's just great, now what are-"

"So that's what that light was for."

"Are you kidding me? This is unbelievable, and he's got the kid going to MIT while I get-"

"How far are we from the hospital?"

"Hospital? Are we here?"

"Not yet sweetheart…too far to walk."

"How far?"

"Our exit is in 3.2 miles, then less than a mile off the interstate."

Myelin started to get out of the Caravan.

"What are you gonna do?"

"I'm gonna flag down the next trucker and you and Camy are going to the hospital."

Myelin put on the flashers and stood in front of the Caravan in the glow of the headlights as a slight mist fell from the black sky. His heart beating faster than it ever had as guilt saturated his soul. He could feel his heart thumping in the temples of his forehead. Char turned to sooth the now restless Camy and saw a truck approaching in the distance. *Please let him stop and help us.*

"How are you feeling, Camy?"

"I feel kind of rubbery."

"Rubbery is good, try to go back to sleep."

The truck roared by making no attempt to slow down. It simply drifted to the left lane and continued on. Char whipped her head around and hoped to see brake lights. She did not. She immediately became terrified by what else she did not see. Myelin was gone.

CARL PEACH'S PLAN

Jake and Eric Stokes were longtime friends of Carl Peach. A couple of years ago their parents died in a freak escalator accident. The circumstances of their death led to a lawsuit, which led to a settlement, which led to the Stokes brothers moving to West Covina, California and purchasing a Harley Davidson dealership, which led to an open invitation for Carl Peach to join them. Carl now felt this would be the perfect time.

Carl was not about to leave Penny's body in his mother's garage. He knew if he did that it would only be a matter of time before the long arm of the law would grab hold of him. His mother had left him $642 cash. And he knew her car was sitting at his uncle's house and the spare keys were hanging on the decorative hook by the back door that spelled out the word *keys*. He wasn't about to waste any of that $642 on special plastic barrels or flesh-eating acid for some cockamamie plan his mother got from a basic cable original series. Oh no, absolutely not. His plan cost $15.99 + tax.

Carl took the bus to his uncle's and procured his mother's car. He then went to Menard's and purchased a box of 32 count super heavy-duty contractor grade trash bags. Once back at his mother's, he split and laid three of the super heavy-duty contractor grade trash bags on the garage floor. He was very impressed by their thickness and durability. He then placed his mother's 3X5 patio table on top of bag-lined floor and covered it with two additional bags. He then grabbed eight of his mom's best bath towels, three buckets of water, soap and shampoo and bleach and sponges and scrub brushes. Once in the garage with all of his necessary supplies he locked himself in by nailing the people door shut and unplugging the overhead door opener. He then stripped naked, placing his clothes in another one of his superior trash bags and tied it shut. Next, he placed Penny's body on top of the trash bags on top of the patio table.

The Plan: Cut Penny's body up into twenty-five pieces and place each piece into an individual super heavy-duty contractor grade trash bag and tie it shut. He would then clean everything up, including himself, put all the bags on the floor and table along with all the cleaning supplies into the twenty-sixth bag. Get dressed, pry the nails out of the door, plug the overhead door opener back in and open the overhead door. Put all twenty-six bags into his mother's car's trunk. Pour the buckets of bloody water down the storm sewer behind the garage, rinse them out. Lock up the house and garage and head to West Covina, California. It was about a 2,000-mile trip. Carl planned on pulling off the interstate every seventy-five miles or so, finding a garbage can and throwing one of the bags into it. Carl felt his plan was ingenious and would someday end up on a TV show like *Unsolved Mysteries*. He soon discovered his plan was not without problems.

Problem Number One: As Carl approached Penny's body with his father's old circular saw in his hand he felt uneasy. At first, he wasn't sure what was making him feel so uncomfortable. Was it the fact that he was about to use a dangerous electric power tool for the first time in his life and he was doing so naked and his intent with the aforementioned circular saw was to cut his girlfriend into twenty-five pieces. He did not consider that being the cause of his anxiety. Nope. Carl decided it was because her face was visible. After some careful thought he decided to cover Penny's face with one of the super heavy-duty contractor grade trash bags. Now he would only have to cut her into twenty-four pieces and only stop about every eighty miles to dump a bag.

After covering Penny's face by securely bagging it and duct-taping around her neck, Carl discovered problem number two. As Carl stood there naked and stupid, Penny lay on the table in light gray, stained sweat pants and a dingy even more stained white t-shirt, completely covered with black lines. Carl had used a tape measure to divide Penny's body into twenty-five semi-equal parts and a black sharpie to make cut lines. It was the most he had ever used math in his life. But now having used one of the twenty-five bags to cover Penny's face, he would be slicing her up into only twenty-four pieces. Instead of placing two body pieces into one bag, because that thought had never occurred to Carl, he remeasured Penny into twenty-four semi equal parts and made new cut lines, this time with a red sharpie.

NOW

Char flung open her door to go look for her brother. Camy sensed that something was afoot and attempted to sit up, but her head was too heavy and her body too sleepy and rubbery. She drifted. Char's door did not open completely. Almost completely, but not quite. It stopped short when it collided with the crown of Myelin's skull. He was on all fours, crawling toward Char's door when she flung it open. Now he lay on his side in the fetal position as an annoying drizzle filled the night's atmosphere. Char heard the thump and soon after saw her brother.

"Oh my God, Melvy!"

Gasp, gasp.

"What happened?"

Gasp, gasp.

Char rolled him onto his back and cradled his head. "What's wrong? What happened? Did that truck hit you?"

"No." Gasp. "Heart attack." Gasp. "Can't-"

"Shhh, shhh, stop talking. Breathe through your nose."

"I can't-"

Another truck blasted by as Char cradled her brother, rubbing his hair, trying to soothe him.

"Shhh, calm down."

Gasp.

"Breathe in…breathe out…breathe in…breathe out."

Gasp.

Char considered, *Heart attack? Panic attack? Stroke?*

Camy's shadow fell over Char.

"What happened?"

"I think he's having a panic attack or something. Get some water. Breathe in…"

Sob. Gasp. Sob.

SEVEN HOURS EARLIER

The circular saw was old. The circular saw blade was dull. The circular saw blade ripped through the flesh just below Penny's left knee. Cotton and skin and blood and bone shrapnel flew everywhere. Once about half way through the bone Carl had to apply great pressure. Even if the blade had been brand new, Carl was not using the proper power tool to cut up a body. Far from it. Which he was about to find out. The blade made it through about 95% of the bone when it kicked back violently. This really spooked Carl and his naked body. He put down the saw and grabbed Penny's foot. He gave it a twist and a pull. The bone severed but the muscle and tendons stayed connected.

Carl felt his stomach start to turn. He threw some water on his face from one of the buckets and grabbed his father's hand saw. Back and forth he dragged the blade through his girlfriend's flesh until it finally came free from Penny's bloated corpse. After separating his first section of human, he laid the piece of leg on the bag-lined floor and began to hack it into three separate pieces, having great difficulty in locating the Sharpie guidelines he had made. After some considerable work Carl had his first three bags completed.

Those first three bags of the twenty-four Carl intended to fill were far more difficult and messy then he had anticipated. As he readied himself to cut into a second portion of Penny's left leg he saw something disturbing. Because of the blood spatter, he could no longer see his red sharpie line, so he instead started on Penny's left arm just below the elbow with the hand saw, to keep the blood spatter to a minimum and avoid the dangerous kickback of the circular saw. Back and forth, back and forth he ran the blade across Penny's skin and into her meat. Back and forth, back and forth, through her tendons and her muscle and her ulna, and her radius, until finally it came free. Carl held the lower part of Penny's left arm in his right hand and the bloody hand saw in his left, blood and flesh drizzled on his face and naked chest. Suddenly, something inside of Carl churned. He let go of both the arm and the saw, letting them fall to the floor. He grabbed his stomach and spewed hot vomit on Penny's torso. With the burning rancid taste of partially digested fast food and stomach acid dripping down his palate, Carl wondered, *What's that about?* He quickly surmised, *Oh great, now I'm getting the flu.*

NOW

Myelin was covered in sweat. His breathing was beginning to become normal but he sounded to be getting worse.

"Here's the water."

"Come on, Melvy, calm down. Breathe for me."

"Char?"

"Take a deep breath, Melvy."

"Char, I think he's crying."

He was sobbing to be more accurate. Myelin sat himself up and leaned his back against the front tire. He pulled his knees up high, put his face in his palms and cried like a baby.

Char scooched closer and knelt at his right side. "Melvin?"

Camy crouched down on his left, "What is it? What's wrong?"

"It's all wrong. Everything is wrong. It's all a big lie. It didn't happen like I said. It didn't—" Sobbing, mumbling.

"What didn't happen?"

"—Jody..." sniffing and snorting.

"It's okay, Melvin."

"No, it's not. Jody didn't *accidently* overdose. She did it on purpose. She killed herself. Because of me."

"Don't think that way."

"You don't know that, Melvin."

"No, I know—" sobbing and mumbling.

"??"

"??"

"When I found her...When I found—"

"___"

"___"

"There was a note. She had a note on her chest."

"Oh, Melvin."

"Oh my God."

"It said...It said...Goddamnit, fuck me, it said...*I am sorry, Myelin. But we should have gotten help. We needed help.*

TEN MINUTES EARLIER

"*That's how there is a roof over our heads! Food on the table! Clothes on our backs! And you sit there and say I don't love you? That I don't care that you're sick?*" His words from five days ago continued to haunt him as he sat alone. *So, I strayed a few times. Said some really stupid shit from time to time. But I have always been there for her. I may not always show it but I do love her. Her and the kids. And this is how she treats me. She asks me for a divorce through voicemail. A goddamned voicemail! That rotten bitch.*

SIX HOURS EARLIER

Carl had thrown more water on his face which mixed with the blood spatters and residual vomit, which gave his entire face a deep reddish hue. He still felt nauseous but knew he had a job to do and that his very future depended on the completion of this job. The task at hand was far more difficult than Carl had envisioned with his prosaic imagination. He decided not to use the hand saw again as it was far too tedious. He instead opted for the far more dangerous circular power saw again. He feared the kickback that had previously intimidated him. He visualized losing control of the saw and having it cut into his naked flesh. Most of his visualizations involved him accidently cutting off his own penis. To combat this possibility his solution was to place the saw in the area he desired to cut and to then turn his back to the saw and engage the blade with his hand held behind his back. He felt this was his second ingenious idea of the day.

He placed the blade between Penny's shoulder and neck, turned his back to the gruesome scene, and pressed the button. The blade immediately sliced through Penny's t-shirt and flesh sending fabric and blood and skin flying in every direction. Carl held the button down and applied pressure as the teeth of the blade went to work on her collarbone. Penny's entire body trembled and shook. Well, what was left of her entire body. The vomit that pooled on her torso spattered here and there. Carl's arm vibrated and he struggled mightily to hang on to the saw and retain control. And then Carl heard a loud crash. The saw slipped from his hand and crashed to the floor, as did Penny's mutilated corpse. The glass table top of Char Peach's patio table had shattered from the violent vibrations and fell to the ground in a million little pieces. Penny was now tangled in the framework of the Costco table, twisted and mangled, her flesh now mixed with tiny bits of glass, while her boyfriend stood over her, his naked body covered with sweat and blood and Penny and traces of vomit, his expression bewildered, his eyes filled with dismay. "Oh, fuck no!" Carl exclaimed to himself and Penny as he witnessed the scene. "Mom's gonna be pissed."

NOW

As Myelin's sobbing began to simmer down and his sisters comforted him, Char spoke in a soothing voice.

"Melvy, honey…Can I ask you something?"

"Uh huh…"

"Are you high right now?"

"—"

"Why would you ask him that?"

"Melvin, you're all coked out, aren't ya?"

"Char?!"

"Hush…answer me, Melvin."

"—Maybe a little."

"Goddamn it! I fucking knew it. A little, my ass. All those *(coffee)* stops. How could I be so stupid? How dare you! Risking our lives! Driving like that." Char's words were accompanied by punches in the arm and slaps in the head as Myelin defended himself and Camy stared in disbelief.

"All right! All right! I'm sorry. I'm not proud. I told you I've been living a lie. You guys aren't perfect either. Look at you, Camy. You said we would have plenty of warning before you went septic."

"Sepsis."

"Whatever."

"That's true, Camy, I looked it up."

"I'm feeling better now."

"You're high on Oxycodone."

"Well, we are a few miles from Erie Christian Hospital right now, and guess what? That's where you're going."

"No, I'm not. How far away from Chic—"

"Too far!"

"Why would you risk your life like that?"

"I want to see my doctors!"

"But to risk your life."

"What life! I got no life."

"You got a better life than me. I'm going home to an empty house. I got a son that won't have anything to do with me. I made my wife kill herself and now my little princess is gone."

"Yeah, you don't even want to know what's going on at my house right now. You got it pretty good, sister."

Camy began to weep.

"Well, I know. You've been through a lot. The cancer and all that…but you got a great husband and great kids-"

"My kids are selfish brats!"

"Camy?"

"I called them from the hotel. That's who you heard me talking to. Two of them didn't even realize I wasn't home."

"Oh honey, that's just how kids are sometimes. Don't let it get you down. And you got yourself a great man."

"Yeah, you guys are the best couple I know."

"I'm leaving him."

"What?"

"No way. Why?"

"Ask Stefon."

"Who's Stefon?"

"His lover."

"??"

"??"

"Yeah, my lovely husband is a fucking homo."

Camy hung her head and bawled. Myelin and Char enveloped her and the three embraced as one.

"I overheard him on the phone with Stefon" – *sniffle, sob*—"and… and…and…"

"Oh, poor baby."

"And he wished I would have died in a car accident."

"I always hated that prick."

"I always had a feeling he was a cocksucker."

"Not helping."

FOUR AND A HALF HOURS EARLIER

Carl had given up on his original plan. The chore was too difficult and the mess was too great. He now had a new terrible plan. He decided to leave Penny where she lay in the mess of shattered glass, severed limbs, and vomit. He decided to douse her in gasoline and burn down the garage and head to California. For some reason he had this notion that if the authorities were unable to identify the victim then they could not file murder charges.

I don't have any idea how he arrived at that belief, but believe it, he did. So, in order to protect himself and his mother from any future charges he cut off all ten of Penny's finger tips and put them in a zip lock bag. His plan was to dump them along with her fingerprints in the ocean once he arrived in West Covina, California, for the fish to eat. I also don't have any idea why he thought it was a good idea to drive two thousand miles with a Ziploc bag of fingertips in his pocket. I mean he would pass an incredibly vast number of bodies of water with aquatic life during his journey, but his heart was set on the Pacific Ocean. I'm sure he also did not realize that West Covina is two hours inland from the ocean.

Then there was the matter of the dental records. Although he briefly considered it, Carl decided not to travel to California with Penny's jaw in a zip lock bag. Instead, he stood over her head, which was still covered with a super heavy-duty contractor grade trash bag, with his father's ten-pound Craftsman steel sledge hammer. He held the heavy sledge high over his head like he was at a carnival strong man attraction. One…Two…Three…

NOW

As the Smathy siblings embraced on their knees on the shoulder of Interstate 90 somewhere between Cleveland and Toledo a strange feeling came over them. It was a feeling they could vaguely recognize but not remember. It was the perception of compassion without the bullshit of deception. The last time the three of them shared this attribute was when they were little children, before they decided to not reveal all they feel. Before they decided that sometimes it is better to save face, or spare feelings, or exaggerate accomplishment than to be frightfully and painfully honest. The Smathy siblings now shared pure unadulterated understanding.

"Okay, guys," Camy winced and broke their huddle, "let's get back in the van and get me to the hospital."

"We can't-"

"Van's out of gas."

"Are you fucking kidding me?"

"It's okay, it's okay, I'm gonna flag down the next truck and the two of you are getting to the hospital."

"What if they don't stop?"

"Truckers always stop. It's in their DNA."

"Really, because three of them have passed us by since we pulled over."

"Seriously though, guys," Char spoke in her, *I am the oldest and I am commanding your undivided attention voice*, "the three of us, we have all been through so much and we have to realize we are each other's greatest advocates. We can't lie to each other anymore! We can't keep things from each other! We have to all promise to be honest to one another from now on."

The three of them reflected on the words of Char Peach as an approaching truck's headlights appeared on the interstate horizon. Each of the three of them decided right then and there that they had something important that they had to share with their siblings. The three of them chorused their confessions.

Camy, "I puked up some blood in the van and I think my colon just exploded."

Char, "There is a dead girl in my house."

Myelin, "I'm probably gonna finish this coke."

THREE AND A HALF HOURS EARLIER

Carl Peach pulled out of his mother's driveway in his mother's car, as smoke slipped out the tiny gaps of the garages overhead door, which would soon be followed by flames, which would soon be followed by fire trucks, which would soon be followed by the police, which would soon be followed by a murder investigation.

The detectives assigned to the case would determine Penny's identity rather quickly despite the grotesque condition of her body. Less than an hour into the investigation they would find Penny's purse, which contained her driver's license, in the bedroom of Carl Peach, *Person of extreme interest.*

NOW

"It's killing me. Every moment of everyday it is absolutely destroying me. But the bills don't stop coming because you are sick. We are barely hanging on. We are this close to losing what little we have. That's why you have to fight and I have to work." His last face to face conversation with his wife from five days ago kept running through his groggy, confused, angry mind. And now, how could she? To ask for a divorce on a voicemail. And even worse, not have the common decency to answer his calls while he pushed himself hard at work.

She had the nerve to say she was sick and tired of his selfish behavior and could no longer take it. *Selfish behavior? How is busting your ass at work day after day to support your family selfish behavior?* He wished he could be by her side while she battled the cancer that had invaded her body. *Didn't he?*

She went on to tell him that when he returned home she and the kids would be gone. They would be at her parents. That she had already spoken to a divorce lawyer. That it was over. Conrad began to doubt himself. He had been working the better part of five days and his wife's words along with his physical and mental emotion were beginning to get the better of him. *Maybe he had not been there for her as much as he should have been.*

Maybe he couldn't face the truth. Maybe he was running away. Maybe he was running away from the painful truth and hiding at work.

They used to be so close. Even after three children, they still made passionate love together. She would eagerly wait for him to return from work and make him the happiest man in the world. It was after a long trip, while romantically embracing and caressing one another, that Conrad found the lump. He immediately felt the dour presence of devastation. *What about the kids? How could he finish raising the children without Janet?*

Conrad should have pulled his rig into a rest stop, but he did not. He felt he had to push himself. He had to get to Janet and talk some sense to her. Or apologize. Or maybe even plead. It had been twenty-four hours since he had first heard his wife's bitter voice mail. A full day of her not answering his calls. A full day of him listening to her message over and over and over again. A full day of driving. Five days on the road. Exhaustion. Frustration. Anger. Self-doubt. Confusion. And then, Conrad's phone rang. Janet's beautiful face illuminated the screen. Conrad's favorite picture of her. A photo that was snapped years ago. Before children. Before cancer. Before too large of a mortgage and ever-growing debt. Before endless road trip after endless road trip. The phone was too far for Conrad to reach. He had thrown it in frustration over an hour ago and now it sat at the far end of the cab. Much too far to reach, but reach Conrad did. The 60,000-pound behemoth road monster veered. The rumble strips roared, warning Conrad he had crossed onto Interstate 90's shoulder. Under normal circumstances a truck driver as experienced as Conrad would have been capable of negotiating with the laws of physics and correcting the impending doom foreshadowed by the sleeper lines. These were not normal circumstances. Because of his physical and mental state, Conrad overcorrected, the combination of that overcorrection and the shoulder not being clear led to complete disaster. The shoulder's obstruction, which was the final component of Conrad's Calamitous Fortune, was a Dodge Caravan rental vehicle with three people standing outside of it in the black mist of an unforgiving night.

LATER

When Conrad woke up at the Erie Christian Hospital two days later, his entire body ached. His head pounded. His lips were swollen and starved for water. His vision was blurry but slowly began to come into focus. He felt a strange tightness around his right wrist. It was heavy. It was handcuffed to the bed.

Conrad was charged with three counts of vehicular manslaughter. The combination of an illegal driver's log, a bag of speed, an overzealous district attorney, and a merciless judge would send Conrad to prison for eight years after he healed from his injuries.

Myelin would never get to finish his coke. Camy would not get the antibiotics that would have saved her life. Her lovely husband's wish would come to fruition. Char would never see the mess her son left for her.

Lydia would be the Phoenix of our story. She would spend much of her young adult life lonely and family-less, but she would also continue on with her education. She would graduate from MIT and then Harvard Medical. She would go on to do great things. She would become very wealthy and very successful. She would marry three times and fall in love twice. She would birth two loving sons. In her later years she would be instrumental in the development of the artificial spinal cord.

James would lose contact with Lydia soon after their father and aunts were killed. Turned out he was just an asshole.

Janet would be a survivor. She would beat the cancer. She would divorce Conrad while in prison and marry her oncologist. She never did take the kids and go to her parents. At the time, she did not really intend on leaving Conrad, nor had she fallen in love with her doctor yet. She was waiting at home. Feeling alone, feeling depressed, feeling neglected, feeling angry. She left that biting message on Conrad's voice mail because she was starved for her husband's attention. His complete and undivided attention. She wanted to be the only thing in his life that mattered. And for a little while, that night on Interstate 90, somewhere between Cleveland and Toledo, I guess her wish also came to fruition.

"THINGS I'VE HEARD"

"You are mommy's precious little angel, always and forever."

"Who's daddy's big boy?"

"Peek-a-boo."

"I got your nose."

"You are going to be a big brother."

"Give baby a kiss."

"It's okay. Mommy's here. It was just a bad dream."

"Don't cry. Just rub it, you'll be fine."

"Don't be nervous."

"Don't be shy."

"Don't be scared."

"I love you."

"What do you want to be when you grow up?"

"Such a smart young man."

"You are a very gifted young man."

"You will go far if you apply yourself."

"Because I said so."

"Yes, you have to."

"Because he is your brother."

"Sometimes you have to stand up for yourself."

"Don't be scared."

"Don't cry. Just rub it, you'll be fine."
"I love you."
"Such a kind young man."

"Don't be such a pussy, your parents will never know."
"I don't care if everyone else is doing it."
"C'mon, we won't get caught this time."
"What did we say about applying yourself?"
"Are you even trying?"
"If your friends jumped off a bridge, would you?"
"We are very disappointed in you."
"We love you."
"I'm afraid the cast will be on the entire summer."
"It's by Kurt Vonnegut. Give it a try. I think you'll like him."

"Great job, son. We knew you could do it."
"We are so proud of you."
"I hate you. You are the worst brother ever."
"She's cute."
"If you want to use the car, you'll give your brother a ride."
"You look so handsome."
"You guys make a great couple."
"I love you so much. We'll be together forever."
"So what colleges are you considering?"
"Congratulations."
"That's so far away."
"I think we should see other people."
"How are your classes?"
"What is your major?"
"I met somebody else."
"I'm sorry, son. I am here for you."
"There are plenty more fish in the sea."
"I love you."

"Congratulations. That's a very tough internship to get."
"It's so great to have you back home."
"Did you see your brother's new girlfriend? How did he land her?"
"You are doing really well. I think they may offer you a job."
"Please stop, I'm dating your brother."
"The problem is we don't have anything available around here."
"I made a mistake. Please, don't tell your brother. He'll never forgive me."
"Are you willing to relocate?"
"We have to stop doing this."
"Because it's your brother's girlfriend, goddammit!"
"That's so far away."
"We'll miss you."
"We love you."
"Great job, kid, you'll go far in this company."

"We sure miss you."
"Come on, join us for a drink after work. Meet the team."
"You want to meet her, sure, I can introduce you."
"You are so sweet. Thank you."
"Your brother is getting married."
"You are so funny. You make me laugh."
"I'm so glad you made it."
"Your girlfriend is great. Mom even likes her."
"You make me so happy."
"I'm worried about Dad."
"I love you."
"Congratulations, you are the youngest VP in the company's history."

"I'm pregnant."
"Congratulations. She's lovely."
"It's beautiful. Can we afford it?"
"It's a boy."
"Da Da."
"He looks just like you."
"Another great year. We are lucky to have you."

"I'm pregnant."

"You have to get home. It's Dad."

"He's a tough son of a bitch. He'll be okay."

"He's a fighter."

"He's in so much pain."

"He is suffering."

"I'm sorry."

"It's a girl."

"Congratulations."

"What about Mom?"

"I will go anywhere you want."

"We are sorry to lose you."

"Welcome home."

"Excited to have you aboard."

"Welcome home, and thank you, son."

"It's even bigger and more beautiful than the last one. Can we afford it?"

"When I grow up I want to be just like you, Daddy."

"What a good-looking family you have."

"I love you, Daddy."

"Best vacation ever."

"I never dreamed things could be this great."

"It hurts, Daddy."

"It's just a minor surgery. She'll be fine."

"I'm scared, Daddy. Do I have to?"

"There were complications."

"She's a strong little girl. She'll pull through."

"Sometimes these things take time."

"She's not responding."

"She can't hear you."

"Daddy?"

"She's going to be okay."

"I expect a 100% recovery."

"Your little girl is a miracle."

"He is having trouble in school."

"Mr. David is really impressed with you."

"I'm not stupid."

"Your brother wants to start his own business. He has a really good idea."

"We've been trying to land the Wallace account for years, great job."

"I don't get it."

"She is my best student."

"I am trying!"

"There is a special program we believe he would benefit from."

"I'm just too stupid."

"We offer an accelerated program we feel she would thrive in."

"It would cost about eight thousand to get the whole thing started."

"A summer home right on the lake! Can we afford it?"

"I hate school!"

"I'll pay you back. You're the best brother a guy could have. I'll make you proud."

"I don't want your stupid books! I hate reading."

"I'm a little concerned about the numbers this quarter."

"Daddy, I was named team captain!"

"Maybe we get the summer house next year?"

"I hate you!"

"I'm not going to school any more. You can't make me."

"With her grades and athleticism, she'll get plenty of scholarship offers."

"It's the entire industry. These numbers are worrisome."

"Your brother is doing great."

"Without your help I could have never done it."

"We better tighten our belts. I'm afraid we are in for some lean times."

"I want to take you guys out to dinner, to celebrate."

"Thank God for the Wallace account. That will keep our heads above water."

"To my brother, who believed in me and made all this possible."

"Daddy! It's Gramma, I can't wake her!"

"I'm so sorry for your loss."

"She was a great woman."

"At least she went peacefully."

"He's taking online classes, but he doesn't want anyone to know."
"I don't like this new crowd she's been hanging around with."
"The Wallace Company filed bankruptcy."
"We can't weather this storm. We're ruined! Don't you get it? We're ruined."
"We are very concerned about your daughter's grades."
"Mom, Dad, I did it! I got my GED!"
"Mr. David took his own life. His wife found him this morning."
"His name is Foster and he is bad news."
"Even if you do all that, financially, you're in big trouble. I'm sorry."
"What are you guys going to do? Do you have a plan?"
"Because we're in love and want to be with each other."
"You're going to have to sell the house."
"You always said you wanted to do your own thing."
"Sorry to disappoint you, but I'm not going to college. I'm joining the army."
"I'm going to State because I want to be close to Foster."
"Look at me brother. Now is the time. Go for it!"
"You wouldn't understand. We're soulmates."
"You're not getting any younger."
"I hate you."

"It's not a loan."
"We ship out tomorrow."
"Because you're my brother."
"That's so far away."
"It looks like life begins at fifty for you. Congratulations."
"I'm not going back to school. I'm moving in with Foster."
"You should have done this years ago."
"I miss you, Dad."
"The doctor found a lump."
"I'm pregnant, Daddy."
"You have to run the business. We'll get through this."
"I love you."
"It's benign! Thank God."
"He's coming home for Christmas."

"You have a grandson."
"His name is Quentin."
"I love you, Gampa."
"It's the best thing I ever did, Dad. I found my place in life."
"Foster lost his job, again."
"Thank you, Dad. I'll pay you back someday."
"Oh my God, that's right where your son is stationed."
"I've been on the phone all day. I can't find anything out."
"Foster never came home last night."
"Let's play, Gampa."
"Relax, calm down, I promise I'm okay."
"Foster's never coming home. He left us."
"You were right, Dad. The whole time you were right."
"What am I going to do? I ruined my life."
"I told her to come live with us and go back to school."
"You want to buy the summer place now? At our age?"

"I love to fish, Gampa."
"Let's play hide and seek, Gampa."
"I got the job! Can you believe it, Dad?!"
"Can I drive the boat, Grampa?"
"Thank you for the books, Grampa. I never heard of him, but I'll check him out."
"What I really want to do is work for you, Dad."
"He is coming in for two weeks. Let's have everyone out to the lake."
"I'm going into town. Anyone want to come?"
"I'll go with you, I want to stop at the Post Office."
"I'm sorry sir, there's been a terrible accident."
"No Daddy, oh God, no, Daddy!"
"We cannot tell you how sorry we are."
"We feel just terrible."
"Poor guy lost his wife and brother."
"I really miss Gramma."

"I can't believe he's gone. Thank you for all your support and help."

"Hey Grampa, do you want to watch the game?"

"These are such difficult times, for both of us."

"Hey Grampa, do you want to play some cards?"

"Without your company, I don't know how I would have survived these last couple of years."

"Hey Grampa, can you teach me to drive?"

"You can kiss me if you'd like."

"Hey Grampa, is it okay if I bring a couple of buddies to the lake?"

"A partner! Dad, you're making me a full partner! Thank you."

"Her name is Jodi. We'll be in for Christmas. I can't wait for you to meet her."

"Should we keep this a secret? Or should we tell our children?"

"Because it's your brother's widow, Dad, that's why!"

"Dad, this is Jodi."

"Dad, this is Chuck."

"Grandpa, I hate Chuck."

"Grandpa, this is Jennifer."

"Dad, I'm not sure how I feel about Jennifer."

"It doesn't bother me. Sneaking around just makes it exciting."

"Jodi and I are moving to Germany."

"I was accepted to Washington University!"

"What do you mean you're retiring?"

"Let's just stay in bed all day."

"I'd like to run a few more tests."

"I'm sorry, Dad, if the two of you are happy, who am I to judge?"

"I'm so happy we don't have to sneak around anymore."

"Seriously, Grandpa? You and Aunt Joelle! That's cool."

"I think we'd be more comfortable in person. Can you come in?"

"Six months. Maybe less."

"This cruise was a great idea, Dad."

"It's so nice to have both our families all together."

"Jodi and I have a big announcement to make."

"We should do this every year."

"School's going great. One year away from my Bachelors."

"Work has been super busy and I just get a little aggravated sometimes."

"It was a great internship and they really liked me, so that's a strong possibility."

"Well, Heller certainly doesn't respect me like he respects you."

"I never really thought about working with Mom."

"No, Chuck was great, but we just weren't right for each other."

"I guess I'm just destined to be alone."

"It really upset me at first, but I'm happy you and Aunt Joelle have each other."

"You're giving me your car? No way, Grandpa!"

"Dad, why are you giving up the Lincoln? You love that car!"

"Honey, are you okay? You don't look so good."

"I'm so sorry, but there is nothing more we can do."

"Why didn't Grandpa tell us he was sick?"

"Mom, you have to get some sleep."

"Do you think he can even hear us?"

"Mom, Aunt Joelle, you have to eat something."

"I'm here, Dad."

"I love you, Dad."

"I'm here, darling. I'm squeezing your hand. Can you feel it?"

"I love you so much."

"Please, you guys have to get some sleep."

"Why is he moaning?"

"Is he in pain?"

"We are all honestly shocked he has hung on this long."

"Hey Dad, you're a Grandpa again."

"A granddaughter. Her name is Lilly."

"Please darling, don't leave me! Don't leave me like your brother did!"

"Hi Dad. I'm here."

"Aunt Joelle is sleeping. They gave her something to help her rest."

"Mom, you have to eat or sleep or something."
"Dad, your grandson is here."
"Mom you can't stay in this room."
"At least take a walk outside. Get some fresh air."
"I love you, Dad."
"He can't hear you, Mom. He is already gone."
"Please, Mom. I'll stay with him. I'll hold his hand."
"I'll be right back Dad."

"Grandpa."
"I just want you to know, you were the best father a kid could ever have."

"I love you Grandpa."

"Don't worry about Aunt Joelle or Mom."
"I'll take care of them."
"It's okay Grandpa."

HAPPY BIRTHDAY ROGER

ROGER GATLEY STRUGGLED with errant perceptions, which left him restless, as he lay awake in his bed on the eve of his fiftieth birthday. He was unusually agitated and habitually worried. He felt abused: abused by his employer, abused by his government, abused by his God. Normally after a night of alcohol and television Roger would just feel lascivious and sleepy. The moderately-priced wine that Roger enjoyed imbibing in combination with the sexually alluring women that appeared in all popular television programs and mainstream Hollywood movies would generally act as a sort of aphrodisiac. Roger would go to bed with his alcohol-fueled imagination making him feel wanton and unrestrained. After a few minutes of imagined companionship, he would enjoy a restful night. That was not the case on the eve of the Big 5-0.

This evening's viewings consisted of the *American Broadcasting Company's* weak attempt at a situation comedy, and an On-Demand movie provided by the *Comcast Cable Company* for the low, low price of six American dollars, which would simply be added to Rogers's monthly Comcast Cable bill. The movie was called, *The Gift*.

Roger had never heard of it, but it starred Jason Bateman, an actor Roger was very fond of. While trying to determine whether or not to spend the six American dollars, he considered Bateman's work on an absolutely tremendous situation comedy television program called *Arrested Development* presented by the *Fox Network*. *Arrested Development* had been canceled after only three seasons due to unimpressive ratings. The far inferior, formulaic, frustratingly non-funny, situation comedy offered by *ABC* that Roger had just finished viewing was in its seventh season and enjoyed highly successful ratings. Go figure.

Roger nearly decided to not spend his six American dollars on the movie, *The Gift*, when he discovered it was not a comedy, the genre he believed Jason Bateman to most excel in. But then he read a review on the internet that gave *The Gift* four and one half stars. Roger was able to find the review on the internet by using his handheld Galaxy cellular device. The review was posted by nobody Roger had ever heard of and he had no way of knowing whether or not this unknown person and he shared any interest, likes, dislikes, or commonality of any kind, but still the stellar review was enough to convince Roger to part ways with his six American dollars.

Go figure. It was the stranger's on-line review in conjunction with a couple glasses of wine and a complete inability to stomach another network television offering. This evening's episode of *Modern Family* was unusually upsetting to Roger. He wondered why he even still watched the show. The monthly Comcast Cable bill did not have Roger's name on it. Well, it does have his last name. Comcast Cable account number 11036765-1419-3838-1967000001 was under the name of Agnes Gatley. Roger had not seen Agnes in four years. Their last encounter was not a pleasant one.

After the movie, after *Modern Family*, after a bottle of Barefoot Malbec, after thirteen anchovy-stuffed olives, after a one ounce shot of Jameson Irish Whiskey, Roger went to bed in the usual way. Well almost. He staggered to the kitchen to rinse out his stemless wine glass. He relieved his bladder. He set an alarm for 6 a.m. on his handheld Galaxy cellular device. The same device he had used earlier to seek entertainment advice from the mysterious stranger. He attempted to clear his mind of all thoughts that were not attractive. That was generally a simple accomplishment on drinking nights. Roger drank every other night. Never two nights in a row. On drinking nights Roger was rewarded with thoughts of beautiful women. Stimulation. Manipulation. Gratification. Hibernation. The suspension of all voluntary bodily function. But most significantly a moratorium of consciousness, an intermission from worry, a postponement of troubles. Roger triple checked his alarm and then reclined trying to imagine being in the presence and in the desires of Sofia Vergara, but then an uninvited, unwelcomed visitor entered his mind. It was Jason Bateman. The reason for this unwanted appearance was that Roger had really enjoyed the movie and now could not stop thinking about it. Forty-nine minutes into it he felt he did not enjoy it. He lamented parting ways with his six American dollars. It had all been done before. Roger had seen this movie countless times. Over and over again. The same. Different titles, different actors, but the same goddamned movie.

But then, something unexpected happened. There was a change in the narrative and Roger became very interested. Engaged. The movie was nothing at all like what he was led to believe. It was better, so much better than expected. Roger smiled. Roger thought, *Perhaps I should write a review on the internet so that others can enjoy this very fine underrated film. I can write it tomorrow after work.* Then Roger's thoughts became more somber. *Tomorrow. The big 5-0.*

Roger was lonely. He missed Agnes terribly. For the past four years the only companionship he had was what his mind could conjure up. Well, *adult* companionship, anyway. He did have his daughters. When Agnes left him, she also left their two daughters. The girls were basically grown when Agnes left, not that that made it much easier. Nowadays however, Roger had the whole house to himself.

Avril, the oldest, left a year after Agnes did. She was now a junior at USYD, a fine American University. Joelle, Roger's baby, had just begun her freshman year at MXU. The girls were the reason Roger still watched the underwhelming and overrated situation comedy entitled *Modern Family*. The first two seasons the episodes were much better, the plot lines were more original, and the writers were less lazy. And more importantly to Roger, the Gatleys watched it as a family. When Roger watches *Modern Family* now, the unfunny retelling of *I Love Lucy* and *Dick Van Dyke* and even *That's so Raven* episodes, it usually did not affect him so negatively, because in his mind, for that thirty minutes, Avril is lying on the couch, Joelle is in the Lay Z Boy, and Agnes is beside him on the reclining love seat.

Currently, Roger's mind was supposed to be imagining Sofia Vergara in different stages of undress, but instead, it was comparing his life to the Jason Bateman movie and the television sitcom *Modern Family*. His mind produced a collage of unfortunate thoughts: *That's it for me. It's all over. There will be no change in my life's narrative. Nothing unexpected. No plot change. The girls are gone. I will see them less and less. How long before they move far, far away?*

Roger was suddenly feeling depressed. He felt the rest of his life would be filled with nothing other than loneliness and worry. His greatest fear was to continue to exist unspectacularly and then die expectedly. Roger loved his girls more than anything. He feared they only tolerated him, because let's face it, he was their provider. For now. Soon, he thought, they would no longer need him and abandon him.

Nothing could be further from the truth. The girls loved and appreciated their father more than anything. Neither had ever even considered the possibility of Roger not being a major presence in their lives. Roger's compilation of unfavorable ideas continued to hold Sofia at bay: *My job will continue to take me for granted. I'll eventually have to sell the house. My life will be nothing but lonely and awful.*

Then Roger had a refreshing consideration, *My life has been like the first half of the movie The Gift. It has been so formulaic. Boy meets girl. Boy marries girl. They have two wonderful children and live happily ever after, predictable, safe, unspectacular, highly rated by most Americans. Just like Modern Family. But maybe my life could have a plot twist, like in the movie. Something different. Something better. Interesting. Exciting... wait, I already had my plot twist. Agnes. My sweet beautiful Agnes. Oh my God. That was my plot twist. The end to my happily ever after. Goddammit! Why am I thinking like this? This is a drinking night. I am supposed to be at peace with myself, Goddammit!*

Roger was justified in his angry confusion, because he never considered things like this on drinking nights. He only had attractive thoughts and restful sleep. Every other night however, Roger's mind would race with depressing circumstances and constant worry. He called them worries, but actually they were fears. Roger was constantly afraid of things going wrong. His fears controlled him. His fears defined him. His fears made him like so many other Human Beings. Unoriginal. Unspectacular. Captive.

Roger rubbed his tired eyes hard with the palms of his hands trying to erase the unwelcome thoughts in his head. Soon the only thought that remained was that of the gorgeous Sofia Viagra. His libido, however, was still not fully committed to his weary mind's agenda. Suddenly, Sofia had another visitor and it shook Roger to his core. The actor that portrayed her fictional husband, Ed O'Neill, suddenly stood before Roger's mind's eye in all his superannuated glory. O'Neill appeared just as he had in the show from earlier in the evening. Ancient and decrepit. His stomach distended and over ripened. *This man is grotesquely obese.* His jowls and chins had begun a full invasion of his neck. His breathing looked labored, his eyes squinted and strained. His spine had begun to curve, seeming to prefer the ground to the sky. *Oh my Lord. Is this what I have to look forward to? What happened to the fit and trim, spry young man from Married with Children? How long ago was that? It doesn't seem all that long ago. How old is Ed O'Neill? How long do I got? Is that hair coming out of his ears?*

Roger sat up in bed to grab his handheld Galaxy cellular device and ask the internet just how old Mr. O'Neill is. After acquiring the important information he sought, he rechecked his alarm three more times to assure himself that his unscheduled trip on the internet did not queer the agreement he had previously made with his devices clock. It had not. *69. I got less than 19 years before...*Roger's worries of aging became more intense as he considered that the *American Broadcasting Company* probably employs an entire crew of professionals just to make Ed O'Neill look as good and young as possible. *Hair stylist. Make-up artist. Nutritionist. Personal trainer. And that's the best they can do? Oh my Lord, how terrible am I going to look?*

It was time to bring out the big guns. Again Roger rubbed his eyes to erase his thoughts. All of them. Even Sophia. He now brought someone else to the center of his mind, the kind and caring, beautiful and sexy, Helen Lovely.

Helen worked at Vicious Corp as did Roger. She had started working there five years ago, which was Roger's fifteenth year with the company. She was the personal secretary to Roger's boss Mr. Medium. This was right around the time things started going bad with Agnes. She was sympathetic and understanding. During those dark times she was Roger's only ray of sunshine. They were never super close or anything. She just always knew the exact right thing to say and made Roger feel respected and defined, maybe even beloved. And her beauty was beyond reproach. The thought of Helen Lovely calmed Roger and soothed his savage breast. He did not imagine her in various stages of undress. He simply imagined being with her. Being part of her life. Roger soon fell asleep, un-frustrated but definitely dissatisfied.

* * * * * * * *　* * * * * * * * *　* * * * * * * * *　* * * * * * * *

Agnes DeLint, who later became Agnes Gatley, was the worst thing that ever happened to Roger Gatley. But not until long after she was the best thing that ever happened to him. He truly loved everything about her and she loved him deeply despite his constant worry and lack of confidence. They had two marvelous daughters, more house than they needed, and just enough money. Life was splendid. Life was predictable. Life was happy. Until the day that one of Roger's many fears came to fruition. Agnes became sick. The kind of sick that does not end with getting better.

Medical science had yet to come up with a cure for what had invaded the lives of the Gatleys, but it had developed some very, very expensive ways to keep Agnes sick longer. There were some extremely painful and difficult and invasive treatments that succeeded in keeping Agnes sick for almost ten months. Vicious Corp had provided the Gatley family with a top rated health insurance provider for the low, low price of twenty-three percent of Roger's income. Before taxes, of course. The premium was so painless, it was almost delightful. But not to Roger.

Roger never liked seeing the large amount of cash deducted from his weekly paycheck, but he realized it was a necessary evil. Roger prayed they would never need their health insurance to the extent that they did once Agnes began her treatments and procedures and medications, but need it they did. For the first time Roger was delighted to have paid so much money for such a grand health insurance plan, because he was under the impression that he had an agreement with the health insurance company. Roger thought the deal was this: I give you 23% of my money and if anyone in my family ever gets very sick or suffers a catastrophic injury you will pay whatever it takes to make them better. Or as better as possible. Roger failed to read the one hundred and thirty-eight pages of fine print.

In case you have been fortunate enough to never find this out, the situation is as follows: it seems the grand insurance companies of the United States take some of that premium money they collect and hire a slew of very intelligent people with a great eye for detail whose only job is to pore over mountains and mountains of contracts and paperwork and find any possible way to legally avoid the actual paying of any of their customer's medical bills. Any loophole. No matter how immoral or heartless. Even if it bankrupts their customers. Even if it kills their customers. Literally. Any way to get out of holding up their end of the deal is acceptable: preauthorization failure, provider is out of network, coding errors, form errors, typos, experimental treatment or medication, and of course my personal least favorite, First you need a referral in order for doctor to *Do No Harm.*

It wasn't long before the girl's college funds and the Gatleys home's equity were gone. But the ten extra months afforded to the dying Agnes Gatley were filled with many great memories for Roger and his girls: Cleaning up vomit and feces, having their hands squeezed tightly by Agnes as unbearable pain ripped through her failing body, endless days and nights in hospital rooms staring down at someone who was really no longer there. When science could no longer keep Agnes sick and she finally died, Roger told no one that he actually felt as though a tremendous weight had been lifted from his tired shoulders. He mistakenly felt that feeling of relief was a betrayal of his *true love,* when it was actually a release from the grips of a terrible sickness that he and his daughters were also the victims of. Agnes was gone long before she left. In order to alleviate his guilt Roger spared no expense on her funeral arrangements.

Roger received a rather substantial check from their life insurance company. Life insurance companies have a more difficult time getting out of their agreements with their customers, but believe me it's not from lack of trying. Death is just harder to argue than sickness and treatment. Roger gave a healthy portion of his financial windfall to the funeral director who made Agnes look as pretty as you can make a dead woman look, which he must have been successful at, because several women in attendance at the wake of Agnes Gatley commented on how good she looked, just before she was sealed in a very expensive and impressive cherry wood casket, trimmed in gold with solid copper hardware and maroon velvet interior and then buried six feet under the earth's surface and covered with dirt and stones and clay and a complete ecosystem of bacteria, fungi, protozoa, nematodes, arthropods, earthworms, and other creepy crawly insects, all of which will eventually make their way into the very expensive final resting place of Agnes Gatley, at which time she will become part of their ecosystem. Then, Roger marked the spot on the earth's surface with a rather costly smooth rock that boasted her name and ranks, complete with many adjectives *loving wife, devoted mother, neat sister, moody daughter* and the dates of her existence. The funeral director informed Roger that all of his choices were both excellent and outstanding and really showed he cared. *And in no way did he appear relieved that Agnes no longer suffered a painful existence among the living.*

Anytime Roger started to feel a little hinky about the amount of money he was spending on his dead wife, the funeral director would reassure him that Agnes would have wanted it this way. Roger figured the guy was full of shit because he was pretty sure, given the choice, the way Agnes would have wanted it would involve her still being alive and healthy, but he felt guilty about being relieved that he no longer had to watch his once beautiful and happy wife suffer and cry and deteriorate and not get better, or have to watch his daughters watching his wife, or clean her vomit and feces, or help her eat and dress and bathe and he also deeply feared what other people would think if he did not give his wife's soon to be rotting corpse the very best of everything.

Not all of Roger's settlement money went into the hole that now housed his wife's decaying body. Most of what was left went to a very fine American learning institution. Avril was accepted into the thirty-eighth ranked American University a year after her mother's prolonged death. The University of Suck You Dry was well worth the investment. Roger knew Avril was receiving a quality education at USYD and her future, though motherless, would be limitless.

For the first three years after the death of Agnes, right alongside the tremendous guilt Roger felt was a relentless fear that he might make a mistake in providing the finishing touches of raising their daughters alone. He did not feel guilty about keeping Agnes alive her final months, pushing countless treatments and medications and procedures even though they both knew their efforts would be fruitless and the situation was hopeless, because society had told them both that their actions were proper and expected. Roger had also come to terms with the sense of relief he felt after the end of Agnes. The guilt that Roger carried for those first three years was because of unkept promises he had made to the love of his life. Vicious Corp, the company Roger works for is in the business of addiction. They manufacture some useless product or provide some pointless service that people believed, due to an incredible advertising campaign and social media blitz and celebrity endorsements from the right celebrities, they absolutely could not live without.

Roger worked in the logistics department at the Chicago office. He was a good employee and made a livable wage. A few months before Agnes became ill, Roger had come up with a plan that would really streamline some of whatever the hell it was that Vicious Corp did. Roger's plan was more efficient than the system the company currently used. It would save Vicious Corp both time and money. Lots of money, Roger told Agnes his ideas while complaining about his job. Despite his wife's urgings he never presented his idea to the company. He would always tell Agnes that now was not the time to introduce major changes in his company's business model, what with her being so sick and all. Truth was Roger was afraid to tell Mr. Medium his plan. What if he missed some obvious obstacle? What if it didn't work? What if it angered Mr. Medium or even worse, Mr. Big, the company CEO? Besides, he was hired to perform a job, not change his job completely. It probably would not work anyway.

But before Agnes died she made Roger promise to tell Mr. Medium his idea. She expected big things to come from it. That was not all Roger promised Agnes before she left him. Agnes also made him promise that if Vicious Corp did not use his new system, that he would bring his ideas to one of their major competitors, The Merciless Company or Cruelty Incorporated. That's how much Agnes believed in her man. Nearly three years after the corpse of Agnes Gatley was deposited into the earth Roger still kept his idea a secret. That's how much Roger did not believe in himself. Then Joelle, with her 4.67 GPA and a near perfect 34 ACT score was accepted to the thirteenth ranked American University. Compared to USYD, MXU was even *More Expensive*. If Joelle was going to attend MXU, Roger would need a raise. A big one.

It was a warm spring morning when Roger decided he would have to demand a raise. He was a loyal and competent employee with nineteen years on the job. After exchanging a few nervous pleasantries with the lovely Helen Lovely he marched into Mr. Medium's office full of fear and void of confidence. After several minutes of throat clearing and jumbled words and ums Roger requested that his weekly wages become slightly more significant.

Mr. Medium was a good egg. He liked Roger and recognized him as a valuable employee. He also had sympathy for Roger. He noticed how lost Roger seemed since Agnes had passed three years earlier. But there was no way Mr. Medium could offer Roger more money.

Roger did not take it very well which turned out to be very good for Roger's future. After expressing his extreme displeasure and being asked to calm down several times, Roger decided to tell Mr. Medium why Vicious Corp could not afford to pay him more money. He first explained how inefficient their current system was and then in a rather animated and bois- terous manner introduced his idea. Roger raised the volume of his voice to an almost threatening tone and his body gyrated in a very unnatural way. During the uproarious scene a small amount of spittle was unintentionally jettisoned from Roger's mouth and landed at the very center of Medium's desk, which both men witnessed and both men decided to pretend they did not, notice that is.

It was quite a display of unsure confidence, solely driven by anger and worry and desperation. Mr. Medium could not get a word in edgewise until he finally shouted, "Roger, I think you should calm yourself down. Take the rest of the day off. You are making me feel nervous. I've never seen you like this before. Please don't make me call security."

Roger left Mr. Medium's office feeling a sense of relief he had not felt since his wife died. It felt so liberating to finally share his idea with someone other than Agnes. But now, as he left Medium's office, something looked odd. It was Helen Lovely. She was so much more captivating than usual. She was on the phone. She spied Roger out of the corner of her eye. Upon recognition she did a quick double take with an excited smile of accep- tance. It was only for a moment that Roger enjoyed the radiant beauty of Helen Lovely, because after a couple of seconds he became consumed with worry about the repercussions of his animated and boisterous manner. Just as Roger's confidence and relief retreated so did Helen's smile.

That night Mr. Medium called Roger at home. Upon seeing Medium's digits displayed on his Galaxy handheld cellular device, Roger immediately feared being fired via telecommunication. But that's not why Medium called. His words to Roger were accompanied with excitement. "Roger, your system, I was thinking about it, and I think it can really work. Be in my office at 8 a.m. tomorrow. We are going to place a call to Mr. Big."

Mr. Big was skeptical at first, but then decided to give the new system a shot. Roger's plan was slowly implemented at the Chicago office and within four months it was a huge success. Roger was given his raise.

Mr. Big was very happy. Several weeks later, after ironing out a few bugs, Mr. Big made a call to Roger. Mr. Big was on a family vacation in Cabo San Lucas. Roger was at his desk feeling proud of his accomplishment. Mr. Big told Roger he wanted to implement his system company wide. Next week he was sending Roger four junior executives to train and soon one of them would introduce the new system to the LA office, one to the New York office, one to the London office and the fourth would stay on as Rogers's assistant. *An assistant!* Roger thought as Big continued, "Listen Roger, I have big plans for you. Mr. Medium is a couple of years away from retirement. So I need you to hang on and work with me a little here. Okay, buddy?" *Buddy!* Roger could barely conceal his excitement. *Why didn't I listen to my beautiful Agnes sooner?*

Later that day Mr. Big made a very difficult decision based solely on the projected success of Roger's great idea. He and his family were having an incredible time in a beautiful villa right on the ocean. Mr. Big took a quiet time out from his family vacation to run the numbers one more time. He was positive that based on the millions Vicious Corp would save using Rogers new system; he could definitely buy the Cabo San Lucas Villa. A third vacation home is a very difficult decision to make, but thanks to Roger, this one was a no brainer.

That Monday Roger received his four junior executives: Mr. Young, Mr. Younger, Mr. Youngest and Mr. Fetus. Roger was not sure how he felt about them at first. They seemed fairly intelligent and willing to learn. All four of them had exceptional hearing and constantly boasted about it, saying "I hear you, man." They were also very good at being physically fit and extremely handsome and preferred punching knuckles as opposed to the basic white-man handshake. Roger was most fond of Mr. Fetus, although it did annoy him when he would slip on the embryotic fluid that was now occasionally found on the office floor.

Roger's Galaxy handheld cellular device announced it was 6 a.m. by playing an electronic version of Reveille. The two triple checks of his alarm had worked. It was a Friday. It was Roger's big 5-0. It was Roger's last day with his junior executives in training. Despite the annoying and hazardous embryotic fluid, Roger had requested Mr. Fetus to stay on as his assistant.

The sound of Reveille meant it was now time for Roger to perform his daily morning rituals. Roger got out of bed and stood still for a few moments giving his knees and ankles a chance to catch up. He walked to the bathroom with his usual morning limp. He stripped naked and took a seat for his morning constitutional. Even though he was the only person in the house he still shut and locked the bathroom door.

As he sat staring forward at the ceramic tiles that were badly in need of a re-grouting, he continued his thoughts from the night before, but with a more positive angle. *Agnes dying was a definite plot twist in the life of Roger Gatley. A devastating terrible plot twist. But it was not my only one. How about being lucky enough to meet Agnes in the first place. That was an incredible plot twist. There was nothing formulaic about Agnes. And my girls, Avril and Joelle, they changed everything. And eight months ago when I told Medium my idea…now that was a game changer – a plot twist in progress.*

Roger's thoughts were interrupted by a series of offensive vibrations and electronic beeps. It was his cellular device. It was a text from Joelle. *Happy Birthday, Daddy! Call you later.* Roger worried. *What is Joelle doing up so early? Is everything okay? Why is she going to call me later? Does she want me to call her now? Why hasn't Avril texted me yet? She is my early riser.*

Roger's fears were interrupted by the completion of his task at hand. Now came the hard part. Although not considered difficult by the vast majority of Human Beings, lately Gatley found it quite a challenge. People do it every day without even thinking about it. For most, muscle memory alone could complete the next part of Roger's morning ritual. Not for Roger though. Not anymore. He had to be very careful and plot out each and every one of his movements.

A little over a year ago, when Roger was in fear of turning 49, thinking he was becoming too old too quickly, and his appearance and the shape he was in supported his fear, that's when it happened. The terrible bathroom incident. Roger is still not sure why it happened. He was in severe pain and/or unabated discomfort for over three weeks. He missed five days of work. He only knew that he now lived in fear of a reoccurrence of the unfortunate event.

He had several theories as to why the simple act of attempting to wipe clean the area from which he expelled his dietary waste resulted in such a cruel and unusual punishment.

At the time the event took place, Roger, like most Americans in their late forties, had put on a few pounds. Perhaps he had not battled the punishing effects of age with enough vigor and was no longer in the minimum required shape to perform even the simplest of physical activities. Maybe he simply sat there for too long a period of time and his body had become cold and stiff, perhaps even experiencing the beginning stages of atrophy. At the time Roger liked to read while doing his business and the book he was regarding at that particular juncture was an extremely large one with a word count of 577,608, by one of his favorite authors, David Foster Wallace. At times, while enjoying some of the more interesting chapters, Roger would find himself losing track of time and even completely forgetting that the main reason for his visit to the lavatory had finished some time ago.

Roger no longer read while in the bathroom. Absolutely not. In and out as quickly as possible. He would also now perform a few quick stretches before his post defecation maintenance. A sort of warm up, if you will. He theorized that the severe strain he suffered may have been brought on by the combination of two acts, not just one. First, lifting and moving the rather corpulent novel he was reading for nearly thirty-eight minutes from his lap to the sterile safety of inside of the bathroom sink vanity, a sort of fecal free safety zone for his publications of choice, which he could reach from an awkward position while remaining seated. And second, the action of stretching slightly more than he had in previous attempts to reach around his ever expanding gluteus maximus.

The incident occurred in the superior region of the trapezius muscle, somewhere between the attachment points of the right lateral clavicle and the acromion and spine of the scapula. In case you are not following me, what I'm attempting to say as eloquently as possible is that last year Roger Gatley severely pulled a muscle while wiping his ass.

Roger now went to great lengths to prevent such an incident from ever happening again. So far he had been successful in that endeavor, but unfortunately Roger now belonged to a small demographic of middle aged American males that feared taking care of their bathroom business.

Thankfully, on the morning of his fiftieth birthday, the incident would not repeat. After a triumphant attempt at carefully maintaining the area in question, Roger stood in front of the bathroom sink, fully naked, behind the closed and locked bathroom door of the empty house he currently inhabited alone, looking at himself in the mirror that was also the door of the medicine cabinet that hung above the sink. His reflection looked back. Roger found himself in the same staring contest he found himself in every morning, one he was sure to lose. Roger would always look away first, because every day, more and more, he hated the face that looked back at him. It had lines and bags and worries and wrinkles and a forehead that grew and grew. He saw his own reflection as a guarantee that he would spend the rest of his life alone. *No woman would find this appealing. Especially a woman as spectacular as the lovely Helen Lovely.* Roger was far too hard on himself. What he was becoming made him fearful of the future. Roger's reflection, on the other hand, never looked away. It accepted him for who he was and what he looked like.

For a man in Roger's mental state, there was another unfortunate aspect to his morning bathroom rituals. As he stood there fully nude and fully engaged in an ill-fated staring competition, to his left was the toilet and sealed bathroom door, to his right, the bathtub, which in lieu of a shower curtain boasted sliding glass doors, one of which was a full length mirror that Roger was not fond of viewing. There are some human bodies that look better with their clothes off. Most of them, however, appear far more pleasing to the eye with their clothes on. The latter definitely applied to Roger. Not that he was ugly or extremely obese or grotesque. He wasn't. It's just that gravity and years and Twinkies and beers had a thing or two, or three or four, to say about his appearance. He had some flaws. Flaws that clothing offered an adequate camouflage. It was nothing to obsess over, but at times he certainly did.

After conceding the staring contest to his reflection, Roger caught a glimpse of his full body profile in its most natural state. Ed O'Neill once again invaded his mind. Wanting to look at the age of fifty the way you did at age twenty, or thirty or even forty is as inauspicious as attempting to out-stare your own reflection. Enough self-imposed disappointment. It was time to shave.

Roger had this very strange habit he had begun implementing as part of his shaving routine a few years ago. You may find it rather disgusting or weird. What Roger would do was this: Just before he would lather on the shaving cream, he would stand in front of the bathroom sink, once again inspecting his aging face in the medicine cabinet mirror, with his thighs only about an inch away from the cold, imitation marble vanity top, and he would begin to suck in as much oxygen as his lungs would allow. While doing this he would also suck in as much gut as his inners would allow, slightly arching his back and stretching the hamstring muscles behind his knees.

In the shower door mirror, which at this particular fleeting moment Roger was enjoying in his peripheral vision, because this physical contortion immediately made him appear ten years younger and fifteen pounds lighter. Roger definitely enjoyed that. But that's not why he did it. Roger stood just under five feet ten inches tall, which meant before his powerful and exaggerated inhale his testicles hung just below the bathroom sink's cold, imitation marble vanity top.

Once he struck his age and weight-defying pose his testicles would hang just above the cold, imitation marble vanity top, at which time he would lean slightly forward pressing his thighs against the countertops edge and plop them, the testicles, down on the cold, imitation marble vanity top. It felt rather invigorating. He would leave them there, scrotum, penis and all, the complete package, and enjoy a good shave. Pretty gross, huh? But in Roger's defense, he had carried them around for fifty years. A few minutes of daily rest is not the worst thing I can think of.

Unfortunately, this would not be the case today on Roger's fiftieth birthday. He was about to get a surprise. Not a pleasant one. He missed.

Well, kind of. He was unable to raise his package high enough to clear the vanity. He missed once. He missed twice. He was successful upon his third attempt but there was some help in the form of a tiny bit of tip toe action. *What the hell just happened?*

Roger panicked. After a few minutes to think about it, Roger reached what was far too often, his normal conclusion. *Oh my God, I'm dying. Testicular cancer. I must have a tumor in there the size and weight of a golf ball.* As he felt around for the golf ball size tumor he considered other possibilities. *I'm getting shorter. My spine is deteriorating. Spinal cord cancer? That's a thing, isn't it?*

Roger never even considered that this was not an overnight event but a gradual occurrence. He had not had a perfectly clean descent or landing in several weeks. In fact, there had been quite a bit of unnoticed scrotum scrapings on the vanity over the past few days. There were many other factors involved in the unsuccessful plopping tragedy: Gravity, for one is the enemy of all protruding body parts, also the bathroom was seven degrees warmer than it had been the past couple of weeks, during which time Roger had gained eight pounds – eating quite a bit of junk food on his non-drinking nights – missing his wife, missing his girls, worrying about money, expecting more from his employer, and fearing the half century mark. Not to mention the extra weight had increased his stance by 2mm, for a more stable foundation. Nope. None of that. Roger's mind went right to *I'm -Gonna-Die*, as it so often did. Three weeks ago he had a headache that he was sure was a massive brain aneurysm in the making. The internet on his handheld Galaxy cellular device assured him that his fears were not only logical, but also warranted. Two weeks ago he had contracted some severely impactful gastric distress after eating several bowls of five alarm chili (*see:* gained eight pounds in last couple of weeks) which he promised himself were several myocardial infractions, guaranteed to become a full blown, devastating cardiac event, (i.e. a massive fricking heart attack, i.e. dead, dead as he can be, dead I tell you). When he finally belched you would have thought he hit the Goddamned Lottery.

Just six days ago Roger discovered a wickedly large and intrusive hemorrhoid just inside his anal canal (which added more difficulty to his already time consuming anal maintenance program). Roger convinced himself that it was not a hemorrhoid, but instead his incredibly enlarged, extremely cancerous prostrate, that was absolutely going to become detached, fall out and run down his inner thigh, spreading the cancer everywhere. He only prayed that it would happen at home in the shower and not at work, especially not in front of the lovely Helen Lovely. He felt shitting out his diseased prostrate in front of her would most definitely nullify any remote chance he had in ever dating her. In all actuality, that last part would probably be accurate, if such impossibility occurred.

And so Roger shaved and showered in fear, like he had so many other times. *I can't die. Not yet. My girls need me. I have to finish paying for their education.* Even if Roger lived, which he would, finishing paying for their education would prove to be very difficult with his current financial situation, even with the raise he had received just eight months ago. It seemed like all of the bills that Roger received since Agnes first took ill, medical, burial, USYD tuition, MXU tuition, first mortgage, second mortgage, they all had one thing in common - the amount due was always the same, everything you got and then some.

Roger's fear began to morph into self-pity. *That raise was bullshit. The amount of money Vicious Corp is going to make off my idea and they throw me a few table scraps. Mr. Big says work with me for a little while, be patient. And I just sit there like a good obedient little dog. I'm a coward. I'm old and I'm lonely and I let my fears dictate everything I do or say or even think.* Roger hated feeling so negative about himself, but how could he not. A fearful man, a lonely man, these facts were indisputable. And he felt old. He had been telling himself that fifty was old for as long as he could remember. Hell, society has been echoing the same rhetoric, 50 – nothing left to do now except get your AARP card and wait to die.

He had already been over-the-hill for ten years. At least that's what everyone told him at his fortieth birthday party. They even bought a huge array of decorations and very unfunny, unoriginal gifts boasting the same sentiment. His girls had been teasing him for years about being old. Let's face it, here is a man so old that he actually still occasionally watched network broadcast television shows at the time they are originally broadcast, he prefers to read things printed on paper. For God's sake he does not tweet, he is not even positive what an emoji is and has great difficulty in wiping his ass and lifting his nut sack, mutually exclusive of course. An old, lonely, coward – how completely pathetic.

But then toward the end of his shower, Roger remembered something Agnes used to always tell him when his worry began to get out of control and feast on his very existence. "Don't worry so much, Roger; everything's going to be okay."

He heard her voice in his head as if she were right there in the bathroom with him. He repeated her words out loud to no one but himself, "Everything's going to be okay." And then he thought, *but it wasn't and it isn't. You died, you left me. Broke and alone. Everything is not okay.* Roger's tears mixed with the hot water from the shower head as the newly 50-year-old man wept like a child.

Happy Birthday Roger

* * * * * * *   * * * * * * * *   * * * * * * * *   * * * * * * *

The Oxford dictionary defines an epiphany as a moment of sudden revelation or insight.

Any recovering addict will tell you that a *moment of clarity* is when you suddenly get a deep understanding of some truth that has previously been out of reach.

Both terms sound similar and both seem to insist on the action occurring quickly and without warning. I'm not exactly sure which one applies to Roger Gatley, but I am sure at least one of them does, perhaps both. After his shower of immeasurable remorse, Roger sat at his kitchen table and after eighteen minutes of silent reflection he once again said something aloud to himself that more than likely was the most profound sentence he had ever spoken.

"Everything is okay."

That despite all of his worry and loneliness everything really was okay. It wasn't great or ideal, some of it not very good at all, but it was okay. His girls were beautiful and healthy and happy and working toward very successful futures. He had a roof over his head, clothes on his back, food in his fridge, a handheld Galaxy cellular device and an expanded Comcast Cable package that did from time to time actually work.

Then Roger considered his fears, all of his worries and apprehensions and self-doubts and anxieties and nervousness and he realized that they in no way helped in making his life "okay" but that they definitely contributed to his life not being great or ideal or even very good. These negative attributes were a gray cloud that encompassed all of Roger's *true self.* He had been surrounded by this calamitous aura for so long he did not even notice its presence. As far back as his mind would allow him to travel, he could not remember a time when he was not worried or apprehensive or self-doubting or anxious or nervous. His earliest childhood memory brought him back to a kindergarten game of duck, duck, goose. As he sat in a circle with the other children, native American style, two spots away from Dick Nickler, the boy who used to tease him mercilessly, the boy he never stood up to and said ENOUGH, and across from Lucy Jitters, the little girl that he found so beautiful and engaging that he never once said a single word to her. Even all these years later, sitting at his kitchen table, he remembered the fear so vividly – *Please don't pick me. Please don't pick me. What if I fall down or get up too slowly? What if the other kids laugh at the way I run? What if I run the wrong direction? What if Dick Nickler trips me as I go by? Please. Anybody but me.*

Then Roger thought about something much more recent. A time where he may have actually become somewhat slightly aware of the gray mass that had engulfed him for so many years. It was eight months ago, when Mr. Medium had denied his request for a raise. Roger would not stand for it. He shouted. He peeked out from inside his gray prison of limitation and told Mr. Medium his outstanding idea and it felt wonderful. But it was fleeting. Soon after, he was worried about being fired for his mild outburst.

Every epiphany and moment of clarity are accompanied by something else. A decision. Roger's decision was this – ENOUGH!

I refuse to feel this way any longer. I will no longer be a prisoner to my perfidious mind. I will become the type of Human Being I have always envied. I will go to work today with my head held high and demand better compensation for my efforts. Or else. And I will request the company of the lovely Helen Lovely at a non-work related activity. Perhaps din-

THE NAME OF THE BOOK

Just then the hideous vibrating noise accompanied by electronic beeps returned and rang through the kitchen. It was Roger's handheld – you know what it was. The text was from Roger's oldest, Avril, his early riser. It read *Happy 50th Birthday Dad! Have an amazing day Talk later.*

Roger gave no worry to his daughter's current circumstances. He thought, *I certainly will.* And returned Avril's text with thanks and well wishes and even something he had never done before, a couple of smiley faces. I wish someone was there to tell him that those are emojis.

But it did not matter. Roger Gatley was a man on a mission. He drove to work worry free. Not even concerning himself with the unusual noise that was coming from the front end of his vehicle that was traveling down the Eisenhower Expressway at sixty-three miles per hour, a full eight miles per hour over the recommended, posted speed limit. *Sounds like my right front tire might be a little low.*

And that was it, no obsessive unease, no useless worry, he simply assessed the situation. Determined that it did not require his immediate attention, he did not pull over on the side of the Eisenhower Expressway, he continued on, toward his place of employment, Vicious Corp. The unusual noise the front end of Roger's car was making very well could have been caused by a loss of air pressure in the right front tire. Or it could have been something far worse. Roger did not worry about it. Not one bit.

Happy Re-Birthday Roger

* * * * * * *   * * * * * * * *   * * * * * * * *   * * * * * * *

Upon his arrival at Vicious Corp, Roger forgot all about the rattle of his vehicle and went straight to his office where he immediately began…he began, how shall I put this…well, breathing. Heavier than considered normal for a fifty-year-old man sitting at a desk. His heart rate was at 92 beats per minute. You see, unfortunately, as Roger walked through the Vicious Corp parking lot he began feeling a little bit nervous about the two-part mission he was about to embark on. Self-doubt and worry and apprehension began creeping back into Roger's psyche. He could literally see the gray cloud closing in around him. Now he sat at his desk surrounded by the old familiar aura that was delaying the start of his missions. One hour later – 98 Beats Per Minute. Two hours later – 102 BPM.

Mr. Younger announced, "knock knock" as he walked into Roger's office. "Hey there, Mr. Gatley, I know Mr. Medium is going to meet with us later today, but I was wondering…Any idea which office they are shipping me off to?"

Roger just sat there, flush in the face, disappointed in himself, not acknowledging Younger in any way. 106 – BPM.

"Mr. Gatley?"

Roger turned his inattention to Younger as he got up from his desk. "There's something I have to do."

As Roger walked past Younger, out of the office and down the hall toward Mr. Medium's office, the rejected junior executive said, "I hear you, man. We'll talk later then. Good meeting."

Roger saw the lovely Helen Lovely sitting at her desk looking gorgeous as always. 125 – BPM. Standing in front of her desk, chatting her up, was the always perfect Mr. Sensational. 130 – BPM. Roger had never liked Mr. Sensational even though he had no good reason not to like him. He was polite, friendly, sincere and one hundred percent confident. He was the company's top salesman. There were of course several bad reasons not to like him, jealousy being the top one. *Why is he always in the logistics department talking to Helen?* Roger asked himself a rather obvious seeming question.

"Well, there's the birthday boy. Happy Birthday, Roger." Helen spotted Roger and greeted him in her usual delightful way. Mr. Sensational turned and smiled his perfectly handsome face at Roger: with its tired and sagging eyes, retreating hairline, and slightly crooked and very yellowed teeth.

Enough, Roger thought. *Enough.* Not about how Helen had greeted him, but about the negative attributes that were once again trying to hold him captive. Just as he had successfully done at his kitchen table, Roger once again tried to expel what wished to control him. He swallowed hard and attempted to smile back and with all the confidence he could muster up and he said, "Happy birthday to you, too, Helen."

Lovely giggled. Sensational smiled even bigger. Roger corrected himself quickly, "Good morning. I mean good morning. It's your birthday not my birthday. I mean my birthday, not yours. But it is your morning, well really all of ours, the morning. Let's all have a good morning. All of us." 138 – BPM.

"Happy Birthday, Roger." Mr. Sensational gave Roger a warm pat on the back. "How young of a man are you now?"

Roger twitched an agitated twitch and considered misrepresenting the truth, but then decided to side with it. "I'm 50. The big 5-0 as they say."

"Half a century of Roger Gately. Well, that's just outstanding. You know what they say about fifty these days, right Rog?" Mr.S. looked a sly look at Helen, not expecting an actual answer. " Fifty is the new thirty." Roger enjoyed Sensational's comment as Helen smiled large and Mr. S. chuckled hard trying to continue his social observance. "So I ask you, what does that make twenty? The new zygote?" Sensational laughed at his own joke. Helen also laughed because she found it amusing. Roger smiled because he felt it would be rude not to. Mr. S. continued "Well, listen guys, I gotta get going. You all have a good day. And Rog, don't do everything I wouldn't do."

Sensational's departure was followed with thirteen seconds of slightly awkward silence, then, "So how is your birthday going, Roger?" Helen asked.

"Good. Swell. Um – "Roger considered asking Helen on a date right then and there, but then decided business before pleasure. "Can I see, I mean if he's not too busy, Mr. Medium? Well, actually even if he is busy, this is important, unless he is too too busy."

Helen noticed something different about Roger. It definitely wasn't confidence. And it wasn't his extra nervousness, but there was something different. She smiled a pleasant smile at Roger. "He did ask me to hold his calls, but nothing succeeds but a try."

Helen picked up the receiver of her non-handheld-desk phone held it to her ear and rang Mr. Mediums non-handheld-desk phone.

"Yes, Ms. Lovely."

"Mr. Gatley is here to see you, sir."

"Roger? Now? What for? Did he say what for?"

Roger was unable to hear Mr. Medium's end of the conversation.

"No, sir. Just that it was important."

"Oh boy… Tell him no. I mean tell him I am very busy."

Helen looked up at Roger who was beginning to perspire where his hair met his forehead in the most unattractive way. 150 - BPM. "Okay, sir. I'll tell him."

"Roger it's going to be a few minutes. Why don't you have a seat and relax."

"No. No. I'm fine." Roger fidgeted shifting his weight from one foot to the other.

Helen waited thirty-eight seconds and then redialed Mr. Medium. "Yes."

"He says he will wait."

"Wait? What does he mean he'll wait? I could be all day." Medium sounded like he was the one sweating.

"I don't think that's going to matter," in her normal speaking voice. "He seems very determined," in a whisper.

"What do you mean – does he seem angry?"

"Excuse me, sir?"

"Just give me a few minutes."

Helen hung up her phone. "It won't be long, Roger."

This delay was proving to be very harmful to Roger's disposition. The time for action was now. He had to attack his psychological captors. Fifty years a slave – the time for escape was at hand. "Listen, um, Helen," Roger battled hard against his negative forces, trying hard to glimpse beyond the gray cloud of doubt, but his voice still sounded shaken and awkward. "Is there any way that you might want to maybe some time go out to dinner with me?" Shots fired! Missiles launched! Bombs dropped! Take that self-doubt and fear of rejection!

Helen's eyes widened. She tilted her head slightly to the left. "Oh Roger," she said. But it wasn't *Oh, Roger* like a woman who was just sexually gratified, it was *Oh Roger* like a woman who had just witnessed a chubby, nine year old, spectacle-wearing boy, his arms loaded with packages containing very fragile gifts he had just purchased with every last penny he had earned from an entire year of doing chores, the gifts were for his widowed mother for Christmas, and as he carried them, making his way home, very clumsily through the puddles and slush of a melting snow from a storm from one week previous, a car, going too fast for conditions and much too close to the curb, splashed up a tidal wave of filthy cold water and icy sludge, causing him to lose his balance and fall into a mire of disgustingness, only to stagger back to his feet completely drenched and bear witness to an unfortunate array of shattered purchases, which was very difficult to focus on because lying among the destroyed Christmas presents were the young man's broken and now useless glasses. That's the kind of *Oh, Roger*, Roger Gatley had just received.

"I'm sorry Roger, I think you're a great guy, but- *shots fired.* "I'm already in a committed relationship." *Missiles launched.* "Maybe we could go out for drinks or something sometime – as friends." *Bombs dropped.* Take that, confidence. In your face, bravery.

Roger's face became sullen. His heart rate dramatically decreased. His attempted new persona, crippled – It was a direct hit. Helen went to him. She touched him, her hands on his shoulders as she stood before him. "I'm very flattered that you asked me, Roger." He spoke not a word opting to simply stare at the beauty that would never be his to caress and hold and flaunt. "Are you okay, Roger?"

Roger tried to regain some sense of face. "Oh, fine. Absolutely. I just thought – well, I mean – I didn't know – about dinner, I mean a boyfriend. Not me a boyfriend – your boyfriend – that you had a boyfriend."

Helen ran her hands down his shoulders and released her touch. She smiled, "Well – "

"Is it Sensational?" Roger felt the need to ask. Perhaps he thought that could justify his strong dislike for an all-round good guy. Like an imagined *he-stole-my-girlfriend* sort of thing.

Helen half laughed. "I'm not exactly sure what you are asking me. Are you asking if my relationship is sensational or if my relationship is with Mr. Sensational?"

Roger supplied the other half of Helen's laugh. "Mr. Sensational. I meant Mr. Sensational, is he your boyfriend?"

"No, he's not Roger. And I never said I had a BOY friend- " Helen's line rang. She answered. "Is Roger still waiting?" an unrelaxed Mr. Medium asked.

"Yes, he is."

"Okay. All right. Send him in. Let's get this unpleasantness over with."

Roger staggered into Medium's office still woozy from his injuries. "Mr. Gatley, how good to see you. Come in. Come in. Have a seat. What's on your mind today?" Mr. Medium fished. Roger was having trouble remembering this part of his mission. His mind was on his wounds. They were opened and fresh and filled with shrapnel. "Oh, Oh, and I almost forgot, happy birthday, Roger."

Roger sat across from Medium in total silence. *What's wrong with me,* Roger questioned his failure. *I sounded like a complete idiot. A 50-year-old idiot asking a beautiful woman on a date, sounding like a frightened little school boy.* Roger began to finger his gaping wounds.

Mr. Medium mistook Roger's silence for something it was not. It made him feel nervous. "So what's going on, Roger?"

Shoot!. The mission. Roger remembered. *Does it even matter? Should I even bother? Do I really want another rejection today?* Roger inhaled deeply and spoke slowly, sounding accidently menacing. "I'm here to talk about the new system...my new system."

"Well... you know we have some big announcements coming later today. What is it you want to talk about?" Medium asked in a very unassertive tone.

Roger only half heard Medium and did not respond. His eyes appeared fixed on Medium's head, but were not actually focused on it. While Roger's stare was looking through his boss, his mind concentrated on his wounds. The silence and staring increased Mr. Medium's uneasy feeling. "I mean things are going great. Mr. Big is happy. The shareholders are thrilled."

Roger felt a small piece of shrapnel inside his flesh. He wiggled it trying to pull it free. The movement caused him great pain...he thought.

"Why Roger? Have you heard something about today's big announcements?"

Roger tugged hard on the jagged invader imbedded in his open, bleeding gash. *Oh, the pain. The humiliation.* His eyes became more intense as he thought about his wounds and the manner in which he received them. *Complete mission failure.* The staring that was not staring, but actually dazing made Mr. Medium begin to feel as if he were being interrogated.

"Roger...have you by chance already talked to Mr. Big?"

As he continued to work the shrapnel out of his flesh he remembered he was a key player in the current conversation and answered, "Talk about what?" in a bewildered tone.

"The new system implication, and who is going where and…"

"My assistant," Roger exclaimed excitedly as he pulled the shrapnel free and discovered an incredibly obvious secret. *It doesn't hurt. I mean it does hurt, but it doesn't hurt.* No words followed my assistant, just a seemingly cold and intimidating, but unintentional stare. *It only hurts because I say it hurts. My wounds are all… self-inflicted… self-imagined.*

"Yes, yes, your assistant. Well…" Medium stammered.

I was supposed to do two things today. Insist on better compensation for my system and ask Helen on a date. And I did one of them. I did ask Helen on a date.

"Roger, look. I'm not supposed to say anything yet, but I got a feeling you already know something."

How is that a failure? I did what I wanted to do. I overcame my apprehension. My self-doubt. My fear.

"There is not really going to be an announcement today. Nothing's going to happen until Monday."

Just because you try something doesn't mean you're going to succeed.

"Mr. Big himself is coming in Monday."

Roger no longer paid Medium any attention. His wounds began to slowly close. *But you still have to try. That is what matters.*

"He is going to talk to you, personally. Face to face."

You are not a coward if you don't succeed. You are a coward if you don't try.

"It was my idea actually. In fact, I insisted on it."

Helen's not even straight for God's sake.

"You know Roger I have always liked you. You're a great worker. You have never given me any problems. Exceptional. Absolutely exceptional."

I tried. I could have sounded a little more suave. I'll have to work on my confidence. But everything is still okay. Roger's wounds had completely closed.

"Roger. I'm ten months from retirement. What am I supposed to do? I hate this corporate world."

And it only hurts as much as you allow it to hurt.

"It's Friday. It's your birthday. You should just take the rest of the day off. Have a nice weekend."

Mission one accomplished. Time for mission two.

Mr. Medium leaned back in his chair and sighed, exhausted by his soliloquy. "Just… I don't know. What else could I possibly tell you? Just talk to Mr. Big on Monday-"

"Exactly. Mr. Big," Roger interrupted filled with energy, about to break completely out of his prison of worry and doubt. "I know what Vicious Corp is making on my system and what they are going to make and I want, NO, I demand better compensation."

"Roger… "

"Now listen," Roger continued with no comprehension of any of Mr. Medium's previous statements, "I expect nothing less than your full support in this matter. I want to have a meeting with Mr. Big. And maybe you should be there. I am definitely open to your advice on how to proceed."

"Roger, haven't you been listening?"

"Oh Sir, believe me, I have been listening and watching and the time for action is now, right now."

"Roger, I am so sorry."

He sounds like Helen. But that's not acceptable on this mission. I will not take no for an answer.

"Don't be sorry. And I'll tell you something else, today's announcement, he could go ahead and ship Young, Younger, and Youngest out wherever he wants. I don't care. But Fetus is staying. He will be my assistant." Mr. Medium stared at Roger in complete bewilderment not knowing how to react. Roger mistook Medium's expression for one of surrender. He felt he had him on the ropes. His heartrate was back to 120 BPM, but this time it beat with excitement, not apprehension and worry. He sounded suave and confident as he continued his demands. "On that my mind is made up."

"Roger! I just told you there isn't going to be an announcement today!" Medium's voice was raised, not in anger, but in frustration and with more effort in attempted clarification. "Goddammit, Roger, I didn't even want to see you today. Mr. Big, he doesn't care, but I do. I really do. I didn't want it to happen on your birthday."

"What are you talking about?"

"Mr. Fetus isn't going anywhere. He is staying here… He is replacing you. Roger, they're letting you go."

Shots fired.

"What? Why?" Roger began to sink in total disbelief.

"Fetus makes less than half what you make. You are fifty and more likely to become a strain on the company's health care plan. You get five weeks' vacation as opposed to two. It's all money. The whole decision is based on what's better for Vicious Corp's bottom line."

Missiles launched.

The familiar gray began to creep back into Medium's office from under the door as Roger struggled for words trying hard to launch some sort of counter attack. *Say something* "But my idea. My system."

"Exactly, they feel they have already got everything out of you that they possibly can. You have nothing more to offer. They no longer have any use for you. To show their thanks they are going to offer you a one-year severance package, provided you sign a non-compete contract. I'm sorry."

Bombs dropped.

Roger looked around the office as the atmosphere became a familiar fog of gray and then he looked around inside himself. Searching for what to say, what to do, how to react. After a couple of uncomfortable minutes, he thought he had found the perfect words to use in response to this devastating attack. In searching for the proper reaction Roger was very surprised at what he did not find, there was no sign of worry, no apprehension, no self-doubt, no anxiety, no nervousness. The gray had failed to penetrate Roger's soul.

"Fuck that!"

The room brightened at the speed of light. Everything instantly became clear. The gray returned to wherever it had come from and Roger's moment of clarity continued. Mr. Medium misunderstood Rogers's response. "I know. It's terribly unfair."

"No, I mean you could tell Mr. Big to stick his severance pay and non-compete contract so far up his ass that he chokes on it."

"Roger, I know how you feel, but you have to consider- "

"How I feel? I feel fine, Medium, perfectly fine." *It only hurts as much as you allow it to. And no one and nothing can ever stop me from trying.*

Counter attack.

Roger's voice and heartrate began to gradually rise, but his words remained confident and distinct. "What am I, an idiot? I come up with the best idea this company has had in years and they think I'm going to promise not to bring it to their competitors. Please. By the end of next week, the Merciless Company and Cruelty Incorporated will be in a bidding war to acquire my services."

"Now Roger, lower your voice and calm down. A year's pay for a fifty-year-old man is nothing to turn your back on. It's another year of security. And why do you want to get in bed with another one of these corporations. They are all the same. They will chew you up and spit you out. At your-"

"That's where you're wrong, Medium." Roger shot out of his chair, his finger pointing at Medium's forehead. "From now on I negotiate from a position of power. Never again from weakness. Do you know why Medium?" Roger was almost yelling and began to pace in front of the desk, his chair lying on its back from his aggressive departure. "Because of me, that's why! I'm my own security. And I guarantee you I will never again let myself down. Never!"

Medium was starting to feel nervous, so he decided to inform Roger, "Roger, you are starting to make me feel nervous."

That stopped Roger in his tracks and caused him to re-point his finger at Medium's forehead. "And you guys better get ready for failure. Big time failure. Young, Younger, and Youngest, more like Dumb, Dumber, and Dumbest!" Roger was now definitely yelling.

"If you don't calm down I'm going to call security."

"Fetus is the only one worth a damn, and I might just take him with me – Security? What are you talking about? Call security? Are you scared? Are you afraid of me? Do you think I'm going to hurt you?" Roger's yelling continued and his movements and gyrations did appear to come off as a bit threatening. Medium was on his non-handheld desk phone as Roger continued. "I'm not scared. Do you know why? Because everything is okay! I thought Agnes was crazy when she said that everything is going to be okay. But she was right. No! No! She was wrong. Actually she was wrong. Because everything is going to be fucking better than okay! Things are going to be fucking great!"

"Roger please," Medium begged for composure.

"Oh calm down, you big baby. I'm leaving." Roger stormed out of the office slamming the door behind him only to discover several Vicious Corp employees that had been watching the door that did a poor job of concealing Roger's volume, were now watching him. He straightened his tie. He pushed his hair back with his spread fingers. As the small group dispersed, pretending not to notice anything out of the ordinary, Roger beheld the lovely Helen Lovely doing something he had only observed her doing one other time for a brief moment eight months ago. Her beauty was once again radiant. She was glowing. Her skin radiated with a warm brilliance that was intensely vivid and engaging and completely unnatural and impossible, but this time it was not for a couple of seconds. Helen's blazing beauty shown on and on.

Am I in love, Roger wondered? And then from across the room Helen spoke the same two words she had earlier, "Oh, Roger." Except this time her tone was that of a woman who was just sexually gratified.

Are we in love? I never saw Agnes glow and I know I loved her. I said she glowed while pregnant, but not like this. This is...it's...does this mean she is no longer a lesbian? Roger and Helen gravitated toward each other. They stood before one another. They seemed entranced. They were either searching for the right words or enjoying the silence they shared. Before either spoke two men came between them. Mr. Gallant, the head of security and his right hand man, Mr. Sidekick.

Roger suddenly got a case of the Howling Fantods (*aka:* the Heebie Jeebies, the Willies) because suddenly things got weird. Weirder. At first Roger thought maybe he had gone insane, then he believed that he may have become bi-sexual. He wasn't sure what to think, but he definitely felt that he was the only one seeing what he was seeing. The weirder thing was this, in the eyes of our stories protagonist, Mr. Gallant was also glowing, just as brilliantly as Helen. *It can't be love. I know I'm not in love with Gallant. I mean he seems like a nice guy but-*

Mr. Sidekick, as he so often did, took control of the situation. "Hello, Roger. Is everything okay? is there some sort of a problem here?"

Mr. Medium came out of his office with an apologetic tone. "Not really a problem, I just thought Mr. Gatley might need someone to walk him to his car. But I think he's okay now."

Should I say something. How is nobody else seeing this? Maybe there is a radiation leak in the building. Roger noticed Gallant and Lovely making googly eyes at each other. *Maybe it's the two of them in love? But why am I seeing it? What am I, like freaking cupid or something?*

"Let's take a walk, Mr. Gatley," Sidekick did his best Barney Fife imitation.

"I think he is calmed down now," Mr. Medium surmised. "Aren't you Roger?"

"He just came out of Medium's office?" Gallant directed his question to Helen, indicating Mediums office with his left pointer finger.

Helen nodded her head confirming Gallant's assumption.

Are they superheroes? Am I a superhero? Is this my plot twist?

"I'm sure Mr. Gatley can leave on his own." It was very apparent Mr. Medium now felt very bad for having called Security.

"Was he like that when he went in there?" Gallant asked Helen.

Helen shook her head indicating negative.

Aliens? They must be aliens. And only I can see them. This must be my plot twist! Just like in The Gift. Now everything is going to be different. Wow, I sure did not see that coming.

Sidekick placed his hand on Rogers shoulder. "I'll make sure he gets out okay."

"I got this one, Mr. Sidekick." Mr. Gallant pulled rank on his underling and replaced him in escorting Roger by his left arm down the hallway.

"I really don't think that's necessary," Mr. Medium insisted standing next to the dejected Mr. Sidekick.

"I'll go with you." Helen sprinted forward and took hold of Roger's right arm and off they went.

Roger Gatley, our fifty-year-old birthday boy, walked down the hallway and on to a crowded elevator at the Chicago Vicious Corp headquarters for the last time, with a glimmering Human Being attached to each of his arms. Nobody spoke. Although puzzled and confused he was worry free and at complete peace with himself.

The elevator doors opened at the Vicious Corp lobby and things became even weirder still. Roger saw another glowing person in the lobby and another walking by outside the building on the crowded street. They were both strangers to Roger, but both seemed to be smiling in his direction. "Do you want to do it? Or shall I?" Gallant asked Helen.

"No. No. Absolutely I would love to be the one to do it."

As Gallant released Roger's left arm, Helen pulled his right and led him toward the front doors. "Helen," Roger finally spoke, "I have to tell you something."

"Oh no, Roger, I have something to tell you."

And as they exited the building who should they run into but Mr. Sensational. And he was glowing brighter than sunshine. He smiled a radiant smile and patted Roger's left shoulder with great gusto. "Roger, you ole sonuvabitch, I'm so happy for you." And Roger felt none of the usual resentment he harbored for Sensational as Lovely continued to gleefully lead him to his car. *Am I dead? Are we all dead?* When the two of them reached the back of Roger's car, he felt that Helen's smile had delivered him the message that it was now okay to talk, so he said the very first thing that you would naturally think he would say. "Helen, you're glowing."

"I know, Roger," Helen said excitedly.

"And so is Sensational and Gallant-"

"I know, Roger, I know."

"And that guy over there getting in his car."

"I know."

"He's waving to us."

"Wave back Roger. Be polite," Helen said as she waved to the glowing stranger. Roger waved.

"But what? But why?"

"Roger, you're glowing, too."

Roger looked at his hands and yes, he, too, was glowing, not as brightly as the other illuminated people, but definitely glowing.

"Don't worry, Roger. In a few hours you will glimmer as bright as the rest of us," Helen assured Roger.

"Can everyone see it?"

"Only the illuminated can see the illuminated. But Roger you already knew that. Didn't you?"

Roger became hopeful. "Does this mean we can be together?"

"Roger I told you I am in a committed relationship. My girlfriend is not illuminated, but she still makes me happy. I love her. You and I, Roger, we are friends. Really good friends. And now we have something really, really great in common. But don't worry, Roger, you will meet someone. If that's what you want to do. From now on you'll do whatever you want to do."

Roger was both surprised and impressed with himself that Helen's words were not upsetting to him in the least. His second romantic rejection by Helen was far easier than the first. "Does your girlfriend know?"

"Roger, you already know only illuminated people can know about illuminated people."

She was right, Roger did already know. But he didn't know how he knew. "What is this, though? I mean, what are we? Are we saved? Is this a Jesus thing, because I'm not really very religious?"

"I guess you can say we are saved, but not by Jesus. Roger, you saved yourself, just like I saved myself."

Roger was still confused, but not at all aggravated or frustrated. Things were beginning to become more and more clear. "Does everybody get saved?"

For the first time since Roger beheld the glowing Helen Lovely her joyful expression took on a look of disappointment. "I'm afraid not. Everybody has the ability to illuminate or *save* themselves, but only a small percentage of us do." Helen looked into Roger's eyes, her expression turning back into one of happiness and enthusiasm. "Roger, don't you get it? Can't you feel it? You are one of us now. From now on everything is going to be better. Food will taste better, the air will be fresher, the sun will caress your skin like never before, you'll laugh harder, you'll love stronger, you'll sleep sounder, you'll think clearer. I'm so happy to be the one to get to welcome you."

"I feel it, Helen. I really and truly feel it. And I do love this feeling, I love it so much, I just don't... I'm not sure, I don't know what exactly it is that I'm feeling?"

"Roger, you're not afraid anymore."

THE UNCREDIBLE
SHRINKING MAN

DO YOU MIND if I tell you something about your own self? I mean, it's not a for sure fact or anything like that. It's just based on conjecture. I like that word. Conjecture. It's a smart sounding word. I mean, it makes you feel smart when you say it. Conjecture, do you know what it means? It's when you form an opinion without sufficient evidence for proof. I taught my own self that word. I try to learn a new word every day. I'm getting real good at remembering them, too. Do you want to know what today's word is? It's lugubrious. I really sound smart saying that one. It means to look or sound dismal. So, is it okay if I tell you my conjecture?

You look like the real curious type. Shoot, I know that sounds like a silly thing to say. I mean sure, everyone out here is curious. That's why they're out here. Who wouldn't be? With all the police cars and ambulances. Not exactly sure why the fire trucks are here. I mean there ain't no fire. There is not a fire. Ain't no, that's what they call a double negative, it makes you sound stupid. I don't want to sound stupid. I spent a lot of years sounding stupid. But you don't look curious in the same way the rest of them do. Bank robbers, hostages, dead bodies. That's plenty enough to pique anyone's interest, but I can tell by your face that you want to know the whole story.

I see the way you're looking at me wondering what makes me so idiosyncratic. That means special, like unique. Not like retarded. Lots of people used to refer to me as retarded, but I never really was. My own Mama would tell me I was just a little slow. I never much agreed with that, because I could do reading and writing and even math just as good as any of the other kids. It just took me a little longer. I got a high school education. I didn't finish it at the high school though, on account of some things happened. But I finished it at home. My own Mama became my own teacher, too. And after she was done teaching me, I went right ahead and started teaching my own self.

Never stop learning. Right? That's what my Uncle Rory would always say. Never stop learning. So look at me now, sitting on the back of this ambulance with a blanket wrapped around my shoulders, people all fussing over me. I don't know why they gave me a blanket. I wasn't cold or nothing. Or anything. Sorry, double negative again. I guess I'm talking a little nervous like. And now they went to get me coffee. I don't even drink coffee, but when the paramedic lady asked I felt like I would be rude if I said no.

Why don't you come on over and sit next to me and I'll tell you the whole story? Don't worry about that yellow tape. That's the police line, just slip right underneath it. They won't mind. I'll tell them that you are my special guest.

You worry too much. I used to worry a lot. Worry, worry, worry. I would be worried and nervous all the time. My own Daddy, when he would be around, he would tell me, breathe, Angus. Relax and breathe. Nothing's going to be okay. Bad things are always gonna happen. You might as well be relaxed when they do. That's what he said. That's what he said. He would always said stuff like that. But you don't have to worry, on account I can tell you a secret? It's gonna be kind of hard to believe, but do you wanna know what? I'll tell you what. I can stop time. Swear to Pete. Don't believe me? I can prove it. I'll stop everything right now. Freeze the world. 'Cept for me and you. And then you could slip under that police line and come sit here next to me and I'll tell you the whole story...

My name is Angus Wig and it is a pleasure to meet you, although I wish the circumstances were not so harrowing. That means extremely disturbing and distressing. I was held hostage at gun point earlier today. Right there in that bank. I have a safety deposit box in that bank. I'm almost forty years old. I don't live here in the city. I have my own place in the suburbs. It's not far. You can take a bus and then just walk a few blocks. I only lived there for a couple of years. Before that I stayed in the basement at my Aunt Glads'. Glads is not her real name. Her real name is Gladys but everyone calls her Glads. I don't know why on account she doesn't ever seem very glad. I suppose she just doesn't like to use the letter y in her name.

I lived in her basement for thirteen years, but I never did like it very much. She let me live there on account I was her sister's kid and she is a good Catholic Christian lady. My own Mama used to be a good Catholic Christian lady. I lived in my own Mama's house for twenty-four years. I liked it there. Most of the time. We lived farther than the suburbs. But not in the country. My own Daddy would say we was too city slicker to be hill-billies and too hillbilly to be city slickers. That's what he said. That's what he said. He would always said stuff like that.

It's nice to have my own place. I like it a lot. At first I didn't. I was a little lonely and a little scared. But then my cousin Chip started visiting me. He is my Aunt Glad's son. He never did visit me when I lived in his basement. I don't think he cared for me much then. But then when I lost all my weight he took a big interest in me. Aunt Glads and Uncle George took much more of a liking to me also after I moved out and lost all my weight. Maybe they had different plans for their basement and I was messin' it up on them. Can I tell you another secret? I really and truly didn't even lose any weight. Nope. I just pretended to. Swear to Pete. I think another reason they all started taking a liking to me was because I didn't see Uncle Rory any more on account of him being dead and all.

That makes me sad. Uncle Rory was the best friend I ever had. Really and truly the only friend I ever had. Except if you count Macondo. Uncle Rory was from my Gramma's second marriage. That's Gramma Carson. She's the Gramma on my own Mama's side. I never met my Gramma and Grandpa Wig from my own Daddy's side. I'm not even for sure they ever existed. Aunt Glads would always say my own Daddy wasn't even ever born. That he crawled out from under a rock. I know that's silly and untrue, but I've done research on my own Daddy's genealogy and could not find a single thing. He is his family tree. Uncle George says he's a flimflam man and Connor Wig is probably not even his real name.

Anyway, Gramma Carson and my first Grandpa Carson had my own Mama and Aunt Glads and they were all good Catholic Christian people. Then first Grandpa Carson done died. So Gramma Carson was a widow for ten years and then she married my first Grampa Carson's cousin, my second Grandpa Carson. And they made two more babies, my Uncle Rory and my Aunt Bessie. They were Catholic Christians too. When Uncle Rory and Aunt Bessie were teenagers both Gramma and second Grampa Carson died. My own Daddy would say that's all them Carsons is good at, dying. He might be right because twelve years later is when my own Mama died. That's when I had to move in with my Aunt Glads.

I was already born and alive when my Uncle Rory and Aunt Bessie moved in. I was ten years old. They was nineteen and seventeen. My own Daddy was sure surprised when he came home and they was living with us. He was kind of a part time Daddy. Sometimes he was there, most of the time he was not. Most of the time he was nice. I liked him. And I think he sort of liked me. Most of the time. Him and Uncle Rory are the only men that ever liked me. Oh, and Macondo, I guess. Although he probably really doesn't count. And like I said cousin Chip and Uncle George have been taking a real liking to me. But that might be kind of on account of a little trick I'm playing on them. The one about losing weight and all. I guess none of that matters now though. Does it?

My own Mama was pretty sad that her own Mama and second Daddy had died, but she really liked having her own baby sister and baby brother around. Uncle Rory liked it best because he said he finally felt safe. Safe enough to share some secrets he had been hiding. Aunt Bessie ended up liking it at our house too, but her reason for liking staying with us turned out to be pretty awful. I still don't really understand it too much. Even though Uncle Rory tried to explain it to me a few times. But only on red wine nights. That's when he was the hardest to understand, but it was also the only time he would talk about it.

Aunt Glads was mad at my own Mama because she said my own Mama went against Gramma and Second Grandpa Carson's wishes and was only interested in their money and even though she took her brother and sister in she was not being a good Catholic Christian lady on account of Uncle Rory's secrets that he told right out loud to everyone.

Oh shoot. I'm sorry. I do this sort of thing all the time. I get to talkin' and forget all about the reason I started talkin' in the first place. The bank robbery. That's what you want to hear about. How four people ended up dead. Here I am talkin' about Uncle Rory's secrets. Which I guess is sort of related. My own Daddy would always say everything and everybody is related. I don't know about that one for sure, but I figure he was probably right. He usually was. I was thinking about my own Daddy a lot today. On the bus ride to the bank I was thinking about how he would always say he didn't trust any banks and that cash is king. That I do know about. That's why I don't have any credit cards or debit cards or checking accounts or savings accounts. I keep all my cash in safety deposit boxes at all different banks. Stay off the grid, son. He used to say that, too. I would say okay, even though at the time I didn't even know what the grid was. I found out all about it a few years ago. It's one of the things I taught my own self. It didn't matter at the time on account I didn't have any money. Once I got money, though, I went right off the grid. A state I.D., that's all I got.

See, I knew you was the curious type. Sure, I'll tell you Uncle Rory's secrets. Before he lived with us, when he was being raised by Gramma Carson and second Grandpa Carson he went to Catholic Schools on account of being a Catholic Christian and all. Well, there was this priest there, Father Maylay, and all while my Uncle Rory was growing up Father Maylay would diddle him. When my Uncle Rory told my own Mama, she said he had to tell everyone, even the police.

At the time, I did not know what diddle meant. It sure didn't sound all that bad, so I was very confused. A lot of people at the church got mad at my own Mama and Uncle Rory. Even Aunt Glads and Uncle George got mad at them. They said Uncle Rory was a liar and had an active imagination. Their accusations against my uncle seemed mendacious when five other boys said they were also diddled. Mendacious means false.

The TV news came to our house. My own Mama wouldn't let us go on the TV. Aunt Glads and a lot of people at church stayed mad at us. Father Maylay went away. A few years later my own Daddy researched it and found out they sent him to another church on the east coast, he said to get a fresh crop of boys to diddle. That's what my own Daddy said. That's what he said. That's when my own Mama did talk to the news and to some lawyers and that's when we stopped being Catholic Christians and Uncle Rory told his other secret.

Uncle Rory told us all he was a homosexual. I didn't know what that was at the time but I knew I liked Uncle Rory and he liked me so I really didn't care much about it, but my own Mama was very upset. She said all that diddling is what made Uncle Rory turn into a homosexual. My own Daddy said that was nonsense and that people were whatever they were. I don't think she believed it was because of the diddling for very long, because after a few months, when my own Daddy left again, she said she didn't believe in anything anymore. Uncle Rory stayed with us on and off for many years. Mama said he could never bring his friends over. He became my best friend. My only friend. I hate that word...diddle.

When I lived with Aunt Glads I had to sneak to visit Uncle Rory. I met his special friend Dennis a few times. Before Dennis got sick. Real sick. That made Uncle Rory so sad. It makes me sad, too, when I think about it...The things that Uncle Rory wrongly believed were his dreams began to come true, at the same time his real dream was dying...

Have you ever been in a safety deposit room? It is a little private room. There is nothing in it but a table and it is surrounded by three walls of safety deposit boxes. I had just emptied my box. I put the last of the cash in my money belt when I heard the gun shots. I walked out slowly. I heard a commotion that made me palpitate. That means I was trembling.

I saw Mr. Wallace lying on the ground. He had lots of blood coming out through his clothes. His eyes was opened but I don't think he seen anything anymore on account he wasn't moving. Just staring straight up at the ceiling. I liked Mr. Wallace. Mr. Wallace was a black man who used to be a black police man, who got too old to be a black policeman, so he became a black security guard. He used to always tease me about Jane. Jane works at the bank and I always would wait for Jane to take care of me. Mr. Wallace would say it was on account I was sweet on her. I really was not. I mean she was nice to me, but she wasn't always. I knew Jane for a very long time. I went to school with her. I didn't see her for many years, but when I did, it was after I had my own house in the suburbs. She said she was sorry for when she used to be mean to me and wanted to be my friend. I wish she would've wanted to be my friend back in school. Shoot, I wish anyone would've wanted to be my friend back in school, I mean besides Macondo. And Uncle Rory.

Mr. Wallace didn't have it all wrong. I guess I was sweet on Jane when I was a kid. A long, long time ago. Before she fell in with Bryce and Culver. She just let the wrong people lead her. My own Daddy would always say, Angus, now before you let someone lead you, you best make sure they is headed for somewhere you want to go. That's what he said. He would always said stuff like that. He always felt bad for me that I didn't have no friends. Have any friends. Those double negatives are a tricky thing to avoid. He never liked Macondo. I'm not sure if my own Daddy ever really liked me the same as Uncle Rory liked me. I mean he was mostly nice to me 'cept for a couple of times when he would be mean to me. And most times he would be living somewhere else.

Anyhow, Aunt Glads always said he crawled back under the rock he came out from. I liked him, though. I guess if someone doesn't really like you all that much the next best thing is if they feel bad for you. I think that's why Jane wants to be my friend now. Cause she feels bad for me, or maybe just bad for herself. My own Daddy never called me slow like my own Mama did. No, no, he always said I was simple. I like simple. If you look simple up in the Oxford English Dictionary, that's the OED, a lot of scholarly type people call it the OED. That is where I get all my words from. Anyhow, in the OED, the definition of simple tells more about what it ain't than what it is. Not complicated, not difficult, not complex, not artificial. That sounds pretty good, right? Most people prefer simple. They like simple. 'Cept for when it comes to me. When it comes to me, people must prefer difficult. My Uncle Rory used to always say this here world makes it very difficult to be a homosexual and that didn't surprise me. Not one bit. On account this world even makes it difficult to be simple.

There was yelling and crying and cussin'. Everyone was on the other side of the bank 'cept for me and poor old Mr. Wallace. I reckon I really don't know where Mr. Wallace was. It's for pretty sure he wasn't in his body anymore. If he was a Catholic Christian, he was probably on his way to heaven. My own Daddy says we all go to heaven. Not Mama, she says we have to go to purgatory first on account of not being Catholic Christians anymore and being so nice to a homosexual. She says that's okay though, cause it won't be so bad and it would be worth it to have Uncle Rory in our lives.

Aunt Glads says Uncle Rory won't ever be welcome in heaven. I think she is wrong. Even though she is a lot older than me I don't think she is all that smart. She is always using double negatives. I had a real smart sounding good word to describe what was happening in the bank, but I cannot remember it. Oh shoot. Anyhow, there was a bad guy with a gun. He was doing most of the yelling and cursin'. He didn't see me. He was turned around makin' all the workers and customers sit on the floor. He was trying to make them be quiet. He didn't want any talking or crying or sobbing. I think he thought that the louder he got the quieter they would get. It wasn't working yet. Then I noticed Mr. Wallace's gun on the ground about ten feet away from him. So from me it would be about ten feet plus the width of Mr. Wallace's empty body, on account I was now standing right next to him. So yeah, I'd say twelve feet. I've always been pretty good at judging distances. And do you wanna know what? I'm a pretty good shooter too. My own Daddy taught me. I never owned no gun. I mean a gun. But my own Daddy had quite a few over the years.

After…Well after…Something really bad happened to me. My own Daddy said I had to learn to shoot to protect myself from the bad people in the world. He said, Angus Wig, if anyone ever tries to do me or my own Mama physical harm again, I have to shoot 'em until they're dead. That way they won't ever try to hurt us again. And that the world would be a better place without them in it. He would say, now son, if that's a sin, then I say let's commit it. That's what he said. That's what he said. He would always said stuff like that.

I never liked shootin' a gun, even though I got pretty good at it. We would shoot targets and cans and stuff. I ain't never shot any living being. Never ever. But my own Daddy's words were sure going through my head when I was staring at Mr. Wallace's Glock Single Stack 9 mm pistol. My own Daddy would always say he was the most prejudice man on the planet. But he didn't care none about your color or religion or country or even what kind of a sexual you was. No sir. My own Daddy said he saved up all his hatred for one group of people. Bullies. Oh boy, he hated bullies. Intimidators, oppressors, harassers, ain't no room for none of them in my world. That's a triple negative, but that's what he said. That's what he said. My Own Daddy was real prejudice against bullies. The man with his back to me sure seemed like a bully to me.

Tumultuous! That's the word I was trying to think of. The scene at the bank was tumultuous.

Bryce McNulty and Culver Richardson. Those were the two biggest bullies at my school. Shoot, I had a lot of bullies in my childhood. Mean and merciless. That's what most of my peers were to me. Mean and merciless. I always felt a little odd and different. As long as I can remember. Maybe on account of being slow and simple and ugly. Being pudgy didn't help much either. Uncle George said I got a face only a mother could love. When I was in the third grade, long before Culver Richardson came into my life, back when I was sort of sweet on Jane Brooks, the most beautiful girl in school, that's when my first big mistake happened.

I know I talked too loud and acted too young, but Miss Gack could have just let me go to the bathroom. That's when most of the children switched from ignoring and avoiding me to teasing and picking on me. Meanness is just like anger and cancer, if left untreated it will grow and grow. And Bryce McNulty was the number one gardener of meanness at my school, at least until Culver came along.

I didn't do well at school on account of all the distractions. Plus taking longer to learn things in the first place. My pants was always being pulled down, or parts of me would be crazy glued to other parts of me, or I would be made to eat something disgusting, or my head would be stuck in the toilet, or what have you. No sir, school was not a good place for me. I always dreamed about just being lonely. I know that sounds peculiar because most people hate the idea of being lonely, but when my own Mama pulled me out of high school my dream came true. I became mostly lonely. 'Cept for Uncle Rory, my own Mama and once in a while my own Daddy, I was all alone. And it was wonderful. Now I really am all alone. It makes me sad every now and again, but I'd rather be lonely and safe than abused and tormented.

Anyhow, there was a man with a nylon stocking pulled down over his head tormenting a bunch of strangers. Now these strangers were not kind and talkative to me like Mr. Wallace used to be. And they weren't the kind of strangers that wanted to be my friend because they felt sorry for me like Jane Brooks. No, these were strangers that went out of their way to avoid and ignore me: the odd-looking fellow who just didn't fit in with the rest of the world. Anyhow, there was the Glock, just twelve feet away from me. I could shoot that man dead in the back before he even knew I existed. I would be a celebrated murderer. A hero. Loved and appreciated. Comfort and notice, that is what I would receive for the rest of my life. There had got to be twenty people in here. Twenty normal people. Normal looking. Normal thinking. And they would all owe me their lives. That's what I was thinking. But then I realized it was too late.

I got a lot better at learning things once my own Mama pulled me out of school. Now don't get me wrong, I still passed most of my classes while I was in school, it was just a very difficult learning environment. Every day there was a gauntlet that had to be run before and after any academics. Sometimes even during. And at home my own Mama would help me a lot with learning. So would my Uncle Rory from time to time. Not Aunt Bessie. She was never much good at book learning. She never even high school graduated. My own Mama said she had the looks that she could get away with that.

My own Daddy, he knew a lot a lot of stuff. But he always said he knew the kind of stuff they didn't teach at school. And I don't just mean stuff you learn on the streets, although he was plenty street smart. No, no. He knew things about history and such that I have never heard anyone else say. Did you know that Abraham Lincoln was secretly a homosexual, just like Uncle Rory? And that President William Howard Taft, the twenty-seventh president of the United States of America, used to eat seven whole chickens for dinner and had two toilets side by side in the oval bathroom, because one of them would inevitably be clogged.

President Woodrow Wilson, the twenty-eighth President of the United States, had the second toilet removed and replaced with a fine oak magazine rack where he would always have copies of National Geographic, Scientific America, The Atlantic, and Woman's Weekly. He was the first known sitting president to read while taking a dump.

Although my own Daddy has his suspicions about Theodore Roosevelt, the twenty-sixth president of the United States of America. He always knew all kinds of stuff like that. Once, while I was doing a school report on George Washington Carver, he told me the only thing to match George Washington Carver's love for the peanut was his disdain for the cashew. That's what he said. That's what he said. He would always said stuff like that.

I guess the thing I liked the most about my own Daddy was that he always wanted me to be happy. The thing I really didn't care for was that he never really wanted to be part of that happiness. He hated that I couldn't make any friends. It made him sad to think that I was sad. When I told him about my friend Macondo in the second grade it made him very happy. My own Mama never really cared for Macondo too much.

After my bathroom accident in the third grade, me and Macondo became really close. We would spend hours and hours locked up in my room playing, day after day. My own Daddy wasn't around much for a few years. He came back to live with us after second Grandpa Carson died. A house that used to be just me and my own Mama was now full with Uncle Rory, Aunt Bessie and my own daddy. He was really shocked to hear that I was going into the sixth grade and that Macondo was still around and that we was still best of friends. Now if you ain't figured it out yet, I guess you'll be as surprised as my own Daddy was when my own Mama told him Macondo was my imaginary friend. Now in my defense, Macondo was my only friend in the whole wide world so I sure wasn't going to get particular with what type of a person he was. I was just happy to have someone to play with. To be with. To not make fun of me, to not abuse me, to not hurt me.

Where the fuck did you come from!? Put your goddamn hands over your fucking head before I put a bullet in your skull! That's what I heard being screamed at me while I was considering the Glock. I had no idea there was a second man with a gun and nylon stocking mask. That's because he was out of my sight tending to the third nylon masked gunman. *What the fuck! Get over here with the rest of em',* the first gunman hollered at me. I acquiesced. That means to comply without protest.

He's dead! Harold is fucking dead! That goddamn security guard killed him, he kept right on shouting. I took my place among the normal people that I had hoped to save. The second gunman pressed his gun hard onto Mr. Foster's forehead and asked why he didn't tell them there was a second guard. Mr. Foster was the not black security guard. He didn't have his gun. Not anymore.

The first gunman backed toward Mr. Wallace. He nudged his dead body with his foot. He had two guns. A small .38 revolver and a .44 magnum. Just like Dirty Harry. He emptied the .38. Let the bullets hit the bank's hard marble floor and then threw the gun over the teller stations. Mr. Foster's, I'm figuring. Then he did the same with Mr. Wallace's Glock, including the one in the chamber. Then he started kicking poor dead old Mr. Wallace yelling *Fuck! Fuck! Fuck! I got to think! I got to think!* Mr. Foster was crying, saying, *I didn't know. I swear I thought he was gone. He got off a half hour ago.*

The second gun man now was panning us all with a gun in each hand, a Beretta 92 and a Glock 22. I figured one was his and one was his dead friend Harold's. He was plenty pissed and I was plenty scared.

Any more surprises and I start pulling the trigger and ain't no one getting out of here alive. That's what he said. That's what he said. I sure wasn't going to point out his double negative, although I did notice it. That's when I heard the sirens.

My own Daddy said he did not want to hear any more talk about Macondo. Ever. And then he got me a puppy dog to be my friend. A cute little baby pit bull. Although she wasn't really all that little or cute and my own Mama said she looked a little bit north of being a puppy. Her name was Care. My own Daddy named her that on account she was going to grow up strong and take care of me and my own Mama all the times when my own Daddy wasn't around. This was before he had the whole gun idea. And before Care stopped liking me.

At first things were pretty good. Care was a little skittish which was fine with me, but made my own Mama wonder where Daddy got her from. And Macondo, well he just stopped coming around. My time was pretty full, what with Care and now Uncle Rory and Aunt Bessie. Then one day Care just stopped liking me. She went right ahead and bit me. Pretty bad. I had to get some stitches. I guess I was too simple for her, too. I wonder if my own Mama is still in purgatory?

The sirens really made the nylon men angry and upset which made the rest of us even more scared and nervous than we already were. One man actually spoke up and said, *please sir, my wife, she is with child, please let her go.* The nylon men didn't seem to care at all about that. But I thought right away, shoot, that's another life I could have saved if I would have acted instead of considered when I saw Mr. Wallace's gun. I equivocated. That's a good word, isn't it? I could have saved a life that hadn't even started yet. Depending on when you believe life begins. I know Catholic Christians believe it starts at conception. You know my own Daddy's very last words to me was, son, some people say life begins at conception, I say life begins at fifty. Then he was gone. He still ain't come back. I guess there ain't nothin' to come back to anymore, what with our house knocked down and Uncle Rory and my own Mama gone...

My own Daddy was never a Catholic Christian. Not for real at least. He pretended, he said for a little while.

Isn't anything.

There isn't anything to come back to anymore. Oh shoot, double negatives are sneaky sometimes.

My Own Daddy used to say I am not smart enough to not believe in God, but I am absolutely smart enough to not believe in religion. That's what he said. He hated religion. All religion, not just Catholic Christian. He said the invention of religion is man's greatest excuse. He would always said stuff like that.

I wonder how long that man and woman with the unalive baby have been married?

My own Daddy had some idiosyncratic ideas about marriage. You remember what idiosyncratic means, right? My own Daddy said marriage should come with a five-year contract. At the end of the five years you could sign on for another five or renegotiate or just take your talents elsewhere. Back when my own Mama was still a Catholic Christian and still believed in God and stuff, she would get real mad and say that God didn't want it that way. That God wanted you to be married forever. And then my own Daddy would say that's cus God ain't got no wife and then he'd laugh like a son of a bitch. That's what he would always say after someone did something really well – that they did it like a son of a bitch. Ain't got no wife – he would always use double negatives. They never bothered him.

You shut your fuckin' mouth right now or I'll blow you away and your bitch wife! Your goddamned baby doesn't mean shit to me! You all listen real good. I ain't going back to jail and if I don't get out of here alive none of you are! That's what he said. That's what he said. That's what the nylon man said. There were lots of sirens and lots of flashing lights and I could see two dead bodies on the bank floor. Poor ol' Mr. Wallace and Harold, the third nyloned man.

I started getting that really bad feeling again. My insides were all shaking, my throat wouldn't let any air come in or out, my head was all dizzy and my sweat was burning hot. I hated this feeling. I never thought I would have it again. It wasn't the sight of the dead bodies that was giving me my terrible old feeling. It was something else. Some real bad memories were starting to wake up inside me. And then what the nylon man did next nearly stopped my heart dead.

Back when I still went to high school, Culver Richardson would always make me feel that terrible way. What a...What a...Just, such a bad, bad Human Being. I mean, I always got teased and picked on and even abused from time to time. My bathroom accident in the third grade sure made things worse. Do you wanna know what? That was not my only accident either. No, I had a few more. Number ones and twos. It was on account of how nervous and scared I would get. Thank God for Macondo. I would have never made it through without him. I mean I know he wasn't real. Right? Just pretend. But it didn't matter because he would ease my mind.

But anyway, in high school things really escalated. Terrible things. Bryce McNullty and his girlfriend Cara, they were the worst. Always making my life sad and lonely and always embarrassing me. What made it worse was that Bryce became a big football star in high school. Everyone loved him. Everybody. Teachers, parents, everyone but me. I hated him.

Jane Brooks, the girl from the bank and Cara was best friends. I hated Cara too. But back then I didn't much hate Jane. I'm not sure why not. Was that a double negative? Then at the end of sophomore year, Culver Richardson came to our school. He was a great football player, too. That boy was pernicious. That means wicked. Evil. I don't even feel smart when I say that word. It just makes me feel sick.

Things really got worse when Culver and Bryce became best friends. Now when I got farted on in the bathroom stall, I got pissed on, too. Now when I got pantsed, my pants got set on fire, too. Now when my head got shoved in the toilet, Culver would take a dump in it first. Even when I would snitch, not too much would happen, on account now we had the two best high school football players in the whole state.

Culver gave me a new name. Anus Wad, instead of Angus Wig. Sometimes bullies just get allowed to be bullies. It's true. It's true. Especially football stars, and priests too, I guess. Every few years my own Daddy would tell us what new church Father Malay was sent to for a new batch of little boys to diddle. I wish they would of sent Culver and Bryce to a new school. Let it be someone else's turn. I know that sounds mean and terrible. But I just…Well…Shoot, I don't even know.

I remember my last day of high school. A nice sunny day at the end of junior year. School was almost going to be out for summer vacation. I didn't even know it yet, that it was my last day of ever going to school. Culver and Bryce was so busy being everybody's hero that they was abusing me a little less than they was during the football season. Maybe it was because they won our school the championship. Everyone was so happy about that. The championship. I didn't much get it. At first I thought everyone in the school was gonna get a prize or something. Even the teachers and parents, because everyone was sure happy about it. The championship that is. But nope, no one got nothing 'cept for one big trophy at the school and Bryce and Culver got real bright futures. I'm sorry, no one got anything. They said all sorts of college universities were fighting to get them to go to their school and get them a championship trophy, too. I guess.

This is nice. I really like talking to you. You are a real good listener. Don't worry about the time being stopped. I promise it won't hurt anyone. They won't even realize it happened. I won't keep it stopped too much longer. Just until I finish telling you about the bank robbery. But first I got to tell you this one more story. You know who you listen like? You listen just like Macondo used to. I bet you already knew I was going to say that, didn't you?

Uncle Rory didn't pick me up from school that day. He felt real bad about it. Sometimes those guys would pick on my Uncle Rory, too. They would yell fag and cocksucker and there goes Anus Wad, into the homo mobile. Sometimes they would throw stuff at his car, too. Soda pops, or food, like nachos or eggs or this one time a bologna sandwich. Once Culver threw a cat at Uncle Rory's car. I swear to Pete. I swear to Pete. He yelled, here try some pussy you fuckin' homo.

After it hit the hood that cat jumped off the car and ran away, but it ran real funny like. It was hurt. Uncle Rory felt real bad for that cat. Later that night he said he wanted to run Culver right over with his car. I wished he would have, but I'm real glad he didn't. If that makes any sense, on account of Uncle Rory would have had to go to jail on account of he ain't real good a football player. Or a Catholic Christian Preist.

Anyhow, Culver had one of them dirt bike motorcycles. He was sittin' on it talkin' with Bryce and Cara and Jane. Yeah, Jane was there too. Her and Culver had become like boyfriend and girlfriend. That was a real shame. Anyhow, Culver started talkin' real nice to me like, hey Anus where's your fag uncle? Did he forget about you today? Do you want me to give you a ride home? He was trying to sound all sincere. I said no thank you and that I would walk and he said he had to ask me a question first. How would you like to be on the football team next year? That's what he asked. And everyone laughed like a son of a bitch. I'm serious, Culver said, like just for a couple of plays. He said it would be a real hoot.

I had that feeling. Just like I did in the bank. I always had that feeling when Culver was talking nice, because I knew something bad was coming next. He was insidious. Insidious is when someone pretends to be nice, friendly like, maybe even enticing, but really they are just looking to entrap you. To harm you. To destroy you. Just like Father Maylay. Insidious. That word makes me feel sick, too. But first we got to work on your speed, he says. How fast can you run, Anus? I don't want you to be embarrassed at tryouts.

They tied up my hands with a rope and then tied the other end of the rope to Culver's dirt bike motorcycle. Now you try to keep up, Anus, he yelled. I really tried keeping up. I tried my hardest. Once I fell on the ground it hurt so bad. I got my wrist broken and my shoulder separated. I heard Culver laughing and hootin' and hollering. I know I heard Bryce and Cara living it up, too. But I saw Jane's face and she wasn't laughing. Maybe that's why I didn't hate her. The police got involved and everything. They didn't have to go to jail or anything.

Afterward I remember one of the police saying the same thing the football coach and principal would always say, boys will be boys. In the end both Bryce and Culver had to miss the first three football games of the next season, on account they was both suspended. Lots of people were really sore at me for that. People would throw stuff at our house and graffiti our garage.

My own Mama said no more school for you. That's when I started home learning. Me and Uncle Rory became even better friends. My own Daddy was on one of his sabbaticals. He was gone for a couple years. My own Mama and Aunt Bessie didn't think he was ever coming back. He did though. Do you wanna know what? While I was recovering from my injuries, Macondo came back, too. I mean not for real, but for real. It was nice to talk to him again. He looked a little different. A little older, but I was sure happy to see him. Even though I know I really didn't. He only was around for a few weeks. Then he just up and left, just like my own Daddy would always do.

A couple of times my own Mama almost caught me talking to him. Who are you talking to, Angus, she asked. I said I was talking to Care. That was fine with her. That's kind of weird if you ask me. What's more weird to you, talking to a stupid dog that hates you or an imaginary friend that loves you? They didn't go to the championship on account they lost the first three games without Bryce and Culver.

Anyhow, one day I was in my yard. It was the beginning of springtime. All of the sudden Jane Brooks was standing by my back gate. Care started barkin' like a son of a bitch. That scared Jane, but Care was in her dog run. She was locked in there. She was always locked in there on account of a couple months earlier is when she bit me. Care did. Not Jane Brooks. My own Mama said that's an outside dog from now on. That damn dog, shoot, she bit my wrist right after I was all done recuperating and healing. That really upset me.

Anyhow, Jane asked right away if my bandage was because of what they did to me with the dirt bike. Nope, that's something else I said over the barking and barking and barking. Then Jane asked if we could go for a walk. A walk, with me. Can you imagine that? I figured she must have felt very bad for what had happened.

I loved that walk. It was the greatest walk of my life. We didn't even talk all that much. We just walked and walked. She asked me why I didn't go to school anymore. I just said because of my own Mama. I don't know why I didn't tell her the truth. How happy I was that I didn't have to go to school anymore and be the victim of Culver and Bryce and their many evil followers. Or how great it was to not have that awful sick feeling I use to always have. I should have asked her why she liked them? Why she was with them? Why a lot of things? I guess I just wanted to be happy. To be with Jane. To have a small part of a dream come true. In a childhood of nightmares, a dream is the pot of gold at the end of the rainstorm. It felt strange to feel so good. And then our walk ended. It ended in a small clearing, slightly off the path at the Galapagos Forest Preserve, where Culver and Bryce and Cara sat in waiting. Insidious. Ends up Jane Brooks is the most insidious person I've ever met.

That feeling. It invaded my entire body. That's when I found out about the football team didn't win the championship. How I had fucked the high school and even the entire town. They told me I ruined their futures on account some of the universities stopped recruiting them. At first I tried to run but they wrastled me down to the ground and told me how I had to pay for ruining everything. I throwed up on myself. I was so scared. And Jane...Insidious. They stripped off all my clothes and shoved my face in the dirt. This time they wasn't even laughing at me. They was mad, real mad. Culver said this was payback and I should take it like a man and if I told anyone the next time would be much worse. He was holding a hammer, but I didn't think he was gonna hit me with it on account he was holding it by the head, you know, the heavy part. The hitting part. Culver said I fucked them. I totally fucked them. And that now there had to be retribution. That they was gonna fuck me. Culver said but we ain't no fags like your homo uncle so they gonna...They hurt me. They hurt me real bad.

I didn't need to snitch even though I would have, but they already knew who did it when I woke up in the hospital. I had to have surgery on my bowels. I had to shit in a bag for six months. It was connected right to my own intestines. It was awful. I never would have been able to get through it without Uncle Rory helping me so much. Not many people were on their side after that. Not that they was on mine either. I was still Anus Wad.

Years and years later teenagers would occasionally yell that at me. Even when I was living in Aunt Glads basement. But those boys weren't heros anymore. Bryce didn't get in too much trouble on account his family had a little money and he was better at football than Culver. His family moved and he still went to a big university and he even played for the Cincinnati Bengals professional NFL football team for a few years. But not Culver. On account he was a little less good than Bryce at football and his family had no money, Culver went to jail. I heard that even the coach called him a sadistic freak.

I'm sorry 'bout having to tell you all that, but like I said, you look like the real curious type and I really wanted you to understand why I got that terrible, terrible feeling again. I know I could have described it with less details, but I wanted you to feel it. How all my insides were shaking again and my throat was closed up tight. I couldn't even breath. How my head was dizzy and my sweat was burning hot. *I ain't going back to jail,* the nylon man yelled. It wasn't like I was scared I was gonna die, it's more like I wished I could die, I just knew what was coming next was far worse than death. Just like back there at the Galapagos Forest Preserve. *And if I don't get out of here alive none of you are!* That's what he said, just like that. Then he reached his hand around under his neck and pulled off his nylon mask and it all made sense to me. Why that feeling had come back to me. *Who wants to be first to test me?* he asked as he panned the room. He looked right at me and as sure as I am Angus Wig that nylon unmasked bank robber and killer was Culver Richardson. I'm telling you my heart nearly stopped.

You wanna know what else? When I was in the hospital after my bowel operation Macondo would visit me. He was different than he used to be. Even different from earlier that summer. I could tell it was him, though. But here is the weird part, he did most of the talking. It was nice on account I really was not in the talking mood. But I was fine for listening. He would tell me a lot of stuff my own Daddy used to say. Like one thing was if someone called you ugly, that don't mean nothing...anything. 'Cept maybe that the person calling you ugly is angry and mean. But if enough people call you ugly and they all do it all the time, eventually you will actually become ugly. Because if enough people hear it over and over, again and again, they start to believe it, and if enough people believe it, it becomes the truth.

Not the real honest truth, but another kind of truth. The Perceived Truth. And he said the Perceived Truth is the most powerful weapon on earth on account of so many people base their entire lives on Perceived Truth.

When I was little I told my own Daddy that I just hated myself cause I was nothing but a stupid dumb retart and no one would ever be my friend. That's what I said. That's what I said. That's when he first explained Perceived Truth and he told me that I couldn't believe all those angry mean kids at school. That I had to believe the honest truth. That I wasn't stupid or dumb. I was just simple. And being simple was just a fine way to be.

Well, Macondo, he had a real interesting idea on my own Daddy's idea about the truth. He said why don't I start telling people stuff about my own self. Like I was smart and handsome and people really liked being around me. Macondo told me if I told enough people, that it would become the Perceived Truth. He said C'mon Angus, your own Daddy said it was the most powerful weapon on Earth, why not use it to your own advantage? Our advantage.

At that time I thought Macondo's idea was just plain crazy, but then my own Daddy came home and I started to change my mind.

It took a little while for Culver to recognize me. I guess he did have a lot going on with the police and the hostages and a murdered Mr. Wallace and his partner Harold being all the way dead and his other partner being very upset waving two guns around promising Culver that he would not go back to jail.

I wonder if Mr. Wallace's soul and Harold's soul could see each other? I'm pretty sure they would be headed in different directions. I wonder if Mr. Wallace has to go to purgatory first, before heaven. Oh shoot, I could have gave him a message for my own Mama. He could have told her how good I am doing lately, I mean up until being taken hostage and all. *Anus Wad! You gotta be shitting me. That's you, ain't it? Anus fuckin' Wad.* That's what he said. That's what he said.

You know some people don't believe in heaven or hell or purgatory. No they do not. They believe in reincarnation. Could you just imagine if that were true? Maybe in his previous life Culver was teased and picked on and abused like me and that's why he is so mean now. And maybe in my previous life I was like Culver and now I'm paying the price for my cruelty.

No. No way. Impossible. Even in a thousand life times I could never be like Culver Richardson.

I know I seem pretty relaxed and calm now. And I do feel pretty good but I swear to Pete when Culver shouted out my name, well, not really my name, but what he used to call me, I never felt worse in my entire life.

Do you know if reincarnation was a real thing that unborn baby in the bank, well shoot, that could be my own Mama? Or even poor old Mr. Wallace. I just remembered a funny one my own Daddy used to say about reincarnation. He would say I don't believe in reincarnation, but I did in my previous life. That's what he said. Oh my own Daddy, I was sure happy when he came home. It was after I got my colostomy bag off. That's when he told me, son, as soon as you are up to it I'm going to teach you how to shoot. You will never be a victim again. He said that boy Bryce is lucky he moved away and Culver was lucky to be in jail on account of if they was not he would've killed them both, and if that's a sin, then I say let's commit it. Them dirty sick bastards. They will burn in hell. Even the worst is too good for them. To diddle a man's son with a Goddamned hammer! That's what he said. That's what he said. That's how I found out what diddle meant.

I sure do hate that word.

My poor Uncle Rory. And all those other boys the Catholic Christian Church kept giving to that evil Father Maylay. How could they? Why would they? I figure, if you is really good at football or really good at praying you could be as cruel and evil as you want to be. Must be.

A few years before he died, when all the court stuff was going on, I asked my Uncle Rory about it. He said at first Father Maylay was real nice to him and treated him real special. Gave him gifts and everything. He might have been more insidious than Jane.

Anyhow, that's when I started taking Macondo's advice. I told my own Daddy and Uncle Rory and anyone that would listen, how great a shooter I was. Even before I ever fired a single shot. And do you want to know what? It worked. By the end of the first day I was hitting every target my own Daddy would give me. The perceived truth conquered the real truth right before my own eyes. Son, you can shoot like a son of a bitch. That's what he said. That's what he said. Uncle Rory, not so much. He went with us a few times but he was a terrible shot. He would even say, I'm a terrible shot. And the Perceived Truth would win again.

Get over here, Anus! Culver's eyes were deranged. I could feel the heat from his hateful stare burning a hole right through my face. The man with two guns knew all about me. Not the real me, Culver's casuistic version of me. Two Guns starts saying – *No fucking way! This is the guy that cost you your football scholarship! Your career! Your girl! Your life! Fuck, Culver, this is fate! It's Goddamned fate!*

I don't even remember getting up and walking over to Culver, but I remember kneeling down in front of him. I was facing the other hostages. I felt like I was burning up. My insides were shaking. The pregnant lady was crying. Culver was saying something to me but I couldn't understand what. It was all muffled. My ears were clogged with heat. I felt the burn of vomit rushing up my throat. I clenched my teeth and closed my mouth tight to hold it back. I choked, but I kept my mouth shut. Hot puke shot right out of my nose. I swear to Pete. I dropped my head and opened my mouth. Culver grabbed my hair and jerked my head back hard and then I felt the barrel of his .44 magnum pressed to the back of my skull.

Did you know you could barf out your nose? I sure didn't. I guess I never really thought about it. I think I figured it would just go back down to my stomach. Pretty dumb assumption now that I think about it under more favorable circumstances. By the way, casuistic means intellectually dishonest.

Boy, I really like talking to you. You look cold. Are you cold? Here take my blanket.

There, that's better, right?

My own Daddy stayed with us for almost three years that last time. When he taught me to shoot and about guns and all. We went to a lot of shootin' ranges. Everywhere we went he and I would tell the people there that I could shoot like a son of bitch and by the time we left they'd be saying it, too. We would go to a lot of gun shows, too. A gun show ain't really a show, it's just a place where you could buy guns. And sometimes knives and stuff, too. My Own Daddy once bought me a Swiss Comrade Hunting Knife with a strap-on shoulder holster at the Saint Emerald American Gun Show. Anyhow, Macondo sure was right about that Perceived Truth, don't you think? Sure you do. It was kind of strange back then. Macondo would only come around about once a week or so and never at my house. And every time I saw him he would look completely different. And most times he wouldn't even talk to me. He would just look at me. But his looks would sort of have this way of talking to me. They would say, good job, Angus. You're doing a real good job. Sometimes it would take me a little while to even recognize him, but eventually I always did. Maybe it was because he knew my own Daddy didn't care for him.

Don't get me wrong here. I know he is just in my imagination, but I'm just wondering why my imagination did what it did, that's all.

That was a good time in my life. Then right after my twenty-second birthday my own Daddy told me life begins at fifty and I never saw him again.

I don't understand why. And it makes me sad. My own Daddy used to say, Angus, never expect anything from anybody and you'll never be disappointed. That's what he—

Do you want to know the worst part? He didn't even leave alone. He took Aunt Bessie with him. She was pregnant. They ran off together. Aunt Bessie told Uncle Rory she loved my own Daddy. Aunt Glads said my own Daddy had been diddling Bessie for years and years. My own Mama heard her say it and she didn't disagree or anything. I don't get it. How could she fall in love and make a baby with a man that was diddling her? And how could my own Daddy hate Father Maylay and Culver so much when he… I just don't understand.

I'm sorry. I guess I'm still a little shaken up from the whole hostage thing.

So I got a little brother, but I ain't never met him.

Haven't ever met him.

I know a little about him on account of Uncle Rory talked to Aunt Bessie once in a while. I know his name is Fulton Wig and he has a lot of issues. It's sad. He has a lot of physical and mental conditions. They say he is not even capable of communication. I don't know if I believe that. Everyone must be able to communicate in some way or another, don't you think? One time, before I started losing weight and Aunt Glads still didn't like me much, she told me, Angus your half-brother is even worse than you. I guess we found something old Connor Wig is actually pretty good at...making retarts. That's what she said. I don't think I will ever like Aunt Glads, no matter how nice she is to me nowadays.

Later, Uncle Rory also told me my own Daddy left Aunt Bessie and little Fulton when he was just ten years old. Vanished. Just gone. So I guess me and my little brother have at least one thing in common. I'm going to go visit him. But first I'm going to find our own Daddy. I just...

I just...

I don't have any expectations. That's how come I'm never disappointed. But I just want to ask him, why?

I mean Fulton probably wants to know. And just in case he asks I want to have something to tell him.

It probably bothers him a lot. Fulton, that is.

I really thought Macondo would come around a lot after my own Daddy left the last time to start his life at fifty with Aunt Bessie. But he didn't. Not once. Life sure seemed empty. Really empty. Uncle Rory was hardly ever around. My own Mama said he was falling in with a bad crowd and living a reckless life of drugs and alcohol. I guess it was true, because when I asked him he did not deny it. He just told me not to worry. My own Daddy gone. Aunt Bessie gone. Macondo gone. Even Care was gone. She left before any of them. Not that I missed her or nothing after she went and bit me. Or anything. Sorry.

It was back...back to being only me and my own Mama. I spent two years trying to cheer her up. Just one laugh. Just one smile. I never got neither. Then she did what the Carson's was best at. She died. Aunt Glads said she died of a broken heart from that bastard husband. I really don't think she was all that disappointed in him, because I don't think she had any expectations from him. Years and years of past disappointments had extinguished all future expectations. I do agree my own Mama did die from a broken heart, but it was Aunt Bessie that gave it to her. I'm gonna be sure to tell her when I visit my little brother.

Anyhow, while I was kneeling there with Culver's magnum pressed hard against the back of my head, ol' Two Guns started telling Culver to calm down on account he didn't want Culver to shoot me dead. At least not at first. Not that he cared about me or anything. He seemed to be on

Culver's side as far as me deserving to suffer for ruining Culver's life; he was just concerned about the consequences. *What does it matter?* Culver shouted. *We already got a dead nigger! Did you forget about that? One murder! Two murders! Twenty murders! Do you really think it fucking matters?!*

People were crying, Two Guns was considering, the pregnant lady said, *Please God no* and then she covered her eyes with her hands, the bank phones were ringing and then some young man spoke up loudly – there is a difference. A big difference. That's what he said. That's what he said, the young man.

Two guns and Culver glared at him. Two guns with curiosity, Culver with contempt. He said he went to law school and that the number of homicides makes a difference and that what Culver was about to do was premeditated and that was the worst kind of homicide. Punishment wise.

And do you wanna know what Culver said? He said, *you're goddamn right it's premeditated. I been thinkin' about wasting his ass for over twenty years. Just like you wasted my life.* He pushed my head down to the ground so that my whole body was in a tight ball. He smeared my left check into my own vomit. The smell made me want to vomit again. I felt him pulling my hair with one hand and pressing the .44 Magnum at the bottom of my skull with the other. His knee was jammed into my back just below my backpack which was riding up on me.

I was scared and trembling and really uncomfortable, too. *You yourself said it was fate Chronic.* That's what Culver said next. That's what he said. It confused me. Being in my position I thought he was talking to me, like I was *you yourself.* But I had no idea what fate chronic is. It kind of just dawned on me now that he must have been talking to Two Guns because Two Guns did say it was fate, me being at the bank. And Chronic must be his name. Not his real name, his nickname.

It's funny what you think of and when you think of it. When I was lying there in my own puke, I was figuring I was going to die or maybe even something worse. But then I had a funny thought. Not funny like ha ha and not even funny like peculiar. No this was a whole different kind of funny. I'm sure someday I will find a word that describes it but I have not as of yet. Anyhow, it's like when I was a kid, I was jealous of Bryce and Culver. Not that I wanted to be anything like them, because I definitely did not, but I was jealous of what they had. Great looks, great athletic abilities, lots and lots and lots of friends. The prettiest girlfriends. And now there I was, covered in sweat and puke and about to die and I had what Culver wanted. I mean that's why he was there in the first place. I had lots of money right on my own person. Twenty thousand in my pockets and money belt and fanny pack and over a hundred thousand in my backpack. I wonder how Culver would feel if he knew his knee was pressing up against all that money. Shoot, he didn't have to rob the bank at all. He could have just waited for me. He could have pulled me in an alley, robbed me and had his revenge. Easy, peasy, lemon squeezy. It's because he doesn't do his homework. He is not a good planner. Me, I'm a great planner. I can make plans like a son of a bitch.

I wonder how Culver would feel if he knew my today plan. Today was the day I planned to ask Jane Brooks, the love of his life, to run away with me and all my money and live happily ever after. Not for real, but ask her just the same, for the heck of it, and to see what she would say. Oh boy, I bet that would of sure pissed him off.

You know when that law student spoke up at first I thought it was Macondo. I swear to Pete I did. But then I realized it wasn't just me seeing him. It was kind of disappointing. I really miss Macondo. You are probably thinking if he is an imaginary friend why don't I just imagine him? But that ain't how it works. But you already know that, don't you? Sometimes I wonder if its him that imagines me. I know, I know. That's silly talk. Ole Macondo, he is just like my own Daddy. Never around when you need them and guaranteed to disappoint. Well, not always. Most of the time, but not always. Just have to learn to not have expectations when it comes to those two. But I will admit to you right now, I do have just one expectation of Macondo. And I really don't think I'll be disappointed. Not like I was after my own Mama died. I stayed disappointed for over a dozen years living in Aunt Glads and Uncle George's basement. Never once did Macondo talk with me. I do believe I saw him a few times. I mean I'm positive. He looked different every time. But I could tell it was him by the way he looked at me. Once he was a bus driver, one time he was a police officer, and one time even a nurse. A girl nurse. I swear to Pete, ole Macondo has a lot of tricks up his sleeve. I guess my imagination is the limit, huh? But he never would speak to me. Not verbally at least. But I always got the feeling that he was kind of looking out for me and that he really wanted me to know that everything was gonna be okay again, some day. Just like it was before when we all lived together and my own Daddy and everyone thought I was a real good shooter. All I had to do was wait.

Now when I lived in Aunt Glads and Uncle George's basement, they would talk to me quite a bit. They would constantly let me know how dumb I was, how ugly I was, how fat I was, how good for nothing I was, what a sinner me and my own Mama was.

I stayed in the basement mostly. But I wasn't just waiting. I was learning. Never stop learning Uncle Rory always said. I even got me a minimum wage job at the library. I worked there for ten years. I had to give my money to Aunt Glads though in exchange for a place to sleep and a daily dinner. Well mostly. Some days I wouldn't get a dinner on account Aunt Glads would try to help me lose weight. That's why she stopped giving me bus fare, too, so I could get some exercise walking to and from work. What Aunt Glads didn't know is there was free donuts at the library every morning. Some of the other workers would call me the donut disposal. I was never real fat, but I was never really fit and trim either. Mostly I was just how I am right now.

I would sneak and meet Uncle Rory once in a while, too. He didn't have good living arrangements at the time. If he ever did, he said I could live with him. That's what he said. At that time he lived mostly on people's couches and even in a car for a while. Until he met his special friend Dennis. We was going to get a place together. All three of us. But then Dennis got real real sick. So sick that he died. And right around the time he died the Catholic Christian church decided they felt real bad for Uncle Rory getting, you know, I ain't gonna say that word again, but they decided to give him a whole bunch of money. Over two million dollars.

I think Aunt Glads and Uncle George was real sore about Uncle Rory getting all that money from the Catholic Christian church. They read about it in the newspaper and kept asking me if I had heard from Uncle Rory and that they was anxious to talk to him. I kept on lying to them saying I ain't heard from him even though I had, on account I didn't want them to yell at Uncle Rory for taking the Catholic Christian church's money. Until one day Uncle Rory showed up right at their front door in a limousine. He said he had come to pick me up. That is the last time I was ever in Aunt Glads and Uncle George's house.

He told me, grab whatever is important to you. I started grabbing my clothes and stuff and Uncle Rory said, no Angus, not stuff you need. Just stuff that means something special to you. So I grabbed my Swiss Comrade Hunting Knife with a strap on shoulder holster that My Own Daddy bought me at the St. Emerald American Gun Show we once went to before he left for the last time, and a 5x7 picture of My Own Mama in a frame that I made out of uncooked macaroni noodles when I was a little boy, and a Kurt Vonnegut book called *Cat's Cradle* that my Uncle Rory gave me when I was in the hospital having my bowels reconstructed, and that was it.

I was really surprised on account Aunt Glads and Uncle George was being real nice to Uncle Rory saying lies like how nice it was to see him, and they missed him, and have been very worried about him, and what's your hurry, why don't you stay for dinner. I know they was being insidious and so did Uncle Rory because we didn't stay. We left and went to Uncle Rory's brand new two-bedroom condo. The place where I live now. Uncle Rory lived with me for only two weeks. He kept telling me how happy he was to see me, but he sure didn't seem happy. And he kept telling me how everything that belonged to him belonged to me now, too, and that I should never give any of it to anyone.

He introduced me to his lawyer, Charlie and told me that Charlie was a good guy and that he was my lawyer now, too. Imagine that, I got my own lawyer. But then Uncle Rory did something I wish he didn't. Ends up I understand Uncle Rory even less than I understand Macondo or my own Daddy. Uncle Rory went to the cemetery to visit his special friend Dennis' grave and he brought with him his own gun, a .38 caliber revolver. I was surprised he even had his own gun on account he never seemed to like it all that much when we went shooting with my own Daddy and he was a real terrible shot. But I guess he didn't have to be a good shot to do the shooting he was planning on doing. I miss my Uncle Rory.

I really like you. You are a real good listener. Thank you for letting me do all the talking. And don't worry about the time, I could stop it as long as I want to.

No, no, I sure didn't forget about the bank robbery or my almost being murdered up or anything, but I just have to tell you this one part first. I mean you're not going to believe this, but Aunt Glads and Uncle George and even cousin Chip, well they all started treating me real real nice after Uncle Rory shot his own self. Swear to Pete they did and do you wanna know why? It was on account of some advice I got pretty soon after Charlie, my own lawyer, helped me get Uncle Rory all buried up. The funny thing is it was not even the first time I got this advice. For some stupid reason I just stopped listening to it. You know what I'm going to say, don't you? I can tell you do. It was weird though. Really weird.

It was the very first day that I decided to start putting my cash in safety deposit boxes at all different banks. I was on my bus ride home when all of the sudden I got me a case of terrible human urgency. You know what that is, right? I had to fill the potty big and there was no time to be selective about the potty. Finding a toilet was my preponderant mission. That means most important, overpowering even. There was no way I could make it home. So I get off the bus and end up in this pretty dirty public restroom at a combination gas station, fast food restaurant, liquor store.

There was one sink, one urinal and two bathroom stalls and as far as I could tell one light bulb because it was pretty dim in there. Which I guess was kind of good on account there was a lot of trash on the floor, which I found kind of strange on account there was a garbage can there that was not all the way filled up. But what I really didn't like was the fact that someone was already in one of the stalls doing their business. So now I had to do my business right next to someone else doing their business, which I did not like the idea of at all, but I really had no choice in the matter. So I went into the empty stall, which was a handicap stall and the first thing I noticed was that the last person in there neglected to flush their business, so I tried to flush it but the flusher was broken, so now I had to do my business on top of someone else's business, while another someone else was doing their business right next to me, but like I said, I had no choice in the matter, unless you count having an accident in your pants a choice. I did not consider that choice.

So I closed the door and when I went to latch it I noticed that the latch was as broken as the flusher. My insides gurgled a loud gurgle. The other somebody else made a loud sigh. I think somehow my insides knew how close the toilet was and decided on their own that it was time. Latch or no latch. Pants up or pants down. So as I pulled my pants and underwear down as fast as I could I noticed the strangest thing. A condom. An unrolled condom lying right there on the floor in between my feet.

Now I know what condoms are on account of Uncle Rory showed them to me once and told me if I was ever with a special woman or a man and we was going to be intimate with each other in a sexual way that I would have to put a condom on over my penis to protect myself, on account some people might have a bad disease and I could catch it and get real sick and even die. And that is actually what happened to my Uncle Rory's special friend Dennis.

But I wasn't too sure what intimate in a sexual way meant and Uncle Rory said he really couldn't explain it too well at the time on account he had drank too much red wine and too much red wine makes you really sleepy. In fact, it would make Uncle Rory so sleepy that sometimes his mouth would start to fall asleep before the rest of him and that would make it hard to talk and his words would come out all funny and then soon after his eyes would fall asleep, but they would fall asleep one at a time, first the left, then the right, and sometimes it would be a pretty long time before the right eye would join the left eye. When Uncle Rory decided he was too tired to explain intimate in a sexual way half his mouth and half his eyes had been asleep for quite some time. I tried to learn it on my own a few times on the computer, but every time I did I would end up learning about people being diddled instead, which really made me angry, so I just gave up.

Boy, I hate that word.

Hey, you know what I just thought of? If Uncle Rory can't ever get in heaven that means his special friend Dennis can't either, so that means they must be together now in purgatory. But now my own Mama, she only has to stay in purgatory for a while, then she gets to go to heaven. So the part I just thought of is I wonder if my own Mama gets a choice or if she has to go to heaven and be with God, because I think she would rather be in purgatory with her baby brother. I sure hope I get to stay in purgatory because I would rather be with them than be with God in heaven any ole' day.

So who in the heck anyway would go and bring a condom to this dirty old bathroom? I don't think anyone could ever meet someone special to be intimate with in a sexual way in any kind of a public bathroom, no matter how clean or dirty it was. I mean, what I was thinking exactly was that people don't even talk when they is in a public bathroom. You just do your business and get out as fast as you can.

And then it happened…

Don't worry, I didn't mess my pants or anything. I made it. I got my pants down and sat on that toilet seat. I hunched as far forward as I could and stretched my arms out as far as I could on account I wanted to hold the door shut on account of the broken latch. But I couldn't reach the door from where I was sitting. I came up about a foot and a half short. Which I figured was okay because that would still stop somebody from opening the door all the way and walking right on in, I thought. So I held my arms out like that and I stayed as hunched over as I could. My insides made the loudest gurgle ever and my business exploded onto somebody else's business as I looked down at the condom on the floor feeling a combination of relief and embarrassment, when all of a sudden the other somebody else, not the somebody else that filled my toilet before me, but the somebody else that was filling the toilet next to me, he says, *Atta boy.*

I figured there is no way he is talking to me, right? I looked under the stall and seen his left foot. He was wearing a heavy-duty work boot and had a pair of blue work pants pulled down around them. This was definitely a big man.

A few seconds of silence past and then my insides erupted with the most disgusting and embarrassing of sounds and the other somebody else says, *I know exactly how you feel.*

I was scared. I mean you would be scared too, wouldn't you? I remained silent. Well not exactly silent but definitely nonverbal. Every noise my insides made, every sound my business made was accompanied by words of encouragement from the other somebody else in the stall next to me. *There you go kid, let it all out, that's got to feel great, you can't live your life with that kind of stuff inside ya. Great job. You're almost there.*

Then he stood up. Then he pulled his pants up. I stretched as far forward as I could. My body tightened. Then he says, *you ain't got no idea, do you?*

I wanted to stand up and hold the door shut with my entire body, but I wasn't quite finished and I was a bit of a mess, if you know what I mean? But then he says, *oh I'm just playin'. I know how you hate double negatives.*

My body relaxed a little bit. I felt this strange warmth throughout my insides. Now I don't exactly know why I thought this and thinking back it makes me feel pretty stupid, but do you want to know what I thought? What I said? I said, *Daddy?*

I will tell you this, the other somebody else, well, he laughed like a son of a bitch. Then he says, *I'm disappointed in you, Angus. Your own Daddy gave us some great ideas. We had a real good plan. And you were doing it for a while, remember?*

I felt an ease come over me that I ain't felt in years. I wanted to shout it in my outside voice but it only came out in a whisper. Macondo?

Your own Daddy left. Your own Mama left. Now even Uncle Rory left. Don't worry Angus, nothing's going to be okay, isn't that what he used to say? Your own Daddy? But he was wrong, wasn't he? That's what he said. That's what he said. That's what Macondo said. Macondo said to me.

Macondo, I said in my normal voice.

Now you got to stick to the plan, he says.

I remembered it and then I said it right out loud. Perceived Truth.

There you go. Life was pretty good when you told everyone what a good shot you were, now wasn't it? And you were a regular Annie Oakley, weren't you? Why did you stop Angus? Why'd you stop there? That's what you said. That's what you said. I mean Macondo, that's what he said.

Macondo, I shouted. Was that you I seen all those times? Was that you? Why wouldn't you talk to me? That's what I asked. That's what I asked.

You know the world doesn't like you talking to me, he says. Then he says, *I'm not part of its Perceived Truth.* And then he says, *yet.* Then he walks out of his stall and stands right in front of the door to my stall. I can see his huge work boots and I'm going as fast as I can cleaning up so that I can see what ole Macondo looks like now and he says, *Angus you have to stick to the plan. The whole plan. You remember that night in your yard. The three of us. You remember, don't you? How good it made you feel.*

I remember, I'm yelling! I remember! And I swing the door open, but he's gone.

Just gone.

I was pretty sore about it back then, but I'm not anymore. I did get to see him two more times since then and do you want to know what? Macondo was right. About the plan.

Anyhow, so Aunt Glads comes over for a visit and asks how I'm eating. I say fine, but then I say better than fine. I say I'm on a new diet and that I already lost six pounds. And you know what she says? She says, Oh, I could tell. Honey, you look great. Honey? Can you believe it? She called me honey. I mean she always would call cousin Chip honey, but never me. Next thing I know Uncle George and Chip are telling me how great I look and I keep telling all of them I'm losing more and more weight, when really I have not lost a single pound. So they start visiting me once in a while and every time I tell them I lost a couple more pounds and they are constantly complimenting me and even asking me for my diet secrets.

One time I even caught Chip snooping around my room and he says, you must have some secret diet pills or something in here. I say nope. Just a good healthy diet. Aunt Glads even asks me to make her a grocery list so that they can eat like me, so I do. I just write down a bunch of healthy foods and tell them that's what I eat, and they believe me. Perceived truth. But then Aunt Glads is all crying and sad on account she says her and Uncle George are on a fixed income and can't afford the groceries I put on the list. So now like about once a month I give them a list and some money so they can go and buy the food I say I buy, but I don't even really buy it. Well, I guess I sort of do, on account I give them money so they can buy it, but I sure don't buy it for me. Funny, huh?

I almost feel like I am taking advantage of them, but this is kind of an experiment. All they have to do is look in my fridge, but they are just hoodwinked by my Perceived Truth. Oh Angus, you just look fabulous. On and on they go. If you add up all the pounds that I've told them I lost over, shoot, almost two years now, it would probably equal over a hundred, when the truth is I have actually gained about ten pounds. You see, if you just keep telling someone something long enough and with enough conviction, pretty soon they will believe it. And once they believe it, it becomes what my own Daddy called the world's most powerful weapon, Perceived Truth. Just like when so many people used to tell me that I was an idiot.

And when they can't lose weight with their new groceries they start crying, oh Angus you must have another secret. You must go to a gym or something. So I say yes, I go to the gym five times a week when really I never even been in a gym. Not once in my whole life, but now I give all three of them money to go to the gym. They eat healthy food because they believe I do. They go to the gym because they believe I do. But they cannot lose weight and look great like they believe I do. Perceived Truth, ain't it a real hoot?

So, if telling people I am fit and trim works why wouldn't telling people I can stop time work? That's what I have been doing for the last few months, telling all sorts of people that I can stop time. At first I got a lot of weird looks. I mean it is a big one, but just a few days ago I was walking to the store and I passed these two ladies, older ladies, and I heard one of them tell the other that's the fellow that can stop time.

All that being said, it is not really all that crazy then when you think about it, that when Culver had that .44 Magnum pressed into the back of my skull, ready to shoot me dead, that I would yell, I could get you out of this Culver!

He pulled my hair harder and said that's real funny, Anus, because if you think about it, you're the one who got me into this in the first place. I could have been a NFL star.

I know how you can get away, I yelled, with the money and everything.

Two guns, or Chronic, actually, I guess, he yells to Culver, let's hear what the little puke has to say.

Culver says, start talking.

I can freeze time! Everything 'cept for you and your partner and me. And you guys can get away. I swear to Pete, I can freeze time! That's what I said. That's what I said.

Culver pulled me up by my hair. I was back in the kneeling position with Culver behind me and the gun still touching my head. About half the people I was facing turned their heads. The other half looked scared, real scared. Culver was laughing and saying, *I wonder if the man who can stop time can stop a bullet? Anus Wad I sentence you to death for taking from me my two greatest loves- football and Jane Brooks.*

I heard the gun cock.

She's here! She's here! I yelled, Jane is here in the bank! That's what I said! That's what I said!

My head wasn't splattered yet so I kept on talking. I swear to Pete! She works here.

I'm not so proud of this but I can tell you, I was kind of sobbing while I was talking.

What the fuck are you talking about? How? Where?

I was barely able to talk, you know, being so close to getting blasted, but I told Culver that Jane was in the safety deposit room with me. He believed me enough to go and shove the gun in Mr. Fosters mouth. The security guard. The not dead, not black security guard. *Is he telling the truth? Does Jane Brooks work here?*

Shoot, I remember when I discovered Jane Brooks worked here. I have to admit I was just about as surprised as Culver was. Jane Brooks, the woman who led me to slaughter. I did not choose this bank because of her. No. No. It was a complete surprise to me. My first time here I had a backpack full of cash. She did not take care of me, but she did see me. After I left the bank she ran out after me. She told me how sorry she was and that she had changed her ways and that she had found Jesus. I didn't say a word. Not a single word. That's what I said.

But the second time I did. And the third and fourth and every time since. I would come to this bank once a month to visit my safety deposit box, but really it was to visit Jane Brooks. She would come in the room and I would ask her to stay while I tended to my business. Sometimes she could only talk for a few minutes, sometimes more, once for a full half of an hour. I would never let her see inside of my box. I would be very cautious and secretive. She would always tell me how sorry she was and tell me about how she let Jesus into her life. Sometimes she would suggest I do the same. The Jesus thing. It was very difficult for me to trust her, you know, being insidious and all. She would always insist that she was a completely different person than who she was back in school. That she had been reborn. But I remember my own Daddy would always say people are whatever they are. But then I think, I used to be a fat idiot and I'm not anymore. Maybe Jane Brooks knows about Perceived Truth. If she tells enough people she has been reborn into a really great person, then I guess it will become true.

Now don't be sore or anything, but I did tell her about you, Macondo. She says maybe you really do exist, but you are a guardian angel. My guardian angel.

Are you my guardian angel?

I knew it was you Macondo the whole time.

I can always recognize you. And you are such a good listener.

Thank you for letting me do all the talking this time. You got to do it all the last two times. After that time in the bathroom, I started doing that Perceived Truth thing all the time, but the other part of our plan, from when the three of us was in the yard, that took some time. A lot of planning. At first, I wasn't for sure I was even going to do it. Not until the day I told Jane about you and she told me you might be my guardian angel.

After I left the bank I was sitting at my bus stop all by myself. It was very quiet and the air was very still. I was thinking about things. Considering. And then this black convertible pulls up. The driver is the only one in the car. There are no other cars at the light. He looks right at me and do you want to know what he says? He says, you know that sign you've been waiting for? Well I am it. Stop wasting time and do it. Of course you already knew that, because it was you, Macondo. Two weeks later I was on my way to Boston.

Macondo, I think you're the one who made me find the bank Jane works at and I think you're the one who made Culver pick her bank to rob today. It can't all just be coincidence. Dumb Luck? It can't be.

I still don't think Culver believed me or Mr. Foster until he actually saw Jane with his own two eyes. He was pulling me by the hair and cursing at me when we walked to the safety deposit room. He was saying I swear, Anus, if you're lying you will be so sorry. Thank God Jane was there, because if she wasn't then I sure wouldn't be here talking to you right now, Macondo.

Today was the first day I let Jane see my money. She stood there in amazement watching me pack all that cash in my money belt and fanny pack and back pack. I still didn't let her see everything in my safety deposit box. Then, I had three questions for her.

I said, Jane Brooks, would you run off with me and live happily ever after?

Now don't get sore that I asked her such a question. I didn't really want to run off with her on account of it was too late and I was very serious about sticking to our plan Macondo, but I really wanted to know how she would answer.

She told me she couldn't, but would really like it if we could be friends. And she said I could even go to church with her and be saved just like her. That's what she said. That's what she said. I don't even know what she figured I needed saving from?

Boy, when Culver first saw Jane Brooks he sure forgot all about me. He released his hold of my hair and stared in complete disbelief. It was a high school sweetheart reunion.

I remember that night we made the plan in the yard, Macondo, all those years ago like it was yesterday. It was me, you, and Care. She was barking like a son of a bitch. She sure made me nervous. I'm sorry it took so long, Macondo. I guess I just couldn't stop feeling sorry for myself. It was easier in the yard that night with you being right next to me and Care not being a person.

Then I asked Jane, that day you came to my house and you were so nice and sweet to me and then you brought me to Culver and Bryce and they did those terrible sick things to me...Why did you do that? She never did answer me. She just said she was a different person back then. A bad person. An evil person. She started to cry.

And I said, but you acted so nice to me. She cried harder. And then I asked her my third question. *Do you know what insidious means?* That's what I said. That's what I said.

She put her face in the palms of her hands and sobbed even harder. *I'm so sorry Angus.*

She didn't even see me take the final item out of the safety deposit box. It was my Swiss Comrade Hunting Knife with a shoulder holster that I got from My Own Daddy at the St Emerald American Gun show. The same knife I used on Care that night in the yard. That damned dog should have never bit me. I walked up behind Jane. She kept on sobbing and saying sorry and the last thing she said was *Angus I ain't got no excuses for what I done.* I felt kind of bad that her last words were a double negative.

I got to tell you, Macondo, I can't say it felt all that great running my

Swiss Comrade Hunting Knife across Jane's throat. But it felt like it had to be done. Sort of like when I did the same thing to Care. But I'll also tell you when I flew out to Boston to visit Father Maylay, a couple of weeks after I saw you in that black convertible, now that felt pretty nice. He was pretty old and just lying there asleep, but when I held that pillow over his face, he put up a pretty good fight for an old guy. He squirmed and fussed like a son of a bitch. It made me think of Uncle Rory and all those other boys and how much they must have squirmed and fussed. It really made me feel good.

But, Macondo, nothing made me feel as good as when I saw Culver standing over Jane's lifeless body and I took my Swiss Comrade Hunting Knife out of its holster and plunged it into his back again and again and again. I must have stabbed him over a hundred times. And then I took Culver's .44 Magnum and walked back out into the lobby and put two bullets in the back of Two Guns' skull. Everyone cheered and hugged me and loved me. I felt like a hero. Look at me Macondo. I'm a celebrated murderer. Even a couple of policemen said I was a hell of a shot. Perceived Truth, huh, ain't it a hoot?

But there is much work to do Macondo. I am heading to Cincinnati tomorrow to visit a high school football coach. The school boasts that he is helping shape the lives of many young men and I have to put a stop to that. And then I must return to Boston. I've been thinking about it and I have to find the Catholic Christian men that helped protect Father Maylay and kept supplying him with victims. So don't you see, Macondo, I don't have time to sit around here and be celebrated. As much as I would like to, I just can't. But the people do need a hero. And you are pretty good at changing your looks…So why don't you be me for a little while?

Don't worry about Jane. They will think that sicko Culver did that.

What do you mean the people won't believe you exist? Of course they will. You just have to keep on telling them that you do. Trust me. Perceived Truth, there's nothing more powerful, not even actual truth, remember?

Don't you worry, I'm not going to abandon you. I'm not that type.

Thank you, Macondo. I'll see you again, real soon.

THE ABSENT PRETENDER

OFFICIAL TRANSCRIPT

Candidate: Ellis Snowden
Case Worker: Tina Lester
Objective: VDS Determination Interview
Location: Chicago, Exelon, USCA
Findings: CH41/AP86
Note: Equipment Error, Case Worker transcript inaudible

TL:AUDIO RECEPTION ERROR

ES:Well, once I decided to stop pretending that I gave a shit about what other people had to say, my life became much simpler. It's not that I didn't care about anybody; it's just that I didn't want to hear about it anymore. I had been hearing about it for seventy years and I just figured enough already. I was tired of fictitiously congratulating friends and family and neighbors for their accomplishments. Accomplishments that bored me or made me jealous or, quite frankly, I felt they did not deserve. And their kids. What makes them think I want to hear about their children? I certainly don't talk to them about my children. I wouldn't dream of it. Why would I?

And if people aren't going on and on about their incredible feats of gratification, then they're filling your skull with all their problems. Or at least what they consider to be problems. Look, I realize we all have our own crosses to bear. Some heavier than others. Lord knows I don't tell you about the weight on my shoulders, so please don't tell me about yours. Just cowboy up and carry your load. And if it gets too heavy, or you decide you just can't do it anymore, don't open your mouth and start yakking. Just give up. I mean, that's what I decided I'm going to do.

TL:AUDIO RECEPTION ERROR

ES:What do you mean, what do I mean? You know exactly what I mean. Why else would I be talking to you? I'm done pretending.

TL:AUDIO RECEPTION ERROR

ES:Now why would I talk to you about my problems? I just told you I hate when people talk about their problems. And people should really make a more valid attempt to differentiate between what a problem is versus a minor inconvenience, or a slight difficulty. Or a letdown… Or a compromise. Besides, I really don't have any problems. I just told you, I have made my life simple. Very simple.

TL:AUDIO RECEPTION ERROR

ES:I decided to make my life simple six years ago. Just after Debra…Well, the first order of business in simplifying your life is to remove all other people from it. That was far easier to do than I imagined. You see, people engage you less and less when you stop pretending to give a shit about their constant chatter. But I'll tell you what really makes them keep their distance: When you stop pretending NOT to give a shit. When somebody misspeaks, or says something you consider slightly off-putting, when your sensibilities are insulted, or you find their words to be petty or self-aggrandizing, or just dull, and you don't simply bite your tongue and smile as if it does not bother you, but you instead speak your mind and tell them exactly how you feel. Now that really keeps them away. People put up with me for about a year after Debra's accident. I've basically been a recluse for the last five years. Just me and all the disturbances that play out in my mind.

TL:AUDIO RECEPTION ERROR

ES:Just the sort of things that haunt a man who has nothing but time. The sins of the past. My past. My sins. Nothing for you to concern yourself with.

TL:AUDIO RECEPTION ERROR

ES:Sure I'm lonely. But I was lonely long before my voluntary seclusion. That's why I stopped pretending in the first place. The pretending no longer filled the void.

TL:AUDIO RECEPTION ERROR

ES:Well, first off, how bout you take a short break from pretending and stop calling me Mr. Snowden like you respect me. You don't even know me. Other than what my file says. My name is Ellis. Call me Ellis. And I guess you're probably right, I may have another fifty or sixty years to live, but that's not the point. The point is I don't want another fifty years. Hell, I don't want another day. And unlike you, I'm certainly not going to thank Exelon or any of the *United Corporations* for anything. Not for the quality of my life or the quantity of it.

Many people, the over privileged ones, may live longer, healthier lives today, but it is not because of the gracious hearts of evil corporations that govern our nation. It's because of the increased consumerism potential. You can work a lot longer and buy a lot more shit in 120 years than you can in 75 or 80.

TL:AUDIO RECEPTION ERROR

ES:I don't expect you would understand my attitude. You're too young.

TL:AUDIO RECEPTION ERROR

ES:Do you have any idea how unfair it is to have my future, or lack of future be decided by someone that is half my age and less than half my intelligence?

TL:AUDIO RECEPTION ERROR

ES:Oh, please sweetheart, don't get all defensive. It's not your fault. I grew up in a time when states were not owned by corporations. We were a united country. We made our own decisions. We did things that were bad for us. We were wasteful. We were self-destructive. But we called the shots ourselves. We certainly didn't have to meet with a stranger to find out if we were worthy of suicide.

TL:AUDIO RECEPTION ERROR

ES:Call it what you want. It's suicide.

TL:AUDIO RECEPTION ERROR

ES:*Voluntary Downsizing.* Please. You sound absolutely ridiculous when you say that. And with a straight face no less.

TL:AUDIO RECEPTION ERROR

ES:I know more about your job than you do. I've done a lot of research this past year. I know your textbook tells you I am part of the transformation generation. That I may find some of our CEO's decisions difficult to accept. That many of the people from my generation are myopic and refuse to realize that what is good for United States of Corporate America is good for mankind. That the paradigm shift in the matter in which we are now governed may make us feel redundant. And that the new order, the *ever sympathetic* Corporate America in an attempt to be merciful, has decided to allow us to disburse our assets however we wish and then terminate our useless, non-assimilating bodies. *Voluntary Downsizing.* Pending a caseworker's approval. Do I got all that right, honey?

TL:AUDIO RECEPTION ERROR

ES:Isn't it funny though, how almost all of the people requesting and receiving Voluntary Downsizing are unable to afford all of life's new and improved luxuries? All of these new and amazing advancements in healthcare and entertainment and time wasting are just too far out of reach. So the kind and generous states allow them to give what little they have to their children, tax-free, and then put an end to their misery. The incredible shame of not being rich. Seems to me the United States of Corporate America has two agendas. For the rich, it is the advancement of mankind. For everyone else, Aggressive Mediocrity.

TL:AUDIO RECEPTION ERROR

ES:Their lives are not difficult because they can't find happiness. Their lives are difficult because they can't *afford happiness.*

TL:AUDIO RECEPTION ERROR

ES:Well, it is definitely what they believe to be happiness. And it kind of is. I call it synthetic happiness. And it can be a real blast. Believe me, I have had way more than my share of synthetic happiness.

TL:AUDIO RECEPTION ERROR

ES:There are actually three ways you can achieve happiness. You can earn it. You can stumble into it. And you can buy it.

TL:AUDIO RECEPTION ERROR

ES:Oh, hell yeah, I bought tons of synthetic happiness. At one time I owned five homes. I had a mansion in upstate Apple and another in downstate BASF, a beach house right off the coast in Googletown, and cabins in GE Estates and Groupon Village. My family and I, we were living the high life. And I still have plenty of money and more earning potential than ever. That's why you're my caseworker, sweetheart. But synthetic happiness, it's all bullshit, that I can assure you.

TL:AUDIO RECEPTION ERROR

ES:No. Now that's funny. I never earned any happiness. I stumbled into plenty of it though. Val and Marvel when I was a boy. And then Debra. Beautiful Debra and my boys, they are what made life worth living. But they're all gone now.

TL:AUDIO RECEPTION ERROR

ES:Sorry, honey. But the answer is no. Not even when I was at my happiest. I don't mean to break your crayons, honey, but the corporate bail-out of the USA was the worst thing to ever happen to mankind. It was the beginning of the dehumanization of our nation. I mean look at yourself. You are a team player. You believe everything they tell you. You think they give a shit about you. You toe the company line. But what about all the unchosen ones? They don't have a chance. Take away a man's spirit and he is nothing more than skin and bones. A collection of matter. No different than what is in your kitchen garbage can. Kill the spirit. Take out the garbage. Thin the herd. The rich rise to the top and fuck the rest.

TL:AUDIO RECEPTION ERROR

ES:Do you realize that you have approved more Voluntary Downsizing than any caseworker in the country over the last six years? Provided they meet the proper financial criteria, you send them right on through to the afterlife. Their families get to keep what little they have and you feel good about it. But that's not why you have been assigned to me, is it?

TL:AUDIO RECEPTION ERROR

ES:I don't consider myself a rebel or an anarchist. I believe these things because I am a True Human Being. And I also believe the best way I can help mankind and make amends for the life I've lived is by convincing you to allow me to give up. So enough about my views on Corporate America, sweetheart. Let's talk about my death. What do I have to say to make it happen?

TL:AUDIO RECEPTION ERROR

ES:My childhood? You would never understand my childhood. And what does it have to do with anything anyway?

TL:AUDIO RECEPTION ERROR

ES:Okay, fine. Well, for starters I grew up in Begman's Root.

TL:AUDIO RECEPTION ERROR

ES:I know, shocking, huh? Of course that's not what your file says. I'm guessing you never met anyone from Begman's Root.

TL:AUDIO RECEPTION ERROR

ES:Well, some of us did make it out of there alive. Surprise.

TL:AUDIO RECEPTION ERROR

ES:I guess you could say my father was a thief. But he was the worst kind of thief. He spent his whole life taking things that no one else wanted. He worked at the Begman Mill for thirty-three years. He died two weeks after his fiftieth birthday. For his entire life he took all the abuse and injustice and exploitation he could find. He would never ask. He would never negotiate. He would just take it. He took it from the mill. He took it from his wife. He took it from his God. He took it from his father, who incidentally worked at the mill for forty years and died at fifty-six. Shit, my old man, he even took all my abuse. My ungrateful acts of rebellion, my cruel expressions of resentment. He took it all. Take. Take. Take. Yeah, my old man was a selfish bastard.

TL:AUDIO RECEPTION ERROR

ES:I'm sure I would have followed in his footsteps, but I got Lucky. The mill closed during my second year of working there. When I was a real little kid they called Begman's Root a working class neighborhood. I found out as I got older, that what that really means is the people who lived their hung on by their fingertips. All the time. Get hurt, get sick, piss off your boss and you weren't working class anymore. You were poor, hopeless, abandoned. A few years after the mill closed they called Begman's Root a cesspool of human sewage. The mill was gone, leaving only its victims and filth behind.

TL:AUDIO RECEPTION ERROR

ES:I left. My mother moved in with her sister's family and I lived in my car for a while. And then in the park for a couple of months.

TL:AUDIO RECEPTION ERROR

ES:You mean is that when people started paying me for my paintings? I painted or sketched or doodled my entire life. Well, at least whenever I could afford paint or pencils or a sketch pad.

TL:AUDIO RECEPTION ERROR

ES:That's how I met Debra. I was sitting on a bench sketching a picture on a piece of cardboard I ripped from a box someone had thrown away. She liked it. She said I was talented. She was the first person in my life to tell me I was talented. She changed my life.

TL:AUDIO RECEPTION ERROR

ES:I don't want to talk about Debra.

TL:AUDIO RECEPTION ERROR

ES:There's nothing to say other than we met. We fell in love. I moved in with her family. She inspired me to paint and somehow she convinced stupid rich people that my paintings were good enough to pay me money. Lots of money. We were married. We had two sons. We became stupid rich people. Then our sons were taken from us. Then Debra died. The end.

TL:AUDIO RECEPTION ERROR

ES:I said the end. That's all there is to say.

TL:AUDIO RECEPTION ERROR

ES:Well, I suppose we do have to talk about something in order for you to make your *determination*. So fine, I can tell you a little about my youth. I guess it was okay, for being way below the Viable Line. But I can't say for sure, because I spent most of it stoned.

TL:AUDIO RECEPTION ERROR

ES:I was in little league baseball until I was eleven. The fields were shit. No uniforms, hell, we were lucky to have mitts. Some of us didn't. We shared. That's a funny thing about poor people, they are so much more generous than rich people. I have been both, and let me tell you, it seems to me the less someone has, the more they're willing to give. I think maybe, that more and more money and possessions makes us less and less True Human Beings…

TL:AUDIO RECEPTION ERROR

ES:Anyway, it was pretty boring. Then the neighborhood became too poor for baseball.

TL:AUDIO RECEPTION ERROR

ES:I had a friend, Marvel Svanic, his parents were pot dealers. I smoked my first joint with him when I was ten. Drugs are never boring. So that's what we would do. We got stoned. Every day.

TL:AUDIO RECEPTION ERROR

ES:For a while we would just steal it from Marvel's parents. The weed was plentiful and his folk's weren't all that bright. We smoked so much weed, we used to play this game. We would go to the cemetery. Four of us, Marvel, Val, Derek and me. We would sit in a circle and roll three giant bombers. We'd light all three of them at once, so three out of four of us would take a big hit off our joint and as soon as you sucked as much smoke in as your lungs could hold you would pass the joint to whoever didn't have one. And we would just keep going until our fingertips were burning. The second you passed your joint someone would be handing you one. Wow we would get so fucked up.

TL:AUDIO RECEPTION ERROR

ES:It got a lot harder when we started having to buy our dope. Val worked, so he had a little money, but he was saving up for a car. Not like a new car - like a hundred dollar car. Sometimes we would hop the train and go to a rich suburb like Sequoia Hills and do some thieving. Stupid rich people hardly ever lock up their shit. Their charmed life gave them this fucked up sense of security. Stupid rich people…

TL:AUDIO RECEPTION ERROR

ES:I'm not saying I'm proud of my youth, but I'm not ashamed either. That's what we did. That's what our world was. My friends meant the world to me.

TL:AUDIO RECEPTION ERROR

ES:Three of us made it out of Begman's Root. Marvel's parents got arrested about four years before *the Incident*. He was only eighteen. Amazon had just *bought* the Department of Defense. They were offering a great deal for your future. One year of combat overseas, and then they pay for your education and get you a job. Marvel said the deal was too good to pass up and that we should all take it. He's the only one that did. Only twenty percent of those boys made it back. He wasn't one of them. But I guess he did make it out of Begman's Root.

TL:AUDIO RECEPTION ERROR

ES:Val, he made it out, too. Val was always the most motivated one of us. If you're keeping score with money he even did better than me. We still talk once a year or so. He's got a big family. Kids, grandkids. He just signed up for *Pfizer Advanced Life Program*. Big money for that, and he's got plenty of it. So he will be able to play with his great great great grandkids. He is living a charmed life. I'm happy for him. He probably doesn't even lock up his shit anymore. He was at my son's wake. The last time I saw him was at Debra's wake…

TL:AUDIO RECEPTION ERROR

ES:I'm sorry. What was that?

TL:AUDIO RECEPTION ERROR

ES:No, no, unfortunately, Derek never made it out. Two years before *the Incident* my mother died. I was on my way to my Aunt's house to make arrangements. I had just begun selling my art, but I was by no means successful yet. Anyway I'm in my piece of shit car at a red light and there is Derek walking up and down the street selling water bottles. I call out to him. He doesn't respond. I curb my car and go to him. He doesn't even know who I am. His eyes are dead. They are hollow and reveal nothing of the soul they were once the windows to. He just stands there rocking back and forth, holding a bottle of water in one hand while an open palm waits for a dollar in the other one. *Hey man, ice cold water. One dollar*, he says. I give him five bucks and say I'll be back for him. That's the last time I ever saw him.

TL:AUDIO RECEPTION ERROR

ES:Later, I find out from my aunt that Derek has been garbage picking empty water bottles from the neighborhood recycle bins, filling them at the gas station bathroom and selling them to support his habits. Bad habits. His brain is fried she says. Why didn't anyone tell me, I ask. My Aunt says, "Why didn't you ask?" And I ask myself over and over again, why didn't I? I figured he was still living with Alicio. I doubt either of them survived *the Incident.*

TL:AUDIO RECEPTION ERROR

ES:Alicio came later. We started hanging out with him when we were like sixteen. It was after Val bought his first disposable car. That's what we would call them. He would buy a car for fifty to a hundred bucks and we would drive it until it didn't drive anymore. No plates, no insurance. He wouldn't even transfer the title to his name. We would just steal someone else's plates and cruise.

TL:AUDIO RECEPTION ERROR

ES:Alicio introduced us to a new drug. Acid. LSD. It was great. Mainly because it was cheap. Four bucks. That's it. Four bucks and you get this tiny piece of paper, stick it on your tongue and for the next five hours you're trippin your balls off. You probably never did anything like that. Did you?

TL:AUDIO RECEPTION ERROR

ES:Yeah, I didn't think so.

TL:AUDIO RECEPTION ERROR

ES:Illegal, yes. But I wouldn't say reckless.

TL:AUDIO RECEPTION ERROR

ES:Sure, we may have been a little wild, but we were certainly not utterly unconcerned with the consequences of our adolescences…At least most of the time. We just liked to party. It's not like any of us had a death wish or anything.

TL:AUDIO RECEPTION ERROR

ES:We were careful. We would take safety precautions.

TL:AUDIO RECEPTION ERROR

ES:Well, for one thing, we wouldn't drive while we were tripping. A little buzzed, sure – but never completely stoned.

TL:AUDIO RECEPTION ERROR

ES:When I was seventeen, the best place to party was Mandrake Woods. Growing up in the muck and sleaze of Begman's Root made the woods a very special place to us. It was beautiful there. The trees, the creek, the hills. I guess we were like hippies. Mother Nature and all. The woods went on forever, all the way to Iowa. I'm sorry, Seimens... Seimens, what a terrible name for a corporation, let alone a state.

Anyway, Mandrake Woods was our salvation. It sure the hell smelled better than the piss and chemicals that filled the air of the Root. At home, people were right on top of you. Always. At school, at home, at work, on the streets. You could feel the sweat of other people oozing its way toward you. You were engulfed in a mist of carbon monoxide and bad breath. In the woods you were secluded. It was quiet. It was tranquil. We could be there for hours and never see another soul.

TL:AUDIO RECEPTION ERROR

ES:No – just the five of us, girls came later, for some of us. I mean none of us were gay or anything. But, with our brains brimming with illegal chemicals, there wasn't much of a chance to impress the ladies. Nope, just us and our dope.

TL:AUDIO RECEPTION ERROR

ES:We would drive.

TL:AUDIO RECEPTION ERROR

ES:No, I just told you we wouldn't drive while on LSD. We invented a game called acid roulette. We would buy four hits of acid for the five of us. Then we got five little Dixie cups, usually filled with Mogen David wine that Val would steal from his mom, not a lot, just a little. Then we would drop a hit of acid in four of them and just a piece of paper in the fifth. We'd mix the cups up and then bottoms up. Then we would usually fire up a joint and within fifteen minutes we'd know who our designated driver was.

TL:AUDIO RECEPTION ERROR

ES:Sure, you could drive on pot, but no way did Val want any of us driving his car on acid. He used to say the car is disposable, not us. He was right. I'll be honest with you, there was one time I thought I could drive while I was tripping...ends up I couldn't.

TL:AUDIO RECEPTION ERROR

ES:It was a stupid decision. It was a long, long time ago.

TL:AUDIO RECEPTION ERROR

ES:Only once. See I got burned two Saturdays in a row. I was the designated driver. It was unfair I thought. My buddies didn't agree. Why would they? They got to be chauffeured around while they were tripping their balls off. Then Val's car ceased to exist. While he was looking for his next disposable set of wheels we were stuck partying in the slum we called home. I was desperate. I needed a trip to the woods. Then one day Alicio tells us he can borrow his aunt's car. I wasn't getting screwed again. So I got five hits of acid. I didn't tell anyone. They thought one of our shots of Mogen David was just wine and paper. I decided we were all trippin that day and I was driving. I figured as long as we got to the woods before I started peaking and stayed until the acid wore off.

TL:AUDIO RECEPTION ERROR

ES:Peaking, you know. Well, no, I guess you don't. Well, acid kind of creeps its way in, slowly. Your trip gets stronger and stronger, until you peak. I figured I was good. I figured I was invincible. I was seventeen. I was an idiot. I figured wrong.

TL:AUDIO RECEPTION ERROR

ES:Marvel stole a handle of Hanna and Hog Vodka from his older brother. Cheap shit. Real rot gut. We decided to spike a watermelon.

TL:AUDIO RECEPTION ERROR

ES:You cut a small square out of the watermelon. Like you're carvin a pumpkin. I'm sure you've done that. You seem like you have done all that wholesome family shit.

TL:AUDIO RECEPTION ERROR

ES:Oh, relax. Anyway, you slowly pour the vodka in, let it soak in real good. Shake it up a little. And then you eat it.

TL:AUDIO RECEPTION ERROR

ES:No, it was a big mistake. The acid was stronger than usual. At least I think it was. That and the vodka and we smoked a lot of pot. Derek was having a really bad trip and Marvel must have eaten too much watermelon because he started projectile vomiting everywhere. It was time to go home. And like I said, I was an idiot. I was only seventeen. I took a deep breath, put some Led Zeppelin on and started driving.

TL:AUDIO RECEPTION ERROR

ES:We didn't get very far. It was a bad night. A really bad night.

TL:AUDIO RECEPTION ERROR

ES:Ah shit, now I'm a seventy-four year old idiot, because I still think I could have got us home safe. I'm a control freak, I guess. I mean that's what Debra always said. *"Relax. Let go,"* she would always say. *The world does not ride on your shoulders. Put it down...let it happen...*

TL:AUDIO RECEPTION ERROR

ES:...I'm sorry, what was that?

TL:AUDIO RECEPTION ERROR

ES:No. We all got home eventually. It was the next afternoon. It was on foot. Marvel must have lost ten pounds with all the ralphing he was doing. And me and Val had to talk Derek down a few times. He was freakin' out. And Alicio, that asshole. I almost killed that son of a bitch.

TL:AUDIO RECEPTION ERROR

ES:We were still on Kean Avenue. A two lane road with woods on either side of us…and a deer. A fuckin' goddamn deer.

TL:AUDIO RECEPTION ERROR

ES:It came out of nowhere. I was doing fine. And then Bam! It wasn't my fault. I could have been sober as a judge and I still would have hit it. I mean why? There was nothing I could have done. I never even saw it. I heard it. I mean I heard the noise, I felt the impact, and I slammed on the brakes. Such a terrible noise. I still hear it sometimes at night when I'm sleeping. Such a terrible noise…

TL:AUDIO RECEPTION ERROR

ES:We were all freaking out. Val was in the middle of the back seat, trying to calm Derek down, while Marvel was puking out the window. Alicio and I got out to take a look. Then he starts yelling at me, "*Let's go! Let's go! We gotta get out of here.*"

I must have been in shock; I was like, what about your aunt's car?

And you know what that asshole says? "*It's not my aunt's car, you fuckin idiot. I stole it.*" Just like that.

It came out of fucking nowhere. I can't believe I hit it, I told him. He says "*I know, I know, but we gotta get the fuck outta here, or we're all going to jail.*"

So we ran. All of us… We just ran. We left that poor innocent deer. All alone, bloody and dying… We just ran.

TL:AUDIO RECEPTION ERROR

ES:…I was only seventeen…

TL:AUDIO RECEPTION ERROR

ES:Seventeen…

TL:AUDIO RECEPTION ERROR

ES:I'm sorry, I'm fine. At that moment, it was one of the only times of my life I felt like I was not in control. Like someone else was in command of my actions. Not me. Definitely not me. Goddamn, I hate that feeling. Like right now. I guess you're the one in control of my future. My fate. *Let it go. Put it down. Let it happen.* Debra would always say that, but I would never listen. I couldn't. I hate not being in control. I wasn't in control when my boys were taken from me. Or Debra. I'm not sure who was in control that night. The deer? Alicio? It sure the hell wasn't me. There was nothing I could do. I mean, maybe there was. But it was too late.

TL:AUDIO RECEPTION ERROR

ES:Enough of this bullshit about my youth. My teenage years have nothing to do with now. Let's get on with this.

TL:AUDIO RECEPTION ERROR

ES:You act as if you are some kind of a shrink or something. Well, you're not. You're nothing more than a corporate pawn. You weed out the financially inadequate and make sure the big ones don't get away. Trying to pull some childhood trauma out of me. Why? So you can recommend therapy?

TL: AUDIO RECEPTION ERROR

ES:No. No. I don't want any kind of therapy. I want to be reunited with my family and I know exactly what your decision is supposed to be based on, and it has nothing to do with my childhood or what drugs I use to recreate with, or who I chose to consort with during my impressionable years, or where I grew up.

TL: AUDIO RECEPTION ERROR

ES:Do you want to know why everyone thinks I grew up in Chicago? Because I had an agent that felt my incredibly obtuse fan base would enjoy my paintings less if they knew the truth. He hated the truth. That's why I haven't spoken to him in ten years. Although, to tell you the truth, he and I actually had a lot in common. Our ability to avoid that which was accurate and indisputable was one of the things we had in common.

TL: AUDIO RECEPTION ERROR

ES:Okay, whoa, let's step back here a sec. First of all, I wouldn't call myself famous. I am well known in the art world, and because of the praise I receive from the mighty critics, there are lot of people with way more money than common sense that know me and are somehow under the false impression that I have touched their pathetic lives. That my art somehow spoke to them. Or they have the ridiculous notion that they feel what I feel. They make me sick. But that has nothing to do with this. You cannot base your decision on my public notoriety. Or what your employers will think if you allow the termination of a *productive member of society.*

TL:AUDIO RECEPTION ERROR

ES:You do realize that's why you are my case worker. Because Exelon expects you to deny me. A *famous* painter with lots of very rich fans, perhaps some secret unsold work. And no living family. No friends. I'm a gold mine to them. And you. Do you realize that you have never approved anyone above the Viable Line for VDS? Not that you haven't had far more than your share.

TL:AUDIO RECEPTION ERROR

ES:Oh, I guarantee it. I have thoroughly researched your history, probably more than you have researched mine. I'm telling you the more money a *candidate* has, the more likely they are to have an audience with you.

TL: AUDIO RECEPTION ERROR

ES:With you, the poor get an automatic stamp of approval. But have a penny over the Viable Line, and you get denied. *No VDS. You just need some therapy. You have money; don't you realize how happy you should be?*

TL: AUDIO RECEPTION ERROR

ES:I'm sure it's just a coincidence.

TL: AUDIO RECEPTION ERROR

ES:I have lots of money. Money can get you almost anything you want. I wanted information about my case worker.

TL: AUDIO RECEPTION ERROR

ES:I also found out that you are incredibly honest and are considered to have a very high ethics code. You are a slave to your own morality. You don't even realize what a pretender you are.

TL: AUDIO RECEPTION ERROR

ES:You are so self-righteous you cannot even consider the possibility that you are wrong. The faith you have in Exelon as well as all the other Corporations of America is completely undeserved. I think they have actually trained you to believe that you are somehow acting in the best interest of mankind. Why do you find it so easy to understand why an underprivileged person's life is too much of a struggle to be forced to go on, but you can't even acknowledge the possibility of a person with the luxury of money not wanting to continue?

TL: AUDIO RECEPTION ERROR

ES:Then why is it that on the rare occasion that a rich, successful person decides to self-terminate, more times than not, you are the one who ends up hearing their case? And of course denying them while at the same time protecting their assets and the interest of Exelon.

TL: AUDIO RECEPTION ERROR

ES:Can I read this to you?

TL: AUDIO RECEPTION ERROR

ES:It's your job description. It states that regardless of age, sex, religion, or heritage an individual is eligible for Voluntary Downsizing if they have been determined to have a terminal disease or condition that they do not have the financial means to alleviate, remedy, medicate, rehabilitate, or recover; or are over the age of 120 years; or life has become too difficult to continue due to physical pain, mental anguish, or unreasonable limitations. So there it is. Stamp me approved and let's get on with it.

TL: AUDIO RECEPTION ERROR

ES:My life has become too difficult to continue due to mental anguish.

TL: AUDIO RECEPTION ERROR

ES:Of course I know what that means. It's suffering due to depression or fright or anxiety or distress or grief or trauma.

TL: AUDIO RECEPTION ERROR

ES:Which one? Well, take your pick. All of them.

TL: AUDIO RECEPTION ERROR

ES:We don't need to talk more about my life for you to come to a determination. You just have to believe me.

TL: AUDIO RECEPTION ERROR

ES:I already told you I don't want to talk about my boys.

TL: AUDIO RECEPTION ERROR

ES:Did you know that every one of those rich, successful, productive, poor souls that you denied, every one of them ended up killing themselves anyway?

TL: AUDIO RECEPTION ERROR

ES:How could you not realize you should have approved them?

TL: AUDIO RECEPTION ERROR

ES:No, I don't want to talk about my wife. I want you to admit you were wrong. Over and over again you were wrong. Those people did not need therapy. They needed a dignified termination

TL: AUDIO RECEPTION ERROR.

ES:Fine, stand by your decisions, but realize you are nothing more than a puppet for Exelon. Eighty-five percent of their assets went to the states.

Not their children, not their families, not their friends. Their wills are meaningless. Their wishes are ignored. First by you, then by Exelon and all the rest of the Corporate bastards. The Death Tax. What a scam. Oh sure, since Corporate America has taken over, taxes are at an all-time low. As long as you don't die or share. 85% Death Tax, 85% Gift Tax, oh they get theirs, they just gotta wait you out. And they always will. No matter how long you live.

TL: AUDIO RECEPTION ERROR

ES:Again with my wife. Why should I even talk at all? It's obvious you aren't listening. You want to know about my wife? I'll tell you she was the greatest thing that ever happened to me and I was the worst thing that ever happened to her. She was a pretender. Just like you. Just as you pretend Exelon is worthy of your love and admiration she pretended I was worthy of hers. She pretended I was handsome! She pretended I was romantic! She pretended that I was talented, that I was passionate, that I was caring. She pretended that I was her knight in shining armor.

TL: AUDIO RECEPTION ERROR

ES:I thought I was a pretender, too. I pretended I was worthy of such a woman. But, I realized after a while, I'm not a pretender. I'm a goddamned liar.

TL: AUDIO RECEPTION ERROR

ES:Oh, there's a difference. A big difference.

TL: AUDIO RECEPTION ERROR

ES:During the years of my seclusion I assure you, I was not simply counting the passing days.

TL: AUDIO RECEPTION ERROR

ES:I've been painting. I've been pouring out every drop of my soul onto canvas for the past five years.

TL: AUDIO RECEPTION ERROR

ES:Don't believe everything you read. Just because I haven't sold anything since Debra died, does not mean I haven't been creating.

TL: AUDIO RECEPTION ERROR

ES:For me it's just a way to release what's inside of me. For some reason, other people with lots of money appreciate it. They bought a ton of it and allowed me to provide a luxurious life for my family. But now my family is gone and there is nothing left inside of me. It's all on the canvas. I'm done.

TL: AUDIO RECEPTION ERROR

ES:Death just means you're not living anymore. And I'm not, so let's make it official.

TL: AUDIO RECEPTION ERROR

ES:When I first met Debra she was dead. Her family said it was me and my art that brought her back to life. I didn't believe them. I thought they were all full of shit. How could someone so vibrant, so beautiful, so full of life, be dead? It was years later I found out they were telling the truth, when she died the second time right before my eyes.

TL: AUDIO RECEPTION ERROR

ES:She died three times. The third time was permanent. There is no chance of her coming back again. Her body is no good anymore. Useless.

TL: AUDIO RECEPTION ERROR

ES:Your body is your vessel. It's how you navigate through the world of the living. It is how you are acknowledged. How you are appraised. It is the original reason you receive attention and evaluation. No one can ever know what makes up your soul without first recognizing your physical presence.

TL: AUDIO RECEPTION ERROR

ES:Debra's vessel is gone forever. I will never know its warmth again, and without it, Debra can never come back to me. Don't you see? That's why I have to go to her.

TL: AUDIO RECEPTION ERROR

ES:You think you're clever, tricking me into telling you about my wife. Well, you're not. I am saying what my spirit moves me to say. You are not driving this interview. I am.

TL: AUDIO RECEPTION ERROR

ES:You have my complete bio. The way Corporate America sees my life. I'm sure you could figure out what killed my wife each time.

TL: AUDIO RECEPTION ERROR

ES:I would say *Almost* killed her.

TL: AUDIO RECEPTION ERROR

ES:No. That's not what I mean. It totally killed her. Each time she was completely dead inside. Her body was perfect. Her self was dead. Until her hero with the paint brush saved her.

TL: AUDIO RECEPTION ERROR

ES:What I mean is it was *Almost* that killed her. She *Almost* didn't escape. She *Almost* had her head blown off. She *Almost* got her throat slit. She was *Almost* brutally raped. They *Almost* made it. Too many *Almosts*. That's what did her in the first time, all those *Almosts*. And then half a decade later, I saved her.

TL: AUDIO RECEPTION ERROR

ES:For a long time I only got bits and pieces of the story. Some from Debra, mostly from her family. It wasn't until we were married and had both the boys that Debra told me the whole story. Every gruesome detail. Is that what you want to hear? Every disgusting, grisly detail.

TL: AUDIO RECEPTION ERROR

ES:You know I was just starting to find you a little bit less repugnant than I originally thought. But you are a real sicko. Aren't you? Do you get off on hearing the most hideous locked away details of a desperate stranger's life?

Do you enjoy denying them their chance at escape? Shaking the keys of freedom right in their face and then snatching them away.

TL: AUDIO RECEPTION ERROR

ES:Do you have any idea how all the over-privileged people you denied found their freedom? In painful, frightful ways. With guns and razor blades and pills. Left for their loved ones or employees to find them. There was nothing respectful, or humane or clinical about it. It's a nasty thing, suicide. But at least the Corporations got 85% of their shit, huh? That must make it easy for you to sleep at night.

TL: AUDIO RECEPTION ERROR

ES:Whoa. You can't say a thing like that and then switch the subject to my wife's drug use. You say, *you cannot prevent someone from taking their own life, but as a representative of the state, you cannot, and will not condone it if they have too much to live for.* That is complete bullshit. Too much money, you mean. Whatever you say, sweetheart. Toe that corporate line.

TL: AUDIO RECEPTION ERROR

ES:Okay, if it says it in your file, then it must be true. Just like it says I was born and raised in Chicago.

TL: AUDIO RECEPTION ERROR

ES:Well, Debra may have done a lot of drugs in her younger years, but she did not have a *drug problem like me* as you say.

TL: AUDIO RECEPTION ERROR

ES:Debra and I...Our childhoods were nothing alike. She grew up in Westmont. Her parents were not *working class*, they were living class.

TL: AUDIO RECEPTION ERROR

ES:Sure, they had jobs. But they did not have to sell their souls and sacrifice their bodies for them. No. They had enough time and money to enjoy themselves.

TL: AUDIO RECEPTION ERROR

ES: They could have had the perfect little family with nothing but soda pop and cotton candy, but unfortunately, they did sell their souls. Not to their jobs, not to Corporate America. They sold their souls to God in exchange for a false sense of security and superiority.

TL: AUDIO RECEPTION ERROR

ES:They were religious. Super religious. And that's how they raised their four daughters. Or at least tried to. They were far too sheltering, over-bearing, stifling. There was no room for discussion, or differing opinions. Questions were frowned upon. They loved their girls, but they were just too ignorant to reality. And more times than not, very religious parents have very rebellious teenagers.

TL: AUDIO RECEPTION ERROR

ES:Debra and her older sister, Connie, they were the middle two. They were the rebels. Sex and drugs and rock n roll.

TL: AUDIO RECEPTION ERROR

ES:Debra started partying at fourteen. By seventeen ecstasy was her drug of choice. Well, I guess it was actually Connie's choice. Debra liked every-thing Connie liked and hated everything Connie hated. Ecstasy being an example of the former and their parents being an example of the latter.

TL: AUDIO RECEPTION ERROR

ES:Yeah, they were bad teenagers. Later though, after all the *almosts,* Debra got real close to her parents. I guess you can completely disagree with every single notion a person has, you can think them a fool, an idiot, a complete waste of humanity, but if that person is your parent, and they are able to accept you for everything you are, and everything you are not, and they offer you comfort and safety in your most desperate times, I guess you can put all that other shit aside.

TL: AUDIO RECEPTION ERROR

ES:When it was all over Debra needed a soft place to land, and that's what her folks gave her. They gave her a peaceful place to be dead. Rest in peace, right? Then five years later she saw one of my stupid drawings and she was resurrected. Maybe you should bow down before me. I can raise the dead.

TL: AUDIO RECEPTION ERROR

ES:She was supposed to be a senior at Dunbar High School. But she took a year off. Why not? Connie was taking the rest of her life off. It seemed like the thing to do.

TL: AUDIO RECEPTION ERROR

ES:Connie was twenty. She had her own place in the city. Well, not really. I guess she lived with five other misdirected, unmotivated burn outs. It was party time, all the time. Debra went there on a Friday and came home thirty eight Fridays later.

TL: AUDIO RECEPTION ERROR

ES:There was this one guy. A little older than the rest. They called him Cutter. No one knew where he came from, what his story was, or why they called him Cutter. They knew he had X. He sold it cheap and it was good.

TL: AUDIO RECEPTION ERROR

ES:He just started appearing at parties and hangouts and whatever. He was a stoner, like the rest of them. Back then, that was the only qualification you needed to be part of the group. Thing was, he wasn't like them. Not like any of them. Not in any way.

TL: AUDIO RECEPTION ERROR

ES:Connie had a sort of boyfriend, Paulie. Paulie didn't like Cutter. Connie didn't like that Paulie got jealous when he heard Connie and Cutter got real touchy feely at a rave one night. Connie storms out, *'You don't own me!'* she yelled and hit the streets with my little Debra in tow. So who do you think they ran into?

TL: AUDIO RECEPTION ERROR

ES:Yeah, they're not walking ten minutes and he curbs his car beside them. *'What's up, Con?'* Cutter asks all cool and laid back.

Debra hated that he called her Con. She hated it more that he called her Little Sis. The next thing Debra knows she's in the back seat, Connie's up front and they're on their way to Cutter's house.

TL: AUDIO RECEPTION ERROR

ES:Debra got a bad vibe right from the start. She was nervous and suspicious, but she just kept smiling her beautiful smile, trying hard to act cool. She didn't want Connie to think she was square. Cutter had some X back at his place and they were gonna party the day away. Debra felt safe whenever she was with Connie, so she kept her mouth shut and her paranoia to herself. What she really didn't like was that they'd never been to this guy's house before. As far as she knew, no one had. Cutter had only been coming around for a couple of months. He said his crib was about forty minutes away. And fuck, the guy had Tennessee plates. Back then it would have been Tennessee plates, now you would know them as McDonald's plates. This was years ago, honey, long before the Big Mac *saved* the Smoky Mountains.

TL: AUDIO RECEPTION ERROR

ES:Anyway, they get to Cutter's place, but the thing is there is no house. No neighborhood. No nothing. Just trees. The three of them are walking on a trail through the woods and Cutter just keeps saying, *'It's close, not much further.'*

And Debra knows this is fucked and she's waiting for Connie to say something, but she doesn't. She just keeps on walkin'. Arm and arm, snuggled up close with Cutter. Debra lagged about twenty feet behind. Getting more and more nervous. And angry. And confused and scared. Then they turned off the trail.

'C'mon, Little Sis!' Cutter shouts.

Connie says nothing. She doesn't even turn around to check on Debra. She just assumes everything is fine and Debra will continue to follow her, no questions asked, just like always. But that is not what happens.

As Connie and Cutter slip into the woods Debra stops. She yells *'Connie! What are you doing? Stop!'*

Cutter yells back, *'I thought three would be a party, but I guess it's gonna be a crowd!'* and they disappear.

TL: AUDIO RECEPTION ERROR

ES:Debra waits for a long minute. She starts to cry. She chases after them. *'Wait up! Connie! Please!'*

Finally she sees them, walking away from her so close it looks like they are joined at the hip. As Debra gains on them she begins to yell at her sister, *'Connie why are you doing this to me? Please Connie, I want to go home. Why won't you talk to me? What did I do?'*

And finally they stop. Debra never forgot that moment. She said the sunbeams came through the trees like spotlights on a stage. The brightest most intense ray of light blazed down upon Connie and Cutter. Debra had to squint as she looked upon them. She said it looked like something of a supernatural vision. Almost religious. Holy. But God knows it was not. Debra was close enough to almost touch them. She remembers she wanted to punch Connie. To hit her and scream at her. She was so angry at her older sister, her protector, her role model. But when the two of them turned in unison to face Debra, conjoined lovers, Connie and her new boyfriend, Debra faced the new couple and all her questions were answered. Cutter smiled at Debra as if this had all been a joke, his mouth filled with crooked, nicotine stained teeth. Connie offered no smile, as her mouth was filled with the barrel of a midnight black revolver.

TL: AUDIO RECEPTION ERROR

ES:*'Now c'mon Little Sis. Unless you want me to splatter the back of Con's skull all over this fucking forest, get in front of me and start walking.'* That's what that goddamned monster said.

TL: AUDIO RECEPTION ERROR

ES:Are you liking this story? Do you want me to keep going?

TL: AUDIO RECEPTION ERROR

ES:Well now, you certainly do have a dark side. Don't you? Do you enjoy watching the torture this story is bringing me? Do you like seeing me spill my guts out? Oh, I'll keep going, honey, but let me warn you right now, it gets worse. A lot worse.

TL: AUDIO RECEPTION ERROR

ES: So this goddamned maniac had been living in the woods, but not in a house or anything. He brings the girls to a real secluded area, there's a tent with an umbrella chair sitting outside of it and that's it. Except for a shit load of empty beer cans and pints of whiskey and cigarette butts all over the ground. Oh, and there's a body, a sixteen year old dead girl lying about fifty feet away from them. They didn't see it, but the authorities would find it later. Yeah, Debra and Connie were not the first time Cutter had company over. Anyway, when he gets them there he pulls out a huge hunting knife. '*Now you lucky ladies are going to find out why they call me Cutter,*" he tells them.

Still holding the gun on them he forces them both to take off their pants and shoes. They're hysterical. They're pleading. He seems to enjoy that. He tells them it's okay to make noise, but if they get too loud he'll have to stab them in the throat. He makes Debra…he has her kneel down, facing his tent, with Connie standing in front of her. '*Closer,*' he commands, until Connie's panties are pressed right against Debra's face. '*Please, Cutter,*' they beg, '*don't do this.*'

TL: AUDIO RECEPTION ERROR

ES:And then Cutter… that bastard gets behind Debra. He pushes the barrel of the gun hard into the back of her skull. '*Get out of this alive or dead, the choice is yours,*' he promises.

Debra starts whimpering for the mother she thought she hated. Connie is wearing this silky black button down blouse with white pearl buttons. Debra remembers every detail so vividly as she tells me, just as I remember it so perfectly and I am telling you now, even though she only shared this horrific story with me once. Debra's eyes are pressed hard at the top of their sockets as she is looking up Connie's black blouse, trying hard to see her sister's face, looking for direction, assurance, protection. She finds none of it. What she sees instead is the shiny blade enter Connie's blouse and slowly make its way down popping each button so that it falls to Debra's forehead and then to the grass and dirt below. Scraping against her flesh the blade separates the silk and exposes a black satin lace bra.

'*My, My,*' Cutter says, his mouth overfilled with saliva.

Debra feels his hot, pasty drool as it hits the heels of her bare feet. This sick fuck, he takes the point of the knife and sticks it in between Connie's breasts. He puts pressure to the blade and in one quick motion he pierces her flesh and cuts her bra in two. Connie shrieks in pain. She jumps back clutching her wound.

TL: AUDIO RECEPTION ERROR

ES: The next sound they hear is Cutter cocking the gun. '*Now you best calm yourself,*' he commands her. '*You don't wanna be responsible for Lil Sis's head being splattered, do you? Besides, a little blood ain't never hurt no one. And I like my women a little bloody. Now let me take a look at you.*' That's what that goddamned son of a bitch says. I mean what could they do? Those poor girls.

TL: AUDIO RECEPTION ERROR

ES: What that monster does next…Oh Jesus. That son of a bitch, he grabs Debra's hair and pulls her forward. '*All fours,*' he commands, '*get ready to crawl.*' Then he warns Connie, '*I'm watching you. I'm watching you real close. Let's not make Lil Sis get hurt anymore than she has to.*' That's what he says, the fucking deviant.

And then…And then he sticks that blade into the palm of Debra's left foot and slices it open. She cries out for a God she didn't think she believed in anymore. She falls to her elbows. He pulls her up by her hair with his gunned hand. '*All fours!*' he yells.

Debra watches as her bleeding older sister, the person she had idolized all her life. Connie, squats down into a ball, and clutching her wound, she throws up between her knees.

TL: AUDIO RECEPTION ERROR

ES:Cutter does the same to her right foot. He says, *'Now that's just to keep you from running away when I'm busy with your sister.'*

TL: AUDIO RECEPTION ERROR

ES:At this point Debra becomes a zombie. She accepts that this is the place that she and her sister will die. She says looking back at it, that the moment he cut her second foot she stopped being afraid. She just felt disappointed. Disappointed in herself, disappointed in her sister, disappointed at the way they were going to die, at her entire life. She became overwhelmed with regret. She no longer felt human. She just wished it was over already, and that she were dead. She felt selfish. She remembers thinking that if somehow she got a hold of the gun, not that she was planning such an attempt, but if the opportunity arose, she would escape. Without Connie, though. She felt guilty that she considered it, but her escape plan included abandoning her older sister. She would kill herself. She would shoot herself right in the head. Unapproved Voluntary Downsizing. She was ashamed that she felt that way, but it was all she could think to do to make this evil stop. She would abandon Connie. A big part of her disappointment was she felt Connie had already abandoned her by not being her protector.

TL: AUDIO RECEPTION ERROR

ES:Cutter felt comfortable. Two bleeding victims, paralyzed by fear, or disappointment, or whatever. They were now his to do with as he wished. He was in total control. That is the luxury the sisters afforded him. He walked a few feet in front of Debra. He stood in front of his one man tent. Debra watched him with her eyes still pressed against the top of their sockets as the last of her tears and snot fell to the earth. Cutter placed the gun on the umbrella chair he now stood beside. With the knife still in his left hand he kicked off his shoes and began to take off his pants. He tells the girls, *'Now we're gonna have some fun.'*

Debra is staring at the goddamned gun, wishing it was in her hands. In her mouth. Wishing that she could be in control and end this nightmare. To have the ability to never wake up again and remember this terrible moment and all the worse moments that were about to follow. She remembers every detail of that moment. The umbrella chair was red, white, and blue and written in black across the back rest were the words *Land of the Free*. Of course this was back before we sold our freedom to Corporate America. The gun just sat there waiting to be picked up and put to work, as Cutter fumbled removing his pants, his tongue sticking out between his teeth as he continued to salivate. Debra looked over to her useless sister, still squatting in a pathetic ball of despair. She watched as drops of blood ran down Connie's arms and dripped on to the vomit that puddled between her feet. A few flies had already discovered the scene and buzzed around between her knees. Connie was to the right of Cutter, about four feet away from him. '*Little Sis!*' he called out. Debra made eye contact with him. A straight line of grass and dirt between them. '*Crawl to me!*' he commanded as he began to take down his underwear. That's when everything changed.

TL: AUDIO RECEPTION ERROR

ES:Connie was also able to expel her fear, but she did not replace it with disappointment, she replaced it with anger and rage. And her rage took its most deadly form, action. So as Cutter was bent forward with his boxers around his knees, holding his razor sharp blade haphazardly, as he screamed, '*now, bitch!*' at Debra, Connie lunged forward with all her strength and pushed him just below his chest.

You see, this also used to be the *Home of the Brave*. He fumbled to take control of the knife just before contact, but unable to achieve balance with his underwear around his knees, he failed. He fell backward onto his tent, collapsing the fabric down all around him. Connie grabbed the gun and bobbled it as she shouted, '*Run, Debra, Run!*'

TL: AUDIO RECEPTION ERROR

ES:Debra's heart pumped new life throughout her entire body. All of her muscles ached with the possibility of a second chance. She told me, other than our sons, this was the most beautiful sight her eyes ever beheld. Connie had risen like the phoenix and become the hero Debra had always believed her to be. Debra forgot all about her tortured feet and attempted to stand, only to have the hot sting of pain bring her back to her knees. And Debra, my sweet Debra, who I've never known to harm a single living thing, the kindest person I've ever experienced, she screams, '*Shoot him Connie! Shoot that mother-fucker dead!*'

TL: AUDIO RECEPTION ERROR

ES:Cutter just lays there for a couple seconds, shaking his head in disbelief as blood gushes from his mouth. He spits out a chunk of tongue he had bitten off. He slurs insults at his would-be victims. He calls them dirty whores as he takes notice that he has stabbed himself. From her knees Debra sees the knife stuck in his inner thigh. She's crying tears of fear, tears of relief, tears of exhaustion, tears of anger. She continues to beg Connie to kill this scum of the earth and put an end to this nightmare.

Connie cocks the gun. Cutter starts to laugh. He says, '*Con, you stupid bitch.*' He spits more blood and tissue from his mouth as he slurs, '*I can't afford bullets. I spent all my money on X for you junkie whores.*' Click goes the sound of an empty chamber. Click again. Cutter begins to pull the blade from his leg. And click again. Debra is once again filled with dread.

Connie throws the gun with all her might and connects with the side of that bastard's head. She pulls Debra to her feet. She yells, '*C'mon we got to run! C'mon Debra!*' With Connie squeezing Debra tight under her arms they run. Every step burns with pain. Debra says she could feel the gravel and dirt and pebbles from the forest floor invading her body. Her feet felt as if they are growing in size as they are splitting in two. '*I can't!*' she yells.

Connie ignores her complaints and continues to push and prod her little sister. Debra could hear Cutter. He is giving chase. He is gaining. '*Run Debra! Run!*' Connie commands.

Debra's feet become numb with pain. The girls keep running. Debra keeps going as fast as her torn feet will allow. She feels nothing from her knees down. She is hysterical. She keeps going. Unfortunately…Unfortun…The thing is, the girls were running the wrong way. Deeper and deeper into the woods they were headed. Debra's wound is impaled by a large stick. She falls to the floor. She sees the intruder sticking out of her foot, just as the knife protruded from Cutter's thigh.

Acting on pure adrenalin she attempts to pull the stick from her foot. It's in deep. As she tries to work it out it cracks off inside of her. She looks to Connie in pure terror. But Connie is nowhere to be seen. She is gone.

Debra is all alone. She has no memory of when Connie and she separated. She crawls to an uprooted tree and presses her back against it. She pulls her knees up to her chest and hugs them. Her legs all scratched and bleeding. Her feet throbbing and burning like fire. She just sits there and cries. She sits there for almost twenty-four hours. That's how the ranger finds her.

TL: AUDIO RECEPTION ERROR

ES:Cutter caught up to them… Connie didn't make it.

TL: AUDIO RECEPTION ERROR

ES:I'm done with details. She was fuckin' murdered! And the goddamn bastard that did it got away. Free as a fuckin' bird.

TL: AUDIO RECEPTION ERROR

ES:Debra has no idea what happened during Connie's last moments. When that monster got his fucking hands on her. She just kept running. She doesn't know how long. Minutes, miles, hours. She just ran. But that's how my sweet Debra died the first time. Cutter didn't kill her. She killed herself. She was a victim of guilt. The kind of guilt you could never imagine. She says she should have searched for Connie, or tried to get help or something. Anything. Instead she just sat there and waited to be saved. I tell her it's okay. I tell her she was in shock. I tell her not to blame herself. I tell her I love her.

TL: AUDIO RECEPTION ERROR

ES:She stayed dead for five years. She stayed with her parents. They kept praying for Christ to save her, but he didn't. I did. I saved her with a stupid picture drawn on a piece of garbage. How 'bout that? I can't walk on water but I can save a lost soul. Like I told you, I can raise the dead.

TL: AUDIO RECEPTION ERROR

ES:She said my art spoke to her. It was like I was in her head. At the time, I just thought she was kind of hot, real pretty, so I was like, right on. Whatever, right?

TL: AUDIO RECEPTION ERROR

ES:I moved into her folk's basement and they bought me all sorts of paint supplies. They were stoked that I brought their little girl back to life. They told me a little bit about what she had been through. Shit, I kinda think that maybe they thought I was Jesus at first. You know, like the second coming. Then they saw my paintings. That had to freak 'em out. My early stuff was some fucked up shit. Debra said *'Ellis paints how I feel.'* Now I know that definitely freaked 'em out.

TL: AUDIO RECEPTION ERROR

ES:Anyway, Paulie, you remember Paulie, he was Connie's kind of boy-friend, ends up there was more to him than partying. He works at some art gallery. Not an artist or anything, he just works there. So they like my shit. I do a show there and everyone is blown away. Everyone says I paint what they feel. Bullshit, I'm thinking, whatever, but they are actually buying my stuff so I'm like, right on. Next thing I know I got an agent and we're making up a fake story about my past. It's great to come from poor humble beginnings, but not Begman's Root. You know, *the Incident* and all. People think the Root is nothing but addicts and killers and rapists. That's what he tells me. I'm thinking you dirty mother-fucker and then he hands me a nice check, so I'm like right on.

TL: AUDIO RECEPTION ERROR

ES:Enough already. You got me to open up and spill my guts. I told you some real gut-wrenching stuff. You know my story. I'm consumed with guilt, just like my wife was. It's my fault my boys' lives ended so young, so tragically. And I cannot bear it anymore. They're gone and it's all my fault. So what do you say, sweetheart? How 'bout you approve my *Voluntary Downsizing* and you can get on with your life and I can get on with my death.

TL: AUDIO RECEPTION ERROR

ES:What in the hell do you mean it's not my story?

TL: AUDIO RECEPTION ERROR

ES:What happened in the woods was my wife's story, sure, but the point is we both had to live with unbearable guilt. Her with her sister, me with my...with my sons. The deaths of Jody and Colin haunt me every day. I can't live with it anymore. Not without Debra. I've done it for six years already. It's enough Goddamit. Enough.

TL: AUDIO RECEPTION ERROR

ES:*Reasonable human expectations versus karma,* what the fuck is that supposed to mean?

TL: AUDIO RECEPTION ERROR

ES:What? *Debra's guilt is more warranted because her inaction may have actually had a direct effect on Connie's death?* So you are trying to say Debra was a worse person than I am. She is more of a killer than I am. Is that what you think? You're just out of your mind. You just want the state to get my shit! Well, it ain't gonna happen. That I promise you.

TL: AUDIO RECEPTION ERROR

ES:Debra's guilt is more warranted than mine? How dare you. How dare you tell me what emotions I'm allowed to feel.

TL: AUDIO RECEPTION ERROR

ES:Because you don't believe in karma? What does it matter what you believe in? This is about me. My life! My death! And you better start believing in karma, because some day it's going to come looking for you and it's not gonna give a shit if you believe in it or not.

TL: AUDIO RECEPTION ERROR

ES:I don't give a shit what the state's position is on karma. I know what their position on Begman's Root was. Oh yeah, when Exelon purchased our state they were going to make life better for everyone. They were going to clean up the Root. Do you have any idea what *the Incident* even was? Do you honestly believe the corporate accounts of what happened. It was involuntary downsizing. It was economic cleansing! It was a fuckin' massacre!

TL: AUDIO RECEPTION ERROR

ES:Again, I'll be honest with you. And I say this with a heavy, guilt-ridden heart, but the really sad thing is the Incident was great for my career, the great liar that I am. It inspired me. Me, the great crusader for the poor, the broken, the forgotten. I kept my mouth shut and I painted. Some say it was my best work. I painted what I felt. I emptied my soul on those canvases and you want to know what my soul said? Eat the rich and fuck Exelon and all the rest of the Corporate States of America. Disembowel the evil corporation that bought my state and killed my people. Those paintings went for more money than anything I ever sold.

TL: AUDIO RECEPTION ERROR

ES:It shames me to say this, but two of those paintings hang in the lobby of Exelon headquarters. They helped pay for my first summer home. Such a liar I was.

TL: AUDIO RECEPTION ERROR

ES:You know how my boys died. How could you think that was just a coincidence? That's karma. The sins of the father. That's exactly what that was. My precious boys paid for my sins.

TL: AUDIO RECEPTION ERROR

ES:Colin and Jody. My boys. I know every parent thinks this, but my boys, they were a gift to this world. Who knows what great things they would have accomplished? We were the perfect little family. Health and love and money. The three key ingredients to the perfect life. Some art critics said I had lost my edge after the boys were born. That my paintings were too happy. Maybe they were right. It didn't matter though. The legend had already been born. Once one dumb ass, high society idiot has an Ellis hanging in his mansion, then every one of them rich lemmings needs one, or two, or even three. I was in high demand. I was nationwide.

TL: AUDIO RECEPTION ERROR

ES:A car accident. Yeah, I suppose that would be true, but do you know why? Me, that's why.

TL: AUDIO RECEPTION ERROR.

ES:Jody had just graduated from the University of AT&T. He had been accepted to the Baxter International School of Medicine. We were celebrating. By then we owned five houses. We were out in the country, upstate Apple. Just the five of us.

TL: AUDIO RECEPTION ERROR

ES:Colin's girlfriend Sarah. She was a great lady. I have no idea what became of her. I know she married Colin's drummer, Alfred. After that... who knows? Yeah, Colin and Sarah, I thought they would give Debra and me the most beautiful grandchildren, but...

TL: AUDIO RECEPTION ERROR

ES:Huh? What? I'm sorry. Colin was twenty-four. Such a great musician. What incredible music he would have gifted us all with. Instead he and Jody decided to drive into town and pick up some venison steaks for dinner. Colin was going to grill them. That boy was a helluva cook, too. Sarah had never had venison. I teased her and called it a Bambi Bar-B-Q.

Debra worried. *'You can't drive, you've been drinking,'* she said.

'Two beers,' that's what Colin said and then I said it too. *'Don't worry, he's a big boy.'*

So they left. Debra, Sarah and I, we were relaxing in the pool. Not a care in the world. I remember, I was wondering what lie I would paint next.

TL: AUDIO RECEPTION ERROR

ES:It was more like four beers, but he wasn't drunk. It says as much in the police report. He didn't lose control because he was drunk.

TL: AUDIO RECEPTION ERROR

ES:The police found flesh and blood on the bumper. A trail of blood leading into the woods. My boys. My beautiful boys. They were my best friends. They paid for my sin. I was the one who drove too fucked up. It was all my goddamned fault.

TL: AUDIO RECEPTION ERROR

ES:Didn't you read the report? It was a deer. A fucking deer. He swerved to avoid hitting a goddamn deer. He lost control...

TL: AUDIO RECEPTION ERROR

ES:Message received. That's what I should have done all those years ago. Could of saved us all so much pain. So that's the guilt I live with every day. And I don't want to live with it anymore. I want to go to them and tell them I'm sorry. Tell them it was all my fault. I have to tell Debra. I'm so sorry.

TL: AUDIO RECEPTION ERROR

ES:Well, yeah, yes of course, that's when Debra died the second time.

TL: AUDIO RECEPTION ERROR

ES:No, my art didn't save her a second time. Not at all. It did become honest again, though. Once again, everything I put on that canvas came from inside my dark and tortured soul. The critics loved it. My fans had to have it. I was bigger than ever and at the same time I felt smaller than ever.

TL: AUDIO RECEPTION ERROR

ES:THB, that's who resurrected Debra the second time. Do you know who they are?

TL: AUDIO RECEPTION ERROR

ES:Sure you do. I'm sure your employer has trained you to hate them. Well, let me tell you something, THB is the only true charity organization that's left in this world. The states hate them because that charity status prevents them from getting a share of all that money. And there is a lot of money that goes through THB.

TL:AUDIO RECEPTION ERROR

ES:But it is so much more than money. True Human Beings. People helping people.

TL:AUDIO RECEPTION ERROR

ES:We got a letter from them a couple of weeks after we buried our sons…
It just said, '*If you want to talk, we are here for you.*' I was like, what the fuck
is this bullshit?

TL: AUDIO RECEPTION ERROR

ES:I find out a few weeks later that Debra's been calling. While I'm in my
studio putting all of me into my art, she's been talking to these… people.
Well, she called them friends. And it's been helping her, you know, deal
with things.

TL: AUDIO RECEPTION ERROR

ES:When she tells me about this, she says she wants us to get involved.
Right away I figure it's a scam. But it's not. It's real. It's people helping
people. There's no pressure. No meetings. It's not a cult or anything. It is
exactly what it claims to be. True Human Beings.

TL: AUDIO RECEPTION ERROR

ES:These multibillion dollar corporations may have ended disease for the
rich, but there are still plenty of people out there who need help. And
that's what Debra and I did for the next seven years. When we sold our
first summer home, you know what we did with the money? We paid the
mortgage of a widowed mother of two. Our second summer home put
four deserving kids through the University of YUM Brands. And our third
summer home, that was little Eddie Husker. A ten year old boy with brain
cancer- his family couldn't afford the cure. So we sold our place in upstate
Apple and he is alive today. At least last I heard he was. Like I said, I have
removed people from my life, or at least encouraged them to remove me
from their lives.

TL: AUDIO RECEPTION ERROR

ES:You know the corporations hated that. Even though they had to pretend to admire it.

TL: AUDIO RECEPTION ERROR

ES:Oh, indeed they did. But they had to protect the lie. The lie that people like you believe. That the USCA is all about its people and not about the bottom line.

TL: AUDIO RECEPTION ERROR

ES:Well, you know how it goes, if enough people believe in a lie it becomes the truth. The gospel according to everyone. Not quite everyone. Not the True Human Beings.

TL: AUDIO RECEPTION ERROR

ES:Why do you think the USCA gets almost all our money when we die? Feed the beast.

TL: AUDIO RECEPTION ERROR

ES:Bullshit to keep the states running. Every state has been running on a surplus for years. When I was a kid all the states had deficits. All of them. Great big deficits. Until the corporations saved the country. They started trimming away the *fat*. Now all the states are profitable. Less *dead weight* equals more money, right? The only money they cannot touch are registered charities, and, of course, the assets of a Voluntary Downsizer. Gives their children a chance to become economically viable, to live above the Viable Line, but the corporate pigs will still get it, sooner or later.

TL: AUDIO RECEPTION ERROR

ES:Funny how people below the viable line have a 95% approval rate for Voluntary Downsizing.

TL: AUDIO RECEPTION ERROR

ES:The states have tried to stop THB, but they can't. We have become too big. We help too many people. They secretly spread silly propaganda about THB being a cult. They do it covertly. They don't want to be seen as picking on a charity, but they are slowly but surely getting their false message out there. I'm sure you have seen the stories. I promise you they are bullshit. But every day THB touches more and more lives.

TL: AUDIO RECEPTION ERROR

ES:Do you know how many salaried employees THB has? Do you know how many offices? Buildings? Assets they have? None. Zero. There are coordinators that volunteer from their homes, they find *victims*, people in need of anything: counseling, time, money, whatever. And then there are givers. People like me and Debra. And when a coordinator informs us about a widowed mother of two who has a mortgage she can't afford, we cut a check to THB. THB pays every last cent to the mortgage company and the family keeps their home. And the state gets nothing.

TL: AUDIO RECEPTION ERROR

ES: I'm not entirely sure I believe you. I want to, but it seems unlikely. But let's say I take you at your word and you really do respect and admire THB. Then that means you know what it takes to be a True Human Being. Which also means you know what your decision should be.

TL: AUDIO RECEPTION ERROR

ES:Enough about this. Here it is in a nutshell. True Human Beings gave my wife her life back. We became givers. We lived a simple comfortable life and we helped a lot of people. It allowed me to not dwell on my terrible actions and continue living my lie. I would paint. People would pay plenty of money to decorate their homes with my paintings and I would in turn decorate my life by helping other people with that money.

Then Debra died. I stopped giving a shit about people. I became a recluse. I painted and painted and painted. I can't live like this anymore. I have nothing left to paint. I have to go to my wife and boys and tell them it was my fault and that I am sorry. And what of all my assets? Those paintings are worth millions. It all goes to True Human Beings. The corporations that rule these United States get nothing. And the only way this happens is if you approve me for Voluntary Downsizing. So what's it gonna be? Are you going to do the humane thing? Are you ready to be a True Human Being? Or are you going to do the corporate thing? Are you going to continue to be a puppet of the State?

TL: AUDIO RECEPTION ERROR

ES:No, no, no – see, that wouldn't work. I mean, technically I could donate all my paintings to THB, but they would be next to worthless. Remember, my fans think I come from a poor struggling family in Chicago. When actually I'm from a poor struggling family in Begman's Root. But who would buy a painting from someone from the Root? No one, that's who. We were all cop killers and rapists and child abusers. Anarchists. Evil people looking to overthrow society and destroy life as we know it. Isn't that right? Isn't that what made *The Incident* acceptable? Corporate America spinning the truth to fit their agenda. And that's exactly what they'll do if I donate my art to THB. The rumors start. The spin will begin. The whispers, that become louder and louder. Poor Ellis, he was brainwashed by that insane cult. His once brilliant paintings are now only propaganda for the THB. We all know the corporations control the message. And my *would be* customers, they would believe it. The people I've helped, Debra helped, THB helped – they wouldn't believe it – but they really couldn't afford an original Ellis now, could they? No, my art would no longer be sought after by the people of high society.

TL: AUDIO RECEPTION ERROR

ES:I'm afraid truth is only a lie that enough people believe in.

TL: AUDIO RECEPTION ERROR

ES:Don't you understand? This is the only way. If the state sanctions my suicide, my termination, my Voluntary Downsizing, the value of my paintings triples. Quadruples. Ellis, that poor tortured soul. That incredible artist. And if they do it with the knowledge that I'm leaving all my unsold art to THB –oh my God. I can't even begin to imagine. That would dispel every terrible rumor about True Human Beings. A State endorsement of THB, of people helping people. It might take a while, but as the rich buy my paintings from THB and THB in turn informs them where their money will go, and the stories of the unfortunate souls they are helping, then maybe, just maybe some of them will understand and follow the simple creed of True Human Beings. *If somebody is in dire need of something and you have extra of that same thing, be it money, time, energy, knowledge, patience, or understanding, you should give it to them.*

TL: AUDIO RECEPTION ERROR

ES: That's what I hope will be my legacy. Not my art, but what the money from my art will do to help the helpless, the broken, the forgotten.

TL: AUDIO RECEPTION ERROR

ES: No. C'mon, no, please don't say that. Haven't you been listening? You say I have too much to offer the world, I say I don't. I have painted my last painting. I'm done. I'm finished.

TL: AUDIO RECEPTION ERROR

ES: Happiness? Are you kidding me? The people who purchase my art? Trust me, it does not bring them happiness. It is a status symbol. It's indulgence. It's decadence. My customers have so much money, they are so far removed from sickness and worry and pain and sadness that they could not possibly know what the fuck happiness is.

TL: AUDIO RECEPTION ERROR

ES: I pour my heart out to you. I tell you the guilt I live with every day. I tell you I have to go to my wife and tell her the truth. Tell her how sorry I am. And you say I haven't demonstrated a life too difficult to continue. Well either way this ends. Now you don't have to make your decision until tomorrow morning. So please, for the sake of my family, take the night to think about it. To reconsider. Because I promise you, either way I'm leaving this world.

And if your mind is not changed tomorrow morning I promise you I will destroy every single painting in my studio. Five years of work. Millions of dollars. I'll fucking burn them all and there's not a damn thing you or Exelon can do about it! And that'll be on you! You will deprive the world of ever seeing another Ellis Snowden. The state gets nothing. The rich get nothing. True Human Beings get nothing. We all lose because of you. Five years of paintings, that no one will ever behold. My deepest, darkest reality all right there in brilliant colors and amazing textures.

TL: AUDIO RECEPTION ERROR

ES:Fuck your state appointed psychiatrist! Fuck your group therapies!

TL: AUDIO RECEPTION ERROR

ES:Relax. Relax. You don't have to call security. I'll calm down.

TL: AUDIO RECEPTION ERROR

ES:I told you I'll calm down.

TL: AUDIO RECEPTION ERROR

ES:Okay. There. See? I'm calm. It's just very upsetting. Your decision. It's so unfortunate. It's just…It's just no one will ever get to look at those paintings and lie about them. Rich phony people won't be able to say how much they can relate to me. They can't say I paint what they feel. They can't pretend to know what's inside of me. They're all liars anyway. Because nobody knows what I feel. Nobody.

TL: AUDIO RECEPTION ERROR

ES:Except Debra. I really did paint what Debra felt. I didn't believe her at first. I thought she was just pretending to understand. But she got it. She really felt it. She was the only one. From the very first sketch she saw on that box in the park. I sketched my guilt. And she felt that same guilt, that same exact guilt.

TL: AUDIO RECEPTION ERROR

ES:You know, over the years, I find myself thinking a lot about Connie. I can't help but wonder what she must have felt in her final moments. I don't know exactly what happened, but I do know enough to piece together a pretty clear picture. I know she was doing everything in her power to save Debra. And in that she succeeded. That right there makes her a True Human Being. Debra, with her cut open feet, how much she must have slowed Connie down. I'm sure if Connie would have abandoned her little sister she would be alive today. Debra on the other hand…she would have died at the hands of that madman, but that's not what Connie did. She kept pushing Debra. She did not give up. She would not leave Debra to die alone. She did all she could for Debra and then that bastard, he caught up to them.

Connie must have stopped to face that monster, to give Debra time to escape with her mutilated feet. Debra just kept running. Never even looked back. She has no memory when they separated. She cannot remember when that monster got Connie. I told her over and over, you were in shock. Your body was on automatic survival mode. It doesn't make you a bad person. It's not your fault. You were only seventeen. You were just a kid…only seventeen.

TL: AUDIO RECEPTION ERROR

ES:I think Connie was in shock, too. She was acting on pure adrenalin and instinct. And her instinct was to save her sister first and herself second.

TL: AUDIO RECEPTION ERROR

ES:Fucking Cutter, that Goddamned maniac. Now where he got to her there was a bit of an incline. They were going uphill. Now I don't think that asshole was in the best of shape. That in combination with not wearing pants, a stab wound in the leg, biting off a chunk of his own tongue and probably a little concussed from that gun smacking him in the head, all that might have evened up the odds just a little bit for Connie. She must have given him everything he could handle and then some. She was not going to go quietly. She must have fought like a son of a bitch. I don't know how she got the knife, but when she did, I doubt she hesitated for even a second. Right in the neck she got him. She ripped that jugular right out. Blood everywhere. She was covered in maniac blood.

TL: AUDIO RECEPTION ERROR

ES:Oh no. Cutter never made it out of those woods. Connie put an end to that mad man. That's where the Rangers found him and the knife that tore his neck apart. But Connie was beat up bad. Cut and bruised, just terrible, but she was alive. She started wandering the woods, searching for Debra, hoping to find help, a way out. What must have gone through her head when she found her way out? When she saw the road. How long had she been searching? How helpless she must have felt. And then there was the road. Salvation. The nightmare was over. She would find help. They would find Debra. They would survive. Life would be different. A second chance. Everything is better when you get a second chance, isn't it?

Oh God how incredible it must have felt when she saw the road. Their salvation. What a sight that road must have been... But I fucked up. I fucked it all up. It wasn't...I didn't...Derek was freakin out. He was funckin' hallucinating. He was screaming. And Marvel, he was puking everywhere. I swear to God I never saw her. I shouldn't have been driving. She came running out of the woods. I never saw her. I fucked it all up.

TL: AUDIO RECEPTION ERROR

ES:It was me and Alicio that saw her...lying there. Lying there, covered in blood. All alone. *'C'mon man, we gotta go,'* Alicio said.

I remember asking him, *'Is she alive?'*

Alicio said, *'Do you wanna spend the rest of your life in jail? Stolen car. Drugs. This. We gotta go. Now!'* So we...we got Val and Marvel and Derek out of the back. And. And we ran. We left Connie there. I left her there. Alone. I left her to die. I abandoned her.

TL: AUDIO RECEPTION ERROR

ES:I used to tell myself it wasn't my fault. I was in shock. My body was on automatic survival mode. It doesn't make me a bad person. It's not my fault... The crime my Debra believed herself guilty of...was the crime I committed. She knew the cancer that lurked inside my soul. She felt what I felt. But she wasn't a coward. She wasn't a liar.

TL: AUDIO RECEPTION ERROR

I'm sorry. Please. I'm a mess. I didn't want to get like this. More than fifty years ago. It seems like yesterday.

TL: AUDIO RECEPTION ERROR

ES:The next day Marvel asked what the hell had happened. Alicio said, *'Fuckin, Ellis hit a Goddamned deer.'*

That's when I started pretending. I would only let reality creep out through my brush, my pencil, my fingertips. The pretending offered me a good life. My art gave me relief. It allowed me to release some of the guilt that filled my mind and heart. I didn't even know who Connie was until after Jody was born. A developer had purchased some of the land at Mandrake Woods. It was on the news. I told Debra I used to party there with my friends and then she told me. She told me everything. And I, and I... I told her nothing. I just continued pretending. The perfect husband. The loving father. The great provider. But karma has an everlasting memory. She never forgets. She took my boys. My Debra. My everything... and now... Now, you have to help me. I have to go to them. I have to tell them I'm sorry.

LUCKY

IT IS A staggeringly unfair equation when doing the absolute best you possibly can is added to a highly unfortunate set of circumstances and they equate to the feeling of an overwhelming sense of hopelessness. Somehow the math does not seem to check out, but the equation is accurate, because sometimes the best you can do equals not good enough.

Dymond Washington was a victim of this bad math and the tremendous feelings of guilt and failure would have overtaken her if it wasn't for the anger and resentment that kept her earnest in her task at hand.

Her task was by no means a glamorous one. She was walking. Her legs moved swiftly, while her face portrayed disgust and indignation. If you were to come across her upon the street which she was walking, you would by no means ask her if she knew the time of day. Indeed, you would lower your head to avoid eye contact and continue on your much less tumultuous day. But there was really very little chance of anyone crossing paths with Dymond Washington on this particular day. The streets were empty, except for the horizontal drizzle and the winds, which were currently maintaining between fifteen and twenty-seven miles per hour. The air was thirty-eight degrees Fahrenheit. The fierce spray of water felt almost solid as it bombarded Dymond's uncovered face. It was the only part of her body that showed. This was one shitty day, unfit for any animal to be out in the elements, least of all a Human Being, and a distraught Human Being at that.

Onward she marched with purpose. Her face was numb from the cold.

She was mad at herself having forgotten her scarf. Actually, it was Jayla who had neglected to grab Dymond's scarf, but Dymond could not blame her daughter for the left behind wrap. *Why didn't I put my scarf on the list?* But she did anyway. *Jayla should have known to grab it.*

Dymond did not start this day from her home. She started where she had started her last fifteen days, in the hospital. A cold gust of saturated wind battered Dymond's face for several seconds that seemed never ending. Again, half frozen snot began to leak from both her nostrils. She could not properly tend to it, as her thickly gloved hands were full of meaningless, environmentally irresponsible bullshit. Mostly anyway. She may have had a few documents of importance, but mostly she carried bullshit. She was the middleman, or I suppose the middle woman, so to speak. She began each day with a big collection of garbage, but she would not throw it away. Instead she was charged with bringing it to other people who would throw it away for her. The reason this archaic responsibility still existed in 2017 was because mixed in among the trash there would be an occasional gem or something of necessity.

"Neither rain nor snow, nor sleet nor dark of night shall stay these couriers from the swift completion of their appointed rounds." All Dymond wanted to do was go back to the hospital. She felt she should have never left.

It is a terrible thing when something you hate and despise is essential to your well-being. That was the case with Dymond Washington and her postal route. She spent five days a week for the last twelve years delivering mostly junk mail to the residence of the lily white, upper, upper middle-class neighborhood of Sequoia Hills, a Chicago suburb. She always thought of it as the place the rich white folk lived, where black lives truly did not matter.

Dymond never stopped to think that forming her opinion on an entire group of people with such a broad stroke as she did with the *rich white folk* of Sequoia Hills was the exact same kind of thought process that made her so enraged against the government and police department. Dymond rarely came in contact with any of the residents of Sequoia Hills. The few she did seemed mostly pleasant, however there were others that gave her a look that relayed the message, *What the hell are you doing in my neighborhood?* But most of them were just absent. All of these huge beautiful houses and lavish, nearly palatial estates that seemed to lack life or family or love really puzzled Dymond.

Back at the post office Dymond would enjoy making fun of the invisible residents of Sequoia Hills by imitating her perception of *rich white folk*. Her co-workers would find her buffoonery amusing with the exception of the holier than thou Mary Gibbons.

Mary Gibbons was a middle aged, ginger haired, lily white mail carrier. She is what the USPS referred to as a floater. She did not have a set route. She delivered mail Tuesday through Saturday with a different route each day. With six days of mail delivery and most mail carriers working only five days per week, she would do somebody else's route on their day off. She had done the Sequoia Hills route on Saturdays for the last sixteen years. Because of doing the route on Saturdays, she came in contact with far more residents than Dymond did. And being a red headed white woman made her more widely accepted by the *bad apple* residents of SH.

Mary Gibbons was a very irascible person who did not understand humor. As most things funny are offensive to somebody, all things funny were offensive to Mary. Because Dymond's comedy was at the expense of *rich white folk* Mary accused her of reverse racism. When Dymond told her daughter, Jayla, about Mary's accusation, Jayla opined, 'Wouldn't reverse racism be racial harmony?' Jayla is wise beyond her years.

Someday, my Daryn is going to live in a house like this, Dymond though as she fought through the cruel weather and made her way up another perfect walkway. Dymond was jealous. The people on her route had the money and means to do the one thing she envied most. They were able to not live in fear.

While it was certainly not the case when Dymond was tending to her appointed mail route, she did consider herself somewhat, slightly Lucky as compared to many others in her neighborhood. She didn't always feel that way. Dymond was raised by her very loving, church going grandparents in a two-bedroom apartment with her little brother, Aunt Chloe, and two cousins. She never met her father and her mother was a crack addict. The neighborhood she grew up in was ruled by gangbangers and oppressed by the police.

Under the forceful guidance of her grandparents, Dymond and her two cousins graduated high school. Her brother did not. To him gangbang-ing offered a better and more immediate opportunity. For that decision he was murdered at the age of fifteen. Just before high school graduation, Dymond's mother, desperate and almost dead, stopped using and came to live with them. Soon after Dymond's grandpa died, one of her cousins became pregnant and moved in with the baby daddy. He was a gangbanger. Her other cousin went the way of the pipe. Dymond got a job at Walmart after her graduation and moved in with her cousin and nephew. She met a boy. She became pregnant. She had a baby girl. She met another boy. She got pregnant again. Her cousin's baby daddy kicked her and her daughter and her unborn son out.

She went back to grandma's house. She gave birth to Daryn. Her cous-in's baby daddy was a bad man. One night he got way too fucked up and he started beating on his baby mama and his four-year-old son. He killed the mama and went to jail. Dymond took her nephew in at grandma's house. Aunt Chloe was killed in a hit and run accident. Dymond worked and worked and worked and tried and tried and tried and failed and failed and failed, while her mama and grandma tended to the three children. Her nephew was left severely intellectually disabled from his father's beating. Then one day Dymond was informed she passed the postal exam and began training to be a mail carrier. For the first time in her life, she felt a glimmer of hope. Realistic hope.

Today Dymond makes $49,000 per year, which is far more than most of the residents in her neighborhood. She still lives in the same neighbor-hood, but she now owns a mortgage. The bank allows her to reside in the house with her family in exchange for an outlandish corrupt amount of money. The house is in need of a new roof, new floors and new walls, but it offers Dymond and her family shelter and it is the biggest place she has ever lived in.

Dymond is the main provider in a household that includes her mother, her ninety-one-year-old grandmother, her eighteen-year-old daughter, her seventeen-year-old son and her mentally disabled nephew. When she walks the streets of her neighborhood she feels Lucky, when she walks the streets of her mail route she feels forgotten.

A big part of the reason Dymond feels Lucky in a neighborhood where very few succeed is because she has an ace in the hole. Her son Daryn is brilliant. He is not just the smartest person she has ever met, he is the smartest person the neighborhood has ever known.

Dymond, like her grandparents, stressed the importance of school. With her daughter it was a struggle. At times it appeared it would be a fruitless battle, but last year she received her high school diploma and is currently enrolled at Malcom X College. Daryn, on the other hand took to school *like a fish to water.* He loved learning and was very good at it. While it would be inaccurate to say that Daryn had a photographic memory, he did possess powers of recall that were far beyond that of an average man.

As Dymond struggled on her appointed rounds she was wondering what Daryn was thinking right at this moment. Then she realized that something had changed upon the surface of her face. Although the wind still swirled, the rain had stopped. The majority of the saturation on her cheeks was now caused by her tears. She and Daryn had spent the last few months preparing and submitting college applications as well as researching and applying for scholarships.

Dymond wiped her face with her wet glove and grabbed the next pile of mail from her pouch and tried to compose herself once again by suffocating her sadness and worry with anger and resentment. She noticed what appeared to be a smear of blood on her glove. It was. Her severely chapped lips had given up on holding it together and decided to split open. *Just six more blocks and I'll be done and on my way back to the hospital.*

It was fifteen days ago when Daryn was walking home from school that the universe wadded up a huge ball of unjust calamity and whipped it right at the young scholar's face. It was after five. Daryn was always among the last to leave his school as he would hang out to tutor other students that were in need and more importantly want of his services, or he would find himself talking, learning, laughing or seeking counsel from one of the three teachers at his high school that genuinely gave a shit.

A Chicago police patrol car hugged the curb which Daryn was walking along and shadowed him at a speed that matched his gate. Daryn immediately felt uneasy. He did not turn his head nor change the speed of his stride. He looked straight ahead and continued walking, trying hard not to look suspicious. It was too late for that. Sadly, in the eyes of the police charged with keeping order in a demoralized neighborhood, simply being a resident automatically made you suspicious.

Daryn felt disdain, distrust, and fear toward the police because of the circumstances that surrounded his life. That is what he was conditioned to feel. What made this environment even worse and gave the entire atmosphere a constant *ticking time bomb* mood was that many of the police officers felt disdain, distrust, and fear toward the residents because of the circumstances that had surrounded their lives. That is what they were conditioned to feel.

The police and the residents were in a manufactured war that was fueled by the media and ignored by a government that had no interest in resolving or even recognizing the real problem. It's the cops vs the blacks. That is the agenda of the leaders of conservative white America. Closer to the truth is that society is currently set up to force poor people, stripped of opportunity and forced to live with the fear of being killed, into a manufactured war against an underfunded, undermanned, undertrained police department, that has to work with the fear of being killed and is supposed to keep law in a community, where the most advertised and available opportunities are lawless ones.

Why don't the children of Dymond's neighborhood have the same opportunities as the children of Sequoia Hills? Simple, because the parents in Dymond's neighborhood do not have the means to offer their children the same opportunities as the Sequoia Hills parents. And by means, I mean financial resources. So why don't the parents of the children in Dymond's neighborhood have the same financial resources as the parents of the children in Sequoia Hills? Simple, because the parents in Dymond's neighborhood were never offered the same opportunities as the parents in Sequoia Hills. That's what the world needs to work on, creating opportunities for people who lack opportunities, not perpetuating a war between cops and blacks.

I do not think it's going out on a limb to suggest that if every neighborhood had the same amount of opportunities that every neighborhood would enjoy the same very high rate of success for its citizens.

When survival becomes a struggle, people will do whatever they feel they have to do, laws be damned. For many in Dymond's neighborhood, the most prevalent opportunities are of an illegal nature. The police are sent in to take away those opportunities, but not present any new ones. Tick… Tick…Tick. So, society continues moving backward and its fucked-up agenda flourishes as the media presents the facts that it sees fit to convey its message. The goal: Half the people blame the blacks, half the people blame the cops, while the rich get richer and the poor get poorer. Fifteen days ago, Daryn was a victim of that agenda.

Three blocks to go for Dymond Washington to finish her route. Tears now streaming down her face. The winds began to ease as specks of sunlight peeked through the battleship gray sky. Definitely not a metaphor for Dymond's current life situation. *I should have never went to work today. How could I leave Daryn? I had to. I have to work, bills have to be paid. I've missed so much time already. Jayla is with him. His big sister will care for him. He will be all right. He has to be all right. What if he wakes up today and I'm not there?*

After a long couple of minutes, the Chicago police patrol car sped away. Daryn breathed a sigh of relief. The police were looking for somebody in that area and decided that Daryn was not that somebody. Daryn, however, came across that somebody a few minutes later. Unfortunately, it was at the same time a rival gang came across him with much more aggressive intentions than the Chicago police.

The high powered, semi-automatic assault rifle hung out the window of the slow-moving Chevy Caprice as the sound of gun fire exploded into the air. Daryn immediately hit the ground. He did not do this in an act of self-preservation, for a bullet struck him in the head before his brain even registered the sound of gun fire.

As Dymond walked up the path to the final house on her route she witnessed something that disturbed her to her very core.

Daryn had been in a coma since the shooting, fifteen days ago. His prognosis was dire. One of the few residents of his neighborhood to actually have a viable chance at a real opportunity now clung to life with a fading weak grip.

The final house on Dymond's route boasted a big beautiful bay window a few feet away from the mailbox which offered her an unobstructed view right into the living room. She did not appreciate what she saw.

Even if Daryn survived, what would his life be? Would he ever walk again? Or talk again? Or think again? No matter, Dymond prayed hard for her son to live. She never even considered the possibility that he might become a burden to his mother. A mother that had far too many burdens already.

The front room was almost the size of Dymond's entire house. She spied the warm inviting fire blazing in the huge stone fireplace. The opposite wall had a TV that must have been eighty-three inches. Sportscenter was on. The picture was so perfect the commentators appeared to actually be in the house. And there, right there in the window, so close Dymond could have reached through the glass and touched him, sat a middle-aged man in a recliner, wearing red plaid pajama bottoms and a Chicago Bears sweatshirt, watching the television.

You got to be kidding me? Look at this guy. As Dymond put the mail in the box she was filled with so much resentment for this man who she felt probably never worked a hard day in his life. A life filled with opportunity and money and extreme comfort. *How? Why? It's not fair.*

The man, half in and out of sleep as he watched Sportscenter heard the noise of the mailbox. *It's the middle of the week. It's the middle of the day. How nice it must be?* He turned his head and watched Dymond leave his porch. *What about me? What about Daryn?* As Dymond made her way to the hospital she continued to think about the man in the red plaid pajamas. *I wonder if that son of a bitch realizes how Lucky he is?*

* * * * * * * * * * * * * * * * * * * * * * * * * * * * * * * * * *

Sophie Marquez always considered herself to be a Lucky person. The world would consider her to be an average person. Beautifully average. Her parents were both very hardworking people and showed their daughter tremendous love. She had a brother who was also tremendously loved. Sophie graduated from high school and never even considered continuing her education. She got a job. This was the normal order of things in her community. Her brother went a different route. After high school he moved to Los Angeles to pursue a career as a waiter and ended up making a comfortable living as an actor. Most of his roles did not have names but rather descriptions and/ or numbers, police officer number 2, handsome man in the lobby, angry teacher number 3, but the money paid his bills. Sophie would like to imagine becoming very rich someday, but she realized the chances of that were next to impossible, so instead she spent most of her time being happy and buying a weekly lottery ticket.

Gintaras Bacavis did not consider himself a Lucky person. For the most part his consideration was correct. The world would not consider him to be average because for the first thirty years of his life he was not loved. By anybody. It's not that he was a bad person or that he was hated or even disliked, he just kind of existed. His parents were working class, selfish, functional alcoholics. Gintaras was an accident that forced a marriage that he was reminded of from time to time. His father's brother was a much better person but did not have the time or inclination to care for Gintaras, so he instead turned a blind eye to his nephew's situation. The uncle had a son named Marius who was one year older than his cousin. He realized Gintaras' situation early on. He would look out for his younger cousin upon occasion throughout his life, not out of love, but out of pity.

Marius got a job as a senior in high school on a loading dock of a medical supply company. He was well-liked and would continue working there the first three years of his undergrad. Marius would eventually go on to Harvard Law School and one day have his own practice. But way before that, early on, he got his cousin, Gintaras, a job on the docks at the medical supply company. It would be the only job Gintaras ever held. He was not as well-liked as his cousin Marius. He just kind of existed. That was the way it was until he turned thirty and Sophie Marquez took a job in the office of the same medical supply company.

Sophie stirred feelings in Gintaras that he never even knew existed. He constantly tried to impress her with his unimpressive life. She appreciated the effort and he seemed harmless enough, so she agreed to go on a date with him.

The date went well. He instantly adored her and would do anything for her. Sophie Marquez adored being adored and the two became an item. Their dates were modest but they enjoyed each other's company and felt very comfortable together. They were falling in love. They would go to the White Castle across from Midway Airport, get a Crave Sack, and watch airplanes taking off and landing. They would take long walks along Lake

Michigan. They would visit the rich suburb of Sequoia Hills, pick out their favorite house, and imagine what it would be like to live there. And they kept buying that weekly lottery ticket.

Sophie was five years younger than Gintaras. After five years of steady dating the two decided to get hitched and have a baby. A year later, they were blessed with little baby Gabriela Marquez Bacavis. After thirty years of feeling unlucky, Gintaras spent the next six years feeling like the luckiest man on earth.

The joy of a beautiful daughter brought with it much expense. Sophie was no longer working and the three of them were trying to get by on Gintaras salary alone. It was very challenging. They were beginning to feel the pressure of debt. Gintaras felt the tinge of discouragement invading his Lucky world. But what Gintaras did not realize at the time was that Luck was not done with him yet.

Twenty-six million dollars was the one lump sum Gintaras and Sophie opted for with their winning lottery ticket. All of their problems were gone and all of their dreams realized. Marius set his cousin up with a financial advisor, and a trust lawyer, and a real estate agent, who helped them buy their dream house in Sequoia Hills. The very house they used to sit in front of in Gintaras shitty car and imagine what it would be like to live in such a place.

What they did not realize was that they really would not fit in with the other residents of Sequoia Hills. Sophie's skin was a little too dark and both of their tastes too deficient in quality and their minds intellectually inadequate. They would be shunned. The family would never realize this rejection, however, because they began their residency in the beautiful dream home right around the time Gintaras started coughing and never stopped.

The diagnosis was stage two lung cancer. The doctors put together a battle plan that included radiation, then chemo, then surgery, then more chemo. It would be a long and difficult road, but Gintaras had a chance to beat this terrible disease. With the love and support of his wife and five-year-old daughter, and the financial means to get the best care possible and concentrate only on conquering his cancer, Gintaras was confident.

Then the cure starting kicking his ass. Despite it being far harder than he had ever imagined, his resolve was still strong. Gintaras became violently ill the day after his first chemo treatment. The day after his second they decided it would be better if Gabriela stayed by Grandma and Grandpa's so that she would not bear witness to the sight or sound or smell of the cure for her Daddy's sickness. Gintaras was prepared for the second time around to be as bad as the first. It was not. It was far worse. Still, his resolve did not falter.

The following evening, Sophie was driving Gabriela back to their dream home where Gintaras anxiously awaited their arrival. He felt the laughter he experienced from his little girl's silly antics were by far his best medicine. On that drive home Sophie wondered how the richest time in their life had also become the poorest. How she had never felt unlucky in her life until the diagnosis. *Is the money a curse?* she thought. On that drive home Sophie worried, *what if Gintaras does not beat this? How can I go on without him? He is the love of my life.* On that drive home somebody else fell asleep at the wheel, drifted across three lanes of traffic and collided with Sophie and Gabriela head on.

It was after a period of worrying and unanswered cell calls and more worrying and calling his in-laws and more worrying and going out looking for them and calls from his in-laws and then finally coming upon the accident's aftermath and rushing to the hospital, that Gintaras found out his wife and baby girl had been killed in the head on collision.

Gintaras gave up. He was finished. He refused treatment, he barely ate, he hardly talked. He just waited to die. His only hope was that he be reunited with his Sophie and Gabriela in heaven. His wait for death would not be long.

Marius arranged for Gintaras to have around the clock in home care. The caregivers would offer him pain medicine, which he would refuse, and cook him meals, of which he might take a couple of bites, but mostly they would just be in another room on their phones, waiting for him to die and wondering where their next assignment might be.

There was one caregiver whose presence gave Gintaras a slight sort of fondness. He never really talked to any of them, his depression was too deep. But Renatta had dark brown hair and a very light complexion. She was in her mid-twenties. She reminded him of what his little Gabriela might have grown up to look like.

This one particular day, Marius was going to come over to get Gintaras' finances in order before the inevitable happened. Gintaras did not care. He felt Sophie's parents and Marius could have it all. But on this day, with the Marius visit looming, he was considering leaving some money to Renatta. It wasn't only because she reminded him of what his daughter could have been, it was also because, unlike the others, she was not constantly in the other room on her phone. It would bother him tremendously to hear their trivial complaints about life as they sat in the home of a dying man that just buried his wife and little girl.

As he contemplated Renatta's future he fell in and out of sleep. As he slowly crept out of one of his short sleeps he overheard Renatta's voice from the next room. She was on the phone. *At least she is polite enough to wait until she thinks I'm asleep,* his thoughts defended her.

But then he heard the context of her call. Evidently, she had a child in need of diapers and her husband would be working late this evening. This meant Renatta would have to be the one to stop at the store and purchase the diapers. She was not happy about it. She seemed really put out. *'I'm really not up to it,'* he heard her say.

Oh, poor baby, he thought as he watched the muted screen of his 85" TV. *She is just like the rest.* At that he heard a noise from outside. He turned his groggy head to see the mail carrier make her delivery. *Poor thing out in this weather, and without a scarf. I should leave her my money. Old Marius would love that.*

"Oh, you're awake," Renatta said as she entered the front room.

"Hmmm," Gintaras moaned and as he peered at her and he thought, *I wonder if that son of a bitch realizes how Lucky she is?*

* * * * * * * *   * * * * * * * *   * * * * * * * *   * * * * * * * *

The last thing Renatta wanted to do right now was go to Walmart and buy diapers, but she did not have much of a choice. She had just finished a six-hour shift with a very depressed dying man and her husband had let her down by opting to work a sixteen-hour shift instead of running the *Huggies* errand. She would get in and out of the store as quickly as possible and then rush to pick up her two-year-old daughter from day care. The nasty weather had improved from earlier in the day. The winds had died down, the rain had ceased and the thirty-eight-degree Fahrenheit air no longer carried so much ferocity.

As was always the case, the Walmart parking lot was packed. Being an able minded citizen with all of her faculties intact, Renatta was, of course, repulsed by the idea of having to visit Walmart, but diapers were expensive and here they were the cheapest. She hoped to find a parking spot close to the door. She did. There was one handicap spot open. *Bingo,* she thought.

She also realized she was going to receive quite a few dirty looks for her choice in parking spots, but she tried to convince herself that it would not bother her. But it did. Very much. As soon as she exited her vehicle and began her quick, unencumbered stride toward the doors she felt the heat of angry eyes upon her flesh. *I'll go as quickly as I can,* she thought.

Suddenly Renatta felt capable of reading other people's thoughts. The old lady exiting the store, *shame on you.* The middle-aged man a few feet in front of her, *she certainly does not look handicapped. I hope she gets a ticket.* The attractive woman behind her, *this lady's disability must be a lack of compassion.* The young man employed by the evil empire collecting shopping carts, *seriously??*

Renatta's thoughts defended her actions, *Fuck them. They don't know me. They don't know a thing about me.*

Once inside the store she felt that familiar rubbery feeling that she despised. She grabbed a cart and went right to the diaper aisle. As she placed the box of diapers in the front part of the cart she came to a most unfortunate realization. It was too late. But what was she going to do. Just lay down there in the Walmart aisle and cry like a baby? No. She had to carry on. She had to get those diapers and then go get her daughter. But how? She knew she was going to have to gut it out no matter how bad the pain got. She took a deep breath, put her right hand on her right hip and applied quite a bit of pressure and with her left hand she began to navigate the cart.

She tried to remain calm and was hopeful that she would not collapse in the middle of Walmart, but as she got close to the checkout line she could feel the uselessness of her ligaments and tendons. They were giving way and right now the only thing holding her right hip in its socket was Renatta's right hand. It was starting to hurt. The only thing Renatta could hope for at this point was that it be a subluxation as opposed to a complete hip dislocation and she could somehow make it back to her car.

She made it to the checkout line as her pain began to increase. Renatta now stood in line still holding her hip in place. Standing still was good for retarding the orthopedic event that was inevitable at this time, but it did very little to relieve the pain that was to accompany it. She scanned the front of the store for one of those electric scooters, but this was a Walmart so they were all in use. She was the next in line. The customer ahead of her had about two hundred dollars' worth of completely unnatural and unhealthy food. A bagger appeared and offered assistance. The bagger was the shopping cart gatherer who had witnessed Renatta's parking choice just a short time ago. Renatta heard him whisper to the cashier, "That's her."

The cashier made a very weak effort to be sly when she replied, "Unbelievable, she looks perfectly healthy to me."

Renatta was in great distress upon completion of the transaction. As she walked to her car, now with a noticeable limp, she could feel her right hip attempting to leave its socket with each movement. Her hand continued to do the job of her ligaments and tendons by forcing it back into place with every step. Renatta's thoughts helped occupy her mind from the increasing pain. *Those fuckers all probably think I'm faking my limp now. 'She didn't limp when she came in.'*

Her mind began to formulate a plan. *If it doesn't fall completely out I think I can make it to daycare. Donna will have to bring her out to me and put her in her seat. How will we get in the house? Marge. I'll call Marge.* Renatta was now biting her tongue in an attempt at pain management. She made it to her car door. She flung the diapers onto the passenger seat and then as she twisted to get into the car, holding on tightly to her right hip, catastrophe. Without any warning, her left hip completely dislocated. Intense pain shot through her body. The force of her bite split her tongue. Her ass fell into the driver's seat, both feet still in the parking lot. Stars filled her peripheral vision. She felt as though she would soon pass out from the pain.

That feeling had to be taken seriously because it had happened before, the first time she dislocated her shoulder. She had to complete three tasks before the pain brought her far from the world of consciousness. She had to call her husband. She had to call 911. She had to retrieve the laminated card she made after the shoulder incident so that she would be holding it when the first responders arrived. She fumbled through her purse and retrieved her phone and the laminated card.

The card read…

I have Ehlers Danlos Syndrome

EDS

Do not attempt to treat my orthopedic
conditions with traditional methods

No traction

No surgery

Renatta was a very strong person that considered herself to be a very weak person. She suffered from chronic pain. Every day her joints ached and every day she dealt with that pain and was a productive member of her family as well as society. Unrelated to her EDS, Renatta also had a condition in which an increase in the amount of pain she was accustomed to would occasionally cause a decrease in her blood pressure, which would then cause her to pass out. She had also been known to faint from the sight of blood or finding herself in an extremely anxious situation. This did not make her a weak person. Sometimes her blood pressure just could not keep pace with the events of her day. It appeared this was going to be one of those days.

For anyone who is not familiar with EDS I will offer a quick summary of the syndrome. If you are already aware of the condition feel free to skip ahead to the next paragraph. Ehlers-Danlos Syndrome is an invisible disability. It is rare. It is an inherited disorder. If you have it there is a fifty percent chance that your kid will also have it. There are many degrees of EDS but in general it affects the body's joints, skin, connective tissue, and blood vessel walls. Basically, the victims are too flexible. They suffer from hypermobility. The parts of their body in charge of keeping things in place, fail at doing their job. Joints can dislocate, blood vessels can dilate or even rupture, retina's can detach, all sorts of nasty stuff.

Ehlers-Danlos is just one of many invisible disabilities. There is Rheumatoid Arthritis, Fibromyalgia, Cystic Fibrosis, and Sjogren's Syndrome, just to name a few. Unlike people with visible disabilities such as people who use wheelchairs, amputees, the blind, and so many more who have to constantly prove they are *able* to do things despite their disability, people with invisible disabilities are burdened with constantly having to prove there are some things they are just not *able* to do despite their capable appearance.

Renatta made the card she now clutched to protect herself from well-meaning medical professionals. Years ago she had the misfortune of dislocating her shoulder while visiting a friend in the hospital. While trying to pop it back into place, she became woozy and passed out, on her way to the floor her head banged quite violently on a bathroom sink and she remained unconscious for some time. When she awoke she found her shoulder had been placed in traction. Not a good idea. The traction was stretching her already way too elastic ligaments and tendons. They were stretching something that was already far too overstretched.

She also heard a horror story of an EDS sufferer who was in a car accident. One of her many injuries was a dislocated hip. Unbeknownst to the doctors, as she arrived unconscious, because of EDS this woman dislocated her hip on a weekly basis. She woke up to find they had performed major hip surgery that included some significant drilling and six months recovery. Recovery from a painful event that her body was accustomed to sustaining and repairing on a weekly basis. Renatta feared such a mistake.

As her pain increased and her blood pressure decreased, Renatta felt herself starting to fade away. She touched the screen on her phone to summon her husband. As his line rang she watched a head gracefully glide across the Walmart parking lot. This head did not bob up and down. It floated in a perfectly straight line to a van two rows across from Renatta's vehicle. The head was connected to a body that sat in a Tillite Manuel wheelchair being powered by a SmartDrive attachment. She watched as the van automatically deployed a ramp as the floating head approached. She continued to watch as the chair smoothly rolled up the ramp and then disappeared.

"Hello. Hello. Renatta? Are you there?" her husband called out from the phone as Renatta's world went black. Her final vision was of the van swallowing the ramp back up and her final thought was, *I wonder if that son of a bitch realizes how Lucky she is?*

* * * * * * *   * * * * * * * *   * * * * * * * *   * * * * * * *

Emma Aimison was on the run. Not literally, but she was making a valid attempt to escape her past. She was a high school counselor at a Chicago suburb school. She had been counseling there for less than a year. Previously she lived and worked in Madeira Ohio, a suburb of Cincinnati. She was a high school counselor there also. Emma owned a nice home and vehicle. Most of the money she used to procure those items did not come from high school counseling. It came from Emma's other job. A job she started when she was quite young and naïve. A job she had not done in a few years. A job of which she was now embarrassed and ashamed. Emma Aimison was an Inspirational Porn Star.

Looking back on those days, Emma wondered why she never felt dirty. There she was whoring herself out for the pleasure of others and never even considering the morality of it. She just enjoyed being in front of the camera and it brought her a sense of satisfaction to think she was making others feel good. Not to mention, the money was really good. It never occurred to her that she was betraying the same demographic of which she was a member. Once it was pointed out to her in no uncertain terms, she felt terrible. How could she do such things for such a long time and not know the degradation of her actions? Her parents were even okay with it. Their approval had a lot to do with the muddying of Emma's moral compass.

Her folks were good people. They were very liberal minded atheists, that Emma respected and loved very much, but to this day, they hold no displeasure or regret concerning their daughter's porn career. Emma could not disagree more. It absolutely sickened her that she had objectified herself for so many years. She thought of all of those who had fought for equal rights. She feared how much her actions and the actions of others in her former industry had set the movement back. She swore she would never do it again, but now as she sat in her van in the Walmart parking lot she found herself having second thoughts.

Emma had mistakenly left her phone in the van when she made her Walmart run. She was away from it for twenty-six minutes. When she returned to it, she had two missed calls from two different numbers. Both recorded messages. The first was from her agent. Her former agent. Two years had passed since they last spoke, until last week when he called her with an offer she could not refuse. She refused. Two days later the offer was even better. The refusal more stern. This was his third attempt.

"Emma, doll face, sweetheart, it's (*insert a creepy agent name of your choice here*). Sorry you missed me, baby. And look, I know, I understand you told me you were not interested. Better Human Being. Moral high ground. Objectification. Equal rights, all that jazz, I know I get it. But I remember how shocked you were with how much money they were offering you. Well, guess what sugar pie? They frickin' doubled it! Double! D.O.U.B.E.L. You hear what I'm saying? For one day's work. Two tops, definitely less than a week. Honey. Think of all the good moral, anti-objectification, equal rights shit you could do with that kind of scratch. Huh? Huh? C'mon my precious, I'm sure the camera will still love you. One more time for old time's sake. Call me."

Emma Aimison was a person with a physical disability. Her disability was visible. Very visible. For most people it was the very first thing they noticed about her. For many, there was not a second. Shockingly, in the United States there is a large part of the population that enjoyed the idea of Emma coming out of retirement and degrading herself by having her and her disability objectified.

As Emma sat in her van, with the engine running, the heat on low, still in her parking spot, she felt disgusted. She felt repulsed. She felt tempted.

The next message was much more sobering and brought up another topic Emma was trying to run away from.

"This message is for Emma Aimison. Ms. Aimison this is Detective Herb Katzinburg with the Madeira Police Department. I'm calling in regard to the Burton murder/suicide case. I know you have already been interviewed several times and I have all your statements here with me, but there has been some new evidence and a new person of interest, um...so I would really appreciate a few moments of your time. Just a couple of things you might be able to help us shed some light on. If you would be so kind to give me a call at..."

Emma was lost deep in thought. She sat there with her van idling for more than fifteen minutes. Her mind had carried her far away from the Walmart parking lot. She was not thinking about equal rights movements or the porn world she once lived in or the murder/suicide at the high school she used to work at or Toyota Motor Company. She was thinking about Sydney McMathews. Emma was pulled from her thoughts and brought back to the parking lot by the sound of a siren. An ambulance was entering the Walmart parking lot. There were some people gathered around a car a couple rows away. Emma began her drive home.

Sydney McMathews and Emma Aimison had a lot in common. Both were in terrible car accidents at young ages and both suffered catastrophic spinal cord injuries. Emma was paralyzed from the chest down twenty-two years ago at the age of ten. Sydney, four years ago at the age of twelve. Having Emma for a high school counselor was incredibly beneficial for Sydney. Besides exposing Sydney to a vast amount of adaptation skills, Emma also gave Sydney a proven, realistic goal for what her life could be. Emma was a beautiful, intelligent, confident, independent woman who loved life and all it had to offer.

Emma remembered one of the most difficult times in her life was when she was sixteen. Sixteen is the age that all of her friends began to get a taste of freedom in the form of a driver's license. Emma's family could not afford a car with the modifications necessary for her to drive. Not all of her friends had DL's, so the ones that did would drive the ones that did not, and day after day would be filled with a new adventure. At first Emma would be included in these adventures. They would transfer her into the passenger seat, take the wheels off the chair, put it in the trunk and go. Many times, however, there would be the issue of *not enough room*, or *too much of a hassle*. After the initial novelty wore off, more times than not, Emma would be excluded. This crushed her deeply. It also crushed her that she knew Sydney would soon be experiencing that same exclusion.

Being an inspirational porn star had been very lucrative for Emma and she very wisely saved her money. Until recently, when she spent it. She now owned a beautiful home, completely customized and one hundred percent wheelchair friendly as well as a van modified to fit her specifications. Her salary as a high school counselor was modest, but it paid the bills. Emma now owned more than she had ever dreamed. The cost of her van was eighty thousand dollars. *Sydney would never have eighty thousand dollars for a vehicle.*

The people that wanted Emma to come out of retirement, get back behind the camera and shoot them an inspiration porn video were the folks at the Toyota Motor Company and they just increased their offer from forty thousand dollars to eighty thousand dollars. *Sydney's life has been and will be hard enough. I could make it so much better. But I would have to go against what I believe in...*

Time for another side bar in this story, like the one we did about Ehlers-Danlos Syndrome. I feel that perhaps Emma's career as an inspirational porn star and Toyota wanting her to come out of retirement may need a little clarification. To best understand this, I think we have to step back in history a little bit. I feel we all need to be exposed to some highly shameful intelligence of the way things used to be in the good ole U.S. of A., in order to really appreciate just what the fuck happened. I feel this information will help you sympathize with Emma's current state of mind.

Everybody knows that the United States has a lot of skeletons in its closet that it would rather not discuss. The U.S. is a nation of immigrants. Unless you are of Native American heritage, everyone in the USA are either immigrants or descendants of immigrants, mind you much of that immigration was forced. As we already know, turns out a lot of those early immigrants were complete and total assholes; racist, bigots, elitist, Donald Trump supporters, etc. etc. From slavery and the Trail of Tears to the atomic bombings of Hiroshima and Nagasaki, from the Chinese railroad laborers treatment to Japanese internment camps, to racial discrimination, sexual discrimination, LGBT discrimination and the often-overlooked disabled discrimination.

In the late 1800's many major cities in the United States had what were called *Ugly Laws* that prevented people with disabilities from appearing in public because they were too disturbing to look at. This included crippled children. It also targeted blind and deaf people, and people with intellectual disabilities, as well as anyone born with a physical birth defect.

Historically the laws of the United States completely devalued people with disabilities. They were looked at as objects of rejection, ridicule, and fear. San Francisco passed the first such law in 1867. Nearly every major city followed suit. Chicago's law of 1881 read, *any person who is maimed, mutilated, or in any way deformed are not allowed on the streets, highways, thoroughfares, or public places in the city.*

Are you thinking ancient history? Think again. Most of these laws did not come off the books until the 1970s when the disability rights movement started gaining a little momentum and the Rehabilitation Act of 1973 was passed. Up until then, the *Ugly Laws* were still being used to control the use of public spaces by people with disabilities. These disgusting regulations remained on city books for nearly one hundred years. In the 1960s people who used wheelchairs would gather in front of buildings that were not accessible to them and protest that their civil rights were being violated by not having a way to gain entry. Such protests were legal, but the owners and management of these properties certainly did not want a bunch of maimed cripples disrupting their business. Lucky for them, the *Ugly Laws* were still available. Peaceful demonstration was perfectly fine, provided you were not disturbing to look at. The last Ugly Law arrest took place in Chicago in 1974 when a disfigured blind man was arrested for being too disturbing to look at. Seriously.

But wait, there's more. Eugenics is the *science* of improving the human population by controlled breeding in order to increase the occurrence of desirable characteristics. The method by which this was achieved was by young disabled girls being forced by law to have surgical sterilization. Girls that were blind or deaf or had a mental disability or cerebral palsy or spina bifida or down syndrome or any other disability perceived to be genetic were legally forced to *submit* to a surgical genital mutilation, some as young as seven years old. This was the law in more than thirty states and remained the law in some of them up until the 1980s. The last forced genital mutilation in the United States took place in Oregon in 1981. Seriously. It is still practiced in many other parts of the world.

It was really after World War II, when everyone saw how fucked up the Nazi's were, that much of the rest of the world took a step back and began to consider human rights. The disabled community fought very hard for equal rights and inclusion. Getting the Rehabilitation Act of 1973 passed was a positive start, but it was only a start. While it did give people with disabilities some rights and prohibited some discrimination, it was limited to only federally funded jobs and buildings and programs. So, the fight continued.

ADAPT is a grass roots disabilities rights organization in the United States that began to battle for equality in 1983. Their method was one of non-violent direct action to bring awareness and attention and change to the lack of civil rights experienced in the disabled community. They were instrumental in the passing of the Americans with Disabilities Act.

The ADA was finally introduced to congress in 1988. It was not immediately passed. It remained an uphill battle for the disabled community of the United States. Or at least an upstairs battle. On March 12, 1990, more than one thousand Americans with disabilities descended on the U.S. capitol building to demand their equal rights. Fearing that their voices would go on not being heard by Congress while at the foot of the massive, intimidating staircase, sixty of the protestors threw themselves out of their wheelchairs and began to drag themselves up the eighty-three stairs. "I'll take all night if I have to," were the words of eight-year-old Jennifer Keelan as she dragged herself up the steps with an important message for her congressman.

The spectacle was quite an embarrassment for Congress and with the *Ugly Laws* no longer on the books there was no way of putting an end to this protest. "Let the shameful wall of exclusion finally come tumbling down," were the words of President George Herbert Walker Bush when he signed the Americans with Disabilities Act into law a few months after what became known as the Capitol Crawl.

This is a small part of the history of the disabled community of which Emma Aimison was a member. The actions of these battlers of oppression currently weighed heavy on her mind. She greatly appreciated what they had fought for and every day she enjoyed the fruits of their labor. She fully realized that children with disabilities did not even have the right to an education in the United States until 1975 and was eternally grateful to those who made her current way of life a reality. The other thought that weighed heavy on her mind as she put her Walmart booty away was the way she had previously betrayed those very people and was actually considering doing it again. It wasn't entirely her fault. It was the society she grew up in. It was the world she knew.

When Emma was twelve years old, two years after the horrific car accident that left her paralyzed, her older sister played basketball in a park district summer league. Emma never really liked to participate in sports. They just weren't her thing. Big sister, on the other hand, was a total jock. And Emma loved to watch big sis play. While she watched she began to notice that people had a sort of sympathetic attention they would pay to her. They felt bad for her because she couldn't be out there playing with big sis and company.

Even though Emma had no interest in doing such a thing, she found herself enjoying the attention. She ate it up. So, what was the harm? People would buy her popcorn or soda or ice cream or whatever. *Big deal, they feel sorry for me and want to do something nice. Who cares?*

Emma never considered that the people that did nice things for her could have been doing them for selfish reasons. That doing something nice for the poor little girl in the wheelchair made them feel better about themselves.

That summer big sis and company won the championship. After the trophy presentation, the entire team approached Emma and presented the trophy to her and called her their most valuable player. Emma enjoyed the attention and never questioned its source. *Big deal. Who cares?*

There was a recording of Emma receiving the trophy. It was posted on YouTube. Two years later, it went viral. Emma was the perfect combination of sympathetic and cute.

That video is how Emma Aimison was *discovered* and by her junior year in high school she found herself making money in an industry that she did not even know existed. It started out with *inspirational* posters. A simple picture of Emma and her ever important wheelchair, usually with her arms spread wide, once at the top of a very steep hill that took two strapping young men to push her up, and it would have a caption like, *Yes You Can!* Or, *What's Holding You Back?* Or my personal favorite, *The Only Disability In Life Is A Bad Attitude.*

Emma's first of many TV commercials was for a local gym. They aired it in December and January, resolution season. It started with her waking up in bed, transferring to her wheelchair, and then a montage of her just getting ready for the day, brushing her teeth, combing her hair, tying her shoes, eating a breakfast bar, then she is wheeling down a snow-covered sidewalk. It's just starting to get light outside, the crack of dawn. Then she is riding on this bus looking all tired. And the whole time this inspirational music is playing really quiet, but it is beginning to build. She gets off the bus in front of this building and slowly looks up at the sign and smiles. It's the gym. The music is really pumping now. She scans in her membership card and then they show Emma at a weight lifting machine, doing reps with fake sweat on her forehead with the caption 'NO EXCUSES.'

Emma actually was a member of that gym, but only because in addition to a nice paycheck, she also received a free lifetime membership for her services. She went six times but only used the dry sauna. In all fairness it was the only thing there she could use. There was nothing else there that was wheelchair accessible. The machine used in the ad was actually shot at a nearby rehabilitation clinic. But it didn't matter. None of it mattered. It did not even matter that Emma had never been on a bus. The only thing that mattered in that ad and all of her future ads was that Emma was in a wheelchair and that made people feel Lucky and ashamed and inspired. The gym's January membership was up five times higher than the previous year.

Emma became so popular that she wrote and sang a song. She made a music video. It was terrible. Emma had no talent as a song writer or singer. Didn't matter. The band, the producer, the videographer, and her agent just kept telling her how great she was. I mean after all, she was in a wheelchair. Again, her video went viral. People were inspired by Emma's tremendous lack of talent. At least most were. Soon after her music career started, Emma received a letter from a fellow paraplegic. The writer of the letter was very polite but was not a fan of Emma's work. She was a successful, productive member of society. She was a Physical Therapist at a nearby hospital. She suggested some other videos Emma might find interesting on the YouTube.

The videos were what first introduced Emma to the disability community's history and fights for equal rights. It included the video of eight-year-old Jennifer Keelan's crawl up the eighty-three capitol steps.

Emma was touched, she was awed, she was shocked. She had never considered the disability community even though she was a member of it.

Then there were videos exposing the strange phenomenon of the disabled Americans timeline. How they were once shunned and feared and ridiculed by able bodied Americans and were now incorrectly idolized and infantized by so many. Videos of adults with disabilities out in public being talked to as if they were very young children or being told what a *"great job"* they are doing or how it is *"so good to see you out."* Or they are being treated like saints or heroes because they simply woke up and got out of bed. Americans with disabilities don't just want equal rights…they want to be treated like equals. *Awww, that's so cute…and inspirational.*

Then through the magic of the YouTube Emma Aimison met Stella Jane Young and learned about inspiration porn. Justice Potter Stewart once famously said, "I can't define pornography, but I know it when I see it." Do you? Are you sure? Turns out pornography does have a definition. It is the objectification of one group of people for the satisfaction of another group of people. And we see it far too often.

Stella Young tells us that referring to people with disabilities as inspirational solely or even in part on the basis of their disability is inspiration porn. "I'm not your inspiration, thank you very much." Young challenges that a disability is neither a *bad* thing nor does it make an individual more exceptional than anyone else without a disability. There is nothing wrong with being inspired by a person with a disability, but it is very wrong to be inspired by a person because of their disability. The disability community continues to fight for true equality and inspiration porn is a weapon used against that goal.

This is when Emma discovered that she had been betraying the society that she just realized she had been a member of. She was very disappointed in herself. She may have been the most lucrative inspirational porn star of all time. *Now what?* She considered donating all her now tainted money to the cause and starting fresh. She opted to instead reap the harvest of her misdeeds, move far away, buy a big customized house and vehicle and start anew.

In her defense she did immediately retire from the inspiration porn industry and make a vow to never return. She also now spent most of her free time as a disability rights activist. The idea of helping other people with disabilities was very appealing to Emma, and here was a chance to really help a person with a disability. Directly. How could anyone begrudge her for buying Sydney McMathews an eighty-thousand-dollar vehicle. *But I would betray the equality cause so many have fought for.* Emma struggled. *What would Stella do?* Emma agonized. *But did anyone ever offer Stella 80k for one week's work?* And then right on cue, as if ripped from the pages of some cliché book of short stories, Emma's phone rang. It was her agent. Again.

"Tasteful, sweetheart, baby, did I mention tasteful. I mean this is Toyota. We are talking about a classy company. This ad is going to ooze tastefulness."

"Okay, so tell me what it is?"

"Tell you what what is."

"The tasteful ad, (*whatever creepy agent name you inserted earlier*). What is the ad?"

"Oh, oh, yeah, get this, you're going to be a downhill skier. They got this special wheel chair with skis and you're gonna be flyin' down the hill, be boppin' around the flags and kickin' snow everywhere—"

"I don't know how to ski."

"Who cares. Sweetheart, darling, you won't be skiing. There's a stunt double. They're gonna show you like getting ready. Putting your gear in the truck and taking it out, and, I don't know, probably drinking some hot cocoa by a fireplace afterward, who gives a fuck? And Emma, sweetheart, full winter jacket, gloves, scarf, goggles, there is no way anyone will think this is any kind of pornography like you was worried about before."

"Dammit (*creepy name again*) not that kind of pornography. This is about the objectification of people in wheelchairs."

"Yeah, yeah, right, I'm sorry, I'm joking, bad joke—"

"You don't ever listen to me."

"Oh, c'mon buttercup, I listen."

"So, this is a wheelchair accessible truck?"

"—So, like they do *it* in their wheelchairs?"

"What?"

"The porno?"

"What?"

"What, what? I don't know? I'm just asking."

"See what I mean you don't listen-"

"No, honey cakes, I heard you…It's because, with the winter Olympics coming up."

"Huh? I asked if the truck was wheelchair accessible?"

"Huh? No, fuck no, it's just a regular truck."

"So, it's a truck that I can't even get into?"

"Don't worry about that, princess. They got people for that. If you got to get in there, they'll get you in there, angel cakes. It's Toyota for Christ sake. They got guys that can lift you right in. Strong guys. Nothing to worry about."

"This makes no sense. So they are going to pay me eighty grand to have someone pretend to be me skiing to promote a truck I can't even get into?"

"It's a feel-good story, sweetheart. You are the face of inspiration and they want you."

"I'm not here to make people feel better about themselves."

"No, no, of course not. You're here to make people want to buy trucks."

The conversation went on like this for a little while and then in the interest of moving the story along, once again, right on cue, (*creepy agent name*) brought up the Madeira murder/suicide.

"I hear they are about to name a new suspect. They are saying it might be someone who works at the high school. How bout that sweetie pie, someone you worked with just last year-"

"I have to go." Click.

Emma felt a cold chill. It bothered her terribly that she was among the last to see Chuck Burton alive. She never wondered if she could have handled their final meeting better, because there is no sense in wondering about that which you already know. She could have and should have acted in a much more compassionate and professional matter. What she wondered was if she would have recognized the signs if she would have just bothered to look for them.

This was a young man in deep trouble and yet as he sat on the other side of her desk all she saw was a man of unlimited privilege and opportunity that she held great disdain toward. Emma judged Chuck on his appearance and apparent circumstances in the same way that so many judged her upon meeting her wheelchair and not the person who sat in it. What upset her most were her final thoughts about Chuck Burton as he left her office. *I wonder if that son of a bitch realizes how Lucky he is?*

* * * * * * * *   * * * * * * * *   * * * * * * * *   * * * * * * * *

Young Chuck Burton never understood how blessed he was. He was fortunate enough to be born of and raised by a man who knew everything. Big Chuck. His opinions were always facts that were seldom warranted or justified yet always withstood the scrutiny of others. For some reason the younger Chuck did not look upon this amazing birth right with as much good will as one might suspect.

While there are some parents that do their best to provide a warm, nurturing environment for their children, with a gentle touch of guidance that becomes less and less existent as they grow older, so that they can sit back and count their offsprings' accolades as they enter their late teenage years, Big Chuck had a different parenting method. Big Chuck loved to lay down the law and then hunt for transgressions. Just as some anticipate the success of their children, Big Chuck could not wait for his boys to fuck up. And fuck up they did. Big Chuck's parenting skills shone the brightest when he was enforcing his laws. He had four boys and he was bound and determined to make a man out of each and every one of them.

The younger Chuck was the youngest of big Chuck's four children. Young Chuck always felt that he viewed his father differently than his three older brothers. While they seemed to admire their father, Chuck only tolerated him. While they seemed to respect him, Chuck only feared him.

All four boys excelled at sports. Especially football. His two oldest brothers were ferocious defensive ends. They were violent savages on the field and opposing quarterbacks and running backs paid dearly for engaging in the sport with them. His oldest brother would have gone pro if wasn't for a devastating knee injury in his senior year at Michigan State. The second oldest was in his junior year at Ohio State and very likely to have a shot in the NFL. The third oldest was the runt of the litter, but still an exceptional athlete. He would most likely never make the NFL but was currently quarterbacking the Ohio Wesleyan Battling Bishops varsity team as a sophomore. And then there was Chuck.

Young Chuck disappointed his father more than the other three, because as Big Chuck put it, "You don't have the heart of a man."

Young Chuck was a huge mountain of a young man, but he lacked the Neanderthal genes of his older brothers which made him too timid to play defense, nor did he possess the leadership skills to play quarterback. His father worried about his football future as well as his manliness. The football coach at Madeira high school, who coached all of Big Chuck's boys, insisted dad not worry. "A boy that size. We'll find a place for him."

And that's exactly what coach did. Young Chuck excelled at playing offensive line. It seemed he was not good at leading or attacking, but he was incredibly gifted at protecting things. His senior year football season at Madeira high school was coming to an end. Soon he would be picking from a plethora of universities with big time football programs offering big time scholarships. His father was finally proud of him. At the beginning of the football season, not so much. Chuck was on the verge of quitting the team and becoming the disappointment his father had always predicted.

During his junior year of high school Chuck decided to try his hand at another extracurricular activity he had always found interesting. He joined the Drama Club. He enjoyed it very much and his acting was far better than one would imagine based on his appearance. He had three small parts in three plays. He nailed them. His mother was very impressed. His father and brothers were not in attendance. Coach felt the Drama Club interfered too much with Chuck's demanding football schedule. During his junior year, he missed one practice completely and was late for three others. Senior year, Coach laid down the law.

Young Chuck had to choose between football and Drama Club. Young Chuck chose Drama Club. Big Chuck told his son, "I'm sorry you feel that way."

Whenever big Chuck uttered the words *I'm sorry* they were always followed by the word *you*. He never followed I'm sorry with an I. As in, *I'm sorry you took it that way, I'm sorry you misunderstood me.* Never *I'm sorry I did not take your feelings into consideration,* or *I'm sorry I hurt you.* One of the perks of being the man who knows everything is never having to be really sorry. But Big Chuck wasn't going to let it go that easily. He wasn't going to just sit idly by while his son threw away his dreams. Dad and Coach had a sit down with the misguided youth and explained to him what an idiot he was being and how many incredible opportunities he was throwing away.

Young Chuck held his ground. He explained that he genuinely enjoyed acting better than playing offensive line and that playing football was starting to become very painful. He also revealed his fears of chronic traumatic encephalopathy, the progressive degenerative brain disease said to be caused by constant head trauma. A disease that football players are at an extremely high risk of developing.

Dad and Coach dug in deeper. They assured Young Chuck that there was no real science behind the CTE and football connection and that the Coach along with the team trainers would better manage the pain he felt after games. "Your well-being is my number one priority," insisted Coach.

"You want to go to college, don't you?" questioned Dad.

Young Chuck caved and quit the Drama Club.

Emma Aimison did not know any of this about Young Chuck as he sat across her desk. He was just another gifted jock whose athleticism would carry him through life. Her meetings with the stars of the football team were just a formality. They neither required nor wanted any counseling from Emma. They were going to go to college at whatever university offered them the best scholarship. The academics of the school did not matter. The majors the school offered were of no concern. Football was all that mattered. Emma believed that Chuck Burton perfectly fit this criterion. Emma did not realize that Chuck Burton was a young man in desperate need of help.

Young Chuck got along well with most of his teammates and was fine with the occasional ribbing about his appetite for acting. Every member of the team had a girlfriend and Chuck was no exception. Almost every girl that dated a member of the football team was shallow and vapid and extremely high maintenance. To most of them, appearance was everything and they would spend plenty of time and money to achieve the look of a Barbie doll action figure.

Chuck's girlfriend was one of the exceptions. She was a beautiful girl named Teegan who did not spend time or money on her looks, because she did not believe in her own beauty, but this did not upset her or make her self-conscious, instead her disbelief left her completely uninhibited. She was not a slave to the maintenance of the truth. Nobody knew why Teegan and Chuck dated. They seemed like an odd pairing. Teegan knew why. She was hopelessly, madly in love with Young Chuck. And Young Chuck had a secret about the love-crazed Teegan. And it was the kind of secret he did not plan on keeping much longer.

It was 5:45 pm CST when Emma and Chuck finished their unproductive meeting. She crossed him off her list and was happy to see he was the last of the football team she had to meet with this semester. She always met with them later in the day, after practice, or weight lifting, or violence training, or academic cover ups. Emma was done for the day. She gathered her things and headed home where she would continue her search for a new home. *Chicagoland Area*, she thought. Young Chuck Burton still had another meeting to attend.

Madeira high school's football team was a perennial powerhouse. The man responsible for that was the man Young Chuck was waiting to have a private audience with. Coach was a very busy man and Chuck was his last order of business for the day. Their meeting began at 7:07 pm CST. During Chuck's waiting time in between meetings he went from convincing himself to tell Coach everything, the truth, the whole truth and nothing but the truth, as it would be inconceivably liberating to free himself from the burden of his secrets, to getting cold feet and deciding to keep his mouth shut. Chuck was nervous. Chuck felt cruel and guilty. Chuck felt scared and ashamed.

"Chuckie, my man, how the hell are you?"

"Good, Coach."

"And your folks?"

"Good. Real good."

"Your old man is something else. I really like that man. I tell you Chuckie, you're Lucky to have him."

Young Chuck was there to see the Coach and tell him something he could never tell his dad, but coach's last comment really had him second guessing himself. *How can I tell my father's ally something I cannot tell him?*

"How are your brothers doing?"

The two discussed Chucks brothers for several minutes, during which time Coach regained Young Chuck's trust. *He genuinely cares about us. He remembers everything about every one of us. He has our best interest at heart.* Chuck decided to come clean.

"Coach, I fucked up. I really fucked up." Chuck put his face in his hands and tried hard not to weep.

Coach's facial expression quickly changed from one of jovial conversation to one of deep concern. He jumped up from his chair and came around to the front of his desk. He leaned back on his desk as he supportively rubbed Young Chuck's shoulder.

"It's okay, buddy. Whatever it is you can tell me. I am your advocate, Chuckie. I'm here to help you."

Chuck's glassy eyes took focus on Coach's sympathetic face and he confessed his crime of passion.

"It's Teegan. I really messed things up. I got Teegan pregnant."

Coach did not consider Chuck's words long before he reassured him. "Okay. It's okay. Things like this happen. What's important now is what we do moving forward."

Young Chuck felt some relief from speaking the words and Coach's reaction, but there was more to tell.

Coach began a series of rapid fire questions trying to gauge the situation.

"Do your parents know?"

"No."

"Have you told anyone?"

"No, just you."

"Are you sure it's yours."

"What? Yes. Yes, I'm sure."

"How old is she? Is she eighteen?"

"Not until January."

"Are you eighteen?"

"Not till March."

"Good. Good. Okay your teammates will all be behind you. You know that. But how about her? Do you know any girls that she hangs out with that would be willing to testify that it was consensual?"

"Huh? What?"

"I mean they didn't have to be there during, but right before or right after would be great. Was she drunk?"

"No."

"Were you?"

"No."

"Were either one of you drinking?"

"No, not at all."

"Okay. Good. That's good. The bad thing is the timing. Because of the time of year this is most likely going to come out before scholarship offers. But that's okay. The main thing recruiters are going to care about is consent, so if we can establish consent-"

"Coach!" Chuck aggressively interrupted. "It was consensual!"

Coach's eyes showed signs of skeptical relief. "That's good Chuckie. Real good. But even if it was maybe I should have someone talk to her to make sure we are all on the same page. For your protection. Because sometimes, Chuckie-"

"She's in love with me. She is totally in love with me."

Coach was taken aback by Young Chuck's declaration. He wanted to be relieved but feared Chuck was being naïve. This was not Coach's first rodeo. It was obvious Chuck was extremely upset and becoming more agitated with each passing moment. Coach presented his next statement as tactfully as a man who completely lacked grace and understanding could. "Sometimes Chuckie, when these girls tell mom and dad, they change their story."

Chucks eyes were perturbed and his words stern. "She doesn't have a dad and her mom already knows."

Again, Coach was taken aback. "Okay," he said with some obvious disappointment. "I wish you would have come to me sooner with this."

"What would it have mattered?" That's what Chuck said, but what he wondered was, *would it have mattered? Could coach have prevented one of my many regrets?*

"It just takes our easiest option off the table."

Coach walked back around to his side of the desk, no doubt wanting to put some distance between Chuck's crazy eyes and himself. He took a seat, feeling comfortable having the desk as a barrier. He did not understand Chuck's demeanor, after all he was only trying to help one of his best players.

Coach continued. "In Illinois, you have to be eighteen to get an abortion without your parents written consent, but I know a guy who in certain cases will ignore that regulation. I think Ginger would have been one of those cases, but it's too late now, with her mom already knowing."

Chucks eyes changed from crazed agitation to profound sorrow. He began to weep but made no attempt to conceal the shame of his tears. He stared at Coach making him feel uneasy. With tears streaming down his cheeks he mumbled her name. *Teegan.*

"Excuse me?" Coach did not hear him clearly.

"Her name is Teegan." Chuck spoke loudly.

"Huh?"

"Her name is Teegan. Not Ginger."

"Oh, yeah I'm sorry. Teegan. Right Tee-"

"And she already had an abortion."

Taken aback a third time. "Huh?"

"Her mother took her yesterday. She asked me if she should do it..." Young Chuck was now sobbing. "I said I don't know...Do what you think is best."

There was the relief Coach was looking for. The problem was solved before Chuck even walked into his office. As Chuck continued to sob Coach wondered, *Why in the fuck would he bring this sort of shit to me. Don't I have enough on my plate? Doesn't the school have counselors for this type of crap?* He knew he had to offer artificial comfort. He went back by Chuck and rubbed his shoulders and he delivered sincere sounding lip service. "You'll get through this. You did the right thing. It was best for everyone."

Chuck composed himself after a few minutes and wondered the same thing Coach did. *Why the fuck would I bring my problems to this inhumane asshole? He is no different than my father.*

Chuck was not unburdened. Chuck did not even tell Coach the full story. Chuck was crushed. He had no one else to talk to. *If only there were someone.* There was. Unfortunately, right now she was at home on Realator.com. Once Chuck pulled himself together he wanted to get away from Coach as quickly as possible so that he could once again fall apart. Dismally, the weight of the three burdens Young Chuck was forced to carry alone was too great. He was unable to get up out of the chair in which he sat.

Chuck's first great burden was that when Teegan called him looking for support and guidance and love, he offered none. He offered no opinion on the life of his unborn child. "I don't know. Do what you think is best." The weight of his guilt completely crushed his heart.

Chuck's second great burden was that Teegan loved him. He did not share these feelings toward her. He liked her very much. She was fun to be around. He treated her well and was happy to have her in his life. He never wanted to hurt her, but now he had brutally wounded her and he knew that was only the beginning. He knew he would hurt her again. The weight of his regret completely crushed his spirit.

Chuck's third great burden was that he was living a lie. He lied to Coach about the night he was with Teegan. They had been drinking. A lot. It was their third time being intimate and all three times alcohol was involved. Imagination was also involved. Chuck did not love Teegan the way she loved him because he was not physically attracted to her. Truth be told, he was not physically attracted to any woman. The objects of his attraction shared a locker room with him and were also the objects of his frustration. In Chuck's world he did not believe gay was a viable option. The weight of his shame completely crushed his soul.

Coach felt Chuck's *sit in* had gone on for too long. He grabbed him under his left arm and helped raise him up while patting him on the back. Chuck felt woozy under the weight of his tremendous burdens. He took a moment to steady himself. "You gonna be okay, big guy?" Coach sort of asked, not wanting a true answer, only wanting the answer that suited him.

Chuck hesitated and then replied, "Yeah, I'll be fine."

What else was he going to say? What else could he say to this poor excuse for a Human Being? What else could he say to anyone in the world in which he lived?

"Good. Great. Because we are going to need you Friday night. Big game."

Chuck was repulsed by Coach, but now he also envied him. Coach was a completely despicable person who lacked even a shred of decency, but he did not have to hide who he was. He could be his real, pathetic, terrible self every day and there were many people that admired him for it. As Coach ushered Young Chuck out of his office, Chuck thought to himself, *I wonder if this son of a bitch realizes how Lucky he is?*

* * * * * * * * * * * * * * * * * * * * * * * * * * * * * * *

Later, as Coach got ready to leave his office he felt as though today was a really good day. The game plan he came up with for Friday night was really solid, and the team had a really productive practice.

Chuck did not head home after his visit with Coach. Chuck spent a little time in the gym and then found himself in the locker room. As Coach walked out of the building and into the parking lot, Chuck sat on the bench in front of his locker. He retrieved two items he had been considering for some time. The first was a box of Hefty extra strong lawn and leaf bags. He took out one bag and then grabbed item number two.

Coach was really on the top of the world as he walked to his car. He was so satisfied with the way the Chuck Burton problem resolved itself. He thought, *that could not have worked out better. I was nervous at first. I didn't know what Chuck was going to throw at me. But it ends up I didn't have to hide anything, or cover anything up, or call in any favors, or pull any strings, or threaten anybody. Hell, I didn't even have to talk to anybody. I guess some things just have a way of working themselves out.*

Chuck put the bag over his head and then as quickly as he could he began tightly wrapping a roll of duct tape around his neck and mouth and nose. The sound of the duct tape unrolling tore through the empty locker room so rapidly it sounded like an electric power tool. Chuck began to feel dizzy and then panic ripped through his body. He felt the plastic of the bag being sucked into his mouth and against his nostrils as his body searched for air. He let what was left of the roll fall to the floor as he sat on his hands in an attempt to prevent himself from saving himself.

Coach began to whistle the Bengals Growl Fight Song as he reached into his pocket for his car keys. No keys. *Must be in my other pocket.* As Coach switched his briefcase of football plays from his left to right hand and then reached his left hand into his pocket he thought, *You know, I am really one Lucky son of a bitch.*

Chuck's air starved body began to convulse. He fell off the bench and onto the floor. He began to frantically rip at the duct tape around his neck and mouth. His mind may have decided to die, but his body was now fighting for life. He fought in the blackness trying to tear the plastic and tape that threatened his existence. Chuck's instincts were never to attack or to lead, but to protect. He now struggled mightily, as his body shook violently on the locker room floor, to protect himself from himself. It was too late, he had sabotaged his own preservation. His hands became uncoordinated. The darkness of the bag was soon replaced with the darkness of death.

The whole thing happened so quickly it is really difficult to describe. He came out of nowhere. His presence afterward is a mystery. Coach felt his keys with the tips of his left fingers and then he instantaneously felt three sharp pains shoot through his lower back. It was his right kidney. He dropped his briefcase and grabbed hold of the wounded area only to feel another piercing pain through his hand and then his upper back. It took nearly two and a half seconds for Coach to realize he was being attacked. During that short time spam, he was stabbed eleven times. The attacker was relentless and stabbed his victim with the speed of a jackhammer. In and out the blade sliced through Coach's flesh.

Coach turned to face his attacker. He was short and stocky. He was much smaller than Coach. The arm that held the blade never stopped moving. Coach was able to lean against his car and give the attacker a mighty kick which sent him crashing to the ground several feet away. Despite his size advantage, Coach was in no condition to give fight. At this point he had sustained thirty-eight stab wounds. Surprisingly, there was not very much blood at this point of the violent ambush. The slices of Coach's flesh came faster than his blood flowed. In the time he fumbled for his keys, his heart began to pump blood through his thirty-eight new openings. Flight was Coach's only option.

He managed to get the door open and his ass fell into the driver's seat when his attacker slammed the car door hard against his legs. The first time causing great trauma and breaking the skin that covered his shin bones. The second time completely severing both his tibias in two. And the third and most ferocious door slamming fractured both fibulas. The attacker then pulled open the door and pounced on his bloody victim and continued to drive his blade in and out of Coach's body and face until both were covered in blood and flesh and intestines.

* * * * * * * * * * * * * * * * * * * * * * * * * * * * * * * * *

Despite the lead that Detective Herb Katzenburg currently wanted to discuss with Emma Aimison, the attacker would never be caught. The police would always be baffled by the crime as well as the connection between the murder and suicide at Madeira high school in the early evening of that Autumn night.

They did not have much to go on. Other than Coach, nobody else saw the attacker. They knew the murder weapon was a Swiss Comrade Hunting Knife, which was unusual, but they had nothing else to go on. Unfortunately for the police, but luckily for the attacker, after he stabbed Coach over one hundred times, nobody was around to hear him say, "You'll never hurt anybody again, Bryce McNulty!"

WHAT IS WATER?

THIS IS THE part of the book where my intensions were to accomplish four tasks. Those tasks were to first introduce myself. After all, we did just complete spending quite a bit of time together. Although I have more than likely never met you, I was extremely open and very comfortable sharing my stories as well as some of my deeply personal thoughts and feelings on a myriad of subjects with you. And if you enjoy reading in the same way I have been known to upon occasion, then you may have been experiencing some of my yarns in various states of undress or while performing certain bodily functions. Please, don't be embarrassed. I really don't mind. I only bring it up because I feel it is almost fair to say that you and I have been somewhat, slightly intimate with each other. I find that kind of funny when you consider we don't even know each other's first names. Don't you think?

After introducing myself, my second task was to sincerely thank you for taking the time to read my stories. I understand how much effort goes into reading a book and the nearly infinite plethora of works you have to choose from and I could not even possibly begin to explain to you just how much I appreciate that. It makes me realize what a Lucky son of a bitch I am.

I was also looking very forward to explaining my relationship with William, our more serviceable than elegant author. Don't get me wrong, I do appreciate William. He adds to my Lucky S.O.B. feeling, but let's face it, no one will ever confuse him with (*insert the name of an author you admire here*). That was to be task number three. Interesting, you picked the same author that I did.

And finally, task number four, the book was supposed to end with a melodramatic clarification as to what water is...or at least what I believe it to be.

But that is not going to happen. I'm sorry. *The Name of the Book* did not come out the way I had hoped. It is because of those bastards at Foster and Von Charles Publishing Company. They omitted one of my stories from the collection. My favorite one. The story that best supported my theory of water. Well, not my theory, just the theory to which I prescribe. It was the story of three families and the different ways they each dealt with the catastrophic fates the universe forced upon them. The name of the story was Catastrophic Fates. CF for short. Anyway, the publishing company said it was too long for this project.

It did not start out that way. I just kept remembering very important elements to the story and William agreed to their importance so he kept editing, adding, and rewriting. The story continued to grow and grow. The bastards at Foster and Von Charles continued to become more and more impatient. Even angry. One of them actually had the nerve to quote Antoine de Saint to William. *A designer knows he has achieved perfection not when there is nothing left to add, but when there is nothing left to take away.* To which I told William to relay, perfection? Who the fuck is trying to achieve perfection? I'm just trying to tell my Goddamned story and I want to make sure the entire story gets told.

So, the bastards checked out CF. So far, they liked it. But they said it was way too long for a collection of short stories. One of them suggested that if William were to eliminate all of my egomaniacal declarations and self-righteous sermonizing that everything would fit into the book quite nicely. To him, I say in regards to his advice, fuck you very much. I am the story teller and I will tell it how I see fit. And furthermore, there has never been a teller of a story who has not had an agenda. I shall end this particular rant before it really begins in order to tell you what the bastards at Foster and Von Charles decided to do. They felt that the CF story was a novel. At least one, more than likely two novels in and of itself.

William was thrilled beyond words. They signed him to a three-book deal with a modest but much needed advance. I on the other hand was quite disappointed. First of all, *in and of itself,* what in the hell does that even mean? Worst idiom of all time. And secondly, I thought my time with William was coming to an end. No offense, William, I understand you are the one writing this and you are a *hail fellow well met,* but this relationship train is just about out of track.

From my point of view, not William's so much, but to me these new circumstances created several problems with the book you are currently reading. Still. Hopefully.

The Name of the Book was originally going to be titled *Calamitous Fortunes.* William insisted it still could. My stance was absolutely not. Here is a snippet of our conversation.

"We can still call it *Calamitous Fortunes.*"

"Absolutely not."

My contention was this, how can it be called *Calamitous Fortunes* without *Catastrophic Fates?* The answer is it cannot.

Here is another snippet of our conversation.

"So, then what do you suggest we call it?"

"Call what?"

I love to answer William's questions with questions and pretend I do not know what he is referring to. And I suppose he knows this now. Our relationship is really more advantageous to him at this point. Anyway, that's when he, William, came up with it, The Name of the Book. After I asked, "Call what?" William responded, with some noticeable aggravation...

"The Name of the Book."

"Perfect."

So that's exactly how that happened. More or less. Our *friends* over at Foster and Von Charles felt the title was interesting enough and would receive billions upon billions of unintended inquiries. Think of how many times around the world per day the question, what is *The Name of the Book?* is uttered. William added the subtitle *A collection of short stories* and *interesting concepts* for clarification. I was in favor of his addition. Somebody at Foster and Von Charles came up with the *self-serving rants.* That I did not care for. I'm sure it was the same bastard who quoted Antoine de Saint. My next protest that upset William terribly concerned the *story* you are currently reading. Still. Hopefully.

I informed William, "You do realize this completely ruins the piece you are currently writing?"

"What piece?"

Touché, William.

"What is Water?"

"How so?"

"Well, obviously you are aware of my four goals in this essay of sorts."

"I am."

"Well then you must also be aware that some of them have now become unachievable."

"How so?"

"For starters, William, I am certainly not going to introduce myself to the reader before they read *Catastrophic Fates*."

"Why wouldn't you?"

"Why wouldn't I... Seriously? Because I am an integral part of the CF story and my identity is kind of a *surprise ending* that may somewhat, slightly change the reader's perception of myself as well as all of the preceding events. That's why I wouldn't!"

"I see your point."

"I would hope so."

"So, should we completely scrap this piece?"

"I don't believe that would be very fair. The reader certainly deserves some type of explanation."

William sighed and wrinkled up the page you are currently reading.

"What are you doing?" I asked.

"Starting over."

"I don't believe there is any need for that. I feel we can salvage this. Let's keep going."

"Seriously?"

"Yes, of course. I feel what we have so far is somewhat slightly interesting and while I absolutely cannot introduce myself to the reader at this point and juncture, and I am currently unable to expound on what water is, nor am I able to explain the intricacies of our relationship, I do believe our enigmatic, perhaps even esoteric, banter is going a long way in divulging some of the fundamentals of our incorporation."

"Incorporation?"

"And I have used somewhat slightly three times in this piece."

"Somewhat slightly?"

"Yes, somewhat slightly, you used it several times in *The Name of the Book* and *CF.* I like the way it flows. I used it because you used it. In a complimentary way. I figured you would enjoy that."

"Complimentary?"

"Would you please stop selecting one of the words from my preceding comments and repeating it in the form of a question? It is really quite annoying. I thought that myself turning a phrase in your style would be complimentary. You are always saying how unflattering and critical I am."

"It isn't mine."

"Well of course it is. Who else would I be complimenting? I mean, they are *my stories*, but they are your words. Mostly. Not right now, but mostly."

"Somewhat slightly is from a David Bowie song."

"Seriously?"

"Unwashed and Somewhat Slightly Dazed."

"But you have used it several times."

"I also like the way it flows."

"But it's not yours."

"It's not yours either, and you just said you used it three times."

"Yes, but I used it as a sort of homage to you."

"Well, I did it as a shout out to David Bowie. All my writings contain shout outs."

"Shout outs?"

"Yeah, you know, like an expression of admiration."

"I know what a shout out is. How many are we talking about?"

"Tons."

"Tons?"

"There is one in *About Love* from Alejandro Escovedo I am particularly fond of."

"And here I thought you were the wordsmith."

"I am. Somewhat slightly."

Well, that's about enough of that. Do you see how aggravating William can be? One of the four tasks that I am able to complete at this time is to thank you. Please allow me to reiterate how much it means to me that you decided to give my stories a shot. And that you still are even at this rather ridiculous part of the book, still, hopefully, means the world to me.

Thank you.

William also thanks you. He wanted me to send extra thanks your way if you actually purchased the book and to ask if you could please recommend it to a friend and maybe even post an on-line review if your feelings were positive about our collaboration. I told him absolutely not. A simple thank you would be much more appropriate.

So, thank you, from William also.

So that's it. My other three desires for this project will remain unfulfilled. Temporarily. It sure seems a bit disheartening to just end it here. But I really don't want to tell you anything more about CF at this time. I prefer you go in fresh. So, what else is there to say at this point?

I wish you well in all of your future endeavors. Be safe, but not so safe you become bored. Have fun. Read on...Live on...

That does not feel right. In fact, it feels wrong. Very wrong. I request that you *read on*...and then leave you with nothing to read. You should have the ability to read CF right now at this very moment. But it is not here. I find these circumstances most unfortunate and hope that you are also somewhat slightly disappointed. I have to stop saying that. It does flow off the tongue quite nicely. David Bowie was quite the wordsmith.

So, what else is there to do instead of sharing CF with you? It can't take up too many more pages or the bastards at Foster and Von Charles will throw a fit. I have already made my appreciation of you clear and to thank you again would borderline somewhere between disquieting and annoying. If you never have had the experience, I can assure you when someone you have been intimate with becomes over thankful it can actually feel downright creepy.

I choose not to say any more about the theory of water, other than all of my stories are about water. And there are other sources available on the

World Wide Web to explain what water is. As William said earlier, I did not come up with what water is. Somebody else told me *this is water.*

And I truly do not want to say much more about my relationship with William at this point. It would not be beneficial to any of us and if I am Lucky enough to have you read CF it could take away from that experience. You may be wondering why I am not acknowledged in the credits of this book. Why I have given William complete ownership of my stories. To put it simply, the only thing I care about is making my stories available to the world. I have no need for recognition or accolades. In a world that is fueled by desire, this is currently my only desire. William writes them for me. Mostly in his own words, but without prejudice. He remains truthful to my feelings whether he concurs or not.

Enough already! Enough about what I cannot or will not do. I have come up with something I can do. This is what I can do. And perhaps it is silly. So, at the risk of being silly, if you allow me a little more of your time I can teach you a game that I have always found quite interesting. Maybe you will also. It is not really a game. It's really an experiment, of sorts, that involves a very important and personal decision on your part. A decision that will tell you a lot about yourself and the people in your life, if you take it seriously.

Let us begin.

The name of our experimental game is *My Top Ten.*

Now, if you are going to participate in earnest I have to request that you suspend disbelief while playing.

Here is the scenario. The Grim Reaper is one hundred percent real. He and he alone escorts everyone from the world of the living to the world of the dead. And Old Grim is pretty tired. He has been working for a very long time without a vacation. He decides he is going to take a little holiday. Three years. Which really is not very long when you consider he has been working pretty much nonstop since the Dawn of Man with the exception of a couple of coffee breaks during the Bronze Age.

Now, Grim is no dummy, mind you. He realizes that three years of no human deaths will wreak havoc on the planet. He has even seen *La Morte in Vacanza (aka: Death Takes a Holiday).* And yes, in our scenario Grim is only in charge of human deaths. His brother, Shril Reaper, is charged with all other animal deaths and his cousin Pedro tends to the plant kingdom. And yes, I have made the Reapers all male. I am sorry if this offends anyone. I am completely in favor of equal rights and can assure you I am in no way misogynistic. It's just when I consider the female gender I think of life and hope, while males on the other hand make me think of violence, brutality, injustice, infringement and cruelty. That pretty much encapsulates death, don't you think?

Anyway, for some inexplicable reason, Grim is really into you. I mean this cat really digs you. He enjoys the cut of your jib. Who knows why. Maybe it's the way you sing in the shower or the private conversations you have with your reflection, because just like Santa Claus, Death is always watching. Regardless the reason, Grim decides to reach out to you and tell you his plan.

After the initial shock of finding out that the harbinger of extermination thinks you are the cat's pajamas you think, *Hmm, this is pretty cool*. But, at the same time you want to make sure he is not *in to you* In To You. Grim assures you that he has no romantic feelings toward you, which is good, because he definitely falls a little short in the looks department. That's why he wears the hood. He is very self-conscience about his appearance.

You ask him about his scythe. He explains to you that he has not used the scythe to reap the dead since the middle 1400s and that today the entire death process is pretty streamlined. Almost completely automated. These days the only thing Grim has to do is a couple of keystrokes on his desktop computer. Despite the fact that his job has become much easier over the past few centuries, he tells you he is in dire need of a vacation. He wants to spend some time among his clientele. Maybe even meet somebody nice. He is not looking for a LTR but is not opposed to a few quick hook ups. He plans on trading in his cloak for some nice skin and spending the next three years in a beautiful beach house he rented in Barbados. He says you are more than welcome to join him for a couple of weeks. All expenses paid. Bring a friend even. You tell him it sounds great and you begin to feel very happy about your new friendship.

Then he tells you the bad news.

During the course of an average year Grim takes out about one percent of the human population. His original pre-vacation plan was on the day before his trip to first wash all the new beach outfits he had purchased for a more comfortable and less stiff fit, and also because, as Grim put it, you don't know who could have tried those clothes on before you purchased them and that's just gross, and then he would pack, put on his new skin, call a Lyft for the airport, and while he waited for the three to six minutes for his ride in one fell swoop take out three percent of the earths human population.

Well to say the least you find this a little upsetting.

Then Grim explains that because he cannot even stand the thought of those long security lines at the airport he has decided to take out five percent of mankind. And because he lives near the same major airport as you do an unfair proportion of these fatalities will be from your general area.

Now you're becoming quite angry at your new friend.

He goes on to explain that he generally gets his list of death candidates one week before their time, but this five percent are just going to be picked at random. And that he can't just take them. They have to die. Some of them will be of natural causes but the vast majority of them are going to have to go in very violent and gruesome accidents and catastrophic disasters. He begins to tell you what he has planned and you say, "When?"

His glib response is "Tomorrow."

You begin to realize that your buddy Grim Reaper has a bit of a dark side.

He then goes on to tell you how Stella from H.R. is not going to like this one bit, but that there is no way they can fire him and if they try to he will sue them for the myriad of labor law violations that have been committed against him in the last century alone. He is very confident.

You begin to cry.

Grim notices your tears and feels terrible for having upset you. Then he tells you the good news.

You are not among the five percent.

But wait. There's more.

Not only are you not among the doomed five percent, but you get to select ten others to be spared.

Let the game begin.

Make your list of ten.

And please, consider it carefully. If you take it very seriously your list may surprise you.

Who will you save?

Will it simply be your ten closest loved ones?

Where will you draw that line?

Who is your eleventh closest loved one?

Do you even like all of your loved ones?

Are any of them toxic?

Do any of them make life more difficult for you?

It's possible that your list of ten may include someone that you don't love, or are not close with, or maybe you save someone you have not even ever met. Perhaps a world leader you feel mankind needs. Or a religious leader. Or an entertainer or artist you really enjoy and feel the need to see more of their work. It's your list. It's personal and can be as private as you choose. The only one you have to share it with is Grim and I promise you he is not the judgmental type.

Do you even like all ten people on your list?

William participated in my game a little while back. He more recently told me that his list is different today than it was two months ago. His previous list included two people that I despise and William was not very fond of. But they were necessary in William's world. They were two of the bastards over at Foster and Von Charles. They were big supporters of William and without them he would not have received his book deal. This I understand. It has been William's lifelong dream to be a writer. They are now off the list. This I appreciate.

Is there someone in your life you are dependent on for your employment or economic security or financial future that you are not particularly fond of but could not maintain your quality of life without? Perhaps your boss or partner or a client or customer or maybe even an attorney or financial advisor or a publisher. Maybe a doctor?

Are they on your list?

Who did they bump to get there?

I know another person on William's list. I am sworn to secrecy and unable to share her identity, but I can tell you she is his secret love. His passion for her is deep but the circumstances of life force him to keep his feelings to himself. With the exception of me. He could not even imagine a world without her in it. I can tell that he is upset that I shared this information. Please disregard.

Do you have an undeclared love? A secret crush?

Are they on your list?

Creating this list is a daunting task. In doing so you may discover things about yourself you previously did not consider. Once your list is complete, ask yourself, is there anyone you can share the entire list with? This is my personal favorite part of the game. Who would you crush by revealing your list?

Are your parents on it? Are all of your children on it? How about their significant others? Did all of your siblings make the list? How many grandchildren do you have? How many friends are in your life? Remember, Grim said most of the five percent were going to die violently in horrific accidents and disasters. Who are you not going to protect?

Once you complete your list and feel *comfortable* with it you can advance to level two of the game if you want to. It is much more difficult and only for exceptionally skilled players.

In level two, you have to cut your list to seven.

There. That ought to do it. I feel much more comfortable ending the book now. I feel this chapter is no longer a complete rip off and no longer feel guilty that I have cheated you. I hope you feel the same.

I will not say goodbye as I feel it is unfitting seeing I have not even introduced myself yet. I feel the best way to end *The Name of the Book* is with a German phrase I am quite fond of.

Auf Wiedersehen.

ABOUT THE AUTHOR

William Christopher Spreadbury (aka: Bill, Will, and upon occasion Willie) is a writer and a pretty groovy dude. He is kind to the elderly and somewhat slightly tolerant of idiots and buffoons. He likes to think of himself as a nice guy and most who know him would agree. He enjoys drinking wine and dancing, but is not very good at either. He has two amazing adult children that make him prouder every day. He calls Chicago home, even though he does not live there. William embraces all that is dark and forbidden within him and pours it out onto his pages. If you are willing to join him on his journey, he will introduce you to the part of your soul you pretend does not exist.

28744984R00207

Made in the USA
Columbia, SC
16 October 2018